The Whisper of Pialigos

Other Books by J Douglas Bottorff

A Practical Guide to Meditation and Prayer
A Practical Guide to Prosperous Living (also in audiobook)
Contributing author to John Marks Templeton's *Laws of Living*
Contributing author to *New Thought: A Practical Spirituality*

The Whisper of Pialigos

a novel by

J Douglas Bottorff

The Whisper of Pialigos

Published by Wheatmark®
610 East Delano Street, Suite 104
Tucson, Arizona 85705 U.S.A.
www.wheatmark.com

ISBN-13: 978-1-58736-711-3
ISBN-10: 1-58736-711-4
Library of Congress Control Number: 2006933783

To Elizabeth

You and I have walked before
Together on some distant shore

Special thanks to
Susan Wenger, Ed Fortson, Deb McCoy, Anita Feuker,
Patricia Bottorff, and Elizabeth Bottorff
for their positive contributions to the evolution of this project.

There is a voice.
A quiet voice.
It calls from the Aegean.
Sublime, little more than a whisper.
The whisper of Pialigos.
Few can hear it, fewer still can understand.
But those who hear, those who understand
will not remain unchanged.

—Pialigarian verse

The Whisper of Pialigos

Prologue

LIGHT ROSE IN FAINT SHAFTS over the horizon and streaked the eastern sky with a hint of morning. Raphael looked up from the screen of his laptop computer and watched a sheet of black ripples make their way over the glassy expanse of the Sea of Crete. He waited as the gust nudged his rented Bayliner one or two meters. Annoyed, he glanced at the GPS to recheck his coordinates. *Latitude: 36°09' 55.49'. Longitude: 24°44' 12.62'*, well within the flight path of the Cessna 172P Skyhawk. He could see by the blipping asterisk on the laptop's screen that the tiny transmitter he had planted inside the right wheel pant of the Cessna produced a strong reading. In a matter of a few minutes, he would have a visual on the plane. Everything was in place. The gust of wind had done no harm.

A work of pure genius, he admitted.

The drone of the Cessna's engine drifted in with the cool morning breeze. Raphael removed a black ski mask from the pocket of his military jacket and slipped it over his head. He pressed the pound key of a cell phone followed by four carefully selected digits, an act calculated to trigger a series of electronic marvels.

THE MIND OF SIXTY-SEVEN-YEAR-OLD ALEXIOS Mikos had just begun to drift when an unexpected burst of static blurted through his headset. Startled, he blinked the glaze from his sleepy eyes. In the next instant, the engine of the 1981 Cessna Skyhawk sputtered.

So did his heart.

Alexios straightened to attention. He toyed anxiously with one sagging jowl while scanning the array of gauges beneath the brow of the Skyhawk's instrument panel. No abnormalities. Forty-two gallons of usable fuel. Engine purring.

A bubble in the fuel line? Possible. The recent engine overhaul would explain it.

Alexios took a deep breath and adjusted the bill of the yellow baseball hat that covered his balding head. *You are much too old for this kind of nonsense*, he told himself. *You should be home in bed with Celia.*

Ten years ago, a solo departure over open seas at 0500 had been as routine as a drive to the office. Now the bane of a decreasing attention span and the handicap of poor night vision were taking their toll on the confidence of the aging pilot.

The journey ... you must enjoy the journey.

He reminded himself of the bit of wisdom he'd tried to instill in the heart of his daughter. He'd had conflicting feelings about her decision years ago to follow him into the realm of archaeology. She would face many disappointments, countless dead ends. "Niki, you will survive in this business," he had told her, "only if you learn to enjoy the process of archaeology. If it is but a single end that you seek, of what value is the journey? Something can be learned even from your failures."

Now, with endless kilometers of vacant sea creeping beneath the Skyhawk, the mainland of Greece nowhere in sight, he was forced to take his own advice.

Alexios removed his trifocals and rubbed fatigue from his baggy eyes. After replacing his glasses, he adjusted the boom of the microphone an inch from his lips, and he punched the transmit button on the control yoke.

"Athens Tower, this is Cessna, Sierra, X-ray, Alpha, Oscar, Papa, requesting a radio check. How do you read?" Only the hiss of static came through the headset. Puzzled, he called again. "Athens Tower, this is Cessna, Sierra, X-ray, Alpha, Oscar, Papa, requesting a radio check. How do you read? Over."

"Good morning, Dr. Mikos."

The voice of an intruder bore the ghoulishly liquid characteristic of electronic alteration.

"Who ... who is this?"

"Does the name *Raphael* mean anything to you?"

Alexios's breath caught in his throat. Raphael was his reason for going to Athens.

"I have … heard the name," Alexios said in as calm a voice as he could muster. He was careful to give no hint that he knew the identity of the man behind the alias, the mastermind responsible for the disappearance of thousands of artifacts from sites throughout the Cyclades. The intruder's voice, he felt, belonged to Gustavo Giacopetti, the agent in charge of Santorini's Department of Antiquities.

"You have heard the name?" The electronic alteration transformed the intruder's laugh into something truly sinister. "I'm afraid with all your busy nosing around, you have done more than that. Look to the top of your left wing strut. You will notice a very small object—a micro video camera to be precise."

Alexios visually followed the strut. Tucked beneath the left wing he saw a black, thimble-sized device that should not have been there. Turning, he stared straight ahead wondering what else Giacopetti had planted on his plane.

"I see you have lost your smile," the ghoulish voice said. "And I am afraid the news I bear will bring little cheer. You see, I have equipped your plane with a substantial amount of explosives. It would be foolish for you to try to fly away."

Explosives? Nothing had suggested that Raphael was a murderer. The intruder was bluffing.

"You have my attention … Raphael. What do you want from me?"

"Today, you have a meeting scheduled with the minister of the Department of Antiquities."

Alexios felt his jaw tighten. How could Giacopetti know of this meeting?

"Your briefcase. I assume it contains some rather incriminating documentation?"

Alexios glanced at the brown leather case on the passenger floorboard and cursed himself for placing it in the camera's line of sight. The briefcase contained enough evidence to prove that Giacopetti's office had routinely altered records from the Mikos excavation at the Pialigarian temple ruins on Sarnafi. Artifacts of immense archaeological value—under Giacopetti's direct supervision—were turning up in private collections from New York to Hong Kong.

"Two kilometers directly in front of you," Raphael continued, "watch for a light."

Alexios squinted anxiously into the distance. Two flashes burst from the predawn sea.

"I see it," Alexios said.

"I assume you have a life vest on board."

"Of course."

"Secure the briefcase in the vest. Assume an altitude of three hundred meters—no less. When you reach my position, drop the case into the water near the boat. If you want to live, Dr. Mikos, do not attempt to empty the case. I am watching."

Alexios glanced at the wing-mounted camera, and then he turned back to the spot where he had seen the light. He could barely make out a white cruiser sitting motionless in the water. As instructed, he dropped the Cessna to three hundred meters, circled, and squinted at the lone figure dressed in military fatigues. The man, apparently anticipating the visual encounter, had his face covered with a black ski mask. He had, however, neglected to hide the registration numbers of his boat, though the numbers were too far away to read. With the plane's left door blocking the camera's view, he eased a pair of binoculars from a pocket in the door and laid them in his lap. At the right moment, he would get the numbers.

"I do not see you equipping the briefcase with your life jacket, Dr. Mikos. Perhaps you are too busy gawking?"

The plane's engine suddenly quit, and the prop stopped dead, leaving only the sound of slipstream just above the incredible silence. Alexios instinctively eased the control yoke forward, tilting the nose slightly down, keeping just enough speed to maintain lift and prevent a stall. He was at the mercy of a madman. Too low to go far, he thought of Celia. How would she get along without him? *This is no time to lose your wits*, he told himself. *The madman is bluffing. It is a demonstration of control. Stay above fifty-one knots. Maintain a straight line until you drop into the sea—if that is what he wants.*

The Cessna continued to sink: two hundred meters … one hundred meters … seventy-five … fifty … steady … twenty-five. At ten meters, Alexios snatched the life jacket from the rear seat, laid it across his lap, pulled snug his seat belt, and prepared for impact.

Suddenly, the engine sputtered to life, obliterating the deafening silence. The vibration tingled through the yoke and into his hands.

Alexios recaptured his breath, increased the throttle, and eased back on the yoke to reclaim as much altitude as his climb rate of 219 meters per minute would allow. He pulled a handkerchief from his back pocket. *I'm too old for this*, he thought again, mopping sweat from his brow.

"Are we in agreement here, Dr. Mikos?"

"Yes. Yes, of course." Alexios's hands still trembled as he snapped the jacket securely around the briefcase.

"Very good," said the voice in the headset. "When you make the drop, do not attempt to leave. We have one further item of business."

One further item? Alexios did as he was told and watched as the case fell within five meters of the port side of the boat. The moment Raphael began to fish it from the water with a grappling pole, Alexios snatched up the binoculars and read the registration: NU739857. He burned the numbers into his memory.

"Excellent, Dr. Mikos," Raphael reported, hoisting the briefcase toward the plane. "It would appear that you have no more business in Athens."

He is telling you to go home, Alexios thought, wanting nothing more than to see the face of his wife of forty-five years. *Do as he says.*

"Yes, Raphael. I suppose Santorini would be the better choice."

"Indeed. But before you go, our final item of business. I believe you have in your possession a certain scroll? I need to take it off your hands."

The scroll! Giacopetti could only be referring to a one-of-a-kind parchment scroll written by the hand of a Pialigarian prophet. He could not possibly know of the scroll. Or could he? Cardinal Salvatore Sorrentino desperately wanted to bury the artifact in the bowels of the Vatican's Secret Archives. It was said of the cardinal that he would employ any means to accomplish his end. Might not he have hired a scum like Giacopetti to locate and retrieve the Pialigarian parchment?

"I have only a photograph of the scroll," Alexios said truthfully. "The parchment itself has not yet been located."

"You are lying, Doctor. I know the scroll exists, and I know that you have it. But then, I assumed you would not be anxious to share your little treasure." There was a pause. "How was your overnight visit with your daughter?"

Alexios's breath grew shallow. Had his telephone been bugged?

"Leave my daughter out of this."

"I understand that Dr. Nicole Mikos holds a key position at the excavation of Knossos. You were there to admire her work? You must be very proud that she has followed so successfully your own footsteps."

Alexios felt the murderous flare of his nostrils.

"I told you to leave Niki out of this," he demanded again. "She does not know where the scroll is."

"Perhaps she does not," the voice said.

Bastard! Alexios struggled to control his breath. "All right," he said, desperate for a plausible story. "The scroll is locked in a vault in my business office at Fira. I will get it for you. I give you my word. But you must promise that you will bring no harm to my daughter."

"Admirable behavior, Dr. Mikos. Now, go to your office. Wait for my call. Twelve o'clock sharp. Do you understand?"

"Yes, of course," said Alexios. "Twelve o'clock shar—"

The normal background chatter suddenly returned to the headset. His radio was back on.

The archaeologist banked the Cessna toward Santorini. He was free.

Or was he?

A dark sense of foreboding fell over Alexios as he climbed slowly away from his tormentor. In the moments that passed, a sudden wave of pride for his daughter forced tears down his sunburned cheeks.

Then, his thoughts turned to Celia, and he wondered if he and his wife would ever again share an intimate stroll over the calming beaches of Santorini.

RAPHAEL WATCHED THE CESSNA ASSUME its proper easterly course. He pushed the pound key on his cell phone and waited for a few moments before pressing another series of numbers: 0-3-1-0-5-9. He held his breath through the brief silence followed by the expected click that he knew would translate as another burst of headphone static. More silence. Then, in exactly five seconds, a small flash erased the landing gear of the Cessna, and a glorious globe of orange flame immediately engulfed the plane. The roar echoed delightfully over the stillness of the morning. The sequence had performed beautifully. Raphael made the sign of the cross and watched in congratulatory tears as the flaming debris plummeted into the sea.

Raphael pulled off the ski mask. The gentle breeze riffled the water and cooled the perspiration from his face. His hand shook with exhilaration when he smoothed his hair back in place. With a deep, satisfying breath, he clicked on the boat's CD player. The haunting strains of Yanni rose from the speakers and moved out over the still waters.

For an artifact worth two hundred million American dollars, he thought, twisting the key that brought the boat's engine grumbling to life, *a simple vault will pose no problem.*

Raphael eased forward the throttle and pointed the cruiser toward the wisps of pink that streaked the morning skies over Santorini.

Chapter 1

One year later in the San Juan Mountains of Colorado

"What'cha looking for there, boy?"

My eyes fluttered open to the darkness beneath my hat. Sleep lingered like a cloud caught in a mountain forest. Pine-perfumed air started a trickle of recollections of the hike, lunch, the spot of shade that prompted the nap.

The voice ... was it real or dreamed? No other sounds supported an argument one way or the other. Only the distant cry of a Steller's jay fractured the silence of the evergreen valley.

My fingers were laced over a topographical map that draped like a blanket on my chest. I pushed the map aside and carefully nudged up the brim of my hat. The muzzle of a double-barreled shotgun hovered like an agitated cobra inches from my face. Squinting past the barrels, I could see a pair of gnarled fingers twitching dangerously on both triggers.

In an explosive flurry that sent my hat rolling, I started to scramble to my feet.

"That's far enough, boy." The voice screeched like a hand-cranked siren.

My arms and legs locked. I lay back and swallowed nervously at the sudden dryness in my throat. Whoever was hunkered over the other end of the shotgun knew the advantage of keeping his head below the sun. Blinded, I carefully moved my hand just high enough to diffuse the sun's brightness and coax features from a frazzled silhouette of white, shoulder-length hair.

The beady eyes of a cantankerous old man, his upper lip curled into a snarl, emerged from the glare. A week's growth of tobacco-stained stubble forced severity into his scowl. Thin white arms protruded from the short sleeves of a green, open-necked shirt. A pair of bone white legs in black socks and sandals dropped from rumpled, buff-colored shorts.

After a careful assessment of the situation, I figured I could slap the barrel of the shotgun, jerk it from the old man's hands, and kick his feet out from under him—one quick, disabling move. I was no fighter, no stack of muscle, but I kept my six-foot, 165-pound frame taut enough to handle this skinny old geezer. However, the fall might kill the old bastard, or worse, it might force him to pull the trigger. I'd done enough hunting to know that a blast from the barrel of a twelve-gauge shotgun a few inches from my face wouldn't leave enough brain matter to satisfy a snacking magpie.

My heart was slamming inside of my chest. I eased up on both elbows. The old man stiffened and took two steps back. I studied the eyes. They were fierce as hell, but they didn't strike me as the property of a cold-blooded killer. They more likely belonged to the owner of a hidden whiskey still. Nobody had told the old fool Prohibition was over.

"You government?" The old man spat a string of tobacco juice that hung off his chin like a spiderweb. With a deft shrug of his shoulder, he wiped it away and then nodded toward my map. "If you're government, you best start making tracks. If you're goddamned IRS, you're gonna be walking out of here with a butt full of buckshot no matter what you're up to."

Certain I'd detected a trace of humor in the old man's belligerent squawk, I sat up and plucked a couple of pine needles from the sleeve of my flannel shirt. "Not government," I said. "And I'm sure as hell not IRS."

"What then? Speak up fast, son. Ya git old like me, your fingers start running out of patience quick."

"I'm a novelist."

"Novelist my ass," the old man grumbled. "Got yourself a name, mister novelist?"

"Adams. Stuart Adams."

"Never heard of you."

I couldn't keep from grinning. There was probably more than me that this old geezer hadn't heard of. "I'll have to take that up with my publicist."

"Don't be getting smart with me, boy. In case you haven't noticed, you're sitting at the business end of a twelve-gauge shotgun."

I'd noticed, all right. "Yeah?" I held up my map. Using it and my handheld GPS, I knew exactly where I was. "According to my map, I'm also sitting on public land. Maybe you know something I don't?"

"That's a likely possibility. The problem with you damn yuppie types is you put on your little designer hats, you climb into your gas-sucking SUVs, and you think you're Marlin Perkins. Not one of the lot of you knows how to read a damn map."

Yuppie type? Slowly, I lifted my sweat-stained Orvis from the soft dirt, brushed dust from its wide brim, and placed it snugly back on my head. "Good for trout fishing," I said. "Keeps the sun off my neck. And I doubt that a black, ninety-six, oil-dripping Wrangler etched by sagebrush and still covered in the dust of my last four outings exactly qualifies as a yuppie-mobile."

"I don't give a rat's ass what kind of a hat you wear or what kind of a car you drive. The point I'm making here is you're trespassing. Man's got a constitutional right to protect his property, so you best start talking or I'm gonna start doing some protecting."

"All right." I started to reach for a photocopy of a letter I carried in my shirt pocket.

The old man stiffened and clutched harder at his weapon.

"Look, mister," I said, my fear giving way to annoyance, "I'm not armed, and I'm sure as hell not here to rob you. If you'll just lighten up a little, I've got a letter that'll explain what I'm doing."

"Trespassing, that's what you're doing. I'm not interested in the obvious. Do what you was gonna; just keep your damn hands where I can see 'em."

Still uncertain what the old geezer might do, I carefully lifted the flap on my shirt pocket and pinched out the letter.

He snatched it from my fingers and shook out the folds. "1847?" He squinted his skepticism. "Little old for a letter of introduction."

"If you'll just read it, it'll explain—"

"No," the old man snapped testily, tossing the letter back in my lap. "You read it. Not taking no chances with the likes of you."

"All right. It's dated August 8, 18—"

"I seen that part. Git on with the important stuff."

Stupid old fart. I cleared my throat and began to read.

Dear Theo,

 Since the last time I wrote, things has warmed up some. It ain't like the East out here in these San Juan mountains. Every night is cold and every day is hot. But there are many interestin things to see and lots of good huntin.

 We came upon a most fascinatin find the other day. Apparently there was some elephants that lived in these mountains. We found what appeared to be a tusk and some bones embedded in the rock that must have been as long as a wagon and a team of mules. Neither me or Ned ever seen anything like it. Trevor says he thinks he might have seen a likeness in a newspaper once, but he ain't too sure. We chipped on it some thinkin maybe we could at least get a piece of it. It broke like rock so we didn't try no more. Couldn't haul it out anyway.

 Looks like Ned and Trevor is packin out, so I best follow. Don't know when I'll get this letter posted.

 Your dear brother,

 Warren Henry

 p.s. Still no gold.

"So, it's gold you're after. Isn't that right?" The old man barked it as if he finally had something on me.

"Nope. I'm interested in the mammoth."

"Where'd you get that letter?"

"Garage sale. Found it stuck inside a box of old books."

My girlfriend, Marion Chandler, and I had stopped at the sale at a house in the mountains. I never went to garage sales, but she was looking for an antique lamp and insisted that I pull over. While I waited for her to browse, I spotted the books. The entire box—a dozen or so hardbacks—was marked at five bucks. I didn't even look at them. I snatched up the box and headed for the lady at the checkout table.

Marion was amused. "You're buying something?" she asked, a smile of disbelief crinkling the corners of her eyes. "A little impulsive, isn't it?"

I tossed down my five. "Maybe, but I figure you only live once."

That night I had a chance to sort through my newly acquired collection. It turned out that the only book I might be interested in was the one that lay on top of the pile—a 1940s account of an expedition into the Congo. The rest were old children's books and an assortment of odds and ends of no value to me. I'd just tossed the last book back into the box and was about to throw the rest into the trash when I noticed a yellowed piece of paper sticking out from one of the books, the envelope containing the letter.

The old man was skeptical. "What's a novelist doing looking for a damn mammoth in the middle of the San Juans?"

I stood slowly, brushing a few more pine needles from the seat of my jeans. "I'm looking for a story," I said, an intentional understatement. I saw no need to explain to the old man that I was looking for the *big* book. With ten mid-list novels under my belt, self-doubt was growing faster than the gray was spreading from my temples into the thick tousle of my dark brown hair. Marion insisted that the color transformation complemented my denim-blue eyes and gave me the look, she said, of a distinguished writer. Easy for her to say. At twenty-nine, her crow's-feet didn't remain after her smile was gone. Nor did she have to contend with a salt-and-pepper beard that, two days neglected, could turn the face of her so-called distinguished writer into something resembling the haggard mug of a destitute drunk. The truth was, Marion and me were marching to the ticks of two very different clocks.

"Story, huh?" The old man relaxed a little. Skepticism faded from his eyes when he clicked the shotgun's hammers to their safety position. "What do you know about that feller who wrote your letter?" His tone was a little less abrasive, borderline conversational.

"Warren Henry?" I slipped the letter back into my pocket and recalled some of my Internet research. "Not much. I managed to track down a great-great-granddaughter who knew that Warren and a couple of friends had gone west looking for gold. He never came back, and they figured he froze or starved to death. Turned out to be right. I stumbled across the story in a defunct Durango newspaper.

Warren Henry's frozen body had been hauled down from the Silverton area. They'd identified him with this letter that I guess never got mailed."

The old man stared at me, sizing me up as if I was part of a problem yet to be worked out. A second later, he surprised me by handing me the shotgun.

"Shoot me if you was going to."

"What?" My eyes flashed between the old man and the shotgun.

"Shoot me if that's what you come here to do."

"You're insane, old man," I said, braver now that I was armed. "I'm not going to shoot you."

"That's good," the old man said with a tinny cackle. He squeezed out a long fart that sounded like a slowly closing door on rusty hinges. "That old gun isn't loaded anyway." He turned and started walking into the trees.

Bewildered, I broke open the shotgun and stared at the circular glare of two empty barrels.

"Get your stuff," the old man yelled over his shoulder. "Got someone you need to meet."

Half annoyed, half curious, I put on my backpack and, shotgun in hand, caught up with the old man. With the exception of the water sloshing in the bottle holster of my backpack, we moved in silence under the canopy of an azure sky. The air was warm, filled with the sweet scent of ponderosa. Scolding chipmunks scurried like tiny shadows through the undergrowth. Aspens quaked in the breeze, which carried a raven's homely message over the valley. A small herd of mule deer, ears pricked in alert, trotted to the far side of a meadow dotted with blue flax, larkspur, yucca, and sporadic clusters of waist-high sagebrush.

Half a mile later, we stood at the opening of a gated stucco wall. I peered through the bars of the iron gate at a footpath that went straight for a hundred feet before disappearing into the trees.

"Where's it go?" I asked.

The old man fished a large key from a crack in the base of the wall, twisted it in the lock, and then spat his juice before pulling open the creaking gate. "If you'll go in, I imagine you'll find out."

I started through, and then I hesitated. Aside from the fact that he hadn't shot me with an empty gun, I had no reason to trust the old man. "After you."

He glared at me. "You think I'm gonna lock you up or what?"

"No, because I don't intend to give you the chance."

He mumbled something about Christ in heaven, unloaded his spent wad of tobacco, and stepped through the gate.

I started to follow but stopped. Images suddenly flooded my mind. With my eyes I could see the gate, but in my mind I was looking at a zigzagging stairway ascending into a towering wall of red cliffs. What the hell was it? I turned, already knowing what was behind me. The image of an ocean flashed through my mind. There was a stone pier with three boats, all with masts. They were small with long, pointed bows but not like anything I'd ever seen. They were white with brightly painted images of dolphins on their sides. Their hulls—smooth, not planked—looked as if they were made out of some type of fabric. Beyond the pier, there was a harbor protected from the open ocean by an arcing seawall of rock. Even the air was damp, salty, and filled with the cries of gulls. Impossible.

I shook my head, blinked, and started to rub my eyes but stopped. The mental picture, or whatever the hell it was, suddenly vanished. Pier, boats, harbor—everything was gone. Trees now stood where, seconds earlier, an ocean had glistened beneath the sun. The air was dry, not a trace of humidity. Baffled, I turned back to the stairs and the red cliff. They were gone. The only thing I saw was that grumpy old man standing just beyond the iron gate, glowering at me through eyes squinted with impatience.

"You coming or not?" the old geezer squawked.

I just stared at him for a few seconds, trying to get my bearings. If he saw shock in my face, he didn't show it.

I followed him into a courtyard whose centerpiece was a white marble fountain with three urn-bearing cherubim pouring water into a lily pond. The buzz of bees stirred amid sprays of pansies, geraniums, and marigolds. A rainbow of roses threaded through a lattice gazebo and climbed over arbors that covered various points of the flagstone walkways.

I couldn't believe what I was seeing. The house was a mansion with a dormered, red tile roof and vine-covered walls of stucco. Slightly recessed leaded windows added contrasting shades of sunlight to the superstructure. An eight-foot, stucco-and-rock wall, interrupted on at least three occasions by iron gates, surrounded the several acres of yard, gardens, and various outbuildings that made up the estate. I tried to blink it away, but this time the mansion and all its quiet splendor remained.

A Mediterranean villa in the heart of the San Juans?

I followed the old man to a side entrance of the house. We passed through hallways of polished wooden floors, past rooms filled with exquisite statuary, priceless paintings, and ornate vases gracing marble pedestals. One room was a menagerie of big game trophies— lion, grizzly, rhino, leopard, and water buffalo. Another, a billiard room, contained a massive fireplace and one solid glass wall with a stunning vista of the mountains. We walked over Persian carpets and beneath crystal chandeliers, passing enough antique furniture to furnish a Kuwaiti palace. The writer in me wanted to wander off in every direction, linger, study the view, the art, the antiques, and the taxidermy, shoot a game of pool, or maybe even dive into one. But the old man, apparently accustomed to life in a world-class museum, marched past everything that did not relate to his single objective, whatever the hell that may have been. Judging by his attire and frazzled appearance, I figured him for an employee of the estate, janitor maybe.

We traveled the entire length of the house, arriving at the glass doors of an immense solarium. My companion threw open the doors and, with a tilting head gesture, motioned me in. I was beginning to trust him, so I stepped in.

The warm musty air of a rain forest engulfed me like a damp blanket. Condensation on the glass ceiling beaded and dripped with leathery splashes over a room bristling with vegetation: ferns, mosses, banana trees with clusters of green fruit, vines with orchids. A blue and yellow macaw winked from a branch, while a four-foot iguana sunned on a slab of sandstone. A small waterfall tinkled into a brook, snaked through the foliage, and then disappeared through a fissure in the lichen-covered rock.

Impressive as it was, the feature that turned my head, drew me in short, unbelieving steps, had nothing to do with waterfalls, flora, or fauna. I was staring dumbfounded at the fully erected skeleton of a mammoth. The thing was huge, at least twelve feet at the shoulder, with tusks that jutted twenty feet or more from the skull. Its overall length, I figured, would equal that of Warren Henry's wagon and mule team.

The old man, his eyes beaming with gratification over my open-mouthed shock, stood at the door grinning for a long time before he spoke.

"Mr. Adams," he said finally, "I'd like to introduce you to Manfred."

Chapter 2

"THIS THING ISN'T SUPPOSED TO be in the San Juans," I said, recalling my vain search for evidence that the beast had once inhabited the region's prehistoric past.

"Funny," the old man said, his voice thick with contempt. "That bunch of academics at the Museum of Natural History told me the same thing." Nodding to the skeleton, he gargled out a chuckle. "Guess somebody forgot to tell old Manfred he wasn't supposed to be here." He fished a pouch of tobacco from the pocket of his shorts, plucked out a wad, and stuffed it into his cheek. He leaned against a table and folded his arms. "Since I'm making introductions, Barnes is the name—R. Wesley Barnes." The old man made no move to offer the customary handshake. Instead, he lifted a tin can from the table and spat into it. "In case you haven't figured it out, I own the place."

I stared at R. Wesley Barnes for as long as it took to elevate the old man from janitor to estate owner. "It's a pleasure," I said finally, handing him the shotgun. "I think."

Barnes, grinning, leaned the gun in a corner and raised the tin can high enough to indicate the mammoth. "You're looking at ten years of digging and another five fitting the pieces together. Reassembling a creature like that isn't as easy as a man might think."

Contemplating the task raised no images of *easy* in my mind. "I take it you're a paleontologist?"

"Nope."

"Then how do you know it's right? Did it come with a set of instructions?"

"It's right," Barnes said, annoyed by the suggestion. "I learned a long time ago that a man can teach himself just about anything he sets his mind to. I know the bones in that creature better than I know the back of my own hand, probably better than that bunch of half-wits that say it isn't supposed to be here in the first place."

"Have you told anyone?" I unshouldered my backpack and fished out a palm-sized digital Nikon. "You've got a first here, a chance to rewrite a few textbooks." I started to snap a shot.

"I don't think taking pictures is a good idea," Barnes said. "Fact is, I didn't find it on my land."

"Was I close?"

A slight grin emerged on Wes Barnes's face. "Not bad for a yuppie that don't know how to read a damn map."

"So, I *was* on public land."

Barnes hoisted himself to a seat on the edge of the table. "Don't want to mess with the lawsuits. Damn lawyers. I don't trust any of 'em no further than a hog can throw a horseshoe." Red heat rose through a web of tiny veins in his cheeks. "But there's no use blowing the old ticker over it. Fact is, I got me a bigger fish to fry." He scratched at the stubble on the side of his neck and studied me through a green-eyed glare. It was a long few seconds before he asked, "Adams, you a trustworthy man?"

I huffed out a laugh. "Didn't shoot you, did I?" I returned the Nikon to my pack, wondering why he'd asked the question.

"Nope. Guess you didn't." Barnes hesitated another moment, then scooted off the edge of the table, and stepped from the solarium. He returned with a file folder in one hand and a three-foot roll of yellowed paper in the other.

The yellowed paper that Barnes unfurled over the table was a map of the Mediterranean region. He secured the map's edges with a couple of empty flowerpots, and he used a long fingernail to tap a tiny, inked-in dot north of Crete's eastern shore. "This little island's called Sarnafi. Not even on the map. Got me a house on the west side." He gave me another wary exam before handing me the file folder. "Here, have a look."

I opened the folder and found two items. The first item, a glossy eight-by-ten, black-and-white photograph, appeared to be that of an ancient document, riddled with holes, bearing some type of writing.

The second item was a sheet of paper containing a paragraph of typed text. The sentences of the text were broken with brackets and periods, indicators normally intended to show missing words.

"What would you say if I told you that you were looking at a section of a parchment scroll produced by the hand of an Atlantean prophet?"

"Atlantean?" I asked, looking up abruptly. "You mean the *Atlantis* kind of Atlantean?"

Barnes didn't answer or even flinch. In fact, the old man's face was serious enough to send every one of my red flags straight up their poles. I closed the folder, stepped to the mammoth, and thumped one of the ribs with a middle knuckle. It made a deep, vibrating sound.

"Next thing you're gonna tell me is you took old Manfred down single-handed—with a letter opener."

"I should have figured you for the skeptic," Barnes said. "Can't say I blame you. Hell, every other year some yahoo comes up with a new theory on Atlantis."

"You're carrying the baton this year?"

Barnes spat impatiently into the can. "If you don't want to hear about it, I'd just as soon save my breath."

There was enough sincerity in the old man's indignant glare to convince me that I should at least hear him out. "All right, Barnes. I'm listening."

The indignation eased as the old man reclaimed his seat on the table next to the map. "In 1942, I was a Navy Communications Operator aboard the aircraft carrier USS *Wasp*. We were on assignment delivering Spitfires to Malta for the British when we got word that the Greek underground had ferried an American intelligence agent—codenamed Seagull—to an island in the Aegean. Seagull needed to be picked up. I volunteered as radioman for the mission. Our plane was a *TBD-1A Devastator*, an underpowered, experimental torpedo bomber that the Navy had retrofitted with pontoons and a bracket to winch it on and off the carrier. Once Seagull was safely on the plane, I was supposed to radio back a message: *The bird is in his nest.*

"We flew in under the cover of dark. Things were going fine until a German gunboat came around the beach and splashed a light over our plane. All hell broke loose. The Greeks tried to hold off the

Germans long enough for us to get into the air. The Devastator had three seats: pilot up front, radioman in the middle, gunner in the rear. Seagull was scrambling into the rear gunner's seat when he took a bullet to the back. Just before he died, he slipped me a packet of undeveloped film from a Minox."

"The camera favored by spies," I said, recalling the predecessor to my palm-sized digital. I'd learned of the Minox while doing research for my fourth novel, *The Bolivian Exile.* "Got a film cartridge the size of a button."

"You got it," Barnes confirmed. "There were a dozen of these cartridges, but the one that had the picture of the scroll was separate from the rest. Seagull begged me not to hand it over to my superiors, said when the time is right, the world needed to see. The message of this scroll, he insisted, had the power to change everything. Then, with his last few breaths, he muttered something about a volcano and a cave with a plastered hole in the wall. Of course I figured he was delirious. I didn't have the foggiest notion of what he was talking about—least not until I had one of my buddies develop that film. When I saw that photograph, I started putting things together. Seagull must have found this scroll, but circumstances didn't allow him to take it. He photographed it, hid it in the nook of a cave wall, and then plastered the hole. Probably intended to go back for it after the war."

"And you're thinking Seagull's volcano is Santorini?"

"We think Santorini is the volcano he was talking about, but we don't think the scroll is there."

"Why not?"

"Seagull's island was smaller. Even in the dark, I would have been able to see Santorini's horseshoe shape. We didn't go to Santorini that night. I can tell you that for sure."

"But, Barnes, you were the radioman. You would've had the coordinates of your pickup point."

"Normally, yes. In our case, only the pilot was privy to that information. Unfortunately, Dan Bradshaw was killed on his next mission. And since I could have been court-martialed for treason for keeping that little film cartridge, well, I wasn't anxious to ask too many questions of the men in charge.

"Anyway, Santorini was sporadically active when Seagull was in the region. He could have easily seen the plume from Sarnafi. What's more, we've uncovered some ruins there: the remains of a Pialigarian temple and a pier. But the clincher for me was the cave. When my partner told me he'd found one, I bought the island."

Barnes's unyielding eyes and elaborate surroundings were the only things keeping my skeptical tendencies in check. I glanced at the photograph. "The Minox cartridge holds about fifty shots. Why is there only one?"

"Film cartridge got nicked by a bullet. I was lucky to get one picture out of it. Damn shame, too. We think the entire scroll might have been on that roll."

Plausible, I thought, pulling the sheet of paper with the paragraph from the folder. "Translation?"

"We think it's close," Barnes said. "The scroll was written in a script known as Linear A, first discovered on clay tablets at the Minoan ruins of Knossos, in central Crete. I'd made a few contacts in the archaeological community to help me with a translation, but no one recognized the script. In the mid-fifties, I ran into an archaeologist named Alexios Mikos. Mikos introduced me to a couple of his colleagues that deciphered a later, similar script known as Linear B. The translation you got there represents their best guess."

I read the fragmented translation.

[…] my beloved […] [I have] been away from you […] think. These many years […] to a most remarkable […] name, and […] wonderful revelation which he has named, The Three Measures of Wisdom. In a strange twist that […] directed by the hand of the Great Mother, I believe […] recovered the knowledge that made our ancestors a great and prosperous people. […] intends to […] to a life of […] to reconcile myself with the priests so that I may satisfy this deep […] return to you. Should […] prevent me from fulfilling this dream, I send […] contains the knowledge, I am certain, that was lost to our ancestors in the […]. I have written […] the language of our ancestors, knowing that […] will understand them. If I am unable to return, […] this document with an authority whose mind has not been corrupted by the false teachings of the priests […] perpetuating the great lie. Instruct our advocate to […] that I have written, that they may bring our people out of this dark night of ignorance.

The paragraph was proof of nothing. "And you were skeptical of my letter of introduction?" I said, adding my best sarcastic smile.

There were no apologies in Barnes's shrug. "So, what do you make of the message?"

I scanned the document again. "Looks like some guy's been away awhile. Learned about this *Three Measures of Wisdom* from somebody. Thinks some goddess led him to it. Seems to think it's the wisdom that made his ancestors great. Must have been fighting with his priests. Looks like the guy intended to come back to save his people." I looked up at Barnes. "Atlantis is going to rise again, right?"

"Look at the facts, Adams. The script is early Minoan. *Santorini* is the modern name for the volcanic island of Thera—center of ancient Minoan civilization. Thera, classified as a super volcano, erupted in 1628 BC, a cataclysm that made Mount Saint Helens look like the pop of a firecracker. The blast destroyed everything in the vicinity. Excavations at Akrotiri, on the southern shore of the island, show an advanced enough society to make a lot of archaeologists suspect that Thera was the likely basis for Plato's story."

I frowned, but it wasn't the Minoan/Atlantean connection that caused it. I'd seen enough of the PBS documentaries to know the plausibility of the theory. Of all the endless speculation on Atlantis, Thera as the probable location of the lost continent was, to me, the most compelling. No UFOs. No energy vortexes. Nobody jetting around in nuclear backpacks. Advanced for the times, the Minoans were an art-loving, extremely prosperous, seafaring community who enjoyed the amenities of hot and cold running water and flushing toilets. The strangest thing about those people was their love for the sport of bull jumping. But even that, I figured, wasn't unlike the freestyle bullfighters that had emerged within the American rodeo. *Cowboy protectors* they were called, evolving from rodeo clown to competitive sportsmen in their own right.

What bothered me was Barnes's time line. I glanced again at the period-riddled paragraph. "You said this thing wasn't translated until the fifties?"

"That's right."

"Then if Seagull found it in the early forties, why would he have told you that it was something the world needed to see? How could he have known that?"

There was something bordering on admiration in Barnes's smile when he said, "A man with a sharp mind. I like this about you. After the war, I did a little research on Seagull. His name was Lawrence Bernard Stevenson, a brilliant old boy with a PhD in philosophy. In addition to being *the* most respected asset in America's pre-CIA intelligence community, Dr. Stevenson had a deep interest in archaeology. What's more, he was a renowned expert in prehistoric forms of writing. Leading scholars of the day consulted him frequently for his paleographic expertise. As far as the general world of academia was concerned, Linear A had never been deciphered. But you take a man with a mind like Stevenson's, and, well, I'm guessing he knew things your average academic didn't."

"No mammoths in the San Juans?"

"Exactly. Whatever Seagull knew, he figured it was important enough to pass it on with his dying words. That's got to be worth something."

Barnes had developed a pretty neat and logical package. But there was still one thing that made no sense. "You've got a lot of pieces to a very intriguing puzzle, and it looks like some might even fit. But there's one piece, an odd one, that I haven't quite figured out."

"What's that?"

"Me. Why are you telling me all of this?"

Grinning, the old man pushed himself off the table. "I was wondering when you were gonna get around to asking. Grab your purse, Adams. Got something else I want to show you."

I followed Wes Barnes down the hallway to a large, oak-paneled office that had the sweet-musty smell of a library. With the exception of a window that arched to just below the twelve-foot ceiling, three of the walls were lined with books nestled in oak shelving. The fourth wall was home to a copier, a fax machine, and a smattering of other office equipment. At the center of the room sat an executive desk. The only items on the desk were a brass lamp and a laptop computer. A ticker tape feed crawled across the screen of the laptop.

I planted both hands on either side of the computer and studied the colorful display of bar graphs, charts, and floating symbols.

"So this is how you pay your rent?" I said, partly joking but mostly envious.

Barnes grinned proudly. "Adams, you've been talking to an orphan boy from a poor southern town who barely made it through the eighth grade. Had to figure out some way to put a roof over my head. It's a simple matter of learning how to play the game. It's like the song says, you've got to know when to hold 'em, know when to fold 'em. You take a man that knows what he's doing, hamburgers and microchips can produce a pretty damn good life. These days I leave most of the holding and folding to my firm in Atlanta." He nodded to the laptop. "I drop in once in a while, check out the action. I see something interesting, I buy it. Just kind of tinker around, really. I don't need the money or the stress. Besides, I got me a more interesting way to spend my time." Barnes stepped to one of the bookshelves and passed a hand over a row of books. "Tell me what you see here, Adams."

I stepped over, scanned the line of books, and stopped when I came to the spine of one I recognized—mine. Then, I saw another, and another, and I kept going until I realized that all ten of my novels were nestled on that shelf. "I'll be damned. Someone actually does buy those things."

Barnes removed *Rendezvous with an Angel* and leafed to my picture on the back page.

"You knew it was me?" I asked.

"From the instant you lifted your hat." A yellow-toothed grin came over the old man's face. "Adams, you may find this to be a rather unbelievable matter of coincidence, but I've been looking for a writer of your caliber, someone who can reach an audience, help me tell this story."

The odd piece to the puzzle suddenly fit. "You're looking for a ghostwriter?" I said. I couldn't keep the contempt out of my voice. "I do the work, you get the glory, that it?"

Of course Barnes wouldn't understand why I wasn't smiling. Youthful ambition, a few too many beers on the golf course, and a chronically hyper entrepreneur named Steve Faust—he got rich in offshore investing—enticed me into the murky bog of one such project. Faust, assuming the world wanted to read every boring detail of his miserable, self-indulgent life, hired me to perform the deed. In my entire career, I had never done so many rewrites or come so close to committing murder.

"Can't help you, Barnes," I said, tossing the file folder on the desk. "Been there, done that."

"So, you think I'm looking for glory, do ya? Well, I don't need or want any of your damn glory. I don't even want my name on the damn book—outside or in. I'm looking at this thing as a possible opportunity to give something back to the world. The Pialigarians are our only link to the lost culture of the Minoans. But they're a poor people. Their kids grow up and leave the island. There's nothing to keep them there. If they're going to survive, the young people need a reason to stay; they need jobs. But not just any kind of jobs. They need an industry that'll preserve their heritage. I've talked to a lot of people about it, and the only way this is going to happen is through tourism. Adams, if we lose the Pialigarians, we lose a rare link to our ancient past. We need a guy like you to tell their story, to get the world emotionally invested in who these people are. This scroll is going to pique their attention. It'll be the catalyst that's going to help make this happen."

"Yeah? And what if you find this scroll and there's nothing to it? What if it doesn't grab the world by the throat?"

"It'd be your job to make sure that it does."

"I see. Spin a tale, hype it up, build it and they will come. If I was good at doing that, I'd probably make a hell of a lot more money selling used cars."

Barnes fixed his piercing eyes on mine. "I don't think you're going to have to hype anything, Adams. Seagull believed the message of the scroll had the power to change everything. I'm betting on it. I think there's one hell of a good chance that we're on the verge of uncovering the blueprint for a new world order."

New world order? Give me a break. I suppressed a smile, pulled my wallet, and fished out the business card of my agent. "Call Claudia Epstein," I said, holding the card out to Barnes. "New York. You can even tell her I sent you. I'm sure she's got a young writer or two that would love to help you usher in your new world order."

Barnes didn't take the card or return the smile. "A doddering old fart with too much money. That what you're thinking, Adams?"

The definition was close enough. "You've got to admit, Barnes, it all sounds pretty bizarre."

"You have talent, and you're looking for a story. Why else would you be out chasing a damn mammoth that isn't supposed to exist? A guy crazy enough to do that ought to at least be open-minded enough to listen to the deal I'm willing to offer."

Hooking up with a delusional old geezer bent on saving a dying people (not to mention the entire world) sounded like a bad preface to an even worse story. I wanted to advance my career, not nuke it. Barnes was talking fodder better suited to feed the checkout counter tabloids. I could just see it: *Aliens from Atlantis Reveal New World Order.*

Still, my hope of crafting a story of an adventure that I alone could tell had been thwarted by the fact that the old man had beat me to the discovery of the mammoth. Yeah, I could still tell the story, but it wouldn't be mine. The fact was, I had as little now as when I first set out on my quest. Would I have less by giving the old man another five minutes to waste?

"All right, Barnes, I'm listening. Just don't get your hopes up."

"Good," he said, and clasping a wrist behind his back, he began a circular, contemplative stroll, his eyes drifting upward as if it were from the airy heights of the room that he would draw the elements of his proposal. "First of all, I take care of all your expenses: travel, food, the works. For lodging, I put you up at my place on Sarnafi. It's got a view, it's private, and it's close enough to the site to keep you on top of things—perfect place to write a book." Barnes turned to me. "Sound good so far?"

I slid Epstein's card back into my wallet and struck a look intended to convey a specific message: *Good* would begin with a dollar sign followed by a respectable number of digits—preferably five.

Barnes continued. "*If* we find the scroll, and *if* we go to publication, the book goes out under your name. In exchange for your trouble, and your talent as a writer, I will advance you the sum total of one hundred thousand dollars. If we don't find the scroll within a year, you keep the advance and the bragging rights to one hell of a vacation in the Aegean." Barnes turned the full, piercing force of his green eyes directly on me. "So, Adams, does it really matter if I'm a doddering old fart with too damn much money?"

I stood dumb and silent, wondering how high the sudden wave of shock had lifted my eyebrows.

Chapter 3

"SO, WHAT'S WITH THE LONG face?"

Wes Barnes sat in the aisle seat next to me. After he asked the question, he folded his newspaper and laid it in his lap.

We were bound for Rome—our first stop, the Vatican. Cardinal Salvatore Sorrentino, who had learned of the scroll from Dr. Alexios Mikos, had, by letter, invited Barnes to discuss a possible purchase. Barnes, fearing the Vatican might launch its own search for the scroll, hadn't told Sorrentino that he didn't have it yet. Barnes's main interest with Sorrentino was to see what kind of a dollar amount the cardinal was willing to put on the artifact, not with the idea of selling it, but as a way of tapping Sorrentino's expertise to determine the scroll's legitimacy.

I'd been staring out the window, lost in that fuzzy line of a horizon dividing the North Atlantic from the pearl-pink and gray splatters of a late-evening sky, thinking about Marion.

"What makes you think I've got a long face?" I said, turning to Barnes. I figured he had his nose buried too deep in that paper to notice me.

"Let me guess. It's a woman, isn't it?" He grinned softly. The shotgun-toting, tobacco-spitting troll had disappeared. Now clean-shaven, his white hair pulled neatly into a ponytail, he'd taken on an almost dignified appearance. "Usually when a man stares out a window with a face that looks like yours, he's thinking about a woman—wife, I'm figuring."

"Girlfriend, actually. But I'm working on it."

The night before I left for the trip, Marion and I were in bed basking in the afterglow of lovemaking. I was worried about the time away from her, worried what it might do to our relationship. I asked if she'd ever consider getting married.

"I thought you never wanted to get married again," she said. "I quote, 'A creatively gifted sadist couldn't conjure up the kinds of tortures inflicted by a bad marriage,' unquote. Your words exactly."

"That's right. I said a *bad* marriage. That's the exact opposite of a good one."

"What makes you think ours would be a good one?"

"What makes you think it wouldn't?"

She propped her head in her palm, her eyes suddenly clouded with memories of a very oppressive ex. "I don't know," she said, shrugging a bare shoulder. "What's wrong with the way we're doing it now?"

"Nothing. But we've been doing it this way for over two years. I was just thinking maybe we ought to kick it up a notch or two."

She didn't say anything for a long time, a good indication that I'd have been better off keeping my mouth shut.

"Let's talk about it when you get back, Stuart."

That was how we left it. Nothing more said. Just a goodbye hug, a kiss, a good-luck-with-your-story kind of farewell. However, there was something different in the way she acted, a distance in her voice that had me worried.

"Don't tell me. You and your girl fought because she didn't want you going on this trip?"

"Not exactly. She seems to think the time apart will do us some good. Guess she thinks I'm getting too serious."

"Are you?"

"She keeps her apartment in Dallas, but she loves the mountains. Her rent was starting to look like wasted money, so I figured she might as well move in with me. She travels a lot; does interior design for residential offices. Doesn't even know what city she's in half the time."

"Business type, huh?" That information seemed to answer a question for him. "Smart, independent, and aggressive, qualities I truly admire in a woman—long as she doesn't point them at me." He laughed. "Doesn't want to be tied down by children, pets, or a man."

"We've never talked about children or pets. I think she knows I won't tie her down."

"Well, in case you haven't noticed, they don't always say what's on their mind. Where a woman's involved, it helps if you take a course in mind reading."

"Thanks for the advice. I'll check out the community college when I get back."

"I figured a man your age would be well past the dating thing. You ever been married?"

"Once."

"She took you for better or for worse, and you turned out to be a lot worse than she took you for?"

"Something like that." I had it ready, but just then I wasn't in the mood to tick off the long list of details as to why things didn't work out with Alyssa Jackson.

"Been divorced long?"

I'd memorized the math. "Ten years."

"So, you ought to be pretty rested up by now."

"Believe I am."

"This girl of yours. She pretty?"

"Yup."

"And your ex? She pretty too?"

"Kind of lost my objectivity on that one."

"But she started out that way."

"She got my attention."

"You're a sucker for the pretty ones."

"If a woman turns my head, I prefer that it's not because I'm throwing up, if that's what you mean."

He laughed. "Can't say I blame you. I always figured that if a man is going to get married, he might as well get himself the prettiest woman he can find. More than likely, she'll be the last thing he sees when he goes to sleep and the first thing he sees when he wakes up in the morning. By god, she might as well be worth looking at. But, I can also tell you this: it's not all about physical beauty. There's a hell of a lot more to a good woman than her looks."

"I guess you've got a Mrs. Barnes tucked away in that big old house of yours."

"Nope," he said, resuming his scan of the *Times*. "Came close once, but it wasn't meant to happen." He popped a wrinkle out of the newspaper and added, "Don't worry about it, Adams. Things will work out for the best. They always do."

That was all he said.

Outside, the darkness had erased the view. We'd be in Rome by daybreak. I settled back in my seat to try to get some sleep. I wanted to believe Barnes, believe that everything would work out. I just couldn't shake the sinking feeling that something in Marion had changed when I brought up the idea of marriage.

KEEPING PACE WITH BARNES'S STIFF march down the busy corridor of Rome's Leonardo da Vinci airport was no easy task. He'd shot through the plane's door like a steroid-pumped racehorse tearing out of the gate. I scrambled to catch up, yawning, rubbing my eyes, and wishing like hell I'd had another cup of coffee.

"Are we late for something?" I complained. In a near trot, I wrestled with the strap of my backpack that insisted on slipping off every twenty-five steps.

"Partner should be arriving from Athens about now," Barnes said, glancing at his watch. "She'll be coming in at terminal B, gate twelve."

She? Barnes was in such a big hurry he couldn't even keep his genders straight. "You mean, *he*," I said, correcting him. "Maybe if you'd slow down a little, you could remember that your partner is a man."

"My partner *was* a man," Barnes said through a matter-of-fact glance at me, "but now she's a woman, and a damn pretty one at that."

A man that was now a woman? It'd take more than another cup of coffee to sort that one out. Why had I drawn a mental picture of Mikos as a man? Somebody had things a little confused, and I was sure it wasn't me.

"Barnes, you told me Alexios was your partner, and you either said, or you implied, that *he* was a *he*, not a she. That's what I remember."

"Well, Alexios *was* my partner, and he was most definitely a man. But all that changed after the plane crash."

Plane crash? He said it as if I should know what he was talking about. There was nothing in our conversation about a plane crash. I would have remembered. As a kid, I'd seen a small plane go down in the field behind my house. It hit a fence, clipped off a wing, spun, and burst into flames, killing all four passengers. I was the first to the scene and saw the flaming parts of the plane fall away revealing the blackened outlines that were, moments before, living human beings. It was like watching a horror movie, only there was the added smell of burning fuel and the heat of the flames on my face. It took years for the nightmares to go away. I'd wake up in a cold sweat, strapped with that helpless feeling that I should have been able to do something to save those people. No, if Barnes had mentioned a plane crash, I would have remembered.

"You never said anything about a plane crash."

Barnes squinted with a thin hint of surprise—a little too thin in my book. "You sure? I could have sworn I told you that."

"Positive," I affirmed, and I suspected right then, though I had no idea why, that he'd intentionally withheld that information.

"I could have sworn I mentioned it. Alexios went down at sea a little over a year ago. You sure I didn't tell you?"

"Why do I suddenly feel like there's more to your story than you're saying?"

"We've had our problems with the Sarnafi dig. Damned if Athens didn't pull our permit. We can't legally excavate the temple ruins, not even with a teaspoon."

"You can't what?" I was sure I'd heard him right, but it made no sense.

He just shrugged, a lame gesture that did nothing to clear up my confusion.

"Why are you paying me a hundred grand to write about a dig we can't do?"

"Who said we can't do it? I only said our permit for the temple site has been temporarily revoked."

He was dispensing important information far too slowly for my satisfaction. I stopped walking and waited. I wanted his full attention.

He hesitated and then turned to take the few steps back to me.

"Okay, Barnes, I could ask you a lot of questions, but I'd rather you save me the trouble and just tell me the whole story."

"I was getting around to it, but since you're in such a big hurry ..." He motioned with a head gesture for us to continue. "Do you mind if we keep walking?"

I went along, but I slowed our pace, and I could tell it grated on him.

"Smuggling antiquities is a big business," Barnes began to explain. "Over the years, artifacts have been mysteriously disappearing from sites all over the islands—the Cyclades in particular. A lot of people in the business think it's an organized ring, and that the mastermind behind it is a gentleman who operates under the alias of *Raphael.*"

I sensed that he expected I'd heard the name, as if it'd been splashed all over recent headlines. The name meant nothing to me. "Who's Raphael?"

"A lot of people are beginning to suspect Gustavo Giacopetti, the agent in charge of the Cyclades branch of Greece's Department of Antiquities. On the black market, a single artifact can fetch a couple years' worth of government pay, and it would appear that Giacopetti is living well beyond his means. Alexios believed he had proof that Giacopetti was skimming artifacts from a whole slew of sites. Probably had enough to get the bastard indicted. Alexios was on his way to Athens to hand over the evidence when his plane went down."

"You're saying Mikos was murdered?"

"Nobody's proved it."

"What about your site at Sarnafi? I suppose you're going to tell me that Giacopetti is in charge of that one."

"Unfortunately he is. He's the one that got us closed down ... pending further investigation. Somehow that son of a bitch convinced the higher-ups that Alexios was the one doing the skimming. When we get Sarnafi reopened, you can bet that Giacopetti will come nosing around."

Great. A Greek official capable of murder breathing down our necks. Just what I needed. "Does this guy know about the scroll?"

"Scroll? What scroll would that be?" He glanced at me, eyes smiling at his charade of deception.

His levity annoyed me. "But … you told me there was a crew working on the cave."

"That's right. And if you're lucky, we'll get there before they find it. Give you a chance to gritty up your writing with a little archaeological experience."

It was a growing effort to control the anger rising through my confusion. "What about permits, all the legal stuff?"

"Permits? You don't need a permit for wine storage."

"Wine storage?" That was it. I stopped abruptly. "Barnes, would you tell me what the hell you're talking about? You're raising a lot of questions, and if you don't mind, I'd like some straight answers for a change."

He stood there with a grin, and then he slipped an arm around my shoulders and urged me on. Speaking in soft, conciliatory tones, he said, "Relax, Adams. Our cave isn't listed as part of the Sarnafi dig. Government doesn't even know about it. Even if they see us excavating it, everybody knows that the best way to store wine in the Aegean is in caves. Temperature is constant. It's a perfect environment. People have been doing it for thousands of years. Giacopetti comes nosing around, and he probably will, that's the story he gets. Get that memorized and you'll do just fine."

I kept walking, but I brushed his hand off my shoulder. "I see. And if we just so happen to uncover an ancient scroll written by this Atlantean prophet of yours, we quietly set it aside and go on with the work of excavating your wine-storing facility?"

"That's right. Only we set it aside in New York. A friend of mine, Dr. Stanley J. Davis, at the Institute for Minoan Research, will head up the translation process. They'll scan the scroll into a high-resolution digital format for translation and further study. The institute will then hold the artifact until we can get a proper facility built to house it at the monastery on Pialigos."

"Your tourist bait," I said, relaxing a little. There was enough sincerity in his voice to make me believe he'd gotten the point that I was in no mood to be messed with.

"Tourist bait? I prefer to think of it as a future center designed to further the world's understanding of this ancient culture. Whatever you want to call it, we can't let a document of this magnitude end up in a private collection, or worse, get buried by some government bureaucracy … wind up rotting in a warehouse. There'll be a few legal hurtles, but I've already got that one covered: Weathersby & Rollins, a firm specializing in international law. These guys are the best. When the time comes, they'll figure out how to make it happen."

I liked the sound of involved law firms, and translators connected to credible institutes. I might have breathed a sigh of relief on that note were it not for one small detail that he seemed to pass over a little too quickly.

"You said we'd set the scroll aside in New York?"

"That's right."

"With government permission, I presume?"

Barnes scratched the back of his neck as if he was annoyed. "Guess you're not following what I've been saying."

"Oh, I think I follow it all right. You're saying we've got to get this thing off Greek soil … without the Greeks knowing about it."

"Well, I suppose that's one way to put it."

"Here's another way," I said. "It's called smuggling."

"Smuggling? You know, I've never thought of it quite like that."

The shifting of his eyes suggested that Barnes was looking for a plausible lie to support the one he'd just told. I glared at him scornfully, shaking my head with one of those save-your-breath kinds of looks. He responded with an audible sigh, undoubtedly the most honest noise he'd made in the last fifteen minutes.

"Adams, you got any idea what an artifact like this would bring on the black market?"

"Ten, maybe fifteen years?"

He ignored the sarcasm. "Millions. Ten, a hundred, maybe two hundred. Why do you think the Vatican wants first crack at it? If word of this thing hits the streets, people are gonna flock to the islands, and I can tell you they're not gonna be a bunch of UFO buffs in search of the secret vortex that leads to Neverland."

"No. They could be gentlemen associated with customs, the police, or, better yet, the Greek Mafia. Hell, Barnes, do you know how long I've wanted to hook up with an illegal smuggling ring? It's been a lifelong ambition. I've always thought that if I were to ever wind up murdered or in prison, I'd want to make sure I got there smuggling antiquities out of Greece."

Just then, I turned to see two security guards emerge from the flowing crowd. They were heading straight for me. My heart thumped, and every muscle in my body tensed, as if I'd sped over a rise in the road and suddenly found myself staring down the barrel of a motorcycle cop's radar gun.

The guards drew near, smiled cordially, and nodded apologies that the busy airport had forced them to pass so close. They hurried on their way, leaving me in quiet relief, laughing inside myself over the fact that I didn't even need to commit the crime to feel guilty. Some smuggler I'd make.

Barnes must have seen my jaw tighten, heard the breath stop halfway down my throat, and maybe noticed my relieved smile at the guard's passing. His voice burst with amusement when he said, "The problem with you, Adams, is that you're too paranoid. You need to lighten up. Then again, I suppose this whole thing would seem a little adventuresome to a guy whose biggest risk in life is the development of carpal tunnel. You need to get out more. You might discover that if a thing's worth doing, there's likely gonna be a little danger involved. You want a big story? Then you've got to be willing to step out into a bigger arena, take a risk or two." He opened his arms like a water-logged cormorant drying its wings, and he said something I didn't expect. "You ready to give me a farewell hug, is that it? If you want to go, then go. Just write me a nice big refund check, and you can head on back to your mountains."

I just stood there staring at him for a couple of seconds. His theatrics were juvenile as hell, but the set of his eyes was all business. The choice was mine. Going back and fixing things with Marion was a lot better than doing time in a Greek prison. But the idea of a refund … that was the part that troubled me. I'd already developed a certain feeling of warmth knowing that a hundred thousand dollars was sitting in my bank account.

I took a sobering breath. "I just want you to be up-front with me, that's all. Is that asking too much?"

"So I left out a few minor details." He dropped his arms. "You expect a man my age to remember everything?"

We'd started to resume our walk when Barnes suddenly winced and clutched at his stomach. Now what?

"Damn that airline food," he grumbled. "Always gives me the runs."

I watched him scan the airport corridor until his eyes locked on the men's room.

"Adams, if you're still with me on this deal, get on down to B-12 and pick up Niki. I'll meet you at the baggage claim." He started away.

"Niki?" I called out. The name was new to me.

"Alexios's daughter." Barnes shot the words over disinterested travelers that were beginning to fill the space between us. "Dr. Niki Mikos."

"How am I supposed to know what she looks like?" I shouted back.

"For crying out loud, Adams," Wes Barnes screeched, his pinched face suggesting that he was rapidly losing the battle for muscle control, "she looks like a damn archaeologist."

Even through the bustling crowd I was sure I could hear the tinkle of his loosened belt buckle as he disappeared through the restroom entrance.

I stood in that busy corridor feeling more hoodwinked than reassured. Write Barnes his refund check, and get out while you can— that's what my gut was telling me.

I let out a long, tired breath and stared above the passing heads at nothing in the polished granite blocks that formed the walls of the airport.

Then, for reasons that ran counter to all warnings being issued by my intuitive logic, I started shuffling down the corridor toward gate B-12.

At least there was something satisfying in walking at my own pace.

I stood at gate B-12 scanning the group of passengers emerging from the plane. What in the hell is a female archaeologist supposed to look like?

I sized up each of the many types of single women that filed off the plane. One, dressed in a business suit, punched at the keypad of a cell phone as she passed briskly by. Nope.

Another—fair-skinned with long, wavy brown hair, a tank top, cutoffs, and tennis shoes—scanned the waiting crowd, picking her steps as if it was slowly dawning on her that she was in the wrong airport. A possibility, though I figured her skin was too fair for a person who made her living in the sun. I checked her off when a man stepped from the waiting crowd and she fell into his arms.

A college-aged girl with low-slung shorts and a tattoo peeking provocatively from her upper buttocks didn't fit my archaeologist profile, but she did have me wondering what the whole tattoo might have looked like.

Another woman, wearing a baseball hat and dark glasses and pulling a powder gray canvas carry-on, emerged from behind a cluster of gabbling schoolgirls. In her late thirties, she had full, Jagger-like lips, a slender body, and black hair tied in a ponytail and falling halfway down her back. One loose strand escaped the ponytail and dangled at the left side of her face. A sleeveless khaki shirt hung open over a yellow tube top. Khaki shorts fell to just above her knees. She wore a pair of scuffed, lace-up boots with thick socks turned down over the tops of the boots. All her exposed skin—face, neck, upper chest, shoulders, and legs—was deeply tanned. Her plain, tousled appearance suggested that she was a woman more interested in her outdoor career than in making a favorable impression on the public—or a man. An archaeologist if ever I'd seen one.

When she veered from the flow of passengers to an out-of-the-way corner to scan the crowd, I decided it was time to approach.

"Excuse me," I said, stepping in front of the woman. "Would you happen to be Dr. Mikos?"

She peered up at me from behind her dark glasses, her full lips perfectly straight. "That depends on who is asking."

Definitely Greek, I thought, noting the accent. Her tone was stiff, even challenging, maybe a little surprised at being confronted by a strange man.

"My name's Stuart Adams. I'm here with Wesley Barnes."

Mention of Barnes's name drew only a slight rise from one thin eyebrow. She removed the sunglasses and let them dangle from the cord around her neck. Something in her large, dark brown eyes gave me the strangest feeling that we'd met, though I couldn't imagine where.

"It would appear that you are here with no one," she said, searching the empty space around me.

I glanced halfway over my shoulder and nodded in the general direction of the men's room. I was still trying to remember where I'd seen her. "Barnes made a personal stop. He's supposed to meet us at the baggage claim."

"Oh yes, you are the novelist from Colorado."

In the next instant, she was off in a stiff gait that would've smoked the wheels off a lesser carry-on. I clutched the shoulder strap of my backpack and took off like a late commuter running to catch a rolling bus.

"I understand you're working at the site in Knossos," I said, catching up to her and matching her stride as if I was the one who'd set the pace.

"You are familiar with Knossos?"

"Minoan ruins on Crete. Discovered by Sir Arthur Evans. 1900, if my memory serves me right." That was the extent of information I'd retained from a couple of excursions on the Internet.

"I see you are a scholar of sorts," she said, the thin sliver of a smile threatening to soften her face. She put it in check by increasing her pace. "Actually, the site was discovered over twenty years earlier … 1878, to be precise. A merchant from Iraklion, Minos Kalokairinos, first uncovered two of the palace storerooms."

"Oh yeah. I forgot about Minos Kalokairinos."

She ignored my stab at levity.

"Before that, the locals often found ancient artifacts while working in their fields. Evans, of course, is credited for the discovery of Minoan civilization which until that time was, I am sure you already know, mentioned only vaguely through Greek mythology."

"Exactly," I said through a lying grin. "I didn't want to bore you with the finer details."

"Bore me with details, Mr. Adams? Surely you know that an archaeologist is keen on details, *especially* the finer ones. I would assume the same would be true of the novelist."

"Oh, we're keen on details, all right," I said with a laugh. "And the great thing about fiction is that if you don't know it, you just make it up."

"Make it up? In my work, we sometimes get it wrong, but we do not *make it up*. Fabrication is a luxury that no archaeologist can afford."

Where was this woman when they passed out a sense of humor? Something was bothering her, and I had a pretty good idea what it was. With nothing to lose in the popularity department, I decided to test my theory.

"You don't like the fact that I'm a novelist, do you?"

"Why would I care what you do for a living?"

"Because I'm not a scientist. You don't want a novelist telling the world about your scroll. You're afraid all the facts aren't going to be lined up in a nice straight little row."

She stopped and turned sharply toward me, her eyes flaring large, burning with a flame that incinerated all traces of familiarity. "In the first place, Mr. Adams, it is not my scroll. Like you, I was commissioned to do a job. Writing fiction is your specialty. Science is mine. I only hope that you do not undermine the plight of the Pialigarian people or smear the face of science beneath the cheap façade of sensationalized Hollywood entertainment. Atlantis has suffered enough at the hands of armchair amateurs bent on doing nothing more than selling books. If we are lucky enough to find it, the scroll could provide us with concrete evidence that Atlantis was a real place, populated by real people, with living descendants who have real feelings about their ancestry. It was my father's vision to lift this legendary continent from the fantasy realm of science fiction to that of a legitimate archaeological study. But more importantly, we have found a dying people in desperate need of our help. I only hope that when you write your story, you refrain from making up your facts, from displaying these people like ... like some kind of a human curiosity in a circus sideshow. The simple truth, I am most certain, will serve us all quite adequately."

Bingo. Mother Teresa meets Atlantis.

She ended her little sermonette with a sniff and then turned to resume her march, this time at warp speed. I didn't even try to keep up. Her carry-on roared dangerously over the concrete floor, popped over cracks, and buzzed through patches of inlaid brick. I had the feeling that if we didn't get to the baggage claim soon, someone was going to get hurt, and it wasn't going to be me.

We waited in uncomfortable silence for Barnes to arrive. It was with some relief that I finally spotted him coming with the flow of people down the corridor.

The doctor saw him and waved excitedly. "Rufus!"

Rufus? The *R* of R. Wesley Barnes. He didn't strike me as a Rufus.

Barnes, arms open, full of smiles, his yellow teeth reflecting a thin spear of Roman sunlight, embraced a very different woman than the one that had just lectured me. In his arms, she was warm and cuddly as a kitten, borderline cute.

"I see you found my girl from Santorini," Barnes said, as I approached. He patted his purring kitten on the shoulder.

"Yeah," I said. "Guess I know more about spotting archaeologists than I thought."

"Oh, do you now?" Dr. Mikos snapped, the lips going straight again. "What, Mr. Adams, is an archaeologist supposed to look like? We come in all shapes and sizes. Like novelists, no?"

"No. I mean *yes*." What I meant was, I didn't know what the hell I meant. I'd never seen a purring kitten turn so quickly into a hissing tigress. "All shapes. Sizes. All those things."

She gave me a final once-over and then excused herself for the ladies' room. At that same moment I noticed a humongous powder gray suitcase emerge from the cargo hold and tumble like a bloated cow carcass onto the carousel. Even a lowly novelist could deduce by its color, composition, and style that it matched Dr. Mikos's carry-on. Barnes saw it but made no move to get it. I stepped over and winched the behemoth to the floor. She must have packed her whole library. Fortunately, the carcass, too, was equipped with tractor tires.

Barnes, oblivious to my feat, fished out a fresh wad of tobacco and watched the doctor make her way toward the ladies' room. "Ever seen a lovelier woman, Adams?" he asked, stuffing the stringy mass inside his cheek.

I stepped next to him just as the khaki-adorned, boot-clad doctor disappeared through the bathroom door. Seeing no noble reason to dispute the old man's tastes, I decided to play along. "It's a ploy, isn't it, Barnes, using a woman and a hunk of cash to suck me into your little smuggling ring?"

"Worked too, didn't it?" The way he was grinning, a guy might think Barnes was talking about Miss Greece. "Problem is, this woman seems to be having a slight effect on your IQ."

I shook my head and countered with a grin of my own. "Whatever you say—*Rufus*."

Barnes's eyes narrowed into a pair of contemptuous slits. "You know, Adams, I'd rather you didn't call me that. Far as I'm concerned, it could be the name of someone's pet chicken."

"Mother give it to you?"

"Having a bad day, I figure."

"I wonder if that had anything to do with the fact that you just showed up."

He pondered the question long enough for his tongue to work the tobacco into its proper place. "The initial," he said finally, "has a more distinguished ring. Niki's the only one that can roll the *R* off her tongue like it's supposed to go. So, if you don't mind …"

"I'll tell you what, Barnes. You let me know if you've got any more little surprises up your sleeve, and I promise I won't call you … well … you know what."

The lid of one eye fluttered slightly as he considered the proposition. He carelessly spat an uncooperative flake of tobacco over the concrete floor. "Deal."

Dr. Mikos rejoined us, and we were off. Tugging at the slipping shoulder strap of my backpack, cow carcass in tow, I felt as gangly as an orangutan in a bipedal amble.

Falling like a third wheel a few steps behind the arm-locked couple, I was already wishing I were back home working on my future with Marion.

Still, this Greek archaeologist had piqued my curiosity. What, in those big brown eyes of hers, could possibly be so familiar?

Chapter 4

I PICKED UP MY ROOM key at the front desk of the hotel lobby, excused myself from my new partners, and headed up to try to sleep off the fatigue of that twenty-eight-hour flight. The room had a balcony, so I stepped outside to let some of the travel buzz clear from my head. Saint Peter's Basilica, an easy walk from the hotel, stood prominent in the light haze of the late Roman morning. It should have been an awe-inspiring sight, but the uncertainty swirling around Marion, along with the twinge of guilt I felt for being there without her, made it a little depressing.

I let out an exhausted breath that accomplished nothing satisfying. Too tired to sleep, I stepped back into the room, kicked off my shoes, snatched up the laptop, and climbed into the bed to begin the banal task of transferring my longhand notes onto the computer.

There was a knock on the door.

"Yeah?" *Probably Barnes*, I thought, not bothering to get up.

"Mr. Adams, are you awake?"

It was the muffled voice of Dr. Mikos.

What the hell does she want? I rolled off the bed and pulled open the door. She stood in the hallway, barefoot, wearing a white, calf-length bathrobe—I wasn't sure what else. Her hair, free of the ponytail and the baseball hat, fell partially over one eye and spilled down over her shoulders. Her eyes—softer now, even warm, quizzical, almost playful—again evoked that odd sensation of familiarity. The stern scientist was gone, had given way, amazingly, to a woman that was actually attractive.

"I hope I did not bother you," she said, pushing the hair away from her eye, "but I believe I owe you an apology."

"Apology?"

"I fear I did not make a good first impression. As I told you, I am deeply concerned about the plight of the Pialigarian people. But there is more. You may know that my father is dead because someone believed he was in possession of the scroll. Perhaps I am overly concerned about how you will handle this artifact once we find it. I apologize if I came across as arrogant."

"Arrogant? You didn't strike me as arrogant," I lied. "A little anally retentive, maybe. But hey, we all have our faults."

"For what we wish to accomplish with the Pialigarians, a novelist of your stature is certainly the best approach."

An acceptable apology. "Thank you."

"The hotel, it has a wonderful hot tub, quite soothing after a long flight. Perhaps you would care to join me?"

"Join you? In the hot tub?"

Her tone was matter-of-fact, as innocent as if she'd just offered me a slice of pizza. I figured it must have had something to do with that notoriously loose European lifestyle, though she didn't exactly strike me as the loose type. I had to admit that I did have an unexpected curiosity about the landscape beneath that white robe, but my monogamous inclinations immediately ushered an image of Marion—frowning, arms crossed—to the forefront of my mind. And that was reason enough to decline the invitation.

But there was more: I loathed hot tubs. I didn't even know it until Alyssa and I were honeymooning at the Colorado Hotel, in Glenwood Springs. We were on our way to the hot springs pool when I caught my first whiff of the rotten-egg smell of sulfur dioxide. I couldn't get in the water. I started trembling; beads of perspiration broke out across my forehead. The combination of steam and the stink of sulfur was so nauseating that I had to go back to our room.

"Thermophobia." Alyssa's doctor explained it when she mentioned the incident at her next visit. "Fear of heat. Your husband might have accidentally gotten burned in a bath when he was a baby."

I had no recollection of any such incident, but it was a fact that my bathing choice had always been the shower. There might have been some truth to the doctor's explanation.

"Do you not enjoy the hot tub?" Dr. Mikos asked.

"No, I don't enjoy them. They make me sick."

"The hot tub makes you sick?"

"Especially after a long flight. Jet lag, I think. Probably something to do with circadian rhythms."

"Circadian rhythms?" She considered my response with the furrowed brow of a puzzled scientist. "That sounds quite serious. You should probably get some rest. Perhaps another time." She started to walk away and then stopped. "Melatonin."

"I'm sorry?"

"Melatonin," she said again. "It is a hormone produced in the pineal gland that aids in the regulation of circadian rhythms. Perhaps you should consider trying it as a dietary supplement." She turned and walked down the hall. "I will see you in the lobby at one thirty," she called over her shoulder.

"One thirty," I called back.

I closed the door and leaned against it. Jet lag? Circadian rhythms? How in the hell did I come up with that? I hadn't thought about circadian rhythms since I'd learned to pronounce the word in freshman biology. Was I afraid to admit that I had a girlfriend who might take a pretty dim view of me splashing around in a hot tub with a half-naked female, even if she was an archaeologist?

I pushed away from the door and sunk back into the bed. Maybe my biological clock was experiencing a serious synchronizational malfunction.

Or maybe Barnes was right; the woman really was having a serious effect on my IQ.

I STOOD IN THE GLASS-ENCLOSED hotel lobby, hands thrust in the pockets of my slacks fondling loose change, scanning the busy street in front of the hotel. 1:25 PM. The Vatican limo had been scheduled to arrive within the next five minutes. If my calculations were correct, Dr. Mikos, Barnes, and I would be leaving for our meeting with Cardinal Sorrentino at about the same time the 5:30 AM alarm in my bedroom in Colorado would go off. Marion would be there. She'd slap the clock into silence and snuggle deeper into the warmth of the feather comforter. She'd lie there for a while, thinking. About us? By mid-afternoon, she'd be back at her apartment in Dallas. In two days, it'd be San Francisco, bidding another job. That was all I knew of her schedule.

I tugged at the collar of my shirt and coaxed a little more slack into the knot of my necktie. Vatican dress code required that I break a several-year abstinence from wearing my navy blazer and tie. Not that I had anything against dressing up, but T-shirts and jeans usually sufficed for my life in the mountains.

Wes Barnes sat in perfect ease at the other side of the lobby. He was calm, legs crossed, the full spread of a newspaper draped like a drying dish towel between his extended arms. His tie was drawn neatly in place, his hair brushed back in a white wave that fell over the shoulders of his olive green business suit.

The melodic *dong* of the elevator sounded. A dark-haired woman, her eyes alert, brimming with intelligence, emerged. She walked with her head high and confident. She was dressed in a well-tailored burgundy business suit with a white blouse and a skirt cut a few inches above her knees. She wore burgundy heels and had a matching handbag slung over one shoulder. Her hair was swirled into a tight bun. Burgundy highlights blended into her cheeks and full lips and around her dark eyes. I swear I didn't know until the woman crossed the lobby and stopped directly in front of me that I was looking at Dr. Mikos.

"It would appear that your circadian rhythms are more properly synchronized," she said, a surprisingly playful glint of mischief dancing in her eyes.

"I think they'll be fine, Doctor," I said, wondering how I could have so badly misjudged this woman's potential.

In a surprise move, she reached up and retightened the knot of my tie. "Since we are going to be working together," she said, "would it not be more appropriate to drop the formalities? I would prefer that you call me Niki."

"Niki. All right. Come to think of it, the last person that called me Mr. Adams was my ex's attorney. I have no fond memories of that particular form of address."

"Good," she said, smiling. "Then I will call you Stuart."

"Well, well," Wes Barnes said, stepping up to join us. "Rome has never seen a more beautiful woman." He clutched Niki by the shoulders and gave her a light peck on the cheek. "Niki darling, you are a walking dream."

"Thank you," she said through a confident blush. "And I have to say that it is a pleasure to be accompanied by two very handsome men."

A black stretched Mercedes whisked into the pickup area and stopped. The driver stepped from the idling car, pulled open the back door, and stood waiting.

"Your limousine has arrived, Madame," Barnes said in a humorous attempt at formality. Extending an elbow toward Niki, he added, "May I have the honor?"

"It is my pleasure," Niki said, slipping her arm through Barnes's. When the two started for the door, she tossed me a glance over her shoulder. A strange thing happened. An image of the wind-beaten cliffs of an ocean island suddenly flashed through my mind—clear as day.

Who the hell is this woman?

For a few seconds I lingered, pondering the question. With no answer, I hoisted the backpack to my shoulder, and I followed my two companions into the rising heat of the Roman morning.

THE AIR INSIDE THE OFFICE of Cardinal Salvatore Sorrentino was oppressive, warm, and close, steeped in a smell reminiscent of moth-balled leather. Only a needle of the afternoon sunlight managed to penetrate drawn, heavy velvet curtains and illuminate a single spot on the wine-colored carpet. On the far wall, a huge painting of Christ, captured in the agonizing moment preceding his death, hung in pleading silence under a single dim light. I was sure that the tortured eyes of Palol Morelli's fourteenth-century rendition of the Nazarene followed my every move.

Sorrentino, dressed in the black suit and white collar of a priest, stood from behind a fortress of a desk.

"Welcome, my friends," he said offering handshakes, and with a sweeping gesture, he urged us to three leather and brass-tacked chairs fanned before his desk.

Niki took the center seat. Barnes sat to Niki's right, I to her left.

Cardinal Salvatore Sorrentino was a hawkish man, thinned by age, with sparse brown hair combed away from his pallid, liver-spotted forehead. He had penetrating brown eyes that peered from beneath a tangled brow—an appropriate character, I thought, for a man in charge of the Vatican's Secret Archives.

Another man—dark-haired, probably in his early forties, wearing an exquisitely tailored gray and pinstripe business suit—stepped into the room. Sorrentino introduced the man as Inspector Roberto De Santis, "appropriately charged," he assured us, "with security in this department." When the inspector leaned over to kiss Niki's hand, the phrase "appropriately charged" became clear. Through the opening of his buttoned jacket, I spotted an automatic pistol holstered beneath his left arm. De Santis didn't take a seat. Instead, he stood by the door, hands folded in front of him, observing.

When Niki settled into her seat, she crossed her legs, bringing the hem of her skirt several inches above her knee. I masked a stolen glance by scribbling the date at the top of the page in my notebook. She had one hell of a great pair of legs.

"Our interest in this scroll is twofold," Sorrentino said, opening the meeting. "Our most serious concern, Mr. Barnes, is the one that I outlined in my letter to you."

"Heretical Atlantean lore," Barnes said, "might pose a threat to the holy mission of the Church. I believe that's how you put it."

"Your recollection is accurate," Sorrentino said. "However, there is another, shall I say, more academic reason for our interest. As you are aware, the archives teem with fascinating artifacts and literary works, many of which I have been fortunate enough to acquire under my watch. We are most interested, of course, in those relics that concern the affairs of the Church. But we have also managed to acquire many that have little or nothing to do with our history. Some of these represent heresies that are counterproductive to the Church's mission. Apart from these, how shall I say, *substandard specimens*, I am pleased to tell you that we make our extensive collection available to qualified students and scholars of whatever faith they may be."

"And if you deem our scroll a 'substandard specimen,'" Niki asked, "you will keep it away from public and academic view? With all due respect, Cardinal, we feel strongly that whoever houses this scroll must make it available to *all* scholars, as well as to the general public—with security restrictions, of course. We believe the future of the Pialigarian people depends on it."

"Indeed," Sorrentino said, tapping his tepeed forefingers together. "I understand your need as a scientist, as a humanitarian, to make everything available to all interested parties. I am, however, only in a position to assure you that, in the event that your scroll becomes our property, the acquisitions committee will give utmost consideration to your wishes. There are sections of the archives, however, that are of concern only to us. Would one expect less? Now, does your scroll fall into this category? Only a thorough examination of the document will tell." He chuckled coolly. "I pray, Dr. Mikos, that you have not succumbed to the proliferation of rhetoric from conspiracy mongers bent on tarnishing the face of the Church. Show them nine doors, issue complete access to them all. But show them a tenth, put it off-limits for this or that reason, and the conspiracies roll."

"So," said Niki, "you can offer no assurance that the public will be granted access to the scroll?"

She was good.

"Do not be unfair, Dr. Mikos. I have yet to see this scroll of yours. Let us proceed with the intended purpose of our meeting, and *then* we will discuss the finer details." Sorrentino turned to Barnes. "I assume that you have brought the scroll?"

Barnes nodded to me, my cue to pull a copy of the photograph and the translation from my backpack. I handed the items to Barnes, who then pushed only the photograph over the desk to Sorrentino.

"For security purposes," Barnes said, "this is the best I'm gonna do for now. And since I doubt that you can read this thing," he slipped him the translation, "this might help."

Sorrentino, his brow wrinkled into a puzzled frown, gathered the pair of documents into his arthritically gnarled fingers. He glanced at the pages and then at Barnes. "Security purposes?" Waving a hand toward De Santis, he asked, "Did you … did you not assume that we would have proper security? I expected to see the scroll, Mr. Barnes. I … I thought that I made this rather clear."

A brittle moment passed before Sorrentino's eyes dropped to the impoverished copy of the artifact. He started with a perfunctory scan, but I could see that something in the photograph quickly narrowed his gaze. Shifting his eyes to the translation, I noticed that his lips moved slightly with every word. Something was going on in the secret archives of the cardinal's brain that he had no intention of revealing. His eyes suddenly hardened. With a quick, indignant breath he said, "I do not know what you are trying to accomplish here, Mr. Barnes. A photograph is nothing. *Nothing.*" Sorrentino stood and motioned for

De Santis to step over. De Santis studied the photograph, shrugged with indifference, and returned to his place by the door. "You see?" Sorrentino said. "It is impossible to talk business without the scroll." He tossed the photograph on the desk, his eyes filled with suspicion. "You *do* have the scroll, Mr. Barnes?"

"Be kind of hard to photograph a scroll you don't have, wouldn't it, Cardinal?"

It was a standoff. Sorrentino's thin lips trembled as he held a long, scorching glare on Wes Barnes. I knew Barnes would outlast him. I was right. The frustrated cardinal turned to Niki. "I presume that you, Dr. Mikos, have authenticated this document with a thorough examination."

"Unfortunately," Niki said with a professional face that continued to reveal no hint of deception, "I have not yet had the opportunity to view the scroll."

"What!" Sorrentino's right cheek began to twitch with the promise that a full-fledged spasm was imminent. "But I thought—"

"I did not come on this project until recently, *after* my father's untimely death. However, he believed that the scroll is authentic, and I support his belief."

"With all due respect to your father," Sorrentino said, "you are prepared to declare as authentic a document that you have not subjected to even one of your … your scientific tests?"

I was sure the old boy was going to suffer a stroke.

Niki was casual. "Cardinal Sorrentino, have you seen an original copy of even one book in your beloved Bible?"

"I beg your pardon."

"A fair question, I think."

"Of course I have not. The originals have long been lost."

"I see. Perhaps the cardinal has seen a photograph of the originals?"

"You know the answer to this," he snapped.

"Indeed. And yet you are prepared to declare as authentic these documents upon which you base your faith in God? What is the basis of their authenticity, Cardinal?"

"Young lady," Sorrentino's tone rose with the blood in his cheeks, "have you any idea what you are suggesting? To even consider this question is to challenge the very authority of the Church. No, this is worse. It challenges the very authority of God!" He jabbed an unsteady finger toward the ceiling.

Niki, unmoved by the outburst, smiled with the composure of Buddha. God, she was cool.

Sorrentino glanced at his own finger as though he wasn't sure how it had gotten there. He lowered his arm with a deep sigh. It reminded me of someone pulling a lever to release the air from a compressor tank.

"Forgive me, Dr. Mikos, if I have offended you, but you are treading on ground that is very sacred to my heart. You must understand that to question the authenticity of scripture would render meaningless every spiritual value that I have devoted my entire life to upholding."

"Believe it or not, Cardinal Sorrentino, I understand the sensitivity of this matter, but as a scientist, I cannot afford to be chained by dogmatic precedence. My interest lies in uncovering the truth. A spiritual value that can be shaken by truth is, in my estimation, a mere dogma that does not rest on truth."

"Truth? Ah yes. What is truth? Pilate asked this question of the Master himself. Do you know how he, the Master, responded to this question, Dr. Mikos?"

"With silence."

Sorrentino nodded. "Indeed. Perhaps some questions are best addressed with silence."

"Perhaps. But I, Cardinal, have not heard of such a question. You are satisfied to take your scriptures at their face value. I choose to examine them with the same objectivity, the same scrutiny that I will use in examining the scroll."

Sorrentino, suddenly exhausted with the exchange, turned away from us. He had to regroup his thoughts, his composure.

I glanced at Niki, hands folded in her lap, a virtuous air enshrouding her like a white lace veil. Her smile of innocence gave no hint of the fact that she'd just brought a cardinal to his knees. Something told me that he would have found it less humiliating if she'd just stood up and kicked him in the balls.

Clasping a wrist behind his back, Sorrentino stepped toward the portrait of Christ and studied it as though he were considering an invitation to join his Master on the cross. "Well then, I suppose we must deal with matters as they stand." He lingered a moment longer before turning and taking a seat on the edge of his desk. "Mr. Barnes, assuming that you do possess this scroll and assuming that the Vatican would offer to purchase it from you, how would I know that I was purchasing an antiquity *legally* extracted from Greek soil? You can show me the proper permits, I assume?"

That got my attention. I looked up from my note taking, the zing of adrenaline forcing me to shift slightly in my chair.

"You can assume that." Barnes's business amenities were beginning to wear a little thin. I could see his tongue searching his cheek for a fresh wad of tobacco.

"I can check, you know," the cardinal said sternly. "The law, it is quite severe on smugglers."

"I imagine you'd be right about that." Unfazed by the threat, Wes Barnes stood, collected the photograph and the translation from the desk, and handed them to me. "If I ever run into one of them fellows, I'll pass on your warning."

The cardinal's face went white. "You are … you are leaving? But, we have discussed none of the details of a … of a possible …"

"You know where we're staying," Barnes said. "We'll be checking out this afternoon." He removed his tobacco from an inside pocket and stuffed a wad deep into his cheek. "You get any revelations about what you think a scroll like this might be worth, you give me a call."

With a nod to the cardinal, Wes Barnes headed for the door. Niki and I followed.

Chapter 5

"WHAT DO YOU THINK, DARLING? You think the old boy believes we got something?"

The three of us had reached a fair distance from the cardinal's office when Wes Barnes asked Niki the question.

"His face," Niki said, "it was quite difficult to read, but I would say that the cardinal is at least intrigued."

"He thinks we've got something, all right," I interjected, still uneasy with the issue of legality. "He thinks we've got a one-way ticket into a Greek prison."

Barnes chuckled. "Adams here, he's worried about going to prison, becoming the love slave for some convicted Mafia hit man. Hell, Adams, just get you a soap-on-a-rope. That way you won't have to worry about bending over in the shower." He cackled like an insane man.

I pulled off my jacket and went to work loosening the top button of my shirt. "Say what you want, Barnes, but the only bars I want to be looking at are the kind that serve a cold beer." I glanced at my watch. We had three hours to pack before heading to the airport. "In fact, I think I'm gonna start looking for one of those now." I freed the button and jerked the tie from around my neck. It snapped like a whip.

"May I join you?" Niki asked. "I know of a quiet sidewalk café. It is a short walk from here. For me, a glass of wine would be a good thing."

"Sure," I said, pushing aside the image of Marion that suddenly crowded into my mind. "Come to think of it, I don't even know how to order a beer in Rome."

"Birra. Italian for beer."

"Birra." I repeated the word, minus the elegance.

When we approached the limousine, I mustered the courtesy to invite Barnes to join us. "What about you, Barnes? You up to a birra?" I hoped he'd say no.

"I'm afraid not. Dern stomach's still giving me fits. Think I'm gonna head back and have myself a nap."

"You are ill?" Niki was suddenly concerned. "I will go back with you."

"No, darling, you'd better keep an eye on Adams. Make sure he gets to the hotel on time. Hold his hand when he crosses the street. Mountain boy in a big city like this could get himself in trouble real fast."

"You never know," I agreed. "Hell, I might accidentally fall in with a ring of smugglers."

THE HOUR SPENT IN SORRENTINO'S cloistered office had given me a fresh appreciation for the cloudless, blue sky that stretched over the warm afternoon. I inhaled the humid breeze laden with the aromas of baking breads, coffee, and the tantalizing tang of sauces cooking. I watched hunched drivers of mopeds thread dangerously through honking traffic. Dark-suited businessmen with cell phones glued to their ears passed in a stiff hustle. We walked by cigarette-smoking vendors haggling with their customers in a shop-lined piazze. We passed lines of people, young and old, standing before baroque churches waiting for buses to take them to places they needed to be. Students with headsets clamped over bright red or purple spiked hair skated past a beret-clad old man feeding pigeons from a park bench.

The freedom of the open air outweighed the guilt I felt for the fact that it was an attractive woman from Santorini, not Marion, who shared the experience of a casual stroll through streets lined with more history than I could imagine.

However, it was recent history, not ancient, that I was thinking about when I hoisted the backpack over my shoulder. I was captivated by Niki's confidence in an arena that should have given Sorrentino the home field advantage. What made this Greek archaeologist tick?

"You did a pretty impressive job back there," I said.

From the corner of my eye, I watched her remove the clasp that held her hair. She shook it down her back, a sensual, potent signal that she appreciated the compliment and that she was ready to toss the barriers that stood in the way of our prospective friendship. It was a simple act, but it made me feel as if I'd just stepped into privileged territory.

"I was raised Catholic," she said, passing fingers comblike through her fluid hair. "They did not promote Bible study. My father, he was the one responsible for sparking my interest in a critical study of the scriptures. Always he said that if you understood how the Bible was put together, if you could get some feeling for the various intentions and beliefs of the many writers, then you could discern the difference between truth and the theological teachings of the church."

"Well, I think you made quite an impression on the cardinal."

Even as I said it, I had to laugh remembering some of the cardinal's blank and befuddled expressions. I'd never be able to grasp the impact that a gorgeous, intellectually superior woman would have on an old celibate like Sorrentino. We lived on two different planets, he and I.

"Not a good impression, I am afraid. I do not think the cardinal appreciates a mind that is theologically free—especially if that mind happens to belong to a woman."

"Ah, but now your guilt is turning into victimization. I'd put good money on a bet that we're not talking gender issue, here. Sorrentino wouldn't have appreciated your argument if it'd come straight from St. Peter himself."

She flashed a blushing smile. "You are too kind."

"Maybe you're just too modest."

She looked at me as if that would be impossible, and until that moment, I would have agreed. *Beautiful* was the type you hit on in the bar. *Modest* was the type that would listen to you spill your guts when you got snubbed by *beautiful*. I had a feeling that I'd have to invent a new paradigm if I was going to communicate with this woman. For now, it was a lot easier to just change the subject.

"Is Sorrentino really worried that some off-the-wall teaching's gonna pop up and lead their flock astray?"

She fell right in step. "The Church has always had a preoccupation with this concern. The cardinal, he is obviously of the old school, a man who wishes to keep things as they have always been."

"I just can't shake the feeling that the old guy's overreacting. Maybe there's something more—something he's not telling us, some secret stashed behind his door number ten."

"And now you begin to sound like one of the conspirators that the cardinal has so much difficulty appreciating. Perhaps you have some thoughts about who might have produced this scroll?"

"Me?" I was never good at substantiating intuitive feelings. "No. I'm just having a hard time believing that an entity as powerful as the Church is worried that something like this scroll might siphon off their people."

Niki explained. "When it was first suggested that Thera was a plausible location for Atlantis, that the ruins at Akrotiri may have been the very capital of the fabled continent, a great surge of visitors followed that continues to this day. People want to believe in a lost civilization. They want to believe in a golden age, that someone has solved life's many struggles, that things can be better for them than they are now. If they can somehow connect to it, touch the very spot where it happened, it can change their lives. You will see this in places like Machu Picchu in Peru or the great pyramids of Egypt. Visitors from all over the world come by the tens of thousands, often with the hope of connecting to some vortex of power that they believe emanates from these places. From what I have seen at Akrotiri, I can easily appreciate the cardinal's concerns."

We reached a sidewalk café. A smiling waiter with a lot more hair in his mustache than on top of his head greeted us enthusiastically and led us to a table for two. There, with the care of a collector examining a rare piece of china, he assisted Niki into her chair. She was gracious with the extra attention, obviously well practiced in the art of handling gawking Italian waiters.

The first two swallows of beer were exactly what I needed, so I took a third. "This is the kind of thing Barnes is counting on with Pialigos? People flocking to the island so they can see the original charter of their new world order?"

"Would you rather he build a casino?"

"What do the Pialigarians think about it?"

"They know they have to do something. They have been adapting for thousands of years. They are a resourceful people, eager to maintain their ways but realistic in how that may be done."

"Well, if they're going to open their doors to twenty-first-century tourist trade, they'd better be able to adapt." I took another swallow of beer. "But what do I know? I'm just a novelist who's being paid to write a story. Thank God that saving endangered cultures doesn't fall into my jurisdiction. They'd all be in trouble."

Her eyes lingered on mine for a moment before dropping to her glass. I sensed that my lack of concern was a mild irritation to her, but she dismissed it with a sip of wine. "May I ask you a question that is well within your jurisdiction?"

"Sure."

"This morning, you said something about an ex-wife? How is it that a tall and handsome man like you still escapes the clutches of a woman?"

The compliment surprised me. After another swallow of beer, I shot a question back to her. "What makes you think I've escaped?"

She held up her left hand and wiggled an empty ring finger.

"I could ask you the same question," I said.

"But I asked you first."

"Fair enough." I toyed with the condensation on the side of my mug. "I guess it's pretty simple, really. I'm not interested in making the same mistake again."

The instant I said it, I thought of Marion. The words *I love you* had come easily, maybe too easily. Did I even understand what they meant? I'd said that magic line to Alyssa clear up to the end—pleaded with it, actually, as though the utterance of the words every woman longs to hear would make everything work out. I could have said it ten thousand times more, and it wouldn't have made a difference. Alyssa and I were just two very different kinds of people. Was the same thing happening with Marion?

"Mistake?" Niki said. "You ... you fell out of love with your wife?"

"Can you fall out of love, or do you just fool yourself into thinking that you're in it in the first place?"

"I am not sure I understand what you mean."

"It's one of the mysteries of life that I'm trying to solve—a door-number-ten conspiracy. We tried everything: books on communication, counseling, even Bible study." I laughed, thinking how I'd tried to convince myself that a washrag like Reverend Albert Johnston could use the Bible—the product of a male-dominated culture—to unravel, even decipher, the mysteries of feminine behavior. I had the feeling that his own wife, Betty—stoically stuffy, pious as an Inquisition priest—ruled her roost with chains, black leather, and a whip. "Anyway, to make a very long and boring story short, it just didn't work."

"You divorced her?"

"Yeah. After I caught her in bed with the choir director."

"You did not."

"I did."

I'd come home early from a trip and walked in on them in our bedroom. I couldn't grasp what I saw; it didn't sink in until Alyssa gasped, pushed the guy off her, and scrambled to pull up the sheet. I just turned and walked out, too devastated to hear Alyssa screeching out explanations.

Fingers shot over Niki's lips. "Oh my god, the choir director? The one that leads the singers?"

"Apparently teaching church folks how to sing wasn't his only God-given talent. Anyway, that was that, and I guess I'm still sorting through the wreckage trying to figure out what I learned from the whole thing."

Leaning forward, Niki asked, "And what about love, Stuart Adams, have you learned?"

I let one of those nasal wisps pass for a laugh. "I'm not sure there's anything to learn. I don't think love should be like … like skiing."

"Skiing?"

"Yeah. What could be more unnatural than strapping a couple of six-foot boards on your feet and sliding down a mountain at forty miles an hour—standing up? You have to really work on that, overcome your biological aversion to dying. Love shouldn't have to be that way."

"I see. No tutoring necessary."

"That's right. No one has to teach a mother how to love her baby. Why shouldn't it be the same way between a man and a woman?"

With one finger, Niki slowly circled the rim of her wine glass. "Then, am I to assume by this question that you have no, how do you Americans say, other significant?"

"I believe you mean *significant other*. Her name's Marion."

Niki appeared puzzled as she took her next sip of wine. When she returned her glass to the table, she asked, "Then you are telling me that you have not found with your Marion this natural love of which you speak? Or, am I prying?"

I leaned back in my seat and crossed my arms. An answer to a question of this magnitude deserved a lot more preparation than a mere two-thirds of a beer. With Niki's probing eyes suddenly resting on mine like the plotting pens of a polygraph, I didn't figure this was the time to start fishing for a definitive distinction between loving Marion and the possibility that I might be using her to fill a void. I was sure that our relationship ran deeper than that, but Alyssa had shown me how easily a pretty face and a perfect body could subjugate intuitive warnings, at least temporarily. After all, I hadn't asked Marion to marry me until I was faced with the possibility of losing her.

I took another swallow of beer. "Prying," I decided.

The polygraph pens scribbled their response, reminding me that, to a woman, there was no such thing as an evasive answer. In that moment of transparency, I found myself wondering if my half-grin looked as lame as it suddenly felt.

"Forgive me, please," Niki said, laughing at herself. "I am the nosy one, no?"

"Pushing the envelope," I suggested, upgrading my grin to a smile. Anxious to shift the focus away from myself, I said, "What about you? I take it your knight in shining armor hasn't come in and swept you off your feet."

She lifted her glass with the fingertips of both hands and let it dangle a few inches from her lips. "No, he has not, but I do not give up hope." She peered at me, and her lips moved slightly, as if there was something more she wanted to say. Instead, she smiled and raised her glass to offer a toast. "Shall we drink to untutored love?"

Fascinated by her evasiveness, I wanted to push her, turn up the heat a little, but I decided to let her slide, at least for the moment. I hoisted my mug. "To untutored love."

Wineglass to beer mug—a ringing clunk.

When I drained the mug, I noticed that Niki's eyes had suddenly locked on something behind me, her smile turning to a frown. I turned to see a boy—ten or eleven—approaching our table. He had frozen in mid-stride, his eyes shifting nervously.

"Are you okay?" I asked, realizing at the same instant that the boy probably didn't understand English. When I turned to Niki for help, I only heard the scuffle as the boy bolted, snatched my backpack, and dashed off in a dead run.

In the next few seconds, I was in a full sprint pursuing the little weasel through an alley. I followed him into a piazza filled with a colorful maze of milling humanity—shoppers, young lovers kissing, friends sipping lattes, old men casting glances at the open sky, speculating, no doubt, on the capricious nature of the weather. No face revealed anything of a disturbance, nothing beyond life as usual in the eternal city.

Niki, clutching my sport coat, emerged from the alley as quickly as her high heels had allowed. Breathless, she handed me my jacket. "The boy, he got away?"

"Slick little bastard," I grumbled, still scanning the crowd.

"We should go to the police."

"I'm not sure that's a good idea."

"But why? Your notes. Your camera."

"It's the notes I'm worried about. Jesus, I detailed our intentions to smuggle the scroll out of Greece. Add the photograph, the translation, and the account of the Seagull episode I started sketching, and it'd be safe to say that you, me, and Barnes could make pretty likely candidates for surveillance."

"Surveillance? From whom? We will not be looking for the scroll in Rome. What would the Roman police care about what happens in Greece? Besides, do you forget that you are a novelist? Your notes, you simply say they are fiction. Who can dispute this?"

The uneasiness that stirred in the pit of my stomach didn't need specific names or faces of disputing parties. Replacing the backpack would be a lot safer.

Just then, a black Mercedes pulled to the curb. A man in a suit and dark glasses stepped from the rear door—Inspector De Santis, from the Vatican.

"Is there a problem?" De Santis asked as he approached.

"Stuart's backpack," Niki said. "A thief has stolen it."

"Petty thieves," De Santis said, shaking his head. "They prey on the unsuspecting tourists." He leaned close, shifting his eyes between Niki and me. "I trust the scroll was not in the bag."

"Of course not," Niki assured him. "The scroll is in a safe place."

De Santis looked at me. "And the notes of your meeting with Cardinal Sorrentino?"

I nodded. "They were in there."

"I see," De Santis said. "In all confidence, the cardinal has earned his share of political enemies within the Vatican. In the wrong hands, your notes could prove an embarrassment."

De Santis stepped away from us, removed a cell phone from an inside pocket, and punched in a set of numbers. He spoke quietly, urgently, his stiffness, I figured, reflecting the grave concern that must have been in the cardinal's voice.

When the inspector clicked off the phone, he said, "The cardinal, of course, regrets the theft. And now, he worries that word of the scroll will get to the street. There is no question; your backpack *must* be recovered. The chief of police is a personal acquaintance of Sorrentino. The cardinal has instructed me to take you to police headquarters and make a report. Chief Lo Bianco will see to it that every effort is made to retrieve your valuables."

"It's not that big a deal," I said, hoping to dissuade De Santis. "I'm sure I can replace it. Besides," I glanced at my watch, "we need to get back to the hotel. We've got a plane to catch."

"I am afraid you do not understand, Mr. Adams." De Santis lowered his tone. "The cardinal is prepared to offer Mr. Barnes ten million dollars for the scroll. He would rather the existence of this artifact remain unknown."

I think I managed to suppress the wave of shock that threatened to distort my face. Wes Barnes had his answer. The Vatican was willing to pay ten million for a scroll they'd never seen. I was right. Something in the translation had gotten Sorrentino's attention.

"To Cardinal Sorrentino," De Santis continued, "this is a matter of utmost urgency. I will assist you in filing your report. I promise, my driver will return you to your hotel in less time than you can make the walk." He pulled open the front passenger door and motioned to Niki to take a seat. "Please, I insist. This is too important a matter to neglect." Niki slipped into the car. Then, looking directly at me, De

Santis added, "Concerning the contents of your backpack, I advise you to be *very* general with Chief Lo Bianco. Where the police are concerned, a single wrong word can become the pebble that starts an avalanche of suspicion."

He's worried about a pebble, I thought, slipping into the backseat of the car. It felt more like I was on the verge of tipping a damn boulder.

Niki and I followed De Santis through the bustling corridors of police headquarters. Ceiling fans stirred the smell of scorched coffee into the air. Ringing telephones, the quiet clatter of computer keyboards, and a steady murmur of voices tightened the atmosphere. De Santis, obviously no stranger to the place, nodded gestures of recognition to deskbound personnel at every turn.

We entered a reception area where a woman—fifties, trim, pleasant smile, conservatively dressed in a white blouse and blue skirt—sat at a desk. Across the room, I noticed two gorilla-like men in black suits and dark glasses sitting on either side of a door I assumed led to the office of the police chief. It could have been my imagination, but the presence of the two men seemed to bother De Santis.

The woman looked up from a maze of paperwork spread across her desk. "Inspector De Santis," she said in a harried but pleasant greeting. "Cardinal Sorrentino just called. Chief Lo Bianco is expecting you."

"I see he has business with Greece," De Santis said, glancing in apparent recognition at the two gorillas.

"I believe that Mr. Giacopetti is just about to leave," the woman said, picking up her telephone.

Giacopetti? A blast of adrenaline detonated like a keg of powder in my stomach. I was one office away from Santorini's agent for the Department of Antiquities. I turned to Niki. The flare of her nostrils reflected something more than shock at the unexpected encounter. She was about to come face-to-face with her father's murderer.

The receptionist gave us the nod. "Chief Lo Bianco will see you now."

I had a real bad feeling as I followed De Santis and Niki across the lobby toward the office. The gorillas, possibly twins, stood from their seats, stiff and menacing. Both men nodded respectfully to De Santis as he ushered Niki through the door. But when I started to pass, one of them grabbed me at the upper arm.

I had slipped on my jacket to make a respectable appearance before the chief of police. The gorilla had, without explanation, stopped me, pulled open my jacket, and slipped his hands around my waist to pat me down for a weapon.

In a knee-jerk reaction, I grabbed the wrists of the big man. The second gorilla immediately stepped in and clamped a vise-grip on my forearm.

De Santis saw it and quickly intervened. "Vito, Apollo, it is all right. This man is not armed."

The man De Santis called Apollo hesitated and then relaxed his grasp of my arm. Vito turned his wrists slowly, freeing them from my suddenly clammy hands. Even through the dark lenses of the glasses, I could see that Vito's eyes had narrowed into a pair of reptilian slits. I'd just ticked off a killer.

"Do not be offended, Mr. Adams," De Santis said apologetically. "Rome, as you might suspect, is on heightened alert from constant threats of terrorism. These men are trained to take every precaution. They are the bodyguards of Gustavo Giacopetti, Santorini's agent for the Greek Department of Antiquities."

I summoned a shred of calm bravado. "Maybe these gentlemen could use a little training in the art of asking." I pulled open my jacket, but Vito's eyes never left mine. "Suit yourself," I said, suppressing the effects of the chill that crawled down my spine. I buttoned my jacket, nodded to the bodyguards, and stepped into the office.

Chapter 6

TWO MEN WERE ALREADY STANDING—ONE behind a desk, the other beside it—when I entered the room. Both had apparently been too infatuated with Niki to notice my brief delay.

De Santis introduced the man behind the desk—sixties, full face, tired, friendly brown eyes, brown tie loosened at the neck—as Chief of Police Antonio Lo Bianco. The other was Gustavo Giacopetti, a tall, stern man also in his sixties. He had dark, predatory eyes, a thin mustache, and black hair oiled in place. Giacopetti, wearing a charcoal, well-tailored, double-breasted suit, reminded me of a slightly scaled-down Greek version of Saddam Hussein. The guy stood with one arm folded across his stomach, the elbow of the other resting in the palm. In his other hand he held a cigarette, poised near his lips, pinched European-style between his thumb and forefinger.

"Dr. Mikos," Giacopetti said, stepping close to Niki, his head teetering with arrogance, "what an unexpected pleasure." Giacopetti delivered an extended kiss to her knuckles, his eyes slowly dropping the length of her body.

I had an instant disliking for the man. Under different circumstances, I would have been happy to offer Mr. Giacopetti another set of knuckles to kiss.

"Alexios Mikos, he is your father. Am I correct?" Giacopetti asked.

"He *was* my father." Niki pulled her hand away.

"Yes, I remember that dreadful plane crash," Giacopetti said, slightly ruffled by the snub. "Please, allow me to extend my deepest sympathies, belated as they are. A most unfortunate accident."

"Accident? So we were told." Niki's eyes had fixed angrily on Giacopetti's. "Strange that his office was ransacked, his vault emptied the very same day of this *accident*."

"Really?" A nervous smile quivered at one corner of Giacopetti's mouth. "I had not heard that." He took a step back and said nothing more.

Like hell, I thought, watching Giacopetti's eyes shift like a pair of cockroaches looking for a place to hide. The man was a bad liar.

The tension caused De Santis to step in. "My friends have experienced a small problem," he explained to Lo Bianco. "It seems that one of our pickpockets has favored a backpack that belongs to Mr. Adams."

"Yes, the cardinal did call," Lo Bianco said, his head bobbing slightly when he turned to me. "This knapsack of yours, Mr. Adams, I assume it contained valuables?"

I recalled the contents. "Camera, notebook, a photograph, a few other odds and ends inside."

"Mr. Adams is a writer," Niki said quickly, "a novelist from America. The notebook is quite important to him."

"A novelist, is it?" Lo Bianco said, turning back to me. "Often I have myself thought of writing. Crime novels, you know." I smiled with interest, trying to look as if I'd never heard that pat response of someone who'd just learned what I did for a living. Fortunately, the chief was too busy to outline his guaranteed blockbuster. Instead, he laughed tiredly and regarded the stacks of paper that cluttered his desk. "As long as I am in this job, I am afraid that police reports will make up the extent of my writing career. There is always the need for another report." He dismissed the problem with a fatalistic wave of the hand. "So, tell me of this photograph. Was it of a person? Man? Woman?" He smiled at Niki with the warmth of a beaming father. "Your lovely companion, perhaps?"

De Santis intervened. "It is the photo of a parchment that Mr. Adams hoped to authenticate for his research. We at the Vatican were sorry to inform him that his photo was a mere forgery." He turned to me, his eyes showing no hint of the fabrication. "I hope you were not too disappointed," he added.

I shrugged coolly. "Guess I'm not the only one in the world who does fiction."

Lo Bianco bobbed his head, apparently satisfied with the explanation. "So tell me, Mr. Adams, what did this backpack look like? Color? Style?" I described it, and Lo Bianco barked a few orders in Italian into the telephone. "There. If it can be found, we shall find it. And where may we reach you?"

"The Hilton," Niki said.

"And you will be leaving when?"

"As soon as we get back to the hotel."

Lo Bianco chuckled. "I hope you are not expecting miracles."

"We intend to tour the Greek islands," Niki explained. "Stuart is considering the setting for his new book." She scribbled Wes Barnes's name and telephone number on a notepad and handed it to Lo Bianco. "You may reach us here."

Giacopetti's eyes shifted with interest behind slithering tendrils of smoke. He took a final drag from the cigarette, snuffed it in an ashtray, and stepped directly in front of me. "This parchment forgery of yours, where did it come from?"

"I don't know," I said, smelling the stink of tobacco on his breath.

"The parchment itself, you have seen it?"

"I've only seen the picture."

"Your tour, Mr. Adams, it would not, by chance, be for the purpose of locating this … forgery, would it?"

My heart cranked up a couple of beats.

"Mr. Giacopetti," De Santis protested. "I have already explained Mr. Adams's purpose for inquiring about the parchment. Dr. Mikos has told us that he is considering the islands for the setting of his next book. Mr. Adams is, himself, a victim of a crime. I see no need for further questioning of this nature."

"Perhaps you are right, Inspector. But there is a matter that concerns me." Giacopetti took a step toward Niki, tilted his head back, and glared at her down his nose. "Athens has put a stop to your father's work at Sarnafi, am I correct?"

"Of course you know they did," Niki said stiffly. "It was you who propagated the lies that caused it."

"Lies?" He glanced at De Santis and Lo Bianco. "Perhaps not

everyone in our present company is aware that there were items missing from this site. Is this not what the report stated?"

I could see the muscles in Niki's jaw tighten. "What the report fails to say is that the items in question seemed to disappear somewhere between the Sarnafi site and your office. Perhaps, Mr. Giacopetti, there are holes in the floor of your office?"

"Holes, indeed," Giacopetti said with an amused chuckle. "This photograph, it makes me wonder what your father hoped to find on Sarnafi. Pialigarian pottery? An understanding of the Pialigarian social life, perhaps? Or was it, Dr. Mikos, a parchment scroll? Athens, I am certain, would be quite interested to do some intense probing into this matter."

"Athens knows what we do at Sarnafi," Niki snapped. "We hide nothing. They know it, and you know it as well."

I was hoping she'd keep the thing about wine storage to herself. Something told me a shrewd guy like Giacopetti would never buy it. Fortunately, Lo Bianco stood and lightly clapped his hands to signal the meeting had concluded.

"Well, my friends, I believe we have all the information we need. I assure you, Mr. Adams, we will do everything we can to recover your lost property." He turned to De Santis. "Please thank Cardinal Sorrentino for bringing this incident to my attention. I am always happy to assist with matters of concern to the Church."

De Santis made a slight bow. He escorted Niki through the door with me a few steps behind.

"Mr. Adams?" Giacopetti called out.

I stopped, but I only half turned.

"I hope the presumptions under which you intend to visit my country are not as fictitious as I assume your novel will be. We Greeks are an accommodating people. Our prisons are crowded, but we always seem to have room for one more guest."

"I'll keep that in mind," I said, and I walked out the door.

De Santis led us to the car. Explaining that he had further business at the police station, he remained.

We were pulling away when I glanced up to see Giacopetti watching our departure from Lo Bianco's office window. I had a bad feeling that we hadn't seen the last of him.

I slumped back in the seat and stared out the window, nothing

of the passing scenery registering in my mind. I was too busy toying
with the idea of heading back to Denver.

THE TRIP FROM ROME TO Santorini included a two-hour layover
in Athens, adequate time to buy a camera, a notebook, and a cheap
backpack. Engaging in that brief shopping spree provided enough of
a distraction to gloss over most of my worries about Giacopetti.

The Olympic Airways flight from Athens to Santorini—a three-
row commuter—bounced over the air like a pickup truck on a rutted
road. Wes Barnes, intent on passing the forty-minute flight reading
his newspaper, had taken the seat in the single row. Niki, now braless
beneath a red tank top and cutoff jeans, sat in the window seat next
to me, doing her part in keeping my mind off Giacopetti.

The plane passed over the islands of Kea, Kythnos, Serifos, Sifnos,
Kimolos, Milos, and Folegandros. Niki pointed through the sun-
washed glimmer of the water to a cluster of islands.

"There. Santorini."

Red and black cliffs of the horseshoe island jutted a thousand
feet out of the Aegean. I could see whitewashed buildings huddled
precariously close to the cliff edges. Cruise ships, like huge grains of
bleached rice, lay anchored in the cobalt harbor. The bay separating
Santorini from the smaller island of Thirassia and the uninhabited
and smaller still, Aspronisi, was actually the western edge of the volcano's crater. At the center of the crater were two more islands.

"That is Nea Kameni," Niki said of one of the islands. "It only
emerged from the sea just over three hundred years ago. It also remains
uninhabited. Palia Kameni is much older. If you like a hot mud bath,
you go there. Perhaps I can show you—once you recover from your
jet lag, of course."

I was thinking about Marion when I said, "I've made it forty-
seven years without the benefit of a mud bath. I figure I can make
it at least that many more." Still, I couldn't help wonder what Niki
would look like covered in nothing but a thin layer of mud. Rather
than dwell on that one, I took out my pad and pencil. "Tell me about
Thera's eruption."

"We know the people of ancient Thera and most of the other
islands had left their homes. Unlike Pompeii, scientists have yet to
discover even a single corpse in the excavations at Akrotiri, proof that

most of the population escaped. They were warned, we suspect, by a previous eruption. In the post-cataclysm era, the speculation is that many fleeing Minoans integrated with other cultures in much the same way that your North American Anasazi, forced by drought to abandon their elaborate dwellings, might have integrated with the Hopi and other Pueblo tribes. The Minoans did not attempt to resettle Thera. The next inhabitants were Phoenicians, many centuries later.

"The modern Pialigarians maintain that Pialigos has always been the spiritual heart of the Minoan empire. Perhaps they began as a mystical sect of the Minoans, equivalent, say, to the relationship between the Cabalists and the traditional Jew. Anthropologists tend to treat the Pialigarians as a people different from the ancient Minoans. But I believe the Pialigarian roots, which extend back to the time before recorded history, are essentially Minoan.

"The current high priestess of Pialigos, Euphemia, insists that the Minoans once possessed a mystical knowledge that had been the key to their phenomenal success, and that the Pialigarians were the keepers of this knowledge. With the eruption of Thera, the people of the empire dispersed, records were lost or destroyed, and the Minoan form of writing gradually changed from Linear A to Linear B. The most significant casualty of the ancient disaster, however, was the loss of this body of mystical knowledge.

"Sixteen hundred years after the eruption, a young Pialigarian scribe became disenchanted with his post-cataclysmic religion, charging that it had no heart, no wisdom, but consisted only of empty doctrine and meaningless ritual."

"The great lie?" I asked, remembering the broken passage in Barnes's translation.

"We believe so. The scribe's protests earned him the contempt of the priests, and they banished him from the island. According to Pialigarian lore, the scribe wandered around the world in search of the lost wisdom. When he found it, he recorded it on a parchment scroll, in the sacred script of his ancestors—perhaps to give it a more authentic appearance. Returning to Pialigos, he was determined to impart this lost knowledge to his people. The people, astonished by the new revelation, began calling the young scribe the *Prophet*. The priesthood, fearing this charismatic young upstart as a threat to their authority, seized the scroll and condemned the Prophet to death. Before he died, he vowed that he would return and impart the secret knowledge that would restore their empire and bring peace to the entire world."

"Reincarnation?"

"Yes. An accepted tenet of Pialigarian religion."

I stopped writing. "And all the Pialigarians are supposed to recognize this Prophet guy when he shows up? What's he going to do, descend out of the clouds?"

"No. Recognizing him is the sacred duty of the high priestess. She is chosen on the basis of a dream, one that foretells the Prophet's coming. The dream must come when the priestess is but a child, innocent, unable to deceive. All the mothers watch and listen to what their daughters tell them about their dreams. If there is something significant, the mother passes it on to the high priestess. Once the high priestess confirms the authenticity of the dream, the girl is ordained as the *Dream Child.* She is then groomed to succeed the high priestess at her death.

"Euphemia's childhood dream, it was different. She was told that the Prophet would come within her lifetime. And when he comes, he will undergo a test that Euphemia will administer. When he passes the test, the secret knowledge will be restored, and the position of high priestess will come to an end. Every person will awaken, and the new era of a world 'sweet with the fragrance of peace,' as Pialigarian prophecy predicts, will begin." She paused and studied me for a moment before adding, "There is, of course, a more … romantic side to this story, but I cannot tell you about it now."

"Why not?"

"Because."

"*Because* isn't an answer." I'd sometimes use that bit of logic on Marion when she was in one of her evade-through-ambiguity modes. It never worked with her, and I quickly saw that it wasn't going to work with Niki.

"Another time, perhaps," was all she said before she turned back to the window. The plane banked slowly to the right, and Niki pointed to a large mass of land. "The big island is Anafi. If you look very carefully, you can see two tiny islands. The one furthest to the east is Sarnafi. You can just see Carpathos and Casos. Pialigos lies on the Mediterranean side of Casos, two hundred and fifty kilometers from here, a hundred or more kilometers from Sarnafi." She hesitated and then said, "Stuart, I want to take you to Pialigos. I want you to meet Euphemia. We would make the trip by sailboat. We could take the scenic passage, leave from Santorini, go north of Anafi and then south, around Casos. It is a wonderful way to experience the Aegean. It will give you a good sense of the setting for your book."

The intensity in her eyes told me she wasn't going to take no for an answer. Of course, I had no intention of denying myself that opportunity. But I pressed the pencil's eraser to my chin, and feigning a sober, businesslike frown, I said, "I suppose if you twist my arm real hard, you could talk me into it."

Her intensity lightened. She raised a straight-thumbed, girlish fist and shook it menacingly close to my face. "There are better ways of convincing you than a mere twisting of the arm."

"Hey, there's no need to get ugly."

"Then, you will go? Willingly?"

I nodded, and when she dropped her weapon, I added, "The only thing scarier than that fist of yours is the thought of a volcano exploding with us out there in the middle of the ocean. Wouldn't it be safer to take something with wings?"

"Kyropos? Ha! Kyropos is nothing. I grew up on Santorini, source of one of *the* most devastating eruptions in human history. I do not frighten so easily."

The plane began its descent in earnest. Niki sat back in her seat and looked straight ahead, a light smile shimmering over her face. "Of course, if *you* are frightened ..."

I WASN'T SURE HOW OR when it happened, but somewhere on the drive between the Monolithos airport and the docks at Perivolos, I'd fallen hopelessly in love—with Santorini.

Intimate villages, with the clean, whitewashed houses of old fishermen. Lazy burros urged on by small boys with sticks, packing their burdens in large baskets, tripping over rocky paths lined with smatterings of daisies, red poppies, and naked boulders. Tangled, low-cut vineyards scattered in a patchwork of red and black soils. Humid breezes perfumed with thyme, sage, mint, summer savory, lavender, and rosemary. Beaches of white, black, and red sand lapped by sapphire seas, trimmed with shallow ribbons of turquoise.

Something as real and as vivid as a childhood memory called to me from that island. Had I been one of the ancient Minoans forced to flee that thirty-mile plume of killing ash? Had I watched, in a swirl of indefinable emotion, everything I'd known as my earthly home vanish in a roiling fury of flame and froth? I wouldn't have thought so, not in a thousand years. Now, careening over a narrow road through countryside that sparked an inexplicable feeling of having come home, I had to wonder.

At the dock of Perivolos was Nicholas Pappadopoulos, Barnes's Sarnafi groundskeeper. Nicholas—tall, graying, slightly stooped though agile for his age, sun-leathered face, the gentle eyes of a philosopher—helped me transfer the luggage from the cab to his awaiting boat.

A few hours later, we were approaching Sarnafi's western shore. Still some distance out, I could see the home that Barnes had called his "little beach house"—villa, more like it. A zigzagging set of stairs broken by periodic landings provided access to the estate from the sea. Perched high in the cliffs among a swirl of gulls, I could imagine a commanding view of the sea in every direction.

On the beach was a gazebo with a thatched roof and a wooden pier extending about twenty-five yards into the water. A trailer-rigged golf cart awaited us at the dock. Niki, Nicholas, and Wes Barnes stepped off the boat while I stayed on to pass off the luggage to Nicholas. When I hoisted Niki's suitcase, I made a slight grunting sound and joked to Nicholas under my breath that he may need a separate truck for this one.

The philosopher smiled knowingly and, in an equally low tone, said, "Now you understand the reason for the trailer. Before ..." He shook his head like a victim of former atrocities.

When the loading was complete, Barnes and Nicholas boarded the cart. Niki and I opted for the stairs.

On our way up, Niki explained that the estate had started as crude barracks built to accommodate the workers excavating the island's Pialigarian temple. Over the years, it evolved to its present, sprawling, if not haphazard, complex.

Somewhere along the way, she made a curt remark about her mother, Celia, and how they didn't speak much anymore.

"Your mother lives on Santorini?" I asked.

"Chios. Some believe the island is the birthplace of Christopher Columbus. My mother inherited the home where she was born and raised. I think she draws some peace from the surroundings of her childhood, her way of escaping her grief for my father's death. For her, the scroll carries a curse. She is Catholic, you know, prone to superstition. She worries that I will share my father's fate."

"Maybe she's got reason to worry," I said, thinking about Giacopetti and his thugs.

"I do not worry. Why should she? She has always been a worrier. She worried when I was at Knossos. Now she worries for me at Sarnafi. All of my life she worries for me. Worry for this thing, worry for that thing. It does not matter. Worry is what she does the best. Rufus has even offered her an apartment at the villa, just so she can be here to see that all goes well. But she will have nothing to do with him. She has never liked him. I am convinced that she believes he is responsible for taking my father from her—in life, and now in death. My father, you see, he spent a great deal of time away. Always he was searching for the scroll. I think she has resented Rufus for this. And now that my father is gone, her resentment has grown into bitter hatred."

We reached a patio with a half-dozen white metal tables, each sporting a brightly colored umbrella. Barnes sat waiting for us in the shade of one.

Niki flung open her arms and twirled like a dancer. "Have you ever in your life seen a more beautiful place?"

I paused to take in the scene. Each section of the villa claimed its own foothold in the black face of the cliff. Every building—clean, whitewashed stucco, bearing the blue tile roof common to the region—connected to the others by a maze of stairs, patios, bridges, and flower gardens. Flagstone walkways, flanked by turquoise pools, some with tinkling fountains, passed beneath stone arches and vine-covered arbors. The chittering song of finches darting through endless hiding places filled air sweet with the delicate scent of honeysuckle. I would never have known that this was a build-as-you-go project. Every building, from the main house to the toolshed, occupied its space with absolute esteem, specifically placed, I would have thought, by a deliberate fiat of Nature.

"So, this is the little beach house you were talking about?" I said to Wes Barnes.

Barnes stood, grinning slightly. "It's all relative, isn't it, Adams?"

At that moment, a woman, squat, full-faced, with black hair combed tightly into a shiny bun, emerged from inside the house and was making her way toward us. In quick, short steps, she skittered across the patio, buoyant, arms open, her dark eyes glittering with welcomes. For Niki, there were hugs and beefy kisses to the cheeks. I was content to settle for a dainty handshake.

After the flurry of greeting, Niki introduced me to Dora Pappadopoulos, explaining, "She is the villa cook and housekeeper. And Dora, I would like you to meet Stuart Adams. He is a writer from America."

"A writer," Dora cooed. Clasping my hand in both of hers, she said, "and from America?" She winked at Niki, her face bright with the satisfaction of a matchmaking mother. "And such a handsome man he is."

Niki's eyes fluttered with mild embarrassment when she explained flatly, "Stuart has come to write about the dig."

"But of course," Dora said, her gay expression undeterred. Then, with a cook's urgency she said to us all, "You must be starving. Niki, you show our handsome American guest where he will be staying. Then come; I have much for you to eat."

I followed Niki up more stairs, through a covered walkway, to a small cottage perched on the edge of the cliff. She pushed open the door, and we stepped in. My luggage sat in the middle of the sun-drenched wood floor. The ceiling of the main room was log beamed; the walls were plastered and painted in blue pastel. Tapestries bearing images of the frescoes I recognized from my research on Akrotiri hung from every wall. A flower-print grouping of sofa, chair, and low coffee table filled the corner to our immediate left. Straight ahead, just beyond an arrangement of four wicker chairs and a table, I could see the kitchen. To the right of the kitchen was a pair of wooden, glass-paneled doors that opened to an outdoor area, probably a patio. To our immediate right was a high-back, cushioned wicker chair with a small table and floor lamp for reading. Beyond the chair was another door that led to the bedroom. I followed Niki through this door. On the far wall, beyond the bed, there was a writing desk with a window. Outside, the sea stretched into infinity.

On the desk was a copy of a book: *Voice of the Aegean, An Exploration of Ancient Pialigarian Prophesy.* The author was Anna Nicole Mikos. It took me a few seconds to realize that Anna Nicole Mikos was Niki.

"This is yours?" I said, picking up the book.

"Yes. It is my doctoral thesis. My professor encouraged me to publish."

"Why didn't you tell me you'd written this thing?"

"You never asked."

I studied the cover. It was a photograph of Niki taken from behind. She wore a light jacket and shorts. Her hands were in the pockets of the jacket. She stood in the surf looking out into the soft light of an ocean sunset, her hair blowing in the breeze. The cover design was elegantly mysterious, a perfect expression of this woman I had so wrongly misjudged.

For me, the book raised a question. "So, why did Barnes hire a novelist to write about the scroll? Why not his obviously capable partner?"

"You have a much larger following," she explained. "My readers are confined to a handful of academics, mostly critics. Is that difficult to understand?"

"I guess not," I said, but for some reason, I suddenly felt insecure about Barnes's expectations of my commercial value. Maybe it was because I was getting closer to the land of the Pialigarians, starting to realize that they were a real people with real problems. I'd never even met one, didn't know anything about them. But I'd basically accepted the assignment to bring the world to their doorstep. Now I wasn't so sure that I was the right person for the job.

Niki said, "I asked Dora to bring the book here because I thought you would find the information helpful. I told you there was a more romantic side to the story of the Prophet. It begins on page seventy-five—in case you are interested."

I was interested all right. Actually I was feeling a sudden urgency to absorb every shred of information that I could. "Thanks. I'll check it out."

"So," she swept a hand, fairylike, across the room, "you have your own little villa. You have privacy, far away from the rest of the house. Good for writing, would you not agree?"

Sure that my smile was broad enough to add a few more toes to my crow's-feet, I looked at Niki. She was beaming with beautiful, childlike innocence, so eager to please. "It's ... it's great," I said. "I wasn't expecting anything even close to this."

She shimmered with satisfaction. "Come," she said, taking me by the hand. "There is more to see." She led me back through the main room to a wine cabinet that stood in the kitchenette. "Here is wine. On Santorini, there is barely sufficient water for the grapes, but the soil is rich, volcanic, unique in the flavor of the wine. All these wines are world class." She pointed to each type as she described them. "If you like red and dry, there is *Brusko*. A good dessert wine is *Vissando*. You want white and dry? *Nichteri*." Then she handed me a bottle that she'd lifted from the cabinet—not a wine, from the look of it. "Here is a local favorite that is unique to the islands. *Ouzo*. It has the taste of licorice with 45 percent alcohol. Be sure to eat something while you drink it." She smiled mischievously. "Ouzo has a cult following that claims it will make your life calm and beautiful." She took back the bottle and replaced it in the cabinet. "Come. There is one more thing that I must show you."

Chapter 7

WE STEPPED THROUGH THE GLASS-PANELED doors, passed beneath a vine-laced arbor, and walked onto a patio perched at the edge of the cliff. Clusters of potted geraniums and pansies hung from the eave and fluttered in the breeze. We stopped at a waist-high wall and peered over white lines of surf and into the vastness of the ocean that stretched out beyond.

"I never tire of this view," Niki said, her eyes drifting dreamily over the endless blue. "What do you think?"

More feelings of familiarity stirred with the rhythmic interplay of wind and sea. "It's hard to explain," I said. "This place makes me feel like … like there's something more to me … more to all of us than we know. Maybe the Pialigarians are right."

"Right? About what?"

"Maybe we've lived before."

Niki turned toward me and pushed a floating strand of hair out of her face. The softness of her sun-bronzed skin was a pleasant contrast to the harsh backdrop of the black cliffs. "The Pialigarian envisions the soul as being on an evolutionary journey which they depict as a great labyrinth. This journey spans many physical incarnations. With each incarnation, the soul learns something that enables it to advance along its path. We do not come back randomly. We come with a purpose, each with his or her own."

"Do you believe it?"

"I find it a compelling theory, one that seems quite logical, even comforting."

"How is it comforting? I don't know if I could handle the teen years again."

She laughed. "To think that we have as much time as it takes to learn what we need to learn, this is comforting. To the Pialigarian, there is no Judgment Day, no threat of hellfire and brimstone, just a kind of leisurely stroll on our spiritual journey. What about you? Are you wondering if you have lived before?"

"I'm not sure," I said, turning back toward the sea. "I've been having the strangest feelings that I've been here. Not here at this house, but on these islands. It's hard to explain, but it … it feels like I've … come home."

Niki looked at me with something like amused curiosity. "Perhaps you are having a soul memory. Euphemia explained that a soul memory is not a picture retained in the cells of the brain but an experience emblazoned in the heart. Would this describe what you are feeling?"

A seagull rose on the air and hovered close enough for me to see its eye move in the socket. Seeing we had nothing in the way of food, the bird screeched and plunged gracefully into the dizzying depths toward the sea. I watched it for a moment, trying to collect some definite thoughts on the subject. I found none. "I'm not really sure," I said.

"The Pialigarians have a word for intuitive knowing. They call it *Zadim*. The word is a combination of two others: *za*, meaning *life*, and *dim*, meaning *spirit*. *Life spirit*. According to Pialigarian teachings, their deity, the Great Mother, is always calling the souls of her children back to herself through the Zadim. Because they see Pialigos as the symbolic heart of the Great Mother, Pialigarians believe that those instinctively drawn to these islands have reached the final stages of their soul's evolutionary journey. According to this belief, these souls are responding to the very highest calling of the Great Mother, a form of Zadim they have named, the whisper of Pialigos."

"You think this is happening to me?" Something was going on, but I wasn't sure I was ready to go that far with it.

"I cannot say, not with certainty. But it would do no harm to keep an open mind. What I will tell you is this: If, for you, this is a soul memory, if this is the whisper of Pialigos that speaks to your spirit, then I am most happy that you have found your way home."

Our eyes locked, and in that moment it would have been easy to reach over and touch her cheek, to feel the silk of her hair pass through my fingers, to pull her close, press my lips to hers. Something told me she wouldn't resist, so I had to.

"Niki! Signor Adams! Are you coming?" It was Dora, shouting from the main patio two terraces below, shattering the soft tension between us. "You must be starving. Come now; see what I have prepared for you."

"Yes, Dora," Niki called back, waving. Turning to me, she asked, "You are hungry, no?"

I swallowed hard when I nodded. "Yeah."

On the way down, I was afraid to say anything, afraid it might be the wrong thing. But I knew the silence that fell between us was not really silence, that much was being said in a strange, wordless kind of way.

I thought of Marion. Just then, she seemed little more than a distant speck on an infinite horizon.

We were just finishing lunch when the only telephone in the entire villa rang. The telephone—an old black dial unit that rang rather than chirped—was located between the kitchen and the dining nook where we were having our lunch. Barnes explained earlier that he'd had the landline installed in the pre–cell phone era and that, because of the island's isolated location, it had cost him a small fortune. For that reason, he refused to abandon it in favor of wireless technology.

Dora answered on the third ring. "Yes … yes, but of course." She turned to me. "Signor Adams, it is for you. A young lady named Marion Chandler."

I'd given Marion the number, but I didn't expect her to call unless something was wrong. I excused myself from the table and took the receiver from Dora. "Marion?"

"Signor Adams?" Marion giggled. "I love it!"

She was okay. "Yeah, that was Dora. She does the cooking here. Determined to fatten me up too. Hey, how are you doing? Is everything all right?"

"Oh, I'm doing fine, Signor Adams," she said in her best Greek accent. "Are you at a place where you can talk?"

I glanced back at the table where Niki, Barnes, Nicholas, and Dora continued their conversation. "Not really."

"Good. Guess what I'm wearing?"

"Wearing?" *Jesus.* I had to think. It'd be sometime in the morning there. What the hell did she like to wear in the mornings? "Green jogging suit. You just got in from your run."

"Eww, you are way cold."

"Blue tights. You're doing your yoga."

"Noooo … not doing yoga. But you're getting a smidgy bit warmer."

"Okay," I muttered. "Bathrobe. You … um … you must have just stepped out of the shower."

The accent left. "Stuart, baby, what's happened to you? Have those Greek islands done something to your imagination? Think *chemise,* honey … the one you brought home from Victoria's Secret."

I knew the chemise, all right: black silk halter, tied at the back of her neck, front opened like a teardrop exposing a generous portion of her breasts, mid-thigh hem slit to the hip. If she wanted to stop me dead in a mid-sentence edit, all she had to do was step into the room wearing that and her black spike heels. I glanced at my lunch companions again and caught Niki discreetly averting her eyes—not the best time in the world to talk about chemises and spike heels.

I hunkered uncomfortably over the telephone. "You're ruthless, you know."

"Oh, I'm a lot worse than that," she teased. "What else am I wearing?"

"Heels?" My voice was a near whisper.

"Not even heels." With a breathy moan, she added, "I'm lying here on the bed, all by my lonesome, thinking about you. God, I want you, Stuart. I want you right now."

On a scale of one to ten—ten being my point of giving in—her force was about a six-point-five. "I want you too, but that'd be a little hard to manage right now."

"You could do it if you wanted. Book a flight out of there—today."

"Today?" I almost laughed, but I didn't. She sounded like she really meant it. "You're not serious."

"I'm not? I've been thinking about what you said. Stuart, you're right. We need to talk about our future. I know that now. Come home, baby. Come home right now. Let's talk."

She'd kicked up to about a seven-five. "But Marion, I can't just walk out on these people. I've got a commitment here."

"Oh? I guess you don't have a commitment here?"

She lost half a point on that one. Overt guilt didn't work well with me.

"That's not what I'm saying and you know it. Take off a couple of weeks; come to the islands. I'm in a little cottage that looks out over the water. You'd love it."

"Well, who wouldn't? I already told you that I'm buried up to my neck for the next six months."

She could talk a long time about solving impossible problems in her work. Why was this one any different, so insurmountable? Another half-point deduction. Back to six-five.

"What about Jill or Stephanie?" I suggested. "Couldn't they cover for you for a couple of weeks?"

I already knew what she'd say, and she didn't disappoint me.

"Oh right. Like my decorator and architect are suddenly business heads? They wouldn't know the first thing about running this circus."

"Marion, you're not being fair. I told you all about this deal before I—"

"And I still told you to go. I know that, baby. I thought it would be good for you—for us. But it's only been a few days and I'm ... I'm already dying here. What if it takes a year? God, Stuart, I can't take a whole year."

I gave her a full point for taking responsibility and another for convincing me that she really did want me. She was flying on nine, but I was determined to hold my ground.

"I'll get some free time," I said. "So will you. It's not like we can't see each other. The way everyone here is talking, it won't take a year. I'm thinking weeks, a few at tops." No one had actually told me that, but I sensed it was true. "We can handle a couple of weeks, can't we?"

All I could hear was a long, sighing silence. She'd pulled out the big gun. Nine-point-five.

"I suppose."

"It'll go by before we know it. If things here look hopeless, I'll call it off. How's that sound?"

Another silence, then a sniff. "All right, Stuart. If that's what you want. It'll be an eternity." I could hear the rustling sound of her getting out of bed and wished like hell that I was there to pull her back in. "I've got to get ready for work. I just wanted to hear your voice. Come home as soon as you can."

Her tone was soggy with self-pity, a believable attempt to mask strength I knew she had. Still, the charade had its desired impact, and when she gave me a sad kiss through the phone and told me again how much she loved and missed me, I was ready to quit Barnes right there on the spot. She was hitting about nine-point-nine-nine. A puff of wind could have pushed me over. With my last ounce of strength, I said, "I love you too, Marion. I'll call you." I listened until her phone clicked off.

I picked through the rest of my lunch with Marion's aching voice needling my brain. It didn't help that I'd come within a breath of making a pass at Niki. Across the table, Niki showed no signs that anything unseemly had happened between us. Still, I needed time alone with her to assess the potential damage, see if she'd sensed how close I'd come to compromising our professional relationship. We were scheduled to meet at 2:00 for a tour of the cave, a good time, I figured, to make sure things were still in their proper places.

I spent the next hour trying to busy myself transferring notes to the laptop. Everything I'd written about the dig seemed flat, unimportant. I was antsy, couldn't sit still. I snatched clothes from my suitcase, tossed them into drawers, paced from one window to the next, and stared out, seeing nothing. Damn Marion. Why did she have to wait till we were an ocean apart to start talking about our future?

Minutes before 2:00, I grabbed the Nikon, stuffed a notepad and pen in my back pocket, and left the cottage. I found Niki waiting at the patio. Disarmingly cheerful, she gave no indication that anything unusual had happened between us. Maybe Marion's call had given us both a dose of reality. More likely it had just been my guilt-sparked paranoia that caused me to overreact. Everything was fine. The only thing I needed to do was to make sure it stayed that way.

We took the stairs to the beach and had gone three hundred yards when Niki suddenly stopped. "Look," she said, shading her eyes and pointing. "You can see the plume of Kyropos."

I could just make out the darkened smudge barely visible through the quivering distance, not even worth a photograph. But it gave me an idea.

"What makes Barnes think Seagull was talking about Santorini? Why not Kyropos?"

"That is possible, but not likely. There has never been anything of military value on Kyropos. What reason would Seagull have to go there? There are more reasons to believe that his reference was Santorini."

"Such as ..."

"Listen to the talk in any taverna. In this region, when people speak of a volcano, it is always Santorini, never Kyropos. What is Kyropos? Who even cares?" She could have been talking about her hometown soccer team. A foreigner like me would never guess there'd be such a sense of pride in a force capable of obliterating its inhabitants from the face of the planet. She added, "Seagull was a spy, a trained observer. Do you think he would not have known this?"

"Sounds logical," I said, scribbling down key words of her explanation. Not knowing the region and its people put me at a definite disadvantage. I'd never been in a taverna, never heard what the people there talked about. Still, there was something that didn't feel right about her story. The only way I knew to resolve it was to keep asking questions.

"Seagull was dying, after all. Didn't sound like he had much time to go into detail."

"Yes, he was dying," Niki agreed. "Possibly, he was delirious. But we know that Santorini experienced a series of minor eruptions from August 1939 to July 1941, roughly the time that Seagull was in this region. He could have easily seen the column of ash from here."

She started down the beach. I finished writing the dates and caught up to her.

"Okay," I said, as we continued on the beach, "so why are you looking on Sarnafi? Why not Santorini?"

"I am going to show you why. On the ridge, there is a much shorter trail leading from the villa to the cave. I brought you this way so you can see for yourself why we think Sarnafi is the likely location for our scroll."

We came to a group of large stone blocks—black, uniformly cut, half-buried in the sand. Niki stooped by one and ran her hand over the near-smooth surface.

"These blocks drew my father's attention to this island. He recognized the marks of the chisel. You can see the hand of an ancient Pialigarian mason at work here."

To me, the so-called chisel marks were nearly imperceptible lines that only an archaeologist could appreciate. But I snapped a shot and added her comments to my notebook.

"You ask why we look on Sarnafi," she continued, "and not Santorini. My father puzzled over this question for many years. There are no Pialigarian ruins on Santorini. Euphemia has assured us that this is true. Why? We can only guess. But you see, here is evidence of a Pialigarian presence. Pialigarian texts speak of outposts, cave-bearing islands where documents of great importance were safely kept in the event of another cataclysm. This would be similar, perhaps, to the way the Essenes cached their sacred writings in jars in the caves of Qumran. There are many islands in the Aegean. Some have caves. Some have ruins. Sarnafi has both. Add to this the fact that Santorini's ash plume would have dominated the sky during Seagull's time, and you have a compelling reason to begin here. Of course this is not the strongest of evidence, but we have to start somewhere."

I stopped scribbling and tried to assure myself that it was the fault of my untrained eye that I saw only a smattering of large, weathered rocks. "In other words, it's a long shot."

"You are having doubts about this theory?"

"You don't?"

"Okay, it is a long shot. There are no certainties in my field. When you write your novels, you can make them up as you go. I must take the world as I find it. If the archaeologist waits for absolute facts every time before she digs, what discoveries would she make? She often begins her work based on little more than educated speculation—faint chisel marks on the weathered face of a stone. Sometimes she gets lucky, and sometimes she comes up empty-handed. But even when there is no specific find, knowledge is gleaned, lessons are learned, and the scientific database is enriched. Mine is not a profession for the impatient. Nor will it appeal to those who base their happiness on always making specific acquisitions."

"So, what you're telling me is that this whole thing could be little more than an exercise in character building?"

Niki lowered her sunglasses as if she'd discovered an important void in my understanding of humanity, and it was her pleasure to fill it in.

"Would that be such a bad thing? In case you have not noticed, the world is in dire need of people with a little more character." She reset her glasses and added, "Perhaps you should jot this down in that little notebook of yours."

I didn't jot it down, mainly because I figured I already had enough character to get by. Personally, I couldn't see that a few more specific acquisitions—a substantially fatter bank account, for example—were going to do me all that much harm.

Niki started off again. "Come. Perhaps I can bolster your discernible lack of faith."

I followed Niki to an excavation site whose center was a large courtyard surrounded by broken walls with doors and windows framed in thick casings of stone. Weather and extreme age had reduced the building to a pitiful hint of its former magnificence. The courtyard floor was inlaid with black stone, damaged but recognizable.

"Looks like a labyrinth," I said, snapping a shot.

"You are looking at the remains of a Pialigarian temple, officially listed, you should be pleased to know, by the Greek Department of Antiquities." Niki crossed her arms in vindicated satisfaction. "Does this irrefutable evidence appease your skeptical nature?"

I answered with a grin flush with newfound assurance and snapped a few more pictures.

"Come," she said. "I will show you the cave."

We followed a primitive trail that snaked between craggy slopes. Passing through a narrow ravine, we stopped when we encountered another, better-defined trail.

"This is the shortcut back to the villa," Niki explained. "And there"—she pointed to an enormous pile of stone rubble stacked high against the base of the cliff wall—"that is the cave."

I started to raise my camera, but I stopped, confused. All I saw was the collapsed face of a cliff, no cave. I stepped closer to make sure

I wasn't overlooking something. To my right was a smaller mound of stone, about five feet in height. Someone had apparently moved it from the main slide. Was this the extent of the work done by her Cretan excavators? My pillar of newfound optimism wobbled.

"Am I missing something?"

She shrugged. "That depends. What do you think you might be missing?"

"The cave. I don't see it."

"Do you not have eyes?" she said, suddenly defensive. Then she relaxed a little and chuckled. "But of course, you are not an archaeologist. How would you know? The cave is there, beneath the rocks. Do you think I would be excavating a cave that has not collapsed? What need would there be?"

I was trying to reconcile the reality of what I was looking at with the picture of the cave Barnes had painted. They didn't come close to a match.

"But ... but Barnes said you were on top of it, that I'd be lucky to make it here in time to get some hands-on experience."

"Yes. You cannot see that he spoke the truth?"

Was she joking? I waited for the smile to break over her face. All I got was an annoyed frown.

"Why do you stand there staring at me like a dumbo? Does the thought of a little work make you go mad?"

"A little work? No, the thought of a little work doesn't make me go mad. Moving tons of rock by hand? Now that makes me go mad. Niki, even with a bulldozer and a boatload of dynamite—"

"We have considered both. We cannot use either. A bulldozer? How would one get it to this spot? And dynamite? We risk destroying the scroll. We have to do it by hand."

"By hand ... ?" Her indifference suggested a task as simple as sweeping a sprinkle of dirt into a dustpan. I stepped to the smaller pile of stone. "Your so-called crew, did they move these rocks?"

"Of course they moved these rocks. In case you have not noticed, rocks do not move by themselves. Sergios and his son, Christian, they were helping with the cave."

"Were? You mean like ... are no longer?"

Her eyebrows shot up as if she pretended to be suddenly impressed with my acute powers of observation. "How perceptive you are."

"Where are they now?" I asked, noticing clumps of grass growing through the small pile. "Looks like they've been gone for weeks."

"Family matters … on the western shores of Crete. This is why they leave."

"Family matters?" It was the way she broke eye contact that told me she knew more than she was saying. "You're sure that's it?"

She hesitated and tossed back her hair. "Perhaps there was something more."

"I can't wait to hear it."

She blew out an impatient breath. "If you must know, they fear Kyropos. Satisfied? They believe the western shore will provide protection from a tsunami."

"Tsunami? I thought you said Kyropos was no threat."

"I am here, am I not? These men do not share my optimism. Simple laborers, this is all they will ever be."

"Maybe these simple laborers know something you don't."

The risk these guys saw had obviously outweighed the wage they'd been drawing. My guess was that there was some chatter going on in the tavernas that Niki hadn't been privy to. She'd been on Crete, after all.

"What could they know? What man wakes up in the morning certain that he will live to see the night? Am I to crawl into a hole with such cowards and shiver in fear for what I do not know?"

"There are ways of improving your odds," I pointed out. "Like maybe staying out of the path of a nine-hundred-foot wave."

"Ha! This shows how little you know about volcanoes. If you had been observant, you would see that it was not a tsunami that destroyed the temple of this island. It was the death cloud of ash from Thera."

"Death cloud?" Instantly, images of melting eyeballs, shattered teeth, and flesh dripping from my face like liquid wax filled my mind. I could see my pathetically maimed body curled in a fetal position, gasping for breath as particles of fine glass permeate my lungs, coughing black blood, praying for death under the merciless blanket of falling ash. "Hell, that makes me feel a lot better. Incineration and suffocation, that wouldn't be so bad. It's the fear of drowning that keeps me up at night."

"Do you also wish to go to the western shores of Crete where you will be safe? Not even the death cloud could reach you there. Better yet, perhaps you would feel safer back on your mountain in Colorado."

"If I'd known half of what was going on here—no, let me rephrase that—if I'd known half of what *wasn't* going on here, I would have stayed on my mountain in Colorado, and you and me wouldn't be having this ridiculous conversation."

"So, you admit that you are afraid."

"Afraid?" I scoffed at her attempted play on my male ego. "Afraid has nothing to do with it. Look, forget the volcano. Let's get back to the main problem here. Niki, you and me, we can't dig out this cave, not even with your two buddies helping us. Not by hand. It's impossible. You're a scientist. We're looking at a major physics problem here."

She fluttered her eyes shut in defiance, so I waited for them to reopen before I continued.

"Look, here's a mass of rock that has to be moved from here"—I swept a hand over the slide—"to there"—I pointed to the small pile. "Let's call this rock slide *Point A*. That pile is *Point B*. In order to move that mass from Point A to Point B, you have to have a form of energy. You can't use dynamite. You can't use machinery. Your labor force isn't interested in suffocating, drowning, or otherwise dedicating the rest of their lives to moving enough rock to build a major pyramid. Barnes, with all due respect, is too old to be any help. That leaves us. You and me. One man and one woman. Think about it. There's simply not enough energy in one man and one woman to move that mass of rock from here"—I drove a finger—"to there."

"Perhaps if the man were a Greek," she said, crossing her arms and shifting her weight to one leg, "it would be different. You Americans, so smart but so lazy. Get a machine to do your work. This is how you think. If you cannot get a machine, the work, it does not get done. We Greeks, we build great monuments across the whole face of the earth. Did we use bulldozers? No! Did we use dynamite? No! We used our hands. Our *bare* hands."

"You mean you used the bare hands of your slaves," I reminded her. "Thousands of them. And maybe a lightning bolt or two from

Zeus. Now if you happen to know a couple of gods and a few thousand slaves—"

She threw up her arms. "Fine! You will not help? I will do it myself. I will move these rocks from your stupid *Point A* to your even stupider *Point B*. With these hands"—she shook two white-knuckled fists in my face—"I will do this thing. You can sit in the shade and watch. If I must dig alone to get the scroll, then I will dig. You will see."

The idea was so ridiculously childish that I almost laughed in her face. She might have hit me. I needed to find a way to ease her back into the discussion. scientific, rational self back into the discussion.

"What if the scroll's not here?" I asked, calmly. "We do all this work, and the scroll is not here. Niki, we're talking years of work. I'll be pushing a walker by the time we're done."

She lowered her fists, but her eyes stayed locked on mine. "If you would work as hard as you try to avoid it, we would clear this cave long before you need your walker."

It was no use; she wasn't going to budge. Equally clear was the fact that Marion and I would never make it to the end of this job, especially after I'd told her that we were probably just weeks away from finding the scroll. Was I willing to risk losing her for a hundred grand and a story that may not even exist?

"I'm sorry, Niki, but I think you've got the wrong man. I can't do this."

"You cannot do what?"

Her clueless façade was starting to piss me off. "This." I jabbed a finger angrily at the rocks. "We can't do this in a year. We can't do it in ten. The whole thing is nuts. Barnes promised me a story. This is a cartoon. I didn't come over here to do a cartoon."

"Then there is no reason for you to be here."

I hated the sound of it, but I said, "My point exactly."

"And the money that Rufus has paid you?"

"To hell with the money." I turned to leave.

"I know it is your Marion that is calling you home. You had better hurry."

I stopped, spun around, and saw her looking at me like I was a pussy-whipped washrag.

"You can twist it into anything you want," I said, glaring back at her. "The fact is, I don't like being lied to. You want me to write about your scroll?" I nodded toward the rubble. "Give me a call when you find one. Now if you'll excuse me, I've got a flight to book."

I took the shortcut back to the villa, kicking every rock foolish enough to get in my way.

Chapter 8

I WAS SO MAD THAT I wouldn't have shown up for dinner that evening if Dora hadn't gone to so much work. She had the three of us set up in the formal dining room, a windowless interior room with low light she'd enhanced with a pair of candles. A soft piano tinkled quietly in the background. She'd prepared a grilled swordfish and rice entrée that started with a Greek salad and would end with a traditional dessert of rice pudding topped with fresh whipped cream and a sprinkle of cinnamon. It was supposed to be a romantically festive atmosphere. Unfortunately, the dim light combined with our long faces to create a mood more reminiscent of a wake. It was good that no one wore black.

Wes Barnes had on an ivory linen, straight-hemmed shirt with matching trousers and white canvas shoes. Niki wore a slinky knit dress—pink, three-quarter sleeve, mid-calf, slit to the knee—and sandals. I had a brown plaid, short-sleeved shirt with buff corduroy slacks and brown leather shoes. Casual and comfortable we all were—at least on the outside.

Not more than a few dozen words passed between us during the meal. Barnes, sitting across the table from me, cut off a hunk of his fish and chewed in what I hoped was some real soul-searching silence. Niki, her eyes cast downward, took slow, pouting bites. I was so busy kicking myself for nearly blowing it with Marion that I barely tasted my food. Aside from the background music and the light tinkle of silverware, the only other sound was the solemn ticktock of a massive grandfather clock.

I'd made up my mind to return Barnes's money minus the airfare home. The check was folded in my shirt pocket. I had some things to say to Barnes, and the silence was starting to get to me, so I figured now was as good a time as any to plow into him.

"You knew your guys had quit on you. Why'd you tell me they were on top of it, like they were going to find that scroll any second?"

Wes Barnes looked up and stopped chewing. "Guess it don't much matter now, does it?" He washed down his mouthful of food with a sip of wine. "Damn Cretans," he muttered. "Don't think I got an honest day's work out of either one of 'em." He glanced at Niki, pointed. "You mind passing me some of that pita bread, darling?" She did. He plucked a piece from the basket and chuckled as if my decision to leave had proved a pet theory of his. "The yuppie generation, that's what this is all about. Everybody wants everything handed to them." He set down the basket. "Nobody handed me anything, Adams. And nobody's sure as hell handing anything to the Pialigarians. You're whining to the wrong man." He glowered at me for a couple of seconds, sawed off another piece of fish, stuffed it in his mouth, and chewed as if it were something he had to kill.

"I don't care who I'm whining to," I countered. "You know and I know that that cave can't be cleared by two people, not even if one of them happens to be a Greek female."

Niki's eyes popped up like a pair of lit fuses.

"You see, Barnes," I continued, "this is the part that I don't get. The two of you act like moving a few thousand tons of rock by hand is no big deal. So if it's that easy, why don't you go on down and clear it out? When you've actually got a story, give me a call."

"We just might do that," Barnes said. "But I doubt I'll be calling you, not unless you're interested in some instruction on what it means to lend yourself to a cause other than your own comfort and gain."

"We will not be clearing that cave," Niki snapped at Barnes. "You are not going to risk another heart attack."

"Point well made," I said. "Sounds like at least two people in this room are starting to make some sense. And I don't mind lending myself to your cause, but I don't intend to spend the rest of my life busting rock for it."

"I will find someone who is willing to work," Niki said. "You will see." Her eyes flashed with superior confidence and unflagging determination; they were dangerously beautiful in the soft yellow light, but she was still crazy as hell.

That was all anyone said through the rest of the entrée and on into dessert. When I finished, I stood to leave, pulled the check from my shirt pocket, and tossed it on the table in front of Barnes. "I figure this'll even us up."

He picked up the check, studied it, refolded it, and then laid it back on the table. I waited for some reaction. Maybe I was hoping he'd see I was serious and come up with some good reason for me to change my mind, but he just sat there slurping his pudding. I nodded a good evening to them both and turned to leave.

"You will be ready at seven?"

Niki had agreed to ferry me to the dock of Perivolos. From there, I'd catch a cab to the Monolithos airport. Her voice, softened with what seemed like an undercurrent of sadness, stopped me at the door and stirred in me the stinging realization that, after Perivolos, I'd probably never see her again.

"I'll be ready," I muttered, and I walked out.

NIKI HAD JOKINGLY PROMISED THAT the ouzo would make life "calm and beautiful," at least temporarily. Just then, calm and beautiful were two qualities I could use. I was feeling bad about leaving, but I could see no alternative, not with Marion begging me to come home. Barnes would just have to find himself another champion for his damn cause.

I winced at the ouzo I sampled straight from the bottle. Liquid licorice. Over lunch, Nicholas had given me instructions on how to drink it. "Fill a glass to half with ouzo. Top it off with water. Drink it slowly. Do not try to prove your manhood. With ouzo, you will prove nothing." The mix of ouzo and water produced a milky white concoction more suitable to the taste than the eye.

In the bedroom, I'd just tossed a handful of underwear into my suitcase when I noticed Niki's book on the desk. Remembering what she'd said about a more romantic side to her story, I opened the book to page seventy-five.

Konstantina, the high priestess of Pialigos, sentenced Anatolios to being cast, hands bound, into the Pool of Death, a superheated volcanic spring located in the bowels of the sacred cave.

Hands bound? Cast into boiling water? I could almost feel the blistering heat rise in my face. Why couldn't they've done the humane thing and just disemboweled and quartered the poor guy? I countered the heat flash with a sip of ouzo.

Fortunately, there is a romantic element that softens, in a sad kind of way, this rather gruesome story. Pialigarian texts tell of how a young temple maiden—Panagiota, the childhood sweetheart of Anatolios—made the ultimate sacrifice to be with her lover. Given the opportunity to denounce Anatolios as an imposter, she chose instead to be executed with him. Though the details of their deaths are unclear, it was reported to me by the high priestess that two skeletons, still poised in their fatal embrace, lie at the bottom of the pool. The site is closed to any but the high priestess, but all Pialigarians who regard these skeletal remains know that they belong to the condemned couple. Songs and poetry celebrating the bond of these tragic lovers abound to this day. But even for a hopeless romantic like myself, it is difficult to grasp the depth of love that these two people must have had for each other. To choose such a horrible death over life without her lover is an obvious reflection of a level of devotion rarely seen between a man and a woman.

The window curtain suddenly billowed, tapping me on the arm. I turned to look outside. The wind had come up; the sea was restless. Lightning flickered in not-so-distant thunderheads. A storm was moving in, and I didn't want to miss a moment of it. Snatching up the bottle of ouzo, I stepped out on the patio.

Why did I feel such an instant rapport with these two ancient lovers? How could I understand the kind of love they must have had for each other? The feeling was indistinct, like homesickness for a place I'd never been. But the more I thought about it, the more I realized the feeling had always been there, the frail murmur of a steady, quiet voice, but strong. I couldn't turn it off, not even with Marion. And now that I was going back to Colorado to discuss our future together, that murmur had turned to a distinct feeling of reluctance. Why? I didn't want to leave the islands. I didn't understand it, but being there touched something in me, some deep place I only vaguely knew had been empty.

Marion wouldn't fit in here. She thrived on the "circus" that was her business. She needed problems to solve, people to please, and the struggles and strokes that went with the frantic race to get to the top of the heap. I could see it when she came to the mountains. The peace of the *Sangre de Cristos* was a drug shot in her veins. Once she had her mountain fix, she was ready to plunge back into the stink and the noise of the city. These islands were mine, not ours. Marion would never be more than a tourist attracted to shops and nightlife. For me it was empty shorelines, the rush of surf, the cry of a gull, and the sweet fragrance of sage and mint that perfumed the air. I was home.

But I loved Marion. Didn't I? Did I love her as Panagiota must have loved Anatolios? If it came down to it, would I choose death over life without Marion?

The storm was closing in. I inhaled the charged air and chased it with the last swallow of ouzo from my glass. I tested another sip from the bottle. Now it was better straight.

What if I discovered that things would never work with Marion? Would I kill myself? No. I wouldn't throw myself off a cliff or gulp a lethal dose of hemlock. I'd pick up the pieces and move on. We both would. There would be life after Marion.

The wind heaved, threatening to tear the hanging flower baskets from their hooks. Curtains flailed in the windows. A door slammed somewhere in the cottage. I loved a good storm.

The electric buzz of the ouzo kicked in like a truth serum, stirring enough self-honesty to force me to confront another fact. Marion wasn't my only problem. There was Niki. It was no fluke that I'd come so close to kissing her. That wasn't like me. Thinking about her stirred something in me. She was different. She wasn't the stranger she should have been. Why?

The rain started with a few random drops exploding in pings on a metal table. Then, a blinding flash followed by a knee-bending explosion of thunder ripped open the sky, unleashing a horrific torrent. I grabbed the ouzo and dashed inside to close windows.

With the cottage secured, I headed through the flashing room to the reading chair in the corner. I clicked on the light, sat down, and listened for a moment to the sound of rain pelting glass, the thunder rattling windows in their sills. I studied the front cover of Niki's book. What was going through the mind of Anna Nicole Mikos as she stood there looking out over the sea? What was going through her mind now, this instant?

I opened the cover to a page bearing only a short verse:

> There is a voice.
> A quiet voice.
> It calls from the Aegean.
> Sublime, little more than a whisper.
> The whisper of Pialigos.
> Few can hear it, fewer still can understand.
> But those who hear, those who understand
> will not remain unchanged.
> *—Pialigarian verse*

Chills raised the hair on the back of my neck. Had I heard it, this whisper of Pialigos? Had I made a mistake giving in to Marion, quitting before I'd even met the Pialigarians and given things a chance to develop here?

I flipped to the first page of chapter 1. The words moved hypnotically beneath ripples of ouzo. I took another swallow and began to read.

Chapter 9

THERE'S A MAJOR DRAWBACK TO drinking a full bottle of ouzo alone. It's called *the next morning*. For me, this morning had come way too soon, an abrasive intruder as abrupt and as harsh as the knocking at the door that was evicting me from my sanctuary of sleep.

One eye fluttered open. My head hung slightly over the edge of the bed. The first thing I saw was the empty ouzo bottle sitting in the bedroom doorway. I tried, but I could not remember how it had ended up in that particular location—or, for that matter, how it had gotten empty. But there it was, greeting me with a cheery, *Good morning, asshole.* Looking at it made my stomach turn. I closed my eyes, and I would have kept them that way, but another series of rapid knocks, these accompanied by a familiar voice, forced them back open.

"Stuart? Stuart, are you awake? We have to be going soon. You do not want to miss your plane." It was Niki, asking me a very difficult question. "Stuart, wake up." More head-splitting door rapping. "We should be going soon."

She rattled the doorknob. I didn't remember doing it, but I must have locked the door. "I ... I *am* awake," I grumbled. Technically, it wasn't a lie.

"Why do I hear nothing? Stuart, are you ... are you even dressed?"

I looked down at my body and saw that I was still wearing last night's dinner clothes. "I'm dressed. I'm just ... I'm just getting a few more things together."

"I do not hear you moving," she said, her voice climbing to the pitch of doubt. Her tone had a similar effect to the sound of a dog sliding off a tin roof, trying to get a grip. "Stuart, are you up?" More doorknob rattling. "You tell me the truth."

I threw a leg out of the bed and plopped a foot on the floor to make some convincing noise. "I'm up. Just hold your dang horses." I sat up, squinted against the blare of sun, and swallowed hard at whatever was trying to swim up my esophagus. I staggered to my feet and shuffled like a sickly old man to my suitcase. Seizing the handful of undershorts—the sum total of my packing effort—I stepped to the door and threw it open. I held up the shorts as if I were showing off a first-place trophy I'd won in a lying match. "I'm packing," I grumbled. "What's the big hurry?"

Niki stood as still as a stone post. Crisp blouse, shorts, tennis shoes, visor—all white—evoked the image of a fresh field of sun-drenched daisies. I knew I was in trouble when her face morphed from concern to a condition better described as a horrified gape. Her wide eyes scanned me like a bar code and then shifted and locked radarlike on the empty bottle in the doorway. She pushed past me, marched straight for the bottle, snatched it up, and verified its emptiness.

"You ... you drank this whole thing?"

My stomach rolled like a crab boat in a North Sea storm. My vision fuzzed when I said, "If you don't mind, I'd rather not discuss it."

She gave me another scan. I felt like I was being charged double. "Your clothes. You ... you slept in them?"

I looked down and saw half my front shirttail hanging out. Niki was already shaking her head when I started to stuff the shirttail back in.

"You are *not* going to wear that again."

"What's wrong with it?"

"What is wrong with it?" Her voice seethed with disgust. She brushed me aside like a cobweb and started rummaging through dresser drawers, tossing things and muttering what I assumed were Greek profanities. I was about to launch a protest when she turned and thrust a pair of shorts into my hands. "Wear these." She stepped to the closet, snatched out a short-sleeved blue striped shirt, and tossed it over the shorts. "Ten minutes." She glanced sternly at her watch. "You will pack and meet me at the patio in ten minutes." She started for the door and then stopped. "And see that you do something with that disgusting hair. You look like … like a road-killed peacock." She stalked off.

"Well, yes, ma'am," I said to the empty space that her hint of perfume still occupied. I glanced at my reflection in a mirror that hung next to the door. The hair was a little messed up—nothing a splash of water and a baseball hat couldn't fix. But the peacock thing? I was willing to bet that even the great Dr. Niki Mikos had never seen a road-killed peacock standing on its own two feet.

"WELCOME TO THE WORLD OF the living." Niki stood next to the golf cart and trailer rig, arms crossed, regarding me coldly as I approached. Sunglasses did nothing to hide her disgust. I moved toward her with slow, deliberate steps, the inside of my head throbbing like a heavy metal rock concert. I desperately needed to throw up, but I didn't want to give her the satisfaction of knowing I was getting what I deserved.

I shuffled to the trailer with the enthusiasm of a dyslexic on his way to a spelling bee. After hoisting my hastily packed luggage into the trailer, I plopped into the passenger side of the cart. Niki slipped into the driver's seat and stared straight ahead, massaging the wheel as if she couldn't decide which end of me she'd start on. She was either going to jump down my throat or start chewing my ass. Like I needed a lecture. I already had enough self-loathing to swear off alcohol for the next four lifetimes. Anything she could heap on was going to slide right off the pile.

Surprisingly, there was no lecture. Instead, she pulled a folded check from the pocket of her blouse and tossed it in my lap.

"What's this?"

"You have eyes, do you not? Or are they still too bleary to read?"

She floored the cart—a head-jerking, bile-sloshing lunge that nearly caused me to hurl into my own lap.

"Do you mind?" I protested, searching desperately for some part of the scenery that wasn't undulating. I could have been a sack of oats for all she cared. God, I needed to puke, but I fought it with every last ounce of concentration. I unfolded the check. It didn't make sense. It was the money I'd given back to Barnes. "What's this?"

"What does it look like? If it were up to me, I would give you nothing. But the money, it belongs to Rufus, not me. For reasons beyond my understanding, he wishes for you to keep it."

"What do you mean, he wishes for me to keep it? I didn't do anything to earn it."

"I agree 157 percent. But Rufus, he is no ordinary man. If he thinks there is a chance that he has misled you, he will not take back the money. But I tell you, he did not know that Christian and Sergio had quit. Neither of us knew, not until we got here. Nicholas, he tried to call Rufus, but the telephone was down. Giving you this money is his way of apologizing for a mistake he did not make. Giving it back, if you ask my opinion, is his only mistake."

I didn't recall asking, but I had a feeling that the fee for a trip to Santorini was going to be a boatload of unsolicited opinions. "Guess you saw Barnes?"

"While you slept away the morning, we were having breakfast."

"Breakfast?" Even the sound of the word did something to my stomach. It must have done something to my face as well, and Niki didn't miss it.

"Dora cooked up a big, fluffy ham-and-cheese omelet—three eggs, I think—smoked bacon, sausage links, toast, a side of pancakes and maple syrup. And butter, lots and lots of butter."

"May you explode."

"What? You do not eat breakfast, the most important meal of the day? Perhaps you prefer a big glass of ouzo? Better yet, the *whole* bottle." An arm flew up, encompassing the entire universe. "Can you not just taste it now? Licorice. Yum, yum. So good for the stomach, no?"

A wave of sickness rolled over me.

"If you're looking for a reaction, you may just get one—all over those pretty white shoes of yours."

She blew a short, impatient breath. "Men. So stupid some-times."

"You know, I think something happens to you when you put on white. It brings out all your … your pent-up piety."

"Piety? Me? *Ha*! I wonder that men are so much alike. You turn off your brains, and you get drunk all the time. And then you sleep all day. You are lazy. All of you. I do not do any of these things, so I am pious? *Ha!*"

"All right," I conceded, anxious to put an end to the ricocheting sound of her voice inside my head. "We're all stupid, we get drunk, and we sleep all day because we're lazy. It's the holy trinity of characteristics that define the entire male species. Everyone knows it's a well-established, scientifically proven fact. So, now that we got that settled, maybe you can show some pity and cut me a little slack."

Niki's smoldering glare said that she wasn't sure if she was done with me.

I refolded the check, knowing, as I slipped it back into my pocket, that I couldn't keep the money. Maybe Barnes really had thought the cave was farther along than it was. He wasn't trying to trick me; he just didn't know his help had fled. Maybe leaving was a mistake after all.

The cart hissed through puddles left by the storm. I cursed my self-inflicted sickness, cursed the fact that I was more interested in finding a place to lie down than in grappling with the rights and wrongs of my decision to leave. I closed my eyes and tried to sort through the mishmash of a choice I might later regret.

We were just coming around the last bend before the dock when I heard a sound so out of context that I didn't recognize it. Then, at the same instant I knew it was the *ping* of a driver smacking a golf ball, Niki gasped, "Oh my god!" My eyes flashed open; my brain scrambled to take in a scene that was just as unexpected as the ping. Two men in suits and dark glasses stood on the dock; one of the men was still in the upswing stance of a completed drive. I searched the sky, found his ball, and watched it arc slow and high before plunking a respectable distance into the sea. The mystery man, whoever the hell he was, could hit a golf ball.

At the dock, next to Barnes's cruiser, I noticed a sleek black powerboat, a Cigarette boat to be exact. Named for their long, narrow design, Cigarettes were built to smoke on the water—or, more accurately, just above it. I'd watched them race on television. They were the "muscle cars" of the water; their V-hull, closed-bow design, coupled with high-horsepower engines, sent them planing over the water at speeds up to a hundred miles an hour. I remembered the announcer saying that there were two requirements for owning a Cigarette boat: a lust for speed and a hell of a lot of money.

"Do you know those guys?" I asked, glancing between Niki's startled face and the two men.

"I am afraid we *both* know them."

I did a double take. She was right. It was Gustavo Giacopetti who had just made the shot. Vito was the spectator. My heart started pumping even harder when I saw my stolen backpack slung over Vito's broad shoulder.

At the dock, Niki brought the cart to a squeaking stop. We stepped out. I tried to appear casual, but I felt terrible, and my stomach was knotted tighter than a wet rope. Giacopetti, on the other hand, was all smiles, greeting us like old friends on the golf course. He knew we'd seen his shot, and he was gloating.

"You know," Giacopetti said, "I once thought the three wood was the best driver. But now"—he stroked the club as though it were a naked woman—"I think I have found a new love. Big Bertha. Well named, would you not agree, Mr. Adams?"

If he was trying to draw something sexy from the name, we'd obviously hit upon a cultural difference. I had no fond memories of Bertha—the name or the driver. I had an aunt named Bertha. The only thing I remembered about her was that she was fat, drank straight whiskey, smoked like a chimney, and smelled like a locker room after football practice on a hot day. As for the driver, I'd tried Callaway's titanium wonder once, but it was, like most number ones, too long and cumbersome for me.

"A lot of guys I know like 'em," I said, careful to avoid offending Giacopetti's taste in drivers and women, "but you can give me your three wood any day."

"Then perhaps I can make a believer of you." Giacopetti removed a ball from his suit pocket and handed it and the club to me. "Please, be my guest."

I felt bad enough to guarantee a blown shot, which, under the circumstances, would be the most prudent thing to do. I placed the ball on the edge of the dock and flexed the shaft to at least make it look as though I had a good feel for the club.

I prepared for the swing: eye on the ball, head down, left shoulder up, tried to relax my grip. I drew back and intentionally came down with something less than my normal power. The club head glanced off the dock, catching the upper half of the ball. The thing scurried like a little white rat twenty-five yards out into the water. Perfect.

"Damn," I said, handing the club back to Giacopetti. "Same thing happened to me last time."

Giacopetti, obviously pleased at the screwup, shook his head sympathetically. "Perhaps you would like to try another?"

I was about to refuse when Niki stepped forward, surprising us both.

"May I?" she asked.

Giacopetti hesitated. "But of course," he said, suddenly fumbling another ball from his pocket.

I tried to catch her eye and send some signal to mess up. She wouldn't look at me. All I could do was pray like hell that she'd flub the drive. Niki took her stance and, for a painfully long moment, concentrated fully on the ball. I happened to glance at Vito. He wasn't watching Niki. He was looking at me, dead-on, a menacing smile set in his face. No one had better outdo his boss.

I turned back to Niki. In a graceful motion befitting her beauty, she struck with power I'd never seen from a woman. She smacked that ball as if she were teeing off Giacopetti's crotch. The thing climbed in slow motion through the air and sailed as though it'd caught the jet stream. Finally, it dropped, a real bad forty-five yards beyond Giacopetti's.

Niki handed the club to Giacopetti. "Garbage."

My insides cringed. Why couldn't she have waited until *after* I was gone to destroy the ego of her father's murderer? Suddenly Colorado looked like a real healthy option.

An indignant Giacopetti snatched the club and glowered at Niki for an annoyed moment. He turned to his bodyguard, and the big man handed him my backpack. Giacopetti passed it to me.

"As you can see, the police have recovered your belongings. I volunteered to return them to you—*personally*. You will be pleased to know that everything appears to be in order."

I took it and thanked him.

"You are not going to check the contents?"

"I'll take your word for it."

Giacopetti hadn't intended to let it go that easily. "I must confess,

Mr. Adams, I found the beginnings of your story quite fascinating. American spy? A priceless scroll plastered into a cave wall?" He lit a cigarette and blew out a long stream of smoke. "I could not put it down. I read it over and over. I cannot wait to read this book of yours. Even Vito—not an avid reader, mind you—even he enjoyed it. Is this not right, Vito?" The big man cracked an evil grin. "And the journal entries? Quite intriguing. If one did not know that you were a novelist, he might easily suspect that there actually *is* a scroll." He took another puff from the cigarette. "Then, there is the photograph. A hoax?" He frowned. "Of course I have the greatest respect for the opinion of Inspector De Santis. He has a well-trained eye for such things. But now I am not so certain that I share his opinion. You see, Mr. Adams, I took the liberty of having this photograph examined—*by an expert.* He reached a very different conclusion. Linear A? On parchment? An unlikely combination, indeed. Why would a talented forger waste his time creating such a completely unorthodox document? Who would buy it?"

His phony enthusiasm was starting to wear thin. "Look, Mr. Giacopetti, I don't know anything about that kind of stuff. I appreciate your efforts in getting this back to me"—I hoisted the backpack— "but if you don't mind, I've got a plane to catch. We need to be going."

"You sound slightly perturbed, Mr. Adams. I hope you do not mind my taking this liberty with your photograph."

"I told you before, it's not my photograph."

"Yes, of course. According to your journal, the photograph belongs to the very man that owns this estate, Mr. R. Wesley Barnes. He believes that the scroll is here on Sarnafi, in a collapsed cave. Perhaps Mr. Barnes would not mind if Vito and I had a look at this cave?"

"Mr. Barnes would not mind," Niki said, "if you can provide a search warrant of the premises."

"A search warrant?" Giacopetti stepped directly in front of Niki, his eyes crawling up her body like a snake on the hunt. "I see no need to involve the police. You should know that your lack of cooperation could have serious consequences on your ability to work in our country. Of course, it does not have to come to that. Now, I would love to discuss this matter in a more ... *private* setting. Over dinner, perhaps?"

"Rot in hell," Niki said, and she spat at his feet.

Giacopetti forced the indignation from his face. "A woman as feisty as she is beautiful. Qualities I truly admire. It troubles me that I have failed to win your trust. Perhaps if you knew me better—"

"I don't think she wants to know you any better." I heard myself blurt the words. "I sure as hell don't." My heart was hammering in my chest, my breath growing shallow. A flood of adrenaline threw a quiver into my voice. "Why don't you and your friend get back in your boat and putter the hell out of here."

From the corner of my eye I could see Vito stiffen, ready to lunge. Giacopetti looked at me as if I were a foul odor. He tapped me on the chest with the handle of the golf club and nodded toward his bodyguard. "Vito is a very sensitive man, Mr. Adams. Perhaps it would ... *soothe* his concerns, if you were to apologize for your ... *vile* remarks." He took a long drag off his cigarette, and he blew the smoke into my face.

I grabbed the handle of the club and jerked it out of his hand. Vito, his barrel chest nearly popping buttons from his shirt, took a step toward me. I cocked the club, ready to start swinging. Vito's hand slipped beneath his jacket, going, no doubt, for his gun. My heart raced. Giacopetti raised a hand, and the big man froze in readiness.

Giacopetti remained cool. "I see you are fond of this club. Please, consider it my farewell gift." He smiled arrogantly. "I assume you are retuning to America?"

I just stared at him, clinching the club handle to keep my hands from shaking.

"A good choice," he said. He turned back to Niki. "And you, Dr. Mikos, you can be certain that I will be keeping an eye on you." He scanned her body again. "Indeed. If you wish to keep working in Greece, you *will* learn to be more cooperative. I assure you, we are not finished with this matter."

Giacopetti delivered a slight bow, and the men sauntered to the boat. Giacopetti stepped to the helm and brought the engine grumbling to life. He offered a loose farewell salute, pulled away from the dock, and then gunned the Cigarette. In an incredible burst of speed, the boat lifted in the water and disappeared like a tormented demon screaming all the way back to hell. Vito's eyes never left me.

"Bastard!" Niki said, a spasm of repugnance distorting her face. "You should have clubbed that ... that swine. I would do it myself." She turned and started for the trailer. "He has made us late. Now we must hurry, or you will miss your flight." She started pulling my luggage out of the trailer.

I was still holding Giacopetti's golf club. Suddenly it felt dirty in my hands. I flung it as far as I could into the sea. When it hit the water, Niki's eyes shot up.

"Why did you do that?"

A strange thing had happened. The rush of adrenaline had eradicated my hangover. I felt as good as ever. But there was something more—a flash of clarity. Suddenly I knew what I had to do.

I took a calming breath. "I want you to take me back to the villa. There's something I need to tell Barnes."

The puzzlement in Niki's face deepened. "What? But there is no time. You are going to miss your—"

"I'm staying."

It was gratifying payback to watch her jaw drop and her brow furrow, to see my suitcase slip from her fingers and roll over on its side. I couldn't wait to see how she'd manage to take back all the derogatory remarks toward American manhood in general, and mine in particular.

"You ... you are ... *what?*"

"I said I'm staying."

Niki blinked, studying me as if I were some unknown primate species. "But ... but why? Giacopetti ... he will be back. He will make sure that we do not dig out the cave."

"No. Don't you get it? This isn't going to be a case for the Department of Antiquities, and he sure as hell doesn't want the police in on it. He wants the scroll, and he plans on letting you dig it up for him."

I could see in her darting eyes that she'd been so distracted by her contempt for Giacopetti that she hadn't even considered his scheme until that moment.

"I would rather leave it to rot," she said finally.

"Right. You think he'd believe that for a second? I don't, and neither do you. You're going to find that scroll, and you're going to need my help."

"Your help? How are you going to help? You will not lift rocks."

"Maybe I changed my mind."

Niki blinked and stared at me for a long, disbelieving moment. She took the couple of steps that brought her directly in front of me, her face brimming with skepticism.

"You … you will help with the dig?"

After all the barbs she'd thrown at me, it felt good to see her off balance.

"Somebody told me that rocks in Greece don't move by themselves."

"But … but Marion. You told her that you would—"

"I'll worry about Marion," I said, empowered by my own anger for allowing her to manipulate me. I lifted the check from my shirt pocket and held it up as if it were her set of instructions mandating my return home. "I promised Barnes a year. If that's what it takes to find the scroll, then a year it is. I'm not breaking my word."

I tore the check into a hundred pieces and threw it in the water. Tiny fish darted in and nibbled at the fragments.

Niki stared at me for a long, dumbfounded moment. Then, in a very quiet voice, she said, "Stuart, I … I do not know what to say."

"Really? I never thought I'd hear that coming from you."

Her reaction was an open mouth that moved slightly with nothing coming out. With the distinct feeling that neither of us would ever know what words those pretty lips of hers were trying to form, I started for the cart. She grabbed my arm and plunged her eyes deep into mine. Then, with no warning, she took my face in both hands and planted a brain-fogging kiss on my mouth.

Now I was the one who didn't know what to say.

Chapter 10

MARION WASN'T HOME WHEN I called. I filled her machine with a load of apologies and pleas for understanding knowing she was going to be disappointed, probably mad as hell. I'd seen how she was in business. She'd rather lose money than lose a client, and she was not real good at handling rejection. She'd never make it as a writer.

My adrenaline high had flattened into a deep feeling of vulnerability. I shuffled into the cottage, dropped my luggage in the middle of the floor, and tried to melt into the couch. Too hyped with worry to sit for long, I went out to the patio and stared over the water trying to convince myself I'd made the right decision. That night I wrestled with demons, real and imagined, and by sunup, I'd managed only an hour or two of something resembling sleep. I was actually looking forward to hitting the rock pile. Hard labor would do me good and get my mind on something more than the possibility that I'd completely blown it with Marion.

Over the next several weeks, Niki and I fell into a routine. After stuffing us with breakfast, Dora would send us waddling off to the site with the promise of the same treatment for lunch. By sunrise, we'd be whacking, prying, splitting, and heaving our way deeper into the cave. Barnes even ordered a generator and a jackhammer to help with the demolition.

I knew Marion was using her caller ID to avoid me. She wasn't returning my calls. We were having a wordless argument that was growing more heated by the week.

Niki was the bright spot in my life. She could wield a pick, shovel, wrecking bar, and jackhammer as good as any man her size. Even drenched in sweat, covered head to toe in dirt, she could still look good doing it. Just watching her work helped pass the hours and kept my mind off the possibility that our labor might come to nothing.

Barnes was no help, mainly because he'd just barely survived four heart attacks. Doctors said a fifth would probably finish the job, but he was faithful in showing up to cheer us on. Around ten each morning, he'd be at the site with his, "Hello, girls." He'd take a seat in a lawn chair in the shade of a blue tarp. Against doctor's orders, he'd stuff a wad of tobacco in his jaw, snap open the *Times* (at least a week behind), and begin offering solutions to the world's problems that might have had some merit if anybody had been around who cared to listen. Just before lunch, he'd step over, examine our progress, and maybe toss a fist-sized stone or two (that always elicited a scolding from Niki). He'd complete the ritual by saying, "Watching you two girls work has just about worn me out. Why don't we get up to the house and see if Dora will rustle us up a bite to eat?" After lunch, he'd go for his afternoon nap and tend business matters. He wouldn't emerge again until dinner.

Thursdays became our day of rest. Niki and Dora would usually head over to Anafi to shop. Barnes stayed busy in his office catching up on correspondence and various forms of paperwork. Nicholas and I would go down and wait for the mail boat; we'd pass the time killing a couple of six-packs and fishing offshore for sargo, blackfish, doradoes—whatever happened to be biting.

We'd always save a beer or two for Feodor Kabarnos, the burly-browed old postman with sandy hair and scotch-reddened cheeks. Nicholas introduced me to Feodor and told him that I'd come to Sarnafi to write a book. Feodor had seen too much in life to be impressed, but he did show concern when Nicholas told him of my little encounter with Giacopetti. He lifted a pipe from his pocket, lit it, and drew a couple of puffs without taking his eyes off mine.

"You had better watch yourself. Gustavo Giacopetti, he and I were boys together. We fished in the same sea. We worked the same vineyards. I did not like him then; I do not like him now. He is a skunk. Always, he has been a skunk."

When Nicholas explained that Feodor had been the first to suggest to Alexios Mikos that Gustavo Giacopetti was the mysterious

Raphael, Feodor scoffed. "Mysterious? Ha! Giacopetti is as myste-rious as a skunk hiding beneath a wicker basket. Does anyone say, 'What is that mysterious smell?' No. Everyone who gets close enough knows. I too work for the government. I know that no one on govern-ment salary can possibly afford the luxuries enjoyed by this man. Of course he is this ... this *Raphael*. Alexios, he gathered the evidence. He was about to lift the basket, show the world this skunk." Feodor spat with contempt and drilled his eyes deeper into mine. "My friend Alexios, he knew what this man Giacopetti was doing. And now you see, Alexios is dead. On my mother's grave, I swear that Gustavo Gia-copetti is responsible." He pointed the stem of his pipe at my chest. "Listen to what I tell you. If you want to finish this book of yours, you had better watch your back."

Feodor was our eyes and ears on Santorini, a very willing ally for monitoring Giacopetti's whereabouts. "I have friends on every island," Feodor boasted. "Gustavo Giacopetti, he cannot make a move without me knowing. My friends, they call me, I call you."

We all thought it was a little odd that Giacopetti never came.

Tossing rocks all day gave me time to think and work out a few things. I realized that, in a strange twist of irony, Giacopetti had actually bolstered my faith in the scroll's authenticity. His expert had raised a good question: *Why would a forger waste his time creating such an unlikely fake?* The only known specimens of Linear A were on clay tablets, not parchment. The forger would have the dual task of proving the scroll's authenticity *and* convincing a buyer of the origi-nality of an unprecedented combination of text and medium.

Forgery or not, everyone who learned of the scroll's existence wanted it, and they were willing to pay a lot of money, even kill for it. I was beginning to understand that this story was a lot bigger than I had imagined. It was one thing to hear it from a doddering old fart. But to actually feel the fervor of men desperate to get their hands on an artifact this valuable was making a believer out of me. If we found the scroll and I got the story out, there was no doubt in my mind that I was going to be a very rich man.

There was only one problem: I had a nagging feeling that we were wasting our time trying to find the scroll on Sarnafi. Why? Alexios Mikos, who spent much of his professional career researching the problem, believed the scroll was there. Barnes was convinced enough to buy the island. And Niki, a leading expert on Pialigarian culture, had adopted her father's conviction as her own mantra. I had no right to challenge the theory. All I had was a tiny feeling, a grain of doubt next to a mountain of circumstantial evidence. I couldn't even argue a viable alternative. The only way to get past the Sarnafi theory was to plunge into that cave and prove it was empty.

PROGRESS WAS SLOW AND THE work hard, even brutal. I did what I could to keep my optimism and stay focused on the goal instead of on my fear that the silent chasm that had opened between Marion and me was becoming unbridgeable.

It was after 10:00 AM when Barnes arrived with his usual, "Hi, girls." I was hunkered over the jackhammer, attempting to dismantle an unusually obstinate boulder one small chunk at a time. Niki was further breaking down the chunks with a sledge and hauling them off to the ever-growing debris pile.

At around 11:00, we were taking a break when I happened to notice a section of the newspaper that Barnes had laid next to his chair. On the front page was a photograph of Kyropos. The photo was grainy, obviously enlarged. I couldn't make out their facial features, but I could tell it was a shot of a heavily armed group of men and women standing defiantly on the volcano's shores, ash cloud billowing ominously in the background. Something in the angle of the photograph got my attention. I snatched up the paper. The article described the group as members of a radical doomsday cult who called themselves the Children of Light. The name meant something.

Niki saw me studying the newspaper and asked what I was reading.

"Kyropos," I said, still skimming the article. "There's a group of radicals that think the day of Armageddon has arrived."

"They stay on that volcano," Barnes said with a laugh, "and they'll likely get their wish."

"They think the eruption is a signal to take up arms," I explained, "join in the final great battle with the Children of Darkness. They claim they're descendants of the Essenes."

"That is unlikely," Niki said. "The Essenes, they were completely annihilated by the Romans in the first century. It was not ..."

I didn't hear the rest of her explanation. The photograph had triggered something. "I've been there," I said, and even as I heard myself blurt it out, I knew it couldn't be true. Yet the feeling hit with such an absolute burst of clarity that I couldn't stop myself from saying it.

Niki studied the picture and then me. "This photograph was taken from the Rock, the tiny island next to the volcano. You have never been there."

"I know it sounds crazy, but I've seen Kyropos from this angle." In the next instant the image of a bearded man—tall, in his seventies, wearing rough woven clothing—flashed into my mind. "Marcus. This is where I met Marcus."

"Marcus?" Niki frowned. "Who is Marcus?"

"I ... I don't know who he is ... or was. But he and I, we ... we stood together ... right there ... where this photographer must have been standing. Kyropos looked just like this."

Barnes jumped in. "Adams, you sure you haven't been in the sun a little too long? Maybe it's time we take a lunch break. Short nap, maybe."

"I don't need a nap," I said. "Niki, there's something there, something I've got to see." I turned back to the photograph. More images crept into my mind. "There were men. They ... they were asking me questions. And caves. The men lived in the caves ... in the side of the volcano. Children of Light ... these men called themselves Children of Light."

"But the Essenes were not an island people," Niki insisted. "They lived in the desert, near the Dead Sea. And how would you—"

"We've got to go there," I said again, convinced that there was something to the vision.

Niki cupped her hands to form a megaphone and spoke in a singsong tease. "Earth to Stuart. Hellooo. Is anybody home? The cave is still full of rocks. Lots and lots of *biiiiig* rocks."

Her taunting had the effect of a gnat crawling in my ear. "Damn it, Niki, I'm telling you, we're digging in the wrong cave." Suddenly fed up with her little game, I didn't care if she believed me or not. How could I make up something that had never before crossed my mind?

My sudden anger shocked her. She dropped her hands; her face grew serious.

"You cannot know this. Am I supposed to believe that you can just look at a picture in a newspaper and suddenly *know* these things? Are we to drop everything to follow some … some quirky fantasy that happens to pop into your head? Besides," she turned to the photo, "you can see that these people are well armed. It would be too dangerous. We cannot go until—"

"But they're on Kyropos," I argued. "We don't go there. We go to the Rock." I pointed to the picture again. "There's nobody shooting at this photographer. You said you wanted to sail to Pialigos. Let's go see your priestess friend and then head for the Rock. We'll have a look around. That's all I'm asking. If we don't see anything, we'll come back."

She crossed her arms, tilted back her head, and looked down her nose at me, her eyes narrow with suspicion. "This cave has beaten you. You want to quit."

"I want to find the scroll," I said, but I was talking into a black hole. The full, defiantly stubborn force of the Greek conqueror had kicked in. She was set, and arguing with her would qualify as an obvious demonstration of insanity. I stepped back to the jackhammer, shot a final look at her, and started blasting away.

Niki didn't move. She just stood there staring at me. I could feel her eyes: angry, frustrated, and curious. Then, after a few long moments, she stepped over and laid a hand on mine. I stopped hammering. "How certain are you of this … this vision of yours?"

"You want proof?" I said, wiping sweat from my brow with the back of a gloved hand. "I don't have any. All I can tell you is that we're digging in the wrong place."

She stared at me, the muscles in her jaw flexing with suspicion. "All right then, we will find Captain Threader."

The name meant nothing to me, but it brought Barnes slowly to his feet with a face full of doubt. "Blake Threader? Don't you think you'd better—"

"What is wrong with him?" Niki demanded to know. "Captain Blake Threader sailed for my father. He can sail for us."

"That was some years ago," Barnes said. "Nicholas was just saying the other day that he'd seen Threader at the harbor in Santorini. Said things were kind of slipping away from the old captain." Barnes turned to me. "Threader is an American who finished his stint in the Navy and then landed on Santorini, bought himself a boat, and started up a chartering service. Booze took over, and now he runs a small salvage yard at the docks of Santorini's capitol of Fira. Used to be the best in the business, till he started drinking."

This didn't sound good to me. As much as I wanted to check out the Rock, I wasn't anxious to put my life in the hands of a drunken wreck.

"He is *still* the best in the business," Niki insisted. "He knows the sea. He can get us to Kyropos and back in his sleep."

"Yeah, and he most likely will," Barnes said. "But darling, if you want Captain Threader, then you go get him. I'll write the checks, but I won't be making the trip. I've got to keep an eye on the old ticker."

I could almost hear the wheels of Niki's mind whirring away. She locked her determined eyes on mine. "We go. Pialigos first … then Kyropos. We will see if this vision of yours is a soul memory or if it is just a silly ploy to spare your aching back."

NICHOLAS WAS DOING MECHANICAL REPAIRS on Barnes's boat, so Niki and I had to catch a ride to Perivolos with Feodor. From there, we took a taxi to Santorini's port at Fira. The driver let me off at the top of the road that zigzagged down the thousand-foot face of the crater to the docks. My job was to find and hire Captain Blake Threader while Niki arranged for supplies.

I stepped from the cab and then reached back into the seat for my backpack.

"It is a long hike to the dock," Niki said. "I hope you have plenty of water."

"One bottle in the holster, one more inside."

"You may consider renting a donkey for the trip back up the caldera. There are 587 steps in the road. It is much more difficult coming up."

I knew from hiking into the Grand Canyon that coming up would be a lot more difficult than going down. Then I saw a guy about my height sitting on one of those stubby little beasts, whacking it lightly on the rump with a short stick, and barking orders in French, his feet an inch off the ground. Maybe it was an American guy thing, but I couldn't see myself doing that. "If it gets to be too much, I think I'll take the cable car."

"Suit yourself. But I tell you, the donkey trip is an experience every visitor should have at least once in their lifetime."

"Yeah? Is there anything that says it has to be *this* lifetime?"

She was a little puzzled by my reluctance, but she shrugged it off. "You be careful. Watch for Gustavo Giacopetti."

"Yes, mother. Anything else?"

"I am serious," she said. The sternness in her face melted into a smile. "You know how difficult it is to find good help."

I paused at the edge of the caldera to survey the scene. From this height, cruise ships were the size of yachts. The islands of Thirasia and tiny Aspronisi defined the western rim of the caldera. With the exception of Nea Kameni and the smaller Palia Kameni—both had risen from the crater's center in relatively recent times—a five-mile expanse of glimmering sea filled the volcano's interior. The enormity of a blast that could displace that much of the mountain gave me second thoughts about taking a sailboat to Kyropos. If we were anywhere near that thing when it blew, we wouldn't stand a chance.

The descent to the dock was a long, hot trek. Before I knew it I'd emptied my first bottle of water. Forty minutes later, I stood at the dock scanning boats for the thirty-five-foot *Dancing Daphne*, which, according to Niki, Threader had named after a former lover. A fifty-foot dreamboat—*Penelope*—was tied in the last slip. With the hope that Threader had found himself a new girlfriend, I called out for anyone on board. There was no answer. I was about to head for the dock office when I stopped. A quarter mile down the empty beach was another group of boats, a salvage yard from the look of it. Threader's place of business, no doubt.

Every boat was in some stage of disrepair, none appearing seaworthy. With no one around, I started to go, but I stopped when I spotted one boat, battered and loaded with trash, bobbing in the iridescent scum of an oil leak. Most of the paint had flaked off, but there was enough left to make out the name: *Dancing Daphne*.

I stepped in for a closer look. There was a ratty hammock strung between the mast and the bow railing. The hammock's lines, obviously stretched to their limit, hadn't snapped only because the butt of its bulky occupant sank to the deck and relieved the pressure. The buzz of a fly filtered through the fat man's hacking snore. A glint of drool seeped from the corner of his mouth, oozed through a frazzle of white stubble, and dripped to the front of a yellowed T-shirt ready to split under the strain of an oversized belly. The smell of sweat and liquor fouled the air.

I stepped to the deck and picked my way through the maze of rubble toward the sleeping man. A fly crawled over his grizzled face, down a right eye and cheekbone that was black with a fist-sized bruise—a slob, a drunk, and a brawler.

The fly crawled over twitching lips. When it reached his nostril, the man exploded, smacking the side of his own face with enough force to knock him out of the hammock. He went down thrashing on the deck like an overturned tortoise.

"You want more, you son of a bitch?" he yelled in no direction in particular. "I'll give you more."

He scrambled to his feet and launched a softball-sized fist directly at my face. I dodged, and the force of the man's swing sent him tumbling through a tangle of rope and assorted rubbish.

"I'm not here to fight," I said, hoping to dissuade him.

He stood and put a seething, red-eyed glare as squarely on me as he could. He struck a boxer's pose, fists undulating like a pair of pistons. "Slug a man when he's sleeping, will you? Come on, you damn coward. I ain't sleeping now. Try to take a piece of the old captain while he's locked and loaded."

"I don't want a piece of the old captain," I said, raising my hands in a gesture of peace. "And I didn't—"

"Slinking away, are you? Well, son, it ain't that easy. When a man starts something with Blake Threader, he damn well better be ready to dance, 'cause I'm gonna start dancing all over that ugly face of yours."

I didn't consider myself much of a fighter, but there had been a couple of occasions where I'd had to physically defend myself. I was as surprised as anyone that I could hold my own. Threader punched the air with a fake left and launched a slow, predictable right. I pulled back and sank a right-handed package of knuckles in that flour bag gut of his. Threader dropped to his knees; his face went sour. He lunged for the railing, hurling the contents of his stomach into the water.

I took it as my cue for introductions. "Niki Mikos sent me," I said, wincing at the sound of his strangling contractions.

Threader staggered to his feet and wiped his mouth with a hairy arm. Suspicion melted into curiosity. "Niki?" With fingers, he tried to bring order to his sprawling mess of white hair.

"She sent me to hire the services of a Captain Blake Threader. There must be two of you by that name."

"Two of us?" His eyes narrowed with contempt. "I'm Blake Threader, and by god there's only one of me."

I made a head-to-toe pass. "Then she made a mistake."

Threader sniffed and spat a hunk of something over the rail. "There's no mistake," he said in a growl. "If Niki Mikos is asking something of Captain Blake Threader, then by god you've come to the right place."

I huffed out a laugh. "Don't think so. I wouldn't sail in this tub if I could walk on water—which I can't." I turned to leave.

"Well, damn you to hell. You could have fooled me," Threader yelled to my back. "You waltz on my boat like you're the next best thing to Jesus Christ. Daphne is a fine running boat. Little cleanup, that's all she needs."

"Yeah," I shouted back, "nothing a can of kerosene, a match, and a good shove couldn't fix."

I stepped off the dock and headed for the office, hoping to get some recommendations for a respectable chartering service. Niki was going to have to deal with the fact that people change, and not always for the better. I reached for my water bottle to get a drink, forgetting that I'd already emptied it. Still walking, I took off my backpack to get the fresh one. I only half noticed the rumble of a boat that had pulled into the harbor and burbled along behind me. I took a swallow of water. Sensing the driver was pacing me, I turned and almost choked when I saw the black Cigarette.

Giacopetti goosed the motor and made a tight arc that beached the boat parallel to the shore a few yards ahead of me.

"Mr. Adams," he called out. "What a surprise to see you are still in our part of the world."

Apollo and Vito hopped out of the boat, drew their guns, and made sure I saw them screwing silencers into the barrels. Was this intimidation, or did they mean business? Either way, it worked. My heart raced. I swallowed at the dryness in my throat, glanced back at the junkyard, and wished like hell that I hadn't insulted Threader. A drunken brawler would have made a pretty welcome companion just then.

Silencers in place, Apollo and Vito holstered their weapons and gathered like storm clouds in front of me. Their grins were dark, ominous, evil in stereo. Everything in me wanted to run, but where? The main dock was too far away, and I couldn't outrun a bullet. I cursed myself for being so lax. I should have seen the Cigarette in the harbor. This was bad … *real* bad.

"Mr. Adams," Giacopetti said as he approached. "Am I to assume that you changed your mind about leaving?"

"Yeah, I changed my mind," I said, doing my best to keep fear out of my voice.

"You have learned something more of the scroll?"

"I'm not looking for the scroll."

"Oh, but you are, Mr. Adams. You said so in your journal. One year, if my memory serves me. In exchange for a rather handsome fee, you agreed to search for the scroll for one year. I commend you on your rather lucrative arrangement."

"Yeah, well, that's all changed. You say it's authentic. De Santis says it's a fake. Personally, I don't care if it's real or not. I'm not wasting my time with it. I'm over here to write a book, and that's what I'm going to do."

The three men just stood there staring at me, unconvinced. Against the hope that they'd let me go, I glanced at my watch. "Look, I'm supposed to meet someone at the top of the caldera. If you gentlemen will excuse me, it's a long hike and I …" I started to leave.

Apollo grabbed me by the arm. "Not so fast, freak."

I jerked away and met Apollo's icy glare with a little fire of my own. Nothing in his face melted.

"Let us not be the heroic American," Giacopetti said, his eyes growing dead serious. "Honesty, this is all I ask. You are here to search for the scroll. Correct?" He plucked out a cigarette, lit it, and blew a long stream of smoke into the air, this time missing my face. "I am a very reasonable man, Mr. Adams. Tell me what you know about the scroll, and perhaps we can part as friends. Refuse … and, well … a quiet beach like this one offers other ways of extracting information." He nodded to Apollo. Apollo took a step toward me and grabbed the front of my T-shirt.

Instinct kicked in. I surprised Apollo with a left jab straight to his teeth that snapped his head back. Still holding the backpack in my right hand, I flung it at the side of the big man's head. With a dead *thonk*, the holstered bottle found its target.

Apollo scarcely flinched. He ripped the pack from my hand and planted a marble fist in my left jaw. I stumbled back with just enough focus to dodge his left. I countered with a wild right to his ear. I would have done more damage to a concrete block. He answered with a hard right to my gut. I doubled, met a knee to my face, and fell back into a glazed world. He lifted me like a rag doll and held me from behind, giving Vito a clear shot at my stomach. I braced, but that blow and the two that followed turned my legs to rubber. I was going down.

Then, a bloodcurdling scream shattered the air. In the next instant, I saw Blake Threader, armed with a wooden boat oar, hacking Greeks like a madman splitting logs. I heard the sickening thud of wood meeting skull. I saw Vito stagger and then collapse. Apollo tossed me aside and started for his gun. I watched Threader come down with enough force to send the big Greek to his knees. Vito drew and fired. *Pffftt!* A wild shot into the air. Threader spun, splintered the oar over Vito's head, and kicked the pistol from his hand. I scrambled over to snatch it up, staggered to my feet, leveled an unsteady aim inches from Giacopetti's blood-drained face, and hoped like hell he didn't try anything.

I watched Threader tear Apollo's pistol from beneath his jacket and shove the muzzle hard into his ear. I thought he was going to shoot. He didn't.

"Mister," Threader said, "if you want to keep the few brains you got left, you'd better think about your next move real careful like."

Apollo lay still. I could see his eyes shift like those of a cornered hyena. Threader took a few steps back. Dazed, the bloodied Greek came to his feet, his killer eyes searching Threader's, testing. He started to lunge, and Threader fired. *Pffftt.* Apollo shrieked and clutched the side of his head.

I was sure Threader had killed him. My knees went weak. I could hardly hold the pistol. I wanted to throw it away and run as far from that place as I could. I forced myself to stay.

"Next one's going four inches to the left," Threader barked. I could see then that he'd just put a knick in Apollo's ear. Threader turned to Giacopetti. "Unless you wanna start running a help-wanted ad, I'd suggest you pick up your trash and get the hell out of here."

A white-faced Giacopetti nodded. "Apollo! Vito! Do as he says."

I felt huge relief when the battered pair shambled to the boat and climbed in, Apollo still clutching his bleeding ear.

I cleared my throat to make sure I still had a voice. "You might like to join your pals," I said to Giacopetti, still looking at the end of his nose through the trembling pistol sight.

"This time I will have you arrested," Giacopetti snarled back at me.

"You're right about one thing, Giacopetti," I said. "I know where that scroll is, and I'm going to get it. Arrest me and you and your black-market buddies can kiss goodbye any chance of laying your filthy hands on it."

Giacopetti's eyes grew wide and then softened. He wanted to take me then and there, but he just nodded slightly and said, "Perhaps you are worth more to me as a free man. Let me warn you, my American friend; you play a very dangerous game, one, I assure you, that I am quite proficient at winning." He dropped the cigarette and, in a metaphoric gesture intended to send me a message, ground it into the sand with the toe of his shoe. "I will have the scroll, *and* you, Mr. Adams. Of that you can be certain. I … *will* … have you. You have won this day. Next time you will not be so lucky." He lifted his chin. "Now, as you Americans are so fond of saying, have a nice day." He turned and walked casually to the boat.

Chapter 11

MY EARS RANG AND MY head was starting to throb as Blake Threader and I stood watching the black Cigarette disappear from the harbor.

"Better get something for that eye," Threader said. "Believe you're gonna have yourself a worse shiner than me. Come on. I got just the thing."

I followed him back to his boat. The captain disappeared into the cabin and returned carrying a six-pack of beer. He handed me a can, took one for himself, popped it open, and gulped half of it before belching and taking a seat on the edge of the dock.

"I appreciate your help," I said, lifting the can like a toast to him. "Hope you know what you just stepped into."

Threader downed the rest of his beer. "Yup. Believe you just hired yourself a captain." He popped open another can and swallowed as if he were drinking water. "So, Niki found herself a little scroll, did she? That what this is all about?"

I wasn't sure how much to tell him. "It's a long shot. Could be nothing."

"Where we going?"

"Pialigos."

"Pialigos? That ain't nothing. You could charter a damn rowboat for a trip like that."

I hesitated. "Then Kyropos."

"To hell you say! Kyropos is sputtering. Why the devil would anyone in their right mind want to go out there?"

I didn't have a good answer for that one. I would have much rather been talking to the pilot of a seaplane.

"If it's any consolation," I said, "we're not actually going to Kyropos. There's a small island next to—"

"The Rock? That's worse. Ain't nothing but an empty pile of rocks. What makes you think there's a scroll out there?"

Something told me Threader wasn't the type to appreciate my explanation. "It's a long story."

"I see. Don't ask no questions; just sail the damn boat. That it?"

"Something like that."

I watched Threader guzzle more beer. "Don't matter. If that girl wants to go to the edge of Hades, and we ain't gonna be too damn far from it, then I'll take her to the edge of Hades. When we going?"

"Two days." I hoped he'd back out.

"Two days?" Threader turned toward his boat and downed the rest of the beer. He stood, energized, crushed the can in one hand, and tossed it out in the water. "Guess I'd better get to work. Don't worry, Adams. She cleans up real nice. You wait and see."

I studied that heap of flotsam Threader called home. There was nothing in me that believed the captain could be ready, but I at least owed him the chance to prove himself wrong.

"Good luck," I said, and I turned to leave.

"You tell Niki I'll get her there and back safe and sound," Threader called out. "The only thing we got to worry about is that damn volcano. That thing decides to blow, there ain't no place to hide in the open sea. No place. If you don't die in the explosion, you suffocate in the ash. If that don't get you, the tsunami will. It goes, we go. It's that simple. No ifs, ands, or buts about it. It's risky, Adams. Just hope you understand that."

I nodded that I understood, though, having no previous experience with the fury of a volcano, I was sure that I didn't. It added nothing to my comfort to know that a salty old dog like Threader was worried about sailing into the face of that restless beast. Sore and depressed, I shoved the pistol into my backpack and turned to leave. I stopped when I remembered I hadn't thanked the captain for helping me out.

"Threader?"

"Yeah?"

"Thanks for showing up. I may not have fared so well if you hadn't."

Threader laughed. "Maybe you better have a look in the mirror. You might not have fared quite as well as you think."

I OPTED FOR THE CABLE car out of the caldera. Even so, by the time I reached the top, my head felt as if someone had clamped it in a bench vise and whacked it tight with a ball pein hammer. Milling tourists passed in a blur.

The throbbing increased when I spotted Niki sitting on a park bench in the shade of a cypress a few yards away. She wasn't alone. A pudgy, bald-headed, thick-browed, middle-aged guy with a short-sleeved paisley shirt, baggy shorts, and sandals sat next to her—tourist most likely, used-car salesman from one of the cruise ships, getting his kicks by hitting on one of the local beauties.

I started to relieve Niki of the fly, but I stopped. They appeared to be having a deep, possibly intimate conversation. Were they friends? Lovers? The guy didn't strike me as her type. But then what did I know about the types attractive to a Greek archaeologist? It could have been his floppy ears, that dimpled chin, or maybe the big gap between his two front teeth. Hell, it could have been his bone structure for all I knew.

I stopped a few feet in front of the engrossed couple. The guy was the first to look up. He had one of those annoyed, move-along-pal-I-saw-her-first kinds of looks. Then Niki noticed me, squinted, and studied me as if I were some kind of a science project. I tried to smile, but it hurt too much. That's when her curiosity turned to horror. She shot straight off the bench.

"Oh my god! What have you done?"

I almost touched my cheekbone but decided against it. "Got in the way of a fist, I guess."

"A fist? You have been fighting?"

She made it sound like a bad habit of mine. "Actually, I met up with our friend, Giacopetti."

"Gustavo Giacopetti? He did this?"

"He had a little help from his gorillas. If it hadn't been for Threader—"

"Captain Threader? You found him?"

"Yup. He probably saved me a visit to the hospital." I glanced at her gawking companion. I didn't even know the guy, and already he annoyed me. "Looks like you found somebody too."

Niki, still frowning, turned as if she'd just become aware of her tagalong.

"Stuart Adams, I would like you to meet Father Jon Andros, a friend of many years." She reached up and touched my cheek lightly. "We should get some ice."

I liked it that she cared.

"You can call me Father Jon," the guy said, extending his hand to me. "I think Niki is right about the ice."

We shook hands, but the *father* thing just didn't jibe. "Tell me you're not talking about a monk kind of father."

"Why not? Do you wish to make a liar out of me?" The father laughed. "Yes, I am the *monk* kind of father. Why do I gather that this surprises you?"

Something in his tone suggested that he relished the deception. Irreverence for his position, maybe, like he'd been doing it too long. Or maybe not. What did I know about monks? Take all my knowledge, fluff it up, and blow it with a hair dryer, and it'd still have plenty of legroom inside the hull of a sunflower seed.

"Guess I thought you guys wore cowls, counted beads, rode donkeys, walked around with your hands up your sleeves—that kind of thing."

My assessment drew a gratified smile from him, but it drew something else from Niki.

"Forgive him, Father," she said. "I told you he is an American, a *hardheaded* American." She turned to me, her eyes still full of concern. "You are sure you do not need some ice? It will help with the swelling."

At that moment, nothing would have pleased me more than to be lying in a hospital bed with her tending my wounds. Unfortunately, we had a monk to contend with, a monk who didn't look like a monk and who seemed a little too proud of it.

"I don't think the swelling's gonna need any help," I said. "Don't worry, Doctor. I'll live."

"With a fat eye, you will live," Niki said. "But it is your fat eye." She dismissed the problem with an annoyed flutter of her eyelids.

"Father Jon is the only one I can talk to about the scroll. He used to work in the Secret Archives under none other than Salvatore Sorrentino. This is how he first learned of the scroll. He has some information that I think you will find incredible."

Just when I thought a monk in a paisley shirt and baggy shorts was about all the *incredible* I could handle, the father pulled a cigar from his shirt pocket and held it up.

"Do you mind if I smoke?"

Was this guy for real? With a glance, I tried to shoot the question to Niki. She was looking away, intentionally avoiding eye contact with me.

"If it doesn't bother him"—I nodded toward the sky—"it won't bother me."

"Thank you," Father Jon said, and with a thumbnail, he struck a wooden match and lit the cigar. When he closed his eyes and took a couple of thoughtful puffs, he reminded me of a pawnshop owner I knew in Denver.

"Ahhh. Not even God could object to the smell of a fine Cuban cigar.

"I have known Salvatore Sorrentino since he was a monsignor at the Archives," Father Jon explained. "I can tell you that he is a man who will go to any length to preserve the integrity of our theology, including doing business with the notorious Raphael. The cardinal has made a number of secret purchases from this man. Raphael disguises his voice, and couriers always handle the actual transactions, but Sorrentino is quite certain that Raphael and Gustavo Giacopetti are the same man. Who else is in such a key position to acquire the phenomenal quality of artifacts that Raphael so consistently offers? Yet, the cardinal, relishing the benefits of maintaining his surreptitious contact with this mystery man, issued strict orders for me to tell no one. You are the first."

I was sure my face was swollen enough to hide my doubts about that one.

The father went on. "The Vatican's ability to acquire such priceless artifacts, Sorrentino argues, serves a much higher, therefore justifiable, purpose. One such item was a letter written by Flavius Josephus, a Jewish historian born a few years after the crucifixion of Jesus. One evening, after the cardinal had a little too much wine, he told me about the letter. He worried that if it fell into liberal hands, it would force a complete revision of the Church's most sacred doctrines. Sorrentino keeps the letter in a vault in his office. One day he was away, and I noticed he had forgotten to close the door to the vault. I started to lock it, but I could not. My curiosity, I have to confess, got the better of me. I found the letter and read it. It told of the existence of a scroll, written in a strange script, by a foreign scribe with a name none other than *Anatolios*. This scribe, according to Josephus, traveled with our Lord."

I was massaging my temples, doing my best to give the impression that I was interested in the father's story. "Jesus traveled with a secretary?"

"It is quite feasible," Niki said. "In Gethsemane, for example, Jesus took Peter, James, and John to pray with him in his darkest moment. All three disciples fell asleep, and yet the words and actions of Jesus were well documented—in minute detail. By whom?"

"But I don't get it," I said, recalling Barnes's photograph of the scroll. "If Anatolios was a secretary to Jesus, why would he write in an ancient Minoan script?"

Niki agreed. "Aramaic or even Hebrew would make more sense. It does not seem likely that Jesus or anyone else would be able to read such a rare script as Linear A. This makes no sense."

"I have grappled with this question myself," the father said. "Anatolios was undoubtedly bilingual. He may have translated the scroll into the language of his ancestors to give it an appearance of authenticity. Did not our Pialigarian prophet vow to return to Pialigos with the lost knowledge of his ancestors?" He shrugged, and then he waved a finger of warning. "We must tread very carefully. There may be no connection between the letter of Josephus and the scroll depicted in Mr. Barnes's photograph. None whatsoever."

"But what about Sorrentino?" I asked. "He must think there's a connection. Why else would he offer ten million for the scroll? The photograph bothered him. Why?"

"The cardinal is worried," Father Jon explained, "and I can tell you why." He took a puff from his cigar. "According to Josephus, Anatolios and Jesus himself were disciples of a certain Essene mystic."

"Disciples?" I said. "I didn't know Jesus was a disciple of anyone."

"Precisely. And this possibility, I assure you, is what has Sorrentino so upset."

"But why should this be so upsetting?" Niki asked. I sensed that she and the father had discussed this subject before, that she was bringing it up again for my benefit. "Everyone knows that eighteen years of the life of Jesus remain unknown to us. There is persistent speculation that he studied with the Essenes during this time. Why not? Even St. Paul studied under the renowned Gamaliel. Why would Jesus not also have had a mentor?"

"I will tell you why he must not," Father Jon said, his voice suddenly full of more authority than his appearance commanded. "For a man like Sorrentino, it is of the utmost importance to maintain the doctrine of the absolute divinity of Jesus—taught by God, *not* by any man. To the cardinal, the revelation that Jesus was the student of someone would undermine, perhaps even destroy, this most important doctrine."

The paisley shirt was beginning to make a little bit of sense. Intuitively, I couldn't buy into most of the homogenized rhetoric I'd heard in my Bible classes with Alyssa. A God of love ready to sentence me to a life of eternal damnation if I didn't comply? To me, that was like saying you could freeze to death in the middle of an Arizona summer. Through his years of intensive studies, the father probably had learned better than I the political, and very human, forces that lay behind the theology of sin and punishment. Why else would he, in good conscience, shed the beads, the cowl, the donkey? Would I have done less? Maybe I was closer to the father's point of view than I realized.

"So what if he did learn from someone else?" I said. "Would it lessen the value of what Jesus taught, change the good things he did?"

"Not to you and me," Father Jon replied. "But Sorrentino is opposed to considering any variations or modifications of our doctrine. If the scroll reveals a written precedent for teachings attributed as original to the Master, then critics will be quick to point out that the wisdom of Jesus did not come from God but from another man. You can see how the Church's doctrine of the divinity of Jesus could easily be compromised. The cardinal's fear that the foundations of Christianity could be severely undermined is not without merit."

The father had been talking to Niki and me; now he turned to me. "Niki told me of your vision—the bearded man on the island next to Kyropos. You may find this intriguing. According to Josephus, the name of our Essene mystic was none other than *Marcus*."

"Marcu … ?" The name caught in my throat. Now this whole thing was starting to get personal.

"Fascinating, do you not agree? What if Marcus imparted the Three Measures of Wisdom to Jesus and his secretary, Anatolios? This is but one of the many reasons why I am completely intrigued with this scroll. If it truly embodies the teachings of Marcus, teachings that Jesus himself would have studied in the isolated desert environment of this Essene, it would bring us a giant step closer to an understanding of the Jesus of history rather than the Jesus of mere theology." Father Jon took another large puff from his cigar and blew the cloud of smoke over his shoulder. Still looking at me, he said, "I would be honored if you would permit me to join you in this quest for the scroll."

"You mean … you want to go to Kyropos?"

"Yes. I believe I can be of help."

Somehow the concepts of *monk* and *help* didn't coalesce. I shook my head. "It's too dangerous, Father. And I'm not just talking about volcanoes." I pointed to my throbbing eye. "I don't think one of these would look too good on a monk."

"I would agree," Father Jon said, studying the damage. "But you see, Gustavo Giacopetti, he is Catholic. He knows that bringing harm to a man of the cloth would greatly jeopardize his chances of winning an immortal soul. He would not strike me. Perhaps my presence would discourage him from giving you another eye to match that one … or worse."

"Maybe," I said, but I doubted it. "Giacopetti knows what we're after, and there's some pretty big dollar figures floating around this scroll. Millions, maybe. Now I don't mean any disrespect by this, Father, but I know enough about your penance system to figure that a guy with that kind of dough could buy himself a pretty safe passage through your pearly gates. Whack a monk, shell out a few bucks, get your forgiveness, and go about your business. Isn't that how it works, Father?"

"Whacking a monk? Hmm." He stroked his chin. "Whacking a

monk would be quite costly. But you are right. Most any sin is subject to forgiveness, *if* you have enough money. So, allow me to explain something. I do not fear men like Gustavo Giacopetti. Do you know why?"

"No."

"I will tell you. Many years ago, I took a vow to seek the truth, wherever it leads. The truth is my strength, my protection. Something tells me that this scroll contains a truth far beyond anything the world has known. The Three Measures of Wisdom ... perhaps they are the key to Atlantean success. Now I wonder if they are not of even greater value. Perhaps they are the basis of principles out of which the Master formed a more profound teaching, one that is now lost among the thistles of Christian theology. It would mean a great deal to me to know that I did something to help bring the truth of the Master to light. I am begging you to allow me to join you in this quest."

Maybe the guy needed to prove something to his peers ... or to himself for that matter. Then again, he might have been as sincere as the tears pooling in his eyes suggested. Even if he wasn't sincere, what difference would it make?

"If it's okay with her," I said, nodding toward Niki, "it's fine with me."

Niki shot back. "I told the father that he would have to ask you."

"Me?"

"Yes, you."

Niki and I looked at each other for a moment. She was beginning to trust me, and for some reason, that bothered me more than the idea of having a monk tag along.

"All right," I said to Father Jon. "Why not. I just want to make sure you understand that this is no Wednesday night bingo fund-raiser for God. Things could get ugly real fast."

Father Jon's broad smile squeezed a tear down his cheek. "Thank you, Stuart. May I call you Stuart?"

"Please do."

"You worry that things could get ugly? Let me assure you. For me, nothing ... *nothing* could be uglier than a Wednesday night bingo fund-raiser for God."

Chapter 12

TWO DAYS LATER, BY SOME minor miracle, all the swelling and most of the bruise had faded from my eye. Nicholas, having completed repairs on the boat, was driving Niki and me to the dock at Fira. Father Jon was to meet us at Threader's boat. When supplies were loaded, we'd set sail for Pialigos and the Rock.

Niki rode in the front passenger seat. I lay stretched out in the back, catching up on my journal and mulling over the implications of the Josephus letter.

The idea that Jesus might have traveled with a scribe made a lot of sense, especially when Niki explained how many biblical scholars viewed the process of Gospel composition. Mark, she had said, was the first complete Gospel written. The anonymous author, having gathered a list of sayings and other material, added his own narrative to create a coherent story, which he completed around 70 AD. A few years later, Mathew and Luke wrote their Gospels. Each incorporated nearly all of the work of their predecessor before adding their own unique material. John, written twenty years later, came from an entirely different Jesus tradition. Matthew, Mark, and Luke were known as the "synoptic Gospels," because they shared a common source.

It was the "unique material" used by Matthew and Luke that caught my attention. Niki explained that it was made up of various sayings of Jesus—the Sermon on the Mount, for example—and that each writer had incorporated it, more or less, into his own Gospel. Known as *Q* (from the German *quelle*, meaning *source*), this list of sayings was considered the closest to the actual words of the historical Jesus. The individual who first put this group of sayings in writing, however, remained a mystery to scholars.

Could the letter of Josephus and the Pialigarian scroll possibly point to the author of these sayings? Could Anatolios, scribe and possible secretary to Jesus, actually have written the Q source? Had Jesus spent his eighteen undocumented years studying under an obscure Essene mystic named Marcus? Most intriguing, was it possible that the basis of the Nazarene's teachings had their origins in the Three Measures of Wisdom?

My head swam with questions. I tried to heed Father Jon's warning that any connection between our scroll and the letter of Josephus was purely speculative. Still, if even a fragment of our conjecture were true, we were onto something huge. We *had* to find the scroll.

I'd tried to reach Marion a dozen times by telephone. I wanted to tell her what was going on and share my excitement. Had she gotten any of my messages? Why hadn't she returned even one of my calls? I tried to give her the benefit of the doubt. For some reason, Barnes didn't have an answering machine at the villa. Maybe Marion had tried to call but Dora was away from the phone and didn't answer. Frustrated, I decided to send her a letter explaining the phone situation; I told her how much I missed and loved her, that I'd definitely be out of touch while we were off on our little voyage. I kept trying to assure myself that everything was all right with Marion, that she was just throwing a very long and aggravating tantrum. Deep down, I wasn't so sure.

Niki's voice suddenly snapped me to attention. "What is the fire?" she asked Nicholas over the rush of wind, water, and motor.

I sat up to see a thick column of smoke billowing from the direction of Santorini's harbor.

"I do not know," Nicholas said. "A scrapped boat, perhaps. Sometimes they strip them of everything salvageable and then tow them out to set them on fire. Most economical, I suppose."

He was right. Nicholas got close enough for us to see a salvage tug circling a boat disintegrating beneath a storm of orange flame. A group of spectators watched from the dock.

Anxious to see if Threader had kept his word, I searched the dock for his boat. It wasn't there, but Threader was. He stood among the spectators, his fists planted at the waist, his clothes torn and burned. What the hell? Then it hit me. *Dancing Daphne* was ablaze in the harbor.

Father Jon waved from the end of the dock. Nicholas maneuvered close enough for me to throw him a line. The father was far too cheerful to know that our ride to Pialigos was burning before his eyes.

I leaped to the dock and sprinted down the beach toward Threader.

"Where are you going?" Niki shouted. "We still have to unload the boat!"

I didn't stop.

Threader, his face streaked with blackened sweat, glanced at me before turning back toward his mortally wounded vessel. "They damn near got me, Adams."

Niki caught up, breathless, eyes wide with questions.

"Hello, Niki," Threader said, forcing a half smile. "Sorry you got to see this."

"Captain Threader? What is it?" Her eyes darted in many directions. "Why do you say ..."

"I was supposed to be in there." Threader nodded toward the flames. "They tried to block the door, but I busted out."

"Oh my god!" Niki said, gasping. "That is your boat? Somebody ... somebody did this to you?"

"Not somebody. *Giacopetti*. Sure as there's a devil in hell, that son of a bitch done it."

Father Jon joined our group. In silence, we watched the boat sink lower into the water. Then, the bow began to lift. Threader, knowing what was coming, raised his hand slowly, his fingers trembling and then curling into a white fist. The hissing mass groaned and sputtered a final breath before slipping quietly into the tranquil blue of the morning harbor.

Father Jon made the sign of the cross and muttered a prayer beneath his breath. Niki buried her face in her hands, weeping. Blake Threader slipped an arm around her shoulder and looked on as the tug crawled like a beaten dog back to the dock. The dispersing crowd offered hushed condolences, solemn pats to the shoulder, and downcast faces sagging with pity for a broken old seaman whose lifeline to everything meaningful had just unraveled and snapped before his eyes.

I wanted to say something, but none of it would make any difference.

Threader coughed, cleared his throat, and through a raspy chuckle said, "Guess I ain't gonna be much good to you folks now. If I was you, I'd start shopping for another skipper."

"Can't do that, Threader," I said. "We'll figure out something." I didn't have a clue as to what.

"Yeah? You gonna get the father here to raise her from the dead?"

"I believe in miracles," Father Jon quipped nervously, "but I—"

"The *Penelope*," I said. "Is it a charter?"

"Hell yes," Threader snapped. He threw a smoldering glare at the vessel. "She's one of the reasons I'm running a goddamn salvage yard. Guy like me can't compete with the likes of her."

"You know the owner?" I asked.

"Some damn Frenchman," Threader said.

"I know this man," Father Jon piped up. "Philippe Lerfervre. He owns a villa not far from here."

Niki stepped in. "Then you will talk with him. You will tell him that our captain is a seaman of great experience and skill, a captain in great demand."

Threader blew out a chuckle; his eyes dropped. "That'd be spreading it on a little thick, I'd say. Niki, that's awful nice of you, but that was a few years ago. People around here, well, they aren't stupid. They got eyes. They can see that I'm nothing more than a two-bit drun—"

"Enough!" Niki barked.

The word splashed across Threader's face like a bucket of cold water. He looked like a man shaken out of a walking coma.

Niki turned to the *Penelope*. "She is a beautiful vessel. Perfect!" She whirled back toward Threader. "You can sail this yacht, no?"

Threader toyed nervously with his fingers. "Look, Niki, I appreciate what you're—"

She stiffened, daring him to finish his sentence.

He shot a worried glance at the father and me. Our shoulders went up in a simultaneous shrug that said we'd rather eat glass than be on the receiving end of that butt-searing glare of hers.

Then, some remembered shred of dignity seeped into Threader's eyes. He raised his face to *Penelope* and straightened his shoulders slightly, almost confidently. "Hell yes, I can sail her. I do it every time I go to sleep at night."

Niki nodded sharply. "Yes. And if this yacht could dream, she would dream of a captain of your skill standing at her helm, steering her through the great, open sea."

Threader tilted his head like a curious dog, studied Niki, and laughed. "You're funny, girl. You know that, don't you?"

"Perhaps I am funny. But I am serious."

There was no need to convince anyone of that.

"Father Jon!" Niki said, jerking him to attention. "Go! Speak to this owner. Use your influence, whatever it takes. And you"—she drove a stiff forefinger at me—"you will use your American wits to help negotiate the deal. Rufus, he will pay. Whatever it takes, he will pay. And you, Captain, you will dream of sailing the *Penelope* no longer. Come with me. You will have a bath and new clothing fitting for a captain of your stature." She raised an open hand to the *Penelope*. "Today, you, Captain Blake Threader, you will fulfill the dream of this … this magnificent vessel."

It wasn't possible to restore a complete human wreck to its former proud state in a matter of only a few short hours. That's what I believed … until I actually saw it happen. There was no doubt in my mind that if we'd hired another skipper, Threader would have either drunk himself to death or taken the quicker route of putting a bullet through his brain. Captain Blake Threader had gone from a broken, filthy, destitute drunkard to the proud captain of a prize vessel. He stood tall at the wheel of the *Penelope*, the shimmer of purpose burning as bright as the late-afternoon sun in his eyes. Niki had performed a miracle.

I watched her sitting at the deck table next to Father Jon—talking, laughing—and I knew I could feel no more pride for another person than I felt for her at that moment.

Securing *Penelope* was a stroke of luck. The yacht had been slated to go out for the next three weeks, but Lerfevre's client had a last-minute change of plans and had to cancel. Lerfevre's biggest worry, of course, concerned the credentials of our skipper.

Since Lerfervre spoke only French, my American wits were useless in the negotiations. Father Jon, fluent in the language, closed the deal. On the way back to the dock, I asked him what he'd said to convince Lerfervre of Threader's qualifications. The father only said that he'd offered "satisfactory assurances." When I asked how Lerfervre responded to our taking *Penelope* to Kyropos, Father Jon snapped his fingers. "I knew there was something I was forgetting." He smiled. "Oh well, only a minimal confession will be required. A couple of Our Fathers. Three, maybe four Hail Marys. No more." It made me think that a degree in business would come in pretty handy for a guy entering the priesthood.

In any case, we had secured the fifty-one-foot, five-cabin luxury motel on water. By late afternoon, Threader had *Penelope* leaning flat and tight in the wind, cutting through the open sea toward Anafi and the ten-hour trip that would take us to the northern tip of Carpathos.

Threader insisted that *Penelope* was thrilled to be getting back to her roots. When I smiled doubtfully, he explained that the word *yacht* came from the German *jacht*, short for *jachtship*, meaning *hunting ship*. "You can bet your ass she's happy," he insisted. "She's shedding her money-fattened cargo for the chance to go on a *real* hunt."

The plan was to skirt the coastlines of Carpathos and Casos. Once we cleared the southern tip of Casos, we would bear east into the Mediterranean for Pialigos. Father Jon, Niki, and I sat at a table sharing spirited conversation and, compliments of Father Jon's monastery, a bottle of some of the finest, unnamed red wine I had ever sipped. Dry, courage-building stuff it was. I needed it. Doubts about my vision of Kyropos seeped in beneath the thrill of the voyage. One minute it all seemed real; the next, I wasn't so sure.

Hours had passed when Father Jon excused himself for a nap. Niki, wearing a white cotton blouse over a yellow bikini, invited me to join her at the front of the boat. Sitting together, bare legs freely dangling, chins resting on arms crossed over the bow railing, we watched in long silence our blue world of sea and sky pass.

I was lost in thoughts of her and the strange feelings of familiarity that she evoked. Had she played some role in a soul memory that was beginning to ease into my mind from the mists of antiquity? It all seemed so far-fetched, so unbelievable. Yet the bands of stress tightened in my head when I thought of the complications that such a thing might generate in my present situation. If I didn't believe it, why did it worry me?

"What are you thinking, Stuart Adams?"

Niki's voice startled me. I wasn't aware that she'd been watching me. Confused, I needed to talk about my feelings. But not now, not with her.

"Nothing," I said.

"Nothing? Scientific studies have been done. No one can think of nothing, not even you."

"Well, I guess I can't argue with science, can I? Okay, I confess; I was thinking."

"What about?"

"Pialigos," I lied. "You never explained why you wanted to go. You gonna tell me about it?"

"No. You should be happy for the time away from the excavation. You will not strain your back at sea." Her tone was playful but serious enough to tell me she intended to hang on to her mystery.

"You may find it hard to believe," I said, "but I really don't mind a little hard work now and then. I just want it to be worthwhile."

"The American way. The problem with life is that one cannot always know if their labor will reward them with the fruit of a desired end. My father used to say, 'If it is but a single end that you seek, of what value is the journey?' I have never forgotten. When I dig, I dig as if the digging is the joy of my life, the reason for my existence. I give thanks for these fingers that grasp the stone. I rejoice in the arms that enable me to throw it. If I find the scroll, I will celebrate that success is added to my joy. You Americans, you must accomplish to be happy. But then you are not. So you keep going. Again and again you go, always searching for that thing that will make you happy. When will you learn that you do not find happiness? Happiness is *within* you. You bring it like a light to shine on whatever you do. If what you have to do is move stones, then you are happy moving stones. Simple, really. Too simple, perhaps, for the American mind to grasp."

"It's not just us Americans," I reminded her. "I read someplace that your Alexander the Great sat down and cried when he ran out of countries to conquer. Been a long time since any Americans I know have done that."

"He was mad, driven by greed and a need for admiration. He was not a true Greek, at least not in his heart."

"I see. Well, we sure don't want to stereotype and generalize, not when we're talking about Greeks."

The remark drew an indignant glare. She started to respond and then stopped, her face turning soft. "Forgive me. My nationalistic tendencies, I am afraid that they sometimes show."

"Like the mustard on your nose."

"Mustard?" She touched her nose and glanced at her fingers.

"American humor," I said, grinning. It had been a long time since I'd seen anyone fall for that one.

She wasn't amused. "American *boy* humor, no doubt."

I shrugged. "Anyway, I can't say that I agree with your father. If it's all about the journey, then why don't we just sit on this boat and be happy sailing in one big circle for the rest of our lives? I don't know about you, but I want to get someplace, achieve something big, something meaningful."

"And what big thing will you achieve that is so meaningful?"

"I'd find a scroll. Write a story. See my name on the *New York Times* bestseller list. Roll naked in a great big tub full of money. I can see a lot of meaning in doing something like that."

"And when you tire of rolling naked in your great big tub full of money?"

"Never thought that far ahead. Maybe I'd buy the *Penelope* and spend the rest of my life sailing to exotic places."

"Interesting. Does it not occur to you that you are already on the *Penelope*, sailing to one of the most exotic places in the world? You see, you think that you have to get to some other place before you can enjoy what the journey even now freely provides. Will the sea be bluer, the sky brighter because you roll naked in your big tub of money? Are you so consumed with reaching this destination of yours that you fail to see the very things that you would buy sitting in plain sight right under your nose?"

Her logic drove me back into silence. Technically, I already knew that my financial success would do nothing to change the color of sea or sky. I did have a hunch, however, that a tub full of money would go a real long way toward putting a pretty big smile on my face.

WITH A FEW LESSONS FROM Threader, we all took a turn at the helm, sailing through the night. When we reached the mountainous coastline of the Carpathian archipelago—a jagged shadow looming beneath the deep canopy of stars—Threader explained how the islands once provided a favorite hideout for pirates, that the name *Carpathos*, or *Karpathos*, was a derivative of the word *arpakatos*, which meant *robbery*.

Niki added to the history lesson. "Carpathians retain their own dialect and still dress in their traditional costumes. Even their homes, carved from stone, date back to very ancient times."

At first light, we rounded Casos and passed the invisible line dividing the Aegean from the Mediterranean. We arrived at Pialigos under the full blare of the late-morning sun.

Pialigos was smaller than I expected. Like many other islands, it was boulder strewn, splattered with sparse clumps of vegetation, and rimmed in red cliffs lined with thin lips of white sand for beaches. Nestled atop the highest points of the cliffs was the sprawling complex of pinkish stucco buildings with arched windows and red tiled roofs, a fitting setting, I thought, for the ancient heart of Minoan mysticism.

Three small boats lay moored at the pier. Each had a single mast and a long pointed bow, white in color, brightly decorated with painted images of arched dolphins—*exactly* like the ones I'd seen in my vision at Barnes's place in Colorado.

Niki noticed my distraction. "Something puzzles you?"

"The boats," I said, without looking at her. "I've seen this kind before."

Threader, overhearing my comment, explained, "That ain't likely, Adams, not unless you've been on this island. The only place on earth you'll see boats like these is right here. They build 'em just like they did in ancient times: hand-drilled cypress, hand-carved wooden nails, a waxed fabric to waterproof the hull. Fine vessels they are. We could have sailed up to this pier three thousand years ago and seen the exact same thing. You're looking at a living piece of history."

We tied off the *Penelope* and started for the monastery. Threader, popping a beer, stayed on the boat explaining that it'd been a while since he'd spent a night alone "with a lady like this." Nobody tried to dissuade him.

Niki and Father Jon headed for the long stairs that led to the monastery. I lagged a few steps behind, sipping water, absorbing an intensified version of the homecoming sensation I'd felt on Santorini. At one point, I glanced back at the three Pialigarian boats bobbing in their sun-drenched berths. The scene, down to the arching seawall protecting the harbor, was identical to the vision I'd had at Barnes's place.

What was happening to me? The feeling that I knew Niki, the vision of Marcus, the island's welcoming sense of familiarity, and now the recognition of one-of-a-kind boats—these were all like pieces of a frozen block of memory beginning to thaw, titillating drops of recollection still too small to quench my thirst for understanding. And I was about to experience more. Niki and Father Jon had already begun to climb the stairs. I started to follow and then stopped. It was the same stairway I'd seen in my vision.

Niki, shading her eyes, her voice sharp with impatience, called out to me. "Stuart? Why do you stop? We have a long way to go."

"I've been here," I said, climbing past my perplexed companions, taking one, two, even three steps at a time. The sun sucked sweat through my shirt beneath the backpack. I sprinted toward the upper landing, already knowing what I would see. Wheezing, blinking at trickles of eye-stinging sweat, I scanned the area for a small shelter with a tile roof supported by four stone pillars.

It wasn't there. Only the flattened edge of a boulder protruded from the spot where the shelter should have been. An olive grove, overgrown with clusters of tall grass and blooming yucca, revealed nothing familiar.

Niki appeared at the landing, sweating and gasping for breath. "Stuart, why do you run? I can barely—"

"It was here." I pointed to the boulder. "I ... I used to ..." My words trailed off as I circled the rock.

"What? What was here?"

"A shelter. There was a shelter, a gazebo-type structure with a tile roof. I used to come here and ..."

"What? What did you—"

"It's gone," I said, cutting her off. "Everything's gone."

"Gone? What is gone?"

I couldn't remember. My silence, unacceptable to the fact-hungry scientist, forced her to throw up her hands. "I see. Perhaps you are speaking of your mind? Then I would agree. Your mind, it has gone." She gulped air, paced, and wiped her drenched brow with a forearm. "I do not know what to do with you. You make me as crazy as you. This is what you do. Look at you! Sweating like ... like a steamed banana. First you say you remember. Then you say everything is gone. I do not know what to think."

"Forget it," I said, closing my eyes, trying to regain even a shred of the image that had driven me up the stairs. I sat on the boulder in the cooling shade, drenched my parched throat with water, and tried to massage some of the tightness from the back of my neck.

"Forget it?" Niki stopped pacing and stood stiffly in front of me. "In the past fifteen minutes alone you claim that, *one*"—a forefinger flicked out like a switchblade—"you know Pialigarian boats. Impossible! *Two*"—a second finger—"you say you have been on this pier. Impossible! *Three*"—another finger—"you run up the stairs like a madman looking for a shelter that does not exist." All fingers, hands, and arms flew up. "You ask me to forget it? Oh my god! Maybe you were right. Maybe you should go back to your mountain and ... and write your stories. Let this imagination of yours run wild. Forget it? How do you expect me to forget such craziness?"

I just stared straight ahead, made no attempt to answer.

A breathless Father Jon finally caught up. "Forgive me, but I do not wish to die of a heat stroke at such an early age. Have I missed something?" Under the circumstances, his tone was far too cheerful.

"Yes, you missed something," Niki screeched. Still breathless, she leaned stiffly toward the father. "Stuart's mind, it just flew out to the sea." A huge, backward flinging motion of her open palm forced a flinch in one of the father's eyelids. "Did you happen to see it go?"

Father Jon, adapting quickly to the situation, pursed his lips in a manner indicating that he might indeed have seen my mind fly by—or something like it—and that he would be sure to let her know if he saw it again. He allowed his gaze, in a contemplative sort of way, to drift far out to the safety of the sea.

Chapter 13

WE FOLLOWED A WELL-WORN TRAIL that led across windswept slopes, punctuated with scrabbly vegetation and weathered boulders and dotted with occasional stone-and-mud huts with thatched roofs. Primitive as they were, each hut was, without exception, clean and well maintained. I sensed that these were people of integrity, and they were resourceful enough to get by with the little they had.

Aside from the occasional burro, the only livestock I saw was a small herd of shaggy goats with twisted horns nibbling at the sparse vegetation. They were tended by two boys of about ten or twelve years old.

The closer we got to the monastery, the more people we saw. They all bore dark, Grecian eyes and had hair colors ranging from pitch-black to sandy blonde—some even red. Most were older—sixties and over, I guessed. As we passed, they'd stop whatever they were doing, wave, and smile warmly, their faces full of guileless trust. The sight of visitors to their island was obviously a rare and welcome experience. It was a little sad to wonder how long this innocence would last beneath the stampeding feet of tourism.

Soon, a curious group of about a half dozen giggling children—boys and girls—had gathered and was following us at a polite distance. Then, one little girl of about three, urged on by her companions, darted from the group, ran up to me, and tugged on the leg of my shorts. I stopped and knelt before her. She had a button for a nose. Her eyes, large and dark, sparkling with absolute purity, connected instantly with mine. She took my hand and dropped something into my palm—a pink stone, quartz, rounded and polished by the sea. The girl said something that I didn't understand, and then she darted back to hide among her friends. The group scampered off in laughter.

I stood and held the stone in my open palm for Niki to see.

"The pink stone of friendship," she explained. "The quartz is rare on this island, like a four-leaf clover. For the children, this stone would be a great prize. You should feel quite honored that they have given it to you."

"They don't even know me," I said, turning the silky quartz in my fingers. "What'd she say to me?"

"She said, 'You are welcome to our home.'"

"She said that?"

Niki nodded. "You will never meet a more hospitable people. They learn when they are quite young."

I slipped the stone into my pocket and we continued on, but the little girl's haunting eyes didn't leave me.

The main complex of the monastery was a series of simple one and two-story stucco buildings separated by narrow cobblestone streets barely wide enough to accommodate the occasional donkey cart. At the center of the complex was a sunken, circular plaza, a maze of flag-stone walkways surrounding a ten-foot statue of the Great Mother. The space between the walkways teemed with blooming roses. I knew from the description in Niki's book that this was the *Labyrinth of Roses*.

According to Niki, scientists did not know who had carved the robed, serenely smiling deity. They only knew that the white marble had come from the ancient quarry of Naxos. Niki, granted special access to Pialigarian scriptures, pointed out that these writings—some dating back four thousand years—mentioned the statue's existence, proof, she claimed, that supported one of the main points of her thesis.

"Let's see," I said, attempting to paraphrase her argument. "*This statue represents irrefutable evidence linking the modern Pialigarian to Minoan rather than Phoenician ancestry.*"

Her eyebrows shot up. "You read my book?"

"I couldn't put it down. I read it that night I told you I was leaving."

"Yes, I remember. The same night you could not put down the bottle of ouzo."

Just then, a thin, elderly man wearing a straw hat, sandals, a white shirt, and trousers bearing the soiled knees of a gardener waved from among the roses.

"Artemas," Niki called out.

"Niki? I *knew* it was you!" The little man removed his hat as he approached. His head was a sunburned crown of bald surrounded by a band of shortly cropped gray hair. He opened his arms and embraced Niki. "So good to see you, Niki. It has been too long since you have come."

"Yes, Artemas," Niki cooed. "Far too long."

"You have been well?"

"Yes. I have been well." She pulled back and gave him a good looking over. "And you? You are still as young as the last day I saw you."

"Ah, but you are kind," Artemas said, laughing humbly. "Too kind. I am afraid I am not the young man that I once was. My knees, they trouble me."

"Perhaps. But with age comes wisdom, no? Now you are full with the wisdom of the Great Mother."

He waved off the compliment. "Give me the strength and the wisdom to tend my roses. This is all that I ask." He turned to Father Jon. "Father, it is so good to see you again. It has been years."

"Yes, Artemas, years. I think of your island often. Always it is such a pleasure to come."

Artemas turned his curious gaze on me. Curling the brim of his hat in his hands, he said to Niki, "I see you bring another friend."

"This is Stuart Adams," Niki said. "He is a writer from America. I have brought him to meet Euphemia. She is here, is she not?"

"Of course she is here. And she will be delighted that you have come."

Leaving Father Jon and Artemas in the garden discussing roses, Niki and I followed the outer perimeter of the labyrinth. Niki explained how she had often come to Pialigos to walk the labyrinth.

"When I had a problem, I would come here. Walking the labyrinth in silence, you often reach certain points—*stations of remem-*

brance—where a forgotten memory or the inspiration needed to make an important decision suddenly comes. You should try it."

The flagstone path led to the arched gateway of a high wall. Passing through, we stepped into the courtyard of a sprawling though humble residence, circled the house, and then entered the cool shade of an olive grove. At the far edge of the grove, next to a rock wall that followed the lip of the cliff, I spotted a woman profiled in the dappled shade. She stood alone, still, facing the sea, the plume of Kyropos clearly visible on the horizon. She was a slender woman of around fifty, with shiny black hair fixed in a braid that fell far below her waist. Long open curls dangled over her ears, a complement to her high, naturally rouged cheekbones. Her gown appeared to be made of fine silk, ankle-length, with a sash that looped over the right shoulder and spilled well below her left hip. There was a curious mix of human and animal figures embroidered just above a fringed hem. Thin sandals gave her a barefoot appearance. Draped in flowing white, the woman was a silent, ethereal figure, a master's portrait of mystical dignity.

Euphemia still had her eyes closed when we approached. Thinking she was in some kind of a trance, I didn't want to startle her. "Maybe we should come back later," I whispered. But Niki shook her head, placed a silencing finger to her lips.

We waited until Euphemia's eyes fluttered open. She turned to us, her face awash in serenity. "I am so glad you came," she said to Niki in a rich, melodious voice. She took both of Niki's hands and delivered a light kiss to her forehead. She turned to me, her dark eyes smiling with the warmth of an old friend. Still addressing Niki, she said, "This is our writer from America?"

"This is Stuart Adams," Niki said. "And yes, he is the writer that I told you about."

Euphemia stepped in front of me. "The writer who would tell the world of our scroll?"

"That's the plan, assuming there is a scroll."

"I once traveled to America," Euphemia said, "a peace conference held at the United Nations. New York is such a wonderful place."

"Wonderful?" I said, wondering how the woman radiating such a peace-filled countenance could deem as wonderful a place as hyper as New York.

"This surprises you?"

"Your island is so peaceful," I said. "I wouldn't think a place like New York would suit you."

"Peaceful?" She nodded toward Kyropos. "New York does not have a volcano. Any given place in the world can provide many reasons to be upset, Stuart Adams. Peace, it is a fine blanket spread evenly over all the earth. Some choose to partake of it; some do not." A slight breeze stirred the trees. She closed her eyes and inhaled deeply. "This air that I breathe," she said, reopening her eyes, "would it become less because I hold my breath?"

"No."

"And so it is with peace. Its presence is not contingent on certain, shall we say, environmental conditions. Peace, like the air, is always present, here for the taking for all who would choose it."

Suddenly I could imagine a fleet of cruise ships sitting offshore, unloading their cargo like cattle to be herded through a gauntlet of booths stacked with T-shirts, trinkets, and an assortment of Pialigarian memorabilia imported from Taiwan. In a few years, that big-eyed girl who'd given me the pink stone of friendship would be shelling out change for twenties with the ease of a Vegas dealer passing out cards, innocence drained from her eyes.

"And when your island crawls with tourists," I said, "how are you going to keep them from trampling your peace, your whole lifestyle? You might have to start breathing just a little deeper."

"The Pialigarians are a resourceful, resilient people. We have survived a volcano. We can survive the tourists. The Prophet will find a way," she said.

I smiled. "Well, I hope your Prophet has some experience in the tourist trade. He's going to need it if this whole thing breaks open."

Euphemia's gentle expression remained naively unchanged. "I would not expect you to understand or embrace the Pialigarian way." She studied my face curiously. "And yet, I can see in your eyes that you believe you have been here before. Am I correct?"

I glanced at Niki. I wasn't sure how, when, or why, but I knew she'd told Euphemia of my belief that I'd been on Pialigos. How else could Euphemia know?

My look drew an indignant frown from Niki. "Why do you look at me that way?" she demanded. "Do you think that I—"

"Niki told me nothing," Euphemia said. "She does not need to.

In your entire countenance, I see it. You, Stuart Adams, you have the soul of a Pialigarian." The hint of a dare twinkled in her eyes. "Do you wish that I prove this to you?"

"Prove it? How do you intend to do that?"

"Come, I will show you," she said, and she turned to walk away.

"What's she up to?" I asked Niki.

"How would I know?" she snapped back. "Am I also a reader of minds?" Still miffed that I'd silently accused her of being a snitch, Niki skittered off to catch up with her friend.

I took a drink of water and caught a pleasant rear view of my departing companion. But that pleasure was cut short by the unexpected twinge of guilt of knowing I might be the one responsible for opening the floodgates of tourism on this pristine island. I found some comfort in the cold facts. If these people didn't jump into the twenty-first century and develop some major source of income, they'd be going the way of their Minoan ancestors, but with a lot less fanfare. The world had become immune to the sad story of yet another extinction, human or otherwise. Niki was probably the only scientist on the planet prepared to commemorate the Pialigarians' passage, and her book wasn't selling, not to the masses. Nobody really cared.

Nor was it my problem. Empires rise and fall with the tides of time. Cultures vanish. I was being paid to do what I could to bring the world to the Pialigarians' doorstep. It'd be up to them to take it from there.

Another swallow of water. I slipped the bottle back into its holster and started after the two women.

I wished I hadn't seen that little girl's eyes.

I FOLLOWED EUPHEMIA AND NIKI back into the Labyrinth of Roses.

"You will walk the labyrinth," Euphemia said. Removing a long silk scarf from beneath her sash, she stepped behind me and tied the scarf into a blindfold. "When you get to the center, place your hands upon the statue of the Great Mother, and then return to me."

I chuckled beneath the blackness of the blindfold. "You want me to walk the labyrinth … *blindfolded*. You mind telling me how I'm supposed to do that?"

"You will *feel* your way. *Listen.* Let the path speak to you. Clear your mind."

Feel my way? Right. I humored her by drawing an audibly deep breath. Nothing cleared from my mind. I took a step and then another. I took one more, and I caught my toe on the path's stone boundary. Next thing I knew I was going down, grabbing for something to break the fall. What I got was the thorn-laden stalk of a rosebush. Both hands. It happened so fast that I was already on the ground before I realized that my palms were shredded. The pain was excruciating. I suppressed a scream and started picking at the blindfold to get it off.

"Do not remove the blindfold," Euphemia called out. "Ignore the pain. Stand and begin again."

Ignore the pain? The woman must be out of her mind. With my hands stinging, I staggered to my feet. I could feel the blood oozing from my palms, dripping off the tips of my fingers. I'd failed her stupid test. Why go on? But I forced myself to take another step and tried desperately to get even a glimpse of whatever the hell I was supposed to see.

Then, it happened. The whole labyrinth suddenly appeared in my mind. I took a few tentative steps and then a few more; I began walking, slowly, carefully, ready to stop the second my foot touched a rock. It never happened. I followed long arcs and sharp curves until I knew I was within reach of the Great Mother. I extended my arms and felt the cool of the marble come through my hands. The cool turned to a soothing warmth that flowed into my palms and up through my arms. The pain stopped. Unbelievable. I felt for blood that wasn't there. I turned and retraced my steps back to the women.

Euphemia lifted the blindfold. When I looked at my hands, there were no thorns, no ripped flesh, not even the slightest hint of a scratch.

"I ... I don't get it," I said. "My hands should be—"

"Your hands are of no importance," Euphemia said, her breath shallow, her eyes wide and searching.

"Didn't you see? I ... I grabbed a rosebush. My hands should be shredded. Look!" I thrust out my open palms. Euphemia's eyes never left mine.

Niki took one of my hands and examined it. "He is right," she said, her eyes wide with disbelief. "Not even a scratch." She turned to Euphemia. "But I saw it. With my own eyes I saw him grab the thorns."

Euphemia ignored her. "You walked the labyrinth. How did you know?"

"I ... I don't know. The whole thing it ... it came into my mind ... just like you said."

Euphemia studied me for another moment before her eyes darted to Niki's. Neither woman said anything, but their exchanged glances told me that something had passed between them.

"You are an American," Euphemia said finally, "and yet you know the Zadim? How do you explain it? How is it that you know what only a Pialigarian would know?"

"I don't know anything about the Zadim," I insisted. "Swear to God. Never even heard the word until Niki told me about it."

Niki looked at Euphemia. "Do you think? Is this the whisper of Pialigos?"

Euphemia still had her eyes drilled into mine, as if she had bored down deep enough to see a layer of my soul that I didn't know was there. I felt exposed, naked. I shifted on my feet.

"Stuart Adams," Euphemia said, her voice hushed, her eyes flashing with sudden urgency, "there is something that I must show you."

Chapter 14

EUPHEMIA LED THE WAY TO the beach where we walked for a half mile before turning into a narrow canyon. At the end of the canyon was a cave. Inside, the air was stifling, thick with the stench of sulfur dioxide. The walls closed in, and I broke into a sweat; I had to fight the urge to bolt.

Euphemia lit a torch. The yellow light of the flame danced over the walls as we traveled deeper into the hot bowels of the cave. The winding corridor opened into a room the size of a three-car garage. In the center was a steaming pool. I was lightheaded and I could feel large beads of sweat trickle down my face and back. The stench was overpowering. My stomach rolled, and I thought I might be sick.

Euphemia lifted the torch high enough for us to see a tangle of human bones at the bottom of the pool.

Niki edged closer, her fingers touching her quivering lips. "There are two skeletons," she said, her voice cracked, shaking, large tears tracking her cheeks. "Is the other ... Panagiota?"

Euphemia nodded. "Yes."

"She ... she must have loved him very much," Niki said. "It is ... it is such a sad story."

I hated the place. "I don't want to sound disrespectful," I said to Euphemia, desperate for sunlight and fresh air, "but why did you bring us here?"

"Soon enough we will leave," Euphemia said. "But first, there is something more you must see." She walked away with the torchlight. We had no choice but to follow.

We entered a chamber large enough to swallow the light of the flame, a hundred times larger than the first. Euphemia lit a second torch that was mounted in the wall. Another labyrinth, similar to the Labyrinth of Roses, emerged through evil fingers of steam rising in the dim orange light. The spaces between the labyrinth's paths gurgled with boiling water, superheated, I assumed, by volcanic activity. Hell's living room. At the center of the labyrinth, there was another statue of the Great Mother, much larger than the one in the Labyrinth of Roses. The poor lighting gave the face of this statue a sinister appearance, like someone holding a flashlight to her chin. A doorway opened to a chamber in the belly. Inside was a huge stone seat, possibly a throne.

Across the labyrinth I saw a large pale figure, a man, I thought, though he melted into the darkness so quickly that I could not be sure.

"That was Sargos," Euphemia explained, noticing that I had seen him. "He lives in these chambers, for how long no one can say. He does not speak but he is friendly; he will do you no harm."

What kind of freak would live in a place like this? I thought, plagued with the uneasy feeling that we were being watched from the shadows. Could the place get any creepier?

"Aside from Sargos, you are the only outsiders ever to see this," Euphemia continued. "For two thousand years, only the high priestess has entered. In this room, we will conduct our most sacred of ceremonies."

"The Walk of the Prophet?" Niki asked.

Euphemia nodded. "The ceremony will mark the beginning of the new era." She turned to the statue. "You see the throne in the womb of the Great Mother? According to our scriptures, this is where the Prophet will sit to receive the lost knowledge."

"He has to walk this labyrinth to get to the throne?" I asked, still casting glimpses into the dark, looking for movement. I was curious about Sargos.

"Blindfolded," Euphemia said. "In the same way you walked the Labyrinth of Roses."

My interest in Sargos instantly evaporated. "Blindfolded? No wonder it's taking him so long to come back." I meant it as a joke, but nobody laughed.

"Stuart Adams," Euphemia said, "the Labyrinth of Roses has never been walked by anyone wearing a blindfold. Many have tried. All have failed."

"So?" That information meant nothing to me. Why should I care about some offbeat Pialigarian ritual?

"So, the Labyrinth of Roses, it is an exact replica, though smaller, of the Labyrinth of the Cave. And *you* have walked the Labyrinth of Roses."

"I think we already agreed on that," I said. "Why don't you just get to the ..." I stopped. The point she might have been trying to make suddenly hit me like a truckload of gravel. She was trying to tell me that I was the Prophet. "Now wait just a minute. I hope you're not saying what I think you're saying."

Euphemia's eyes flashed, and she opened up like a cloudburst. "You, Stuart Adams, you have responded to the whisper of Pialigos. You are the Prophet, come, as the dream of my youth foretold, to return to the people of Pialigos, to the people of the world, the lost knowledge that our prophecies promise."

The sound of gurgling water harassed the silence. I was too polite to tell her that she was out of her mind. I glanced at Niki for help. Her eyes, wide and searching, were riveted on mine, just like Euphemia's. No help there. I turned back to Euphemia; tension, like the steady rising of water in a teakettle set to a flame, began to build inside of me. The teakettle started to whistle, a wisp of a laugh that escaped my lips. That turned into a chuckle, followed by a full-blown guffaw. Soon, I was convulsing with laughter, bubbling all over the stove.

"It's ... it's a joke, right?" The seriousness in both women's faces made me laugh even harder. "The two ... the two of you got together and ... and you concocted this whole thing." I scanned the flickering walls of the cave. "There's a camera in here. There must be a camera. Like ... like one of those practical joke things ... on television."

"Stuart!" Niki scolded. "You are being foolish and *very* disrespectful. There are no cameras."

"Well then," I said, snickering, doing a poor job of controlling myself, "I do apologize. But ... you both"—another smirk—"you both look so ... serious. Look, Euphemia, I ... I know you want this thing to happen. Real bad. I mean, being a Dream Child and all, it's ... it's got to be tough, a real big responsibility. You've got a deadline.

I understand deadlines. But you're wrong about this—about me. I'm a novelist, not a prophet. I'm not qualified, got no credentials whatso-ever. Now, what you need to do is go back and study your prophecies just a little clo—"

"But you yourself said that you have been here before," Euphemia countered. "Why do you say this?"

The woman was actually serious. "I said I *felt* like I'd been here. I don't know that for sure." I looked at the gnarled fingers of steam rising from the labyrinth. "I'm sure I'd never forget a place like this."

"But you *do* remember," Niki argued. "You have memories. You do not like hot tubs. Why not? How do you explain it?"

"Hot tubs? What do hot tubs have to do with—"

"And you are a writer," Euphemia said. "Anatolios was a scribe."

It was time to end this game, even if I had to do it with a firm hand. "Look, you can twist this thing into your ... your Zadim, call it the whisper of Pialigos, call it past-life memories; you can call it whatever you want." I glanced again at the steaming labyrinth. The thought of walking it made me shudder. "If you think I'm going to walk that thing—blindfolded—you'd better think again, because it's crazy. It's all crazy. No, it's absolutely insane!"

"The Prophet, he cannot fail." Euphemia was unrelenting.

"Yeah? I'll leave it to you to convince him of that. And when you do, maybe you can sell him some retirement property in the Ever-glades."

"Stuart," Niki said, "what if Euphemia is right?"

"Right? Are you crazy too?" I traded glances between the two unwavering women. "Are you both crazy?"

"Then, why do you say that you have been here before?" Niki ticked off her growing checklist. "On the dock, you say it. The boats, you say you know them. At the top of the steps, you say there was a shelter. You have visions of a man named Marcus. You walked the Labyrinth of Roses. How do you know these—"

"Ah, but I was wrong about the shelter," I said, raising a profes-sor-like finger. "Remember? There *was* no shelter at the top of the steps, proof, you see, that I've never been—"

"The steps?" Euphemia asked. "Above the pier?"

"Yes," Niki answered. "The place where the old olive grove now stands."

"Oh, but there *was* a shelter," Euphemia assured me. "I used to play there when I was a child."

"Yeah?" I said, sure that she was lying. "Well, since we seem to like to do tests around here, I've got one for you. Tell me what it looked like."

She cracked off the description. "Four stone pillars and a tile roof. It collapsed in an earthquake. The masons, they carried off the stones for repairs elsewhere."

"You see?" Niki said, driving a finger through the air straight at me. "Exactly as you described. How did you know it was there?"

My mouth went as straight as Anatolios's femur. They had me pushed into the corner with four hands on my throat. "I ... I don't know. Maybe I was here. But I was probably one of the workers. Maybe I'm the one that carried off the stones. For that matter I could have been one of the goats." It was time to end this nonsense. "Look, Niki, it was your idea to come here and talk to Euphemia. The two of you need to get your business done so we can get out of here first thing in the morning. We've got a lot of work to do. Forget Kyropos. I'll move your whole mountain if that's what it takes to find the scroll. But I'm not walking that thing, so forget it. Both of you. Forget all this ... this prophet nonsense. Do your business, get a good night's sleep, and we'll be off bright and early. That's what I signed up for, and that's all I'm doing."

I grabbed the torch from the cave wall and lifted it high enough to scan the shadows for Sargos. Friendly or not, I had no desire to meet up with any lunatic crazy enough to live in a place like this. Seeing nothing, I turned in a huff and I started for the entrance.

"It is too bad," Niki said to Euphemia in an intentionally loud voice, "that this Prophet, he has to come back as an obstinate American."

I ATE PART OF THE evening meal of fish and vegetables, but mostly I just poked around at the food and half-listened to the lively conversation between the two women and Father Jon. My sudden fall from the status of the prophesied messiah to invisible wuss did something to my appetite. I had a desperate need for fresh air, open sky, and a little solitude.

"If you ladies and gentleman will excuse me," I said, standing, "I think I'll take a little stroll."

"Do not fall off the cliff," Niki said. "You promised me that you would move a mountain."

It could have been a Colorado sky: thick and black, streaked with liquid wisps of Milky Way, a countless splatter of stars, the rising rim of a full moon just cracking the horizon, the damp air, warm against my face, sweet with the fragrance of rose and sea.

I walked to the place where the shelter had stood. Far below, I could see the *Penelope*, a ghostly mist against the black water. I imagined Threader down there, sinking ever deeper into the brain-numbing swirl of a drunken stupor, droning on to his attentive "lady" in a monologue of questions about where his life had gone. We would have made good drinking buddies this night.

I let out a deep sigh and sat on the boulder beneath the mystical interplay of moonlight and the ash-tainted atmosphere. I could hear voices in the surf—Euphemia, Niki, Barnes—clamoring in chaotic disarray, like a symphony tuning. I found some clarity when I thought of Marion—the hikes, bike rides, cross-country ski trips, tender moments of talk, sipping wine, making love before the crackle of a pine fire, impervious to the window-rattling assault of a howling blizzard. The memories rolled through my brain in a thick and depressing fog. If there'd been an airport, I would have bought myself a one-way ticket straight to Dallas. Marion and I would talk, get things back on track, and set the stage for our future. We could make it work; I knew we could.

"Do you mind if I join you?"

Startled, I turned. Niki's voice wasn't one of the night sounds I expected to hear.

"Forgive me," she said, emerging from the shadows of the olive grove. "I did not mean to frighten you." She stepped around the boulder, arms crossed, the softness of her moon-splashed beauty instantly lifting some of my fog.

I wanted her to sit, and I wanted her to leave. Just then, I was too screwed up to know what I wanted. I moved to give her room on the boulder.

She sat down, crossed her legs, and laced her fingers over a knee. Her light perfume drifted into my head. Scanning the sky, she said, "It is the most beautiful night, no?"

"I guess that's one thing we agree on. But to tell you the truth, right now I'd rather be watching the moon come up over the mountains."

"Your Colorado nights are as beautiful as this?"

I remembered a night, Christmas Eve, when Marion and I had sat out on my front steps sipping hot toddies, snuggling. "Winter's best. Moon, bright as day, coming up over snowy peaks. Deep black sky. Stars shimmering in the dry, thin air. You can almost hear the crackle of your breath freezing in front of your face. There's no place quite like it."

"And your Marion, you miss her too?"

I glanced at Niki, but she didn't look back. "Yeah. I miss Marion."

"Then, you ... you wish to go back ... to her?"

It was wrong to let feelings between Niki and me go unchecked. I'd gotten caught up in her exotic beauty, entangled in the mystery of her islands. But I knew now that I couldn't just toss out my life with Marion as if it had never even happened. We both needed a jolt back into reality.

"That's the plan," I said. "I'd leave tonight if I could."

"I have angered you. I should not—"

"Look, Niki, this ... this whole prophet thing—it's ridiculous. I shouldn't have told you what I was feeling about this place. It's crazy. I don't know if I'm having past-life memories or if I'm just looking for an excuse to run away from a life I'm not really happy with."

"But, if you are not happy with your life, why do you wish to go back?"

"I'm an American, remember? Always wanting to be someplace I'm not. When I'm there, I want to be here. When I'm here, I want to be there. It doesn't make any sense, but it doesn't have to. Right now, that's what I want. I want to be there. More than anything, I want to be there."

The sigh of a breeze hissed through olive leaves. Niki took in a long breath of her own. "I was ... I was wondering about something. The labyrinth. How did you know?"

"Beginner's luck? Or maybe this place sparks some psychic streak I didn't know I had. Whatever it is, I don't want to read too much into it."

"And the pier? The boats? Kyropos? This man named Marcus?" She turned and looked straight at me, moonbeams sparkling like diamonds in her eyes. "You read nothing into these as well?"

She wasn't asking about boats and volcanoes. She was probing, trying to get me to talk about the feelings I had for her. I wasn't ready to go there.

"Maybe it's just me looking for bluer seas, brighter skies that don't exist. I don't know." And I truly didn't.

"I believe it all means something," she insisted. "There is too much going on inside of you to deny it. This, I feel."

"Well, you sound a lot more certain about it than I do. What if we get to the Rock and it's empty. You still going to enjoy this little journey of yours?"

"Of course," she said, turning back to the sea. Refusing to let go of her optimism, she added, "If we find nothing on the Rock, then so be it. Like you say, we lose little time overall. As I explained to you already, archaeology is a slow and meticulous process. One learns patience. Disappointment frequents my profession, so you get used to it. Yes, I enjoy the journey. Here, now." She turned back to me. "With you."

Damn her!

She took my right hand and, like a gypsy palm reader, traced a soothing finger over the places where injuries should have been. "Incredible that there are no wounds. There should be wounds." She locked her eyes on mine, lifted my hand, and kissed it. I felt the softness of her lips in my palm, the warmth of her breath through my fingers. *Damn her! Damn her!* I was screaming inside, but I couldn't pull away. I didn't want to pull away.

After another kiss, she stood abruptly and took a few steps toward the sea. Her hair floated like black smoke in the breeze. "I am sorry," she said. "I will go if you like."

I was in meltdown. I gulped enough air to resemble a breath and wondered what either of us would do next.

"Niki. I—"

"No, say nothing more. I should not have come. I ... I am sorry."

She turned and quickly disappeared into the shadows of the olive grove.

"Niki?" I called out. "Niki, you don't have to ..." I started to go after her.

Let her go.

I stopped, stunned by the abrupt clarity of the message. It wasn't a voice, just words that blasted into my mind, the pop of a flashbulb in absolute darkness. I blinked. Zadim? I wasn't sure, but the message carried too much authority to ignore it. I eased back to the boulder, sat with my elbows resting on my knees, pushed fingers through my hair, and looked across the sea as though something in that pale distance held the key to what had just happened. All I could see was the moon scattering glimmering fragments of itself all across the water's restless surface.

I closed my eyes, buried my face in my hands, and took a deep breath. I let her go. It was the only sane thing I could do.

Chapter 15

I DIDN'T SLEEP WELL. UP before daybreak, I sat in a claustrophobic cube of a bedroom, hunched over a table, updating my journal. Through a window above the table, I could see the growing light of morning spread slowly over a gray sea. The open view offered some respite from the closeness of the unadorned stone walls that huddled in shadows at my back.

I wrote nothing of last night, nothing of Niki. Saw no reason for it. Her kiss to my palm had been spontaneous, circumstantially provoked, a man and a woman under the intoxicating influence of a Mediterranean moon sailing over open sea beneath a sky full of winking stars. Add a mix of loneliness, uncertainty, and a yearning for a soft touch, and we had an emotional beverage that had momentarily fuzzed recognized boundaries. That's all it was, and writing about it wouldn't make it any different.

I closed the journal and followed the sounds of voices downstairs. Euphemia, Artemas, Niki, and Father Jon had gathered for a patio breakfast of cooked cereal and fresh fruit. I had the cereal with some kind of a soy milk. Bland. I sprinkled in some raisins to get my sugar fix.

The conversation was lively and surprisingly cheerful; it even included the usual banter between Niki and me, as if everything was just as it had always been. Sometime in the night, Kyropos stopped spewing, but there was general concern among the Pialigarians, Artemas in particular, when Niki reaffirmed our intention to sail to the volcano. Tension eased when the old gardener offered a protecting prayer to the Great Mother on our behalf. Everything was again turning in its proper orbit. We had a sunny day, a sea of glass, a dormant volcano, harmony among comrades bound by a high purpose, and the blessing of the Great Mother. Things couldn't be better.

The only discomfort I felt came from Euphemia. She seemed a little distracted over breakfast, disappointed, I was sure, that I'd decided to ignore her interpretation of my destiny. I could feel her eyes, as though she was attempting to silently *will* me to change my mind. Without looking at her, I willed her right back—*Forget it!* I knew she had gotten the message when she insisted on accompanying us on the trek back to our boat.

Our group fell into two distinct divisions. Niki, Artemas, and Father Jon took the lead. Euphemia and I brought up the rear. Euphemia's slower gait was undoubtedly a tactic designed to get me alone—to cut me from the herd, so to speak. She wanted to know every detail of my vision of Marcus and why I thought the scroll was on the Rock instead of Sarnafi. I could tell by her line of questioning that all my answers were going to confirm everything she already believed. But the way I figured it, this was her special little fantasy, and she was welcome to play it out however she wanted. I felt no moral obligation to play along.

We were halfway down the stairs that led to the pier when Euphemia stopped suddenly. She turned, her eyes flashing with frustration, riveted on mine. "Stuart, I want you to listen to me, and I want you to listen carefully."

"Here we go," I said, rolling my eyes in the best politely rude gesture I could come up with.

"You think this is all a silly game, but it is not. You cannot escape your destiny."

"My destiny? You know my destiny? How is it that you've been granted this wonderful privilege, but I don't have a clue?"

"You *do* have a clue, but you do not know that you know."

"I see. That clears it right up." The woman was relentless. I was still trying to be polite to her, but it was getting more difficult by the moment. "What do you want from me? You need a human sacrifice? Appease the Great Mother? Make the volcano stop? Save your little island? Why don't you ask your friendly, nocturnal freak, Sargos, to do your bidding? He probably knows that labyrinth forward and backward."

"The Great Mother requires no such sacrifice," she said sharply. "And Sargos, he is not the Prophet. This involves much more than our little island, as you call it. We are talking about the restoration of the human spirit—a gift that will benefit *all* humanity."

"I see. Sacrifice me and restore the spirit of the entire human race. Now that throws a whole different light on things."

"You mock me."

Her face was red with anger, but I didn't care. All I wanted to do was get the hell away from her and her prophet crap. "Look, why can't you understand—"

"You are the one who must understand. You have no choice. You will walk the labyrinth. You cannot see it now, but you will. You will try to avoid it. You will fight it. You will struggle to convince yourself of another way. There is no other way. A great thing is waiting to happen through you. You think too small, but that must change. You will become restless, filled with anxiety and self-doubt. You have heard the whisper of Pialigos, and now you cannot flee, even though you try. You cannot know completeness until you fulfill this thing that you are destined to do. I am telling you this now as one trained to see and understand such things. But I cannot be your eyes. You have your own eyes. They will open. You will see as you have never seen before. Your eyes, they will be opened!"

The sermon reminded me of a childhood incident, a tent revival meeting I was forced to attend. The speaker raved on about the fires of hell, his voice screeching, his face growing redder, the veins in his neck bulging like a couple of bicycle inner tubes. The guy was a preacher, but I had the feeling he could just as easily have been a chainsaw murderer.

Euphemia was different. She was no raving psychopath. The penetrating fire in her eyes, the flare of her nostrils, and the intensity in her voice were all disturbingly genuine, not an easy thing to put out of my mind.

The first several hours I spent alone in my spot at the bow, thinking, *Marion, scroll, money, Niki, destiny.* That crazy destiny thing. If people really did have destinies, why did mine have to include walking a maze of narrow paths surrounded by deadly pools of boiling water? I was having a hard time believing that the Great Mother, even on her worst day, could cook up a requirement like that.

It was a relief from this line of brain chatter when Father Jon signaled for me to join him and Niki at the table. I was even happier to see the bottle of beer that Threader handed me when I passed him at the helm.

"This man that you saw in your vision," Father Jon began, "what makes you say his name was Marcus?"

I downed a swallow of beer and recalled the experience. "The name just came to me. I don't know how, exactly."

"Did he speak?" Father Jon asked, taking quick, unconscious puffs off a very short cigar.

"No. I just saw his face."

"I have been thinking," Niki said. "I could perform a regression. Perhaps you would remember more of the details."

"Regression?" I asked. "You mean like hypnosis?"

I'd once read a book about people who were trying to recall events from past lives through hypnosis. It was striking, in a humorous kind of way, that in so many of the cases cited the people claimed that in their previous lives they had been famous characters or people of great importance, while their current lives were anything but eventful, let alone influential. Escapism, I remember thinking, came in all forms.

"Yes. Hypnosis," Niki said.

"Come on, Doctor. That's pushing it just a little beyond the realm of your beloved scientific process, isn't it?" I liked her frowning, scientist self. It was a lot safer.

"No one is pushing anything," Niki said, her professional sensibilities bristling like a perturbed porcupine. "I happen to be a certified hypnotist. In the right hands, it is a recognized and respected tool."

"Yeah? I can see it now. You'd have me barking like a dog. Probably put it on video and show all your friends."

"Ha! You already bark like a dog. You need no help from me. Perhaps I would make you chase cars." A maniacal gale of laughter burst from her mouth. "My friends"—more laughter—"they would be quite amused, watching you ... on the video ... chasing cars." When the cackling finally died out, she added, "Perhaps you are having more doubts about this ... this vision of yours? Is this what you are trying to say, now that we are out on the boat, far away from the hard work that you so despise?"

She was cute when she taunted. "You think I said that just so I could get out of carrying your silly rocks?"

She hit me with a level glare. "They are not my rocks. And you yourself said"—she inflected the tone of a whining oaf—"'Niki, there is something out there. Something we have got to see.' Do you not remember? What makes you so sure? You cannot say. Perhaps there are details we can—"

"I didn't have that dorky tone in my voice when I said it. I'm telling you everything I remember. It was clear. I was standing on a beach. I saw Kyropos, *just* like the picture in the newspaper. There was a guy with a beard standing next to me. His name was Marcus. That's it. And if I was under your hypnotic spell, which is *not* gonna happen, I'd tell you the same thing."

"Niki said that Euphemia believes you are the Prophet," Father Jon said, trying to ease some of the tension. "This is … this is quite remarkable that she would say such a thing. A priestess of her stature, she would not make this statement lightly."

It was obvious that Niki had recruited the father to her corner. "Oh, come on, Father. You're not going to tell me that you buy that story, are you? Is there anything in your Bible that says a guy's got to walk through a maze of boiling water to reach salvation?"

Father Jon thought for a moment. "Yes, actually there is. The Master himself said that the gate to salvation is narrow, that the gate to destruction is wide, easily entered. The path to enlightenment, it is indeed narrow, rife with uncertainties and trials of all descriptions. Is this not the symbolism of the labyrinth?"

"Symbolism? I have no problem with the symbolism. Fact is, I kind of like it." The scene inside Euphemia's cave—skeletons rippling in dark, sulfuric stench—drifted into my mind. I took another large swallow of beer to douse the memory, to clear out the smell. It didn't work. "It's that pair of skeletons that bother me. Far as I'm concerned, they look happy enough just like they are. No sense in me being a third wheel."

"Skeletons?" Father Jon asked. "What skeletons?"

"Anatolios and Panagiota," Niki explained. "You know the legend."

"Oh yes, I know it," the father said, recalling whatever version of the story he'd been given. "The Prophet and his lover." He squinted in disbelief. "Euphemia allowed you to see this?"

"Yes," Niki said. "She showed us that this story is not just a legend; it is actually true. We saw their skeletons, in the Pool of Death." She wiped a sudden tear from the corner of her eye.

Why was she so emotional about this thing? Stranger still, why had she so readily joined forces with Euphemia to drag me into all this nonsense? What was it that made this hardheaded logician suddenly go illogical? Nothing about it made any sense. I let out a soft chuckle and accompanied it with a very visible headshake intended to make that very point.

"I don't know about you," I said to Niki, "but I'm having a hard time believing that I was looking at a pair of skeletons that once belonged to me and an old girlfriend."

"Girlfriend?" Niki shot to her feet, her eyes flashing with indignation. "She was more than a girlfriend. Panagiota sacrificed her own life to be with the man she loved." Her lips quivered as she glared at me. Then, she stalked off and sat at the bow of the boat, legs drawn into her arms, staring into the horizon, well out of hearing range.

"Now what do you suppose that's all about?" I asked, all the mysteries of feminine behavior rising into my mind at the same time.

"I do not know," Father Jon said. "The skeletons? Perhaps such a gruesome scene disturbed her."

"I doubt that," I said. "To an archaeologist, a pile of two-thousand-year-old bones is better than sex." I downed the last of my beer. "What is it about women, Father? Why do they always make things so complicated?"

"My son"—a strange air of authority set in—"no creature is more beautiful, or more mysterious, than a woman. That is how God made her."

"Yeah? I doubt that even God can understand how a woman thinks."

"That, only God would know. As for me, I took a vow."

"Let's see now—that's one vow to seek truth and another to avoid women. Maybe that's not a bad combination."

The father frowned and drew a couple of contemplative puffs from his cigar.

"As for me, Father, I vowed that someday I was gonna get this whole woman thing figured out. But I can tell you, I might be an old man before I—"

"Hell, Adams," Threader blurted out from the cockpit, "a guy'd think a fella your age would know something about the fairer sex by now."

I turned to look at Threader standing at the helm. Nothing about that potbellied beer guzzler struck me as an expert on women, but I played along. "Guess you got it nailed, Threader? I don't recall seeing anybody hanging off your arm."

"Nope, you sure ain't." He patted *Penelope's* wheel. "This here's the closest you're gonna see me get to the female kind. I know you wouldn't understand, but when you've had the best, none of the rest of 'em matters—*ever*. But you can bet your ass that I've learned a thing or two about women."

"Yeah? What have you learned, Threader?" This was going to be amusing.

"Well, let's see now, Adams. I believe with you I'm gonna have to start with the basics, so listen carefully. The first thing you got to be able to see in a woman is when she's in love."

"In love? Right. Why was I expecting something profound, man of the world like you?"

"Like I said, Adams. You got to start with the basics. If you ain't got them down, then all the rest is just one big, fuzzy mystery. That's your problem. You ain't got the basics."

"Your point being ..."

"Okay, Adams, I'll spell it out for you. This is really getting down to it. *Pre*-basics, more like it. Women 101 *minus* about fifty-eight. Now listen, and listen good. The girl's in love—with you."

Every muscle in my body stiffened, forcing me to sit up straighter in my seat. I glanced toward Niki to see if she'd heard the comment. She was still looking across the horizon, unmoved.

Sure, I knew there were feelings passing between us, but they were too ambiguous to be defined, at least not with a label as powerful as *love*.

"You're wrong, Threader, out of your mind. I've got a girl back in the States. I already told her that."

Threader chuckled as though he was talking to a half-wit. "That's what you told her? Hell, you're worse off than I thought. You see, Adams, it don't matter if you told her you got *ten* girlfriends waiting back in the States. Love, it don't know how to count. Ain't that right, Father?"

Father Jon perked up. "Indeed. Love, it knows no limitations. On this I can speak with utmost authority." He nodded, as if agreeing with his own statement would lend it more credibility.

"So I'm telling you, Adams," Threader continued, "she's in love with you. You get that one through that thick head of yours, and you understand her behavior. Simple really."

"You best stick to your boats, Threader," I said, anxious to bury this unnerving public discussion. "They're a lot easier to read. If she feels anything, she hates my guts."

"Wrong again," Threader assured me. "If a Greek woman hates your guts, you might wake up one morning with a knife stuck in your neck. You're confusing hate with the fact that she thinks you're a damn jackass. In case you ain't noticed, beautiful women fall in love with jackasses all the time. No, Adams, she doesn't hate your guts. Don't ask me why, but that poor girl's in love with you."

Threader's words banged through my brain like loose shutters in a high wind. I glanced again at Niki, her legs drawn into a ball, staring listlessly over the water.

Maybe this was more serious than I thought.

LATER THAT AFTERNOON, WITH THREADER and Father Jon napping in their cabins, Kyropos now clearly in view, I was taking my turn at the helm, watching a pod of dolphins that had appeared off *Penelope*'s starboard side. The dolphins had paced us off and on for the better part of the voyage. Captivated by their comical antics, these oversized blue-gray rubber pool toys had splashed and giggled their way straight into everyone's heart, especially Niki's.

Niki, wearing her dark glasses, floppy hat, shorts, and a blouse—the tails tied across her waist—sat at the table reading a copy of William Shakespeare's *Troilus and Cressida*, sulking, and doing a real good job of ignoring me.

A steady wind and a straight course gave me plenty of time to come up with a good theory on why I'd made her angry. It had to do with the legend of Anatolios and Panagiota. In that story, she must have encountered her ideal for the perfect relationship. I was taken by it too, at least by her account. Who wouldn't want that kind of love? I had suspicions that she'd done a little doctoring on that obscure bit of history, especially when I remembered that she'd described herself as a hopeless romantic. Embellishments happened. The bond between those two ancient lovers had, in her version, become the stuff of fairy tales and romance novels, of classical heartbreakers like the Shakespearean piece she was now reading—not the kind of love relationships you normally encounter in real life, at least not in my experience. I'd never had a woman that would break a nail for me, let alone die for me.

Niki was young, still waiting for her knight in shining armor to ride up and sweep her off her feet. Now that she was thirtysomething, I figured the age factor was starting to creep in. She was beginning to feel a little insecure, even hypersensitive about whether or not her Mr. Perfect was going to show up.

Her problem aside, I had unintentionally trampled over her romantic fantasy with my off-the-cuff, old-girlfriend remark, so it was up to me to warm the chill that frosted that hollow space between us. The dolphins, I figured, were a good excuse to get us talking; they would give me an opening for an apology.

"Niki, look," I said, pointing to the animals.

Niki, her eyes filled with skepticism, locked on me for an indifferent moment, as if she was weighing whether or not I'd received a sufficient dose of the silent treatment. Apparently I had. She folded her book and stepped toward the helm to join me.

"They are beautiful, so playful. Perhaps they are happy because Kyropos has gone to sleep."

She took a seat close enough for me to catch a hint of her fragrance. I hadn't thought about it until that moment, but her scent had always emitted an air of integrity. It was tasteful, never overdone, the aura of a woman who was confident, secure in her femininity, enough to shake some of the validity out of my theory.

"Maybe," I said, my eyes spending more time on her than on dolphins. "Guess I'm happy about it too. Then in some ways I'm kind of sorry."

"Sorry?" she asked, turning to me, her face fully amused. "Why would you be sorry?"

"Never seen a live volcano up close. Guess I was hoping I'd get a chance."

"I thought you did not like danger."

"I'm not into trying to outrun a pyroclastic flow, if that's what you mean. I didn't say I wanted it to be the *last* thing on earth I'd see."

Niki turned her gaze on the volcano and spoke as casually as if her next question still had something to do with geological anomalies.

"What are you trying to outrun, Stuart Adams?"

I heard the question, but it caught me off guard. I glanced at her, repositioned my hands to the wheel's spokes, and shifted on my feet. I was supposed to be the one controlling the direction of this conversation.

"I make you nervous." She turned toward me, pushing wind-blown strands of hair behind her ear. She'd spoken in a relaxed, analytical tone, like a psychiatrist to her patient. "Why, do you think?"

I swallowed. "Nervous? What makes you think …" *No.* I stopped myself. Here was the opportunity I needed to put this thing on the table, to get it out in plain sight so there'd be no more questions about the way things were. "Okay," I admitted, "you make me nervous."

"Why?" She lowered her sunglasses and looked at me as if she already knew what I was going to say. "What do you think I am going to do?"

I was getting that uncomfortable feeling of being transparent—again. I started to look away, to pretend that some detail in the rigging was about to need my attention, but I was too mired in her quicksand eyes.

"You want to know what I think you'll do?"

Answering a question with a question was a way of buying time to find words to match the sudden burble of emotions I didn't know how to define. How could I say, *You'll make me fall in love with you and complicate the hell out of my life,* without actually saying it?

She didn't wait for me to take a stab at a legitimate response.

"You are afraid that I am going to upset your life."

Her accuracy made me laugh—nervously. "Something like that."

"You worry about your Marion, no?"

Worry? Lately, I'd been thinking a lot about Marion, our relationship, weighing that old "Is it love, or am I filling the void?" question. I'd decided it was neither love nor the fear of being alone that kept me hanging on, even when I knew there were some emotionally important factors missing in the relationship. *Responsibility*, I'd decided. That was the key word that kept bouncing around in my consciousness. I felt responsible for the feelings Marion had invested in me.

I was never one to trick a woman into making her believe I cared for the single purpose of getting her in bed. Sure, I was as taken by a pretty face and a perfect body as the next guy, but I also knew there was a real person behind the physical manifestation, a living soul with needs and feelings that, handled carelessly, could be damaged, even scarred for life. I didn't take that responsibility lightly. It sometimes blinded my better judgment and kept me hanging on long after everything in me was screaming to bail—Alyssa, for example.

Niki, according to my theory, was on a quest for the ideal relationship, and that made her vulnerable. She was testing me, and I didn't want to give her any hint that I was ready to open the door. I was in no position to take on that responsibility.

"I worry about my Marion, *yes*. Before I left, I asked her to marry me, okay?" I saw no need to fill her in with Marion's chilled response. That would only weaken my case.

"Oh? It is strange that this fiancée of yours has not returned even one of your telephone calls."

Strange indeed, I agreed, though I hoped to hide that fact beneath a scowl. The hyper sound of Marion's answering service rolled through my head. *You've reached the voice mail of Marion Chandler, of Chandler & Associates. Your call is important to me. Please leave your name, your number, and a message. I promise I'll get back with you ASAP. Bye-bye.*

Isn't my call important to you? I'd thought every time I heard the thing.

I'd seen the way she treated callers she didn't want to talk to—usually those nervous, pain-in-the-ass clients obsessing over some insignificant detail. She'd fish that chirping cell phone from inside her purse and flip it open to check the caller ID. When she saw it was me, she'd slap it shut—as if I could feel the snap. Captured in that palm-sized, plastic clam, she'd shove me into the dark abyss of her purse, drawing some sense of satisfaction out of sticking me beneath clattering bottles of makeup, nail polish, hand cream, hairbrush, and the seventeen million other objects she'd never leave home without.

"What's she supposed to do," I said curtly, keeping my defenses high, "send a carrier pigeon? In case you haven't noticed, there's no telephone within fifty thousand miles of here."

"She could have called before we left on this trip. There was plenty of time."

Yeah, there had been plenty of time, and if there hadn't, Marion was the kind that would have made time.

"She probably tried to call while Dora was out," I ventured, pumping all the plausibility into my voice that I could.

"I am sure of it."

"I'm sure of it too," I snapped.

"You are sure, or you are just being naïve?"

"Naïve?" I rolled my eyes hard enough for her to see them through my sunglasses. "I really don't see any reason to discuss this with you."

"Why not?"

"Because, that's why."

"Because is not a reason. You said so yourself."

"I don't have to give you a reason. I told you, this is a personal matter. Maybe you Greeks don't understand the meaning of *personal*. It's like, between two people, not three. This is between Marion and me."

"Do not patronize me. I know the meaning of *personal*. I also know that your Marion, she has left you."

"What?" I turned sharply toward her, my lips quivering with words I couldn't find. What do you say when the enemy hits a raw nerve?

I was afraid of losing Marion. Why? The silence of an empty house. Black hole. Not like she was gone on business. That was fasting, choice, agreed-upon deprivation for the larger goal of a greater good. Losing her, on the other hand, would be starvation, stark and merciless terror leading to emotional death. I despised the part of me that needed her. In my strongest moments, I didn't need anybody, but I knew those moments would pass, and all my weaknesses would roll in like clouds driven by arctic winds, full of bone-chilling rain, waves of gray loneliness that'd send me to the telephone punching in her number with urgent force, ready to beseech, to promise the moon and a planet or two.

Who was I kidding? It wasn't all about that noble ideal of responsibility. Fear of the void—that one played a big role.

For a long time, I studied the fiery eyes of my relentless interrogator. I couldn't think of one honest word to refute her. I had but one weapon left—humor.

"You know what you ought to do?"

"No. What is it that I ought to do?" She looked as if she intended to disagree with whatever I suggested.

"You ought to start yourself a psychic hot line. Woman with your talent could get rich in no time."

"Perhaps I should." She crossed her arms defiantly and locked her eyes squarely on mine. "Tell me I am wrong."

I almost wished Kyropos would erupt, just so we could change the subject.

"Look, let's just drop it. Okay? I was showing you the dolphins. Can't we watch dolphins without fighting?"

She did one of those contemplative teeters with her head, a signal to inform me she could go either way. "Okay. We will watch the dolphins." She turned in her seat, both legs folded beneath her, resting her chin on finger-laced hands.

Could there be a more beautiful creature on this planet? I wondered, trying to relax the white-knuckle grip I had on the wheel. This woman was making me crazy.

Then, without warning, the dolphins splashed, as if in a panic, and vanished beneath the waves.

"Did you see that?" I said.

"They have seen a shark."

"How do you know?"

"Who would not know? These waters, they are full of sharks. Reefs, blues, blacktips, even the whites."

"Great whites?"

"Yes." Niki turned toward me and made a ridiculously toothy, biting gesture, clicking her teeth and wrinkling her nose, cute and bratty as she could be.

"You'd make a good one all right," I agreed.

"I would," she said, continuing the shark look, "and I would find you and chomp you right in half."

"That'd be a mistake. You'd have to put up with two of me instead of one."

Her face went flat considering the impossibility of the problem. She turned back to where the dolphins were. "I remember once when I was a little girl, I ..." She stopped suddenly, studying the water.

When I noticed her frown, I scanned the surface half expecting to see the dorsal fin of a great white. The thought of a twenty-foot man-eater swimming beneath the boat induced an entirely new kind of internal shudder and sparked a whole new definition of the creeps.

"This is a very strange thing," Niki said. "The water ... it ... it ripples."

I looked across the rough surface, and I was about to say something when I felt the sea begin to rise, as if a huge arm had passed beneath the boat. The roughness disappeared, as *Penelope* lifted and then fell with the otherwise untroubled water.

"That was no shark," I said, my heart suddenly racing in my chest. Whale maybe? Submarine? A friend had described a similar rising and falling of the sea when a sub passed beneath his Hobie Cat off the San Diego coast.

In the next instant, Threader was on the deck like a captain ready to order his crew to battle stations. Father Jon stumbled out behind him, eyes wide, clueless.

"What the devil was that, Adams?" Threader scanned sea and sky for the enemy.

"Beats the hell out of me. Dolphins took off. Water started rippling in a weird kind of way. The whole sea swelled like a big—"

"My god!" Niki shrieked, pointing to something behind the boat. We all turned to see the back of a giant wave cresting into a thundering wall that continued to move out to sea. "*Tsunami*," Niki said in a borderline whisper. "We have witnessed the birth of a tsunami!"

Chapter 16

THE CHILL DIDN'T REACH THE base of my spine before I felt a subsonic rumble in my gut. I turned just as Kyropos belched a thick cloud of ash. Niki's hands shot over her mouth, an involuntary gasp spilling through her fingers. Awestruck, the four of us watched the huge cloud lumber off and disperse over the sea.

"Tremor must have set off that wave," Threader said, stepping in to take over the wheel. "They don't usually surface like that until they hit a shoreline. No telling what the hell's gonna happen next."

"Maybe we ought to get out of here," I suggested, suddenly feeling vulnerable as a bug bobbing on a cork next to a powder keg with a lit fuse.

"Turn back?" Niki said, her eyes wide with disbelief. "You see a little puff of smoke and you want to turn back?"

"Yeah." Thinking of that hole blasted out of the heart of Santorini made macho pride pretty much a moot issue.

"Hell," Threader said, "we couldn't outrun a tsunami anyway. If we'd been a few miles back, who knows what would've happened. There's a cove this side of the Rock. Our best bet is to anchor there and then wait and see what's gonna happen. Might give us some protection from a blast." He started barking orders. "Niki, Father Jon, we're dropping sails, powering up. Adams, there's shallow rocks that can give us another kind of grief. Git up to the bow and watch. You see anything, shout it out." He grinned. "Doing something constructive might just help firm up that jellified spine of yours."

"Jellified spine my ass," I muttered all the way to the bow. I was mad enough to call for a potluck picnic on the rim of Kyropos; then we'd see who had the jellified spine.

Threader cut the engine and dropped anchor fifty yards from the Rock. We spent the next several hours milling around on the boat, waiting for Kyropos to do something.

"Guess it was just a damn hiccup," Threader announced finally. "Why don't you kids grab your sand shovels and go git your playing over with. Maybe we'll get lucky and get outta here before that damn thing wakes up again."

"You are not coming with us?" Niki asked.

"Nope. Digging and hundred-degree heat don't mix with me. Come to think of it, I may even have myself a swim."

"Don't let the sharks get you," I said. "At least not until we get back."

"Don't worry about me, Adams." He raised the bench seat next to the cockpit and lifted out a lever-action rifle. "Me and Mr. Winchester here, we'd make a pretty unwelcome reception party for a damn shark. Guess that Frenchman wasn't fond of 'em either."

Niki and Father Jon dispersed to their cabins. Threader and I dug out a Zodiac stowed in the forward hull. We inflated the boat with *Penelope*'s compressor, mounted the motor, and slipped it into the water.

Father Jon emerged from below deck wearing a straw hat and carrying a bottle of drinking water in one hand and a canvas bag filled with tools in the other. Niki came up wearing her khaki getup and a baseball hat; a sheathed, foot-long hunting knife was strapped around her waist, and she was toting her own water and bag of hand tools.

"What do you plan on doing with that thing?" I said, nodding to the knife.

"Dig. What do you think?"

I didn't even notice that I was rubbing my neck until I heard Threader chuckling. I glanced at Threader and quickly dropped my hand. "Essential gear for an archaeologist, I guess."

"You carry a pen and notebook, do you not?" Niki nodded toward my backpack. "I cannot dig with a pen, so I carry a knife, a tool of my trade. Do you find that strange?"

"No, guess I don't."

Once loaded, Niki took the throttle of the Zodiac and motored in toward the shore. "In your vision," she said to me, "you say you could see Kyropos?"

"Yeah. It wasn't rocky like this. It was sand. A beach."

"Then we will circle the Rock and find your beach."

She opened up the throttle. Laughing wildly, she sent the over-powered Zodiac slapping across the waves. I held on to my hat and pretended to enjoy the ride, robbing her, I hoped, of the perverted rush she seemed to derive from her control of the throttle.

Father Jon had no need to prove anything. The wind pushed the flimsy brim of his straw hat straight to the sky. He had it cinched so tight that it made his ears stick out. His face was frozen into a wince, his eyes a pair of slits, his full set of teeth clenched hard enough to crack them all. I felt as if I were on a suicide mission with a kamikaze and a smiling chimp.

The Rock's jagged shoreline quickly subsided into sand. Kyropos eased back into view, a dozing giant not to be disturbed.

Then, the hair on the back of my neck went up. Suddenly I was staring at a familiar stretch of beach. I raised my hand. Niki eased off the throttle and drove the Zodiac into the sand.

I walked slowly toward a huge rock outcropping. "There's a cave. Right there." I pointed to the sheer face of rock.

Niki came beside me and studied the spot. "There is no cave. Not here."

Ignoring her, I fell to my knees and began digging with bare hands.

"Stuart, think!" Niki's voice rose in an angry whine. "If Seagull found the scroll in a cave, it would not be filled with sand. How would he find a scroll in such a cave?"

"Perhaps an earthquake pushed a wave over the beach," Father Jon suggested. Nobody acknowledged him. "Just a thought," he quickly added.

"Look at this man!" Niki screeched. "He is possessed with a demon!" She threw up her arms and spun toward the Zodiac. "I will get this stubborn madman a shovel before he breaks every one of his fingers. I will get us all a shovel so we can join in his madness." She kicked through the sand muttering things in Greek.

OVER THE NEXT SEVERAL DAYS Niki, Father Jon, and I managed to excavate the entire cave to the level of its original floor. I was disappointed that all we had to show for our effort were four deteriorated planks, a handful of twine fragments, and a small clay lantern. The lantern, Niki surmised, was first, maybe second century, Jewish in origin. The planks had probably been bound together by the twine to form a crude but functional table. To an archaeologist, the items were tantalizing artifacts that fired the imagination. For a novelist looking for a story, they were like wet tinder on a cold night.

With Kyropos belching ash and sending a spate of tremors through the island, we all decided that we'd pushed our luck far enough. It was time to go back to Sarnafi.

The work had been frantic and exhausting, and on the chance that we might have overlooked something, Niki and I made one last run to the cave. Our inspection confirmed what we already knew: there was no plastered hole in the wall.

We stepped into the shade of an overhang in the cliff. I pulled off my backpack and plopped into the sand. Niki sat beside me.

"What now, Stuart Adams?" Niki said, taking a swallow of water. "Any more visions?"

"Fresh out, I guess. But I have been wondering about something."

"What have you been wondering?"

"This thing about reincarnation. I know I've been here before. But I also know that this is the first time that my physical brain has been here."

"I am glad that you brought it." Niki burst into giddy laughter, fatigue obviously taking its toll.

"I'm not trying to be funny," I said. "You're a scientist. It's the brain that supposedly carries the memory, right? I mean, if a guy gets brain damage, he can actually lose his memory."

Another burst of laughter from Niki. "I am sorry," she said, fanning her face. "Perhaps I have been too serious lately. Do you ..." she smirked. "Do you fear that you have ..." More laughter. "I am sorry. Do you fear that you have ... brain damage?" She buried her face in her hands, shaking hysterically.

I just shook my head. "Thanks for the sensitivity. I hope you set off an earthquake."

The comment sent her into a fetal position, laughing so hard she couldn't get her breath. I passed the time sipping water and looking at the empty sky.

Finally, she straightened, sniffed, and patted her chest. "I am so sorry. Do not take offense. I … I do not … do this often." She forced something resembling a serious look. "Laughing in the face of someone, even you, it is rude. I apologize." She took a quick breath; her eyes flashed large and wet. "I am fine now. What was it that you were saying? Something about"—another smirk—"something about … brain damage?"

"Something like that." I could see it was useless. But in spite of my doubts, I continued. "Okay, I was thinking that maybe there is something to this soul memory thing. How else could I remember this place? It can't be a memory stored in the brain."

"Yes. Yes, it would have to be something like—" Niki stopped. Frowning, she leaned forward and plucked a bit of debris from the sand; it had probably turned up while she was laughing. "What is this? Carbonized wood? Yes, I think so."

"Here I'm trying to carry on a deep conversation about soul memories, and all you care about is a piece of charcoal?"

Ignoring me, Niki rolled to her knees and began sifting through the sand. Soon, she had a large blackened area cleared. "You see? A hearth. Perhaps this is where your friend Marcus cooked his meals. Look"—she held up a charred, slender object—"the bone of a fish."

Suddenly, another picture flashed into my mind. I was sitting before a dozen men dressed in the same type of garment that Marcus had been wearing. Fifty yards behind the men, there was a red cliff wall full of caves—dwellings. I moved out from under the overhang and took a few steps toward Kyropos. Niki followed.

"What is it?" she asked. "Another vision?"

"Kyropos. That's where they lived."

"Who? Who lived on Kyropos?"

"The Children of Light."

"But I told you, that is not possible. The Children of Light were Essenes. The Essenes, they did not live this far west. Do you not remember? They lived near the Dead—"

"How do you explain the clay lamp? You said it was Jewish. The Essenes were Jewish, weren't they?"

Niki didn't answer.

"They were there, Niki," I said, pointing to Kyropos. "I don't know why, I don't know how, but they were there." I turned and took slow steps toward the volcano until I stood knee-deep in the surf.

Niki called from the water's edge. "Stuart, what are you doing? I worry for you. I—"

"It's there," I said in a sudden flood of insight. In that instant, I knew beyond all doubt that we had to go to Kyropos.

THE DRONE OF A MOTOR drifted in above the surf. At first, I thought it was Threader coming around the island to pick us up, but the sound wasn't right.

"A seaplane," Niki said, spotting the aircraft first. "Scientists? Journalists maybe?"

I slogged out of the water and stood next to Niki, watching the plane as it made a low pass before setting down and taxiing to the beach in front of us.

A sudden spurt of adrenaline shot through my veins when Vito and Apollo stepped out. Giacopetti was on their heels. How the hell did he know we were here?

The gorillas drew their guns as the three men approached. This time, they didn't bother to attach the silencers.

"Well, well," Giacopetti said cheerfully, "if it isn't my American friend and his lovely companion." He bowed in mock humility before Niki. "Dr. Mikos, what a pleasure."

"Murderer." The word seethed through Niki's clenched teeth like a poisonous vapor.

"Murderer? Is this any way to greet a fellow countryman?"

"You burned Captain Threader's boat. You tried to kill him."

"Ah yes. I do recall hearing something about a fire in the harbor. An unfortunate turn of luck for the captain, the loss of such a valuable piece of property."

"It was all he had."

"That is most regrettable," Giacopetti said, feigning sadness. "Still, he has his life, does he not? I do not remember hearing anything about a ... *murder*, as you say."

"No thanks to you, he still lives."

"Yes, well, all this talk about the loss of property, it brings up a small matter that, quite frankly, has had both of my good men rather upset. *Pistols*, Mr. Adams. I believe you have a pair that do not belong to you."

"Didn't bring them with me," I said, trying to control a sudden shallowness of breath. Predators like Giacopetti fed on fear, and I was determined to deprive him of the pleasure. "If I'd known you were coming, I would have gladly brought them."

"So poised, you Americans," Giacopetti said. "But then, what would one expect from the country that produced the great John Wayne? Are all Americans so bold, Mr. Adams? Or is it just the occasional fool, like yourself, who dreams of being the tough guy?" He shot me a surly glare. "Yes, well, I do want to trust you. I really do. But if you don't mind, Vito here would like to search you for his gun."

"Actually I do mind," I said, wishing I hadn't left the pistol in my cabin, "but since you've got the firepower ..." I raised my hands.

Apollo kept me covered while Vito stepped in for the frisking. When he finished, Vito drove a fist hard into my stomach. I crumpled, gasping for air.

"Pig!" Niki screamed, falling protectively on top of me. "You had no reason. He has nothing of yours."

With a cruel smile, the big man backed slowly away, snatched up my backpack, and started riffling through it. Finding nothing, he made a shrugging gesture to his boss.

"Perhaps you do not have the pistol after all," Giacopetti said, kneeling in front of me. "But I can see by the pile of sand that you two have been busy little bees, very busy indeed. The scroll, Mr. Adams. Did you happen to find it?"

"We found nothing," Niki said.

"I see. The fruits of the archaeologist's labor, they are sometimes bitter, no? Vito, perhaps you should have a look around, see what kind of nothing our busy little bees have found."

Vito plodded through the sand to the cave.

I regained my breath, but I stayed curled in a ball. I was sure Giacopetti was going to kill us, and I had to do something. Niki's knife dangled from her belt, but what good was a knife against two guns? I noticed something unusual: grains of sand toppling from the edges of our footprints. There was another subsonic rumble and a tremor so slight it would have gone unnoticed if I hadn't been lying on the ground. It stopped. Seconds passed. Then, with no further warning, Kyropos exploded in a horrifying burst of ash and missiles that hurtled like comets in every direction. The sea between Kyropos and the Rock started to swell.

Vito ran out of the cave, and the three Greeks scrambled in wide-eyed terror toward the rocks and higher ground.

"The wave," I said to Niki. "There's another wave. We've got to get to the Zodiac."

Niki turned to see the rising water, her eyes flashing in fear. "Oh my god! We'll never make—"

"The boat," I said, gathering my feet. "Just think about the boat. It's the journey, remember? Time to enjoy it."

Niki smiled, the confidence flooding back into her eyes. I grabbed her hand, and we sprinted for the Zodiac. Shots rang out, and bullets pelted the sand around us, but only for a moment. The Greeks were too busy clambering higher into the rocks to save themselves.

Then, another strange thing happened. The shoreline began to recede, exposing the sea bottom for two hundred yards. The monster wave was sucking up every drop of water in its path. Niki and I tumbled into the boat, covered our heads, and waited. The ground shook so hard it bounced the Zodiac down the empty slope of the seafloor.

"Hang on," I yelled, the terrible thunder reaching a hideous pitch. Gulping what might have been my final breath of air, I held Niki tight and braced for the impact. Seconds passed like hours. Then, the monster curled and fell over us like an imploded building, a terrible crushing blur of blue and white. The Zodiac lifted from the sand like a crippled rocket aimed directly into the cliffs.

In that terrifying instant, there was no doubt in my mind that Niki and I were going to die.

The wave hurled the Zodiac through the air like a fleck of debris. Helpless in its killing grip, we could only cling to each other and wait for death. Eternity passed, but the impact never came. Instead, the horrific thunder settled into a deafening calm.

I lifted my head and squinted hard against the blare of naked sunlight. By some miracle, we were slipping down the back of the wave a hundred yards from the cliffs.

Niki peered over the side of the Zodiac. "My god!" she gasped, her voice cracking with disbelief. "We … we made it."

We sat up, embraced, and laughed and hooted at our impossibly good fortune, but only for a few seconds. A bullet sizzled into the water, leaving a gaping wound across the top of the Zodiac. My jaw tightened with anger when I saw the Greeks standing high in the rocks taking potshots even as the black smoke of their smashed airplane billowed up behind them. Two more bullets sizzled into the water.

"Let's get out of here," I yelled, slapping a hand over the hole.

Niki twisted the starter and cranked the Zodiac full throttle. The Greeks sent a few more wild shots into our wake before scrambling toward the *Penelope*.

It was a credit to Threader that *Penelope* had survived the wave. Unaware that they were about to come under attack, Threader and Father Jon stood on the deck and watched our approach in the wounded Zodiac.

"They must get away from the island," Niki shouted. "Giacopetti will kill them." She lunged to the front of the boat. "You take the throttle."

"I can't take my hand off the leak!"

"Take the throttle, damn it! Now!"

It was no time to argue. I'd barely taken over before Niki was tearing through her canvas bag. She pulled out a flashlight, fell over the hissing hole, and started signaling the *Penelope*.

Threader stood still for a moment and then ducked into the cockpit. A plume of blue smoke went up from the diesel engine.

The pop of pistol fire punctuated the scream of the Zodiac's motor. Threader eased the yacht away from the Rock, pulled out the Winchester, and cracked off three rapid shots, enough to scatter the Greeks and buy time to reach a safe distance from the island.

Niki climbed aboard *Penelope*. The Zodiac had taken at least three hits and was going down fast. Threader tossed a rope around the motor to keep it from sinking. I scrambled off the collapsing boat with the grace of a drunkard doing a jig on a waterbed. We all wrestled the crumpled corpse of the Zodiac on board.

"Damn, girl," Threader said, laughing. "You remembered the code."

"Did I do it right?" Niki asked. "It has been years."

"*Gunfire from rocks.* That's what you said. Remember I told you that you'd need it someday. Girl, you probably saved my life." He scooped her into a bear hug, still laughing.

"I did not know what else to do," she said. "I knew you could not hear me." She turned to me. "The flashlight, it was a code that the captain devised and taught me when I was a child. Not even my father knew. We would talk to each other when he was at sea. No one but the captain and I knew what we were saying."

Father Jon had been standing at the bow of the boat watching the black plume rise from the far side of the Rock. "The smoke, it is from the airplane?"

"I think so," I said. "But to tell you the truth, that wave had me just a little too preoccupied to see exactly what happened."

"Well," Threader said, "we'd better get the hell out of here. Father, if you'll pray real hard, I mean real hard, we may make it before that thing blows."

"Threader," I said, "we've got to go back."

"That's just what I said, Adams. You knock something loose in that noggin of yours?"

"To Kyropos."

Threader froze, his eyes narrowing into an incredulous stare. "To hell you say." He stepped in close to my face, his upper lip contorted into a curl. He spoke in a low tone intended for my ears only. "Are you outta your friggin' gourd?"

"Maybe," I said, unflinching under the gust of his stinking breath.

"What makes you think the scroll is there?"

The rigid set of his eyes told me he wasn't into discussing the validity of visions. I saw no reason to try to make a believer out of him.

"Let's just say I *feel* it."

"You *feel* it, do you?" Threader turned away, scratching the back of his neck, a sarcastic grin cracking one side of his face. He paced in short arcs and glared at me as he spoke. "Let me get this straight. You want me to take *this* boat to the shore of *that* volcano"—he pointed—"risk the lives of *these* people, because you *feel* like the scroll is on Kyropos?"

I met his glare head-on. "That's right."

Threader shook his head, his mouth half open in disbelief. "You sure as hell knocked something loose, Adams." He let out a dismissive chuckle, turned, and stepped into the cockpit. "Since we're getting our feelings out in the open here, let me share one or two of mine. I *feel* like if we don't get the hell outta here right now"—his face grew redder, his voice louder—"it ain't gonna matter if we find a hundred scrolls. We won't be alive to tell about it."

He fired the engine and cranked the wheel to bring the boat to a more favorable angle to the wind.

I spotted the Winchester lying on the table, picked it up, and leveled it squarely between Threader's eyes. I had no idea what the hell I was going to do next.

Chapter 17

"JELLIFIED SPINE, IS IT, THREADER?"

I watched Blake Threader's face tighten with defiance. He killed the engine and stepped in front of me, the gun barrel two inches from his chin.

"Adams, you ain't got the guts to shoot me."

"Turn it around, Threader. *Now!*"

"*Stuart!*" Niki shrieked. "What are you doing? Put the gun away!"

A thin smile came on Threader's face, his unflinching eyes showing no sign of fear. Then, in a quick, single motion, he grabbed the barrel of the rifle and planted a fist in the middle of my mouth. I stumbled backward to the deck. Stunned, it took a couple of headshakes to reengage my brain. I started to stand, but Niki was on me before I could get to my feet.

"Stop!" she screamed in my face. "If you want to fight, go back to the Rock and fight Giacopetti. We will not fight amongst ourselves!" She turned to Threader. "Captain. Put the gun away. Now!"

Threader hesitated, and then he stepped over and slipped the Winchester under the seat. He came back and glowered down at me over Niki's shoulder.

"All right," I said, relaxing under Niki's weight. "It's over."

She stood slowly, poised to spring again if necessary. I propped myself on an elbow and wiped blood from the side of my mouth. Threader's withering stare softened when he leaned down and offered me a hand.

"I owed you that one, pal," he said, pulling me to my feet. "I ain't forgot that little scrap we had on my boat."

My head swirled. My jaw hurt.

Father Jon, his face pale as death, made another sign of the cross. He stepped toward the bow, either wringing his hands or poising them for prayer; I wasn't sure which.

What the hell had I been thinking? I'd never pulled a gun on a man in my life. I wiped another trickle of blood from the corner of my mouth and used my tongue to check for loose teeth.

"Guess I owe everyone an apology," I said, finding all teeth secure. "It was a stupid mistake."

"Stupid is right," Niki said. "Stupid beyond belief."

She had an uncanny talent for driving the point to unsounded depths.

"Now that we got that settled," a victorious Threader said, "let's get the hell outta here." He started for the cockpit.

"No!" Niki planted both fists at her waist.

Threader stopped and turned, his face contorted in confusion. "No? But I thought we just—"

"If Stuart thinks the scroll is there," she said calmly, pointing to Kyropos, "then we will go."

It took quite a long time for Niki's message to travel from Threader's ears to his face. When it finally arrived, his skin tone turned the color of a piece of spoiled bologna.

"But ... but, Niki," he began to plead, "do you know what you're asking? I mean, it's not like—"

She cut him off. "I am asking Captain Blake Threader to reach deep down inside of himself and pull out the great bravery that I know is there. You yourself chided Stuart for a momentary lapse of courage, did you not?"

Threader and I exchanged glances, his bolognafied complexion still intact. I was sure he detected in my eyes the satisfaction of knowing he was getting the well-deserved spanking that he wasn't going to forget any time soon.

He made a lame attempt to defend himself. "Well, yeah, but that was dif—"

She cut him off again. "You are the Captain Threader that I trusted to bring us on this voyage, the same Captain Threader that my father knew and trusted, the same Captain Threader that I have seen spit in the very eye of danger. You are the Captain Threader that I know fears nothing, not even death."

Threader was working real hard to remember that person Niki had just described.

"Oh cripes! Niki, don't do this to me. Look." He pointed to Kyropos. "Look at that thing. It's gonna blow any second. I want you to have your scroll, I really do. But hell, your daddy, he'd never forgive me if I let something happen to you."

He was trying to make it look as though he cared more about her life than his own. It wasn't going to work, not with Niki. I glanced at Father Jon; he was standing silent, his eyes closed, knowing it wasn't going to work. Even Threader, his eyes shifting every which direction, knew it wasn't going to work. Nothing short of doing what Niki wanted was going to work. Everyone knew it. Threader was going down. He needed to accept it.

"If my father were alive, he would not turn away from that stinking mountain. You know that. And if he were here, you would not turn away either."

Threader had the whitish face of a child badly scolded and shamed into submission. Everything about him said he knew he'd have better luck convincing Kyropos to settle down.

"Damn, girl," he said with a capitulating laugh. "I believe you're just as stubborn as your daddy." He turned and stared at that evil gray-black cloud that roiled from the cone of the volcano. Then, I saw a resigned shake of the head. "Hell, if I'm gonna die, I might as well do it with dignity—at the helm of a damn good boat."

Niki stepped in front of him, her eyes filled with premeditated admiration. On tiptoes, she delivered a peck to his cheek, a bit of salve for the welts she'd laid across his ego.

"You are indeed a brave man, Captain Threader. Whatever happens, I will think of you in this way. Always."

Father Jon, still standing alone at the bow, one wrist clasped behind his back, had turned to watch Kyropos. I figured he'd turned away to spare Threader the humiliation of knowing he'd had an audience at his lashing.

Niki called out to him. "And you, Father, you are with us as well?"

I watched the father make one of those contemplative, chin-on-the-shoulder half turns, as though he hadn't noticed the brutality that had just occurred. He let a few seconds pass before he lifted a fresh cigar, still wrapped in cellophane, from his shirt pocket. He turned and ambled over the rolling deck to rejoin us.

Something told me he knew how to answer Niki's question.

"I was going to save this for the trip home," he said, tossing the cellophane to the wind and hoisting the cigar, "but perhaps now is the better time." He lit up and took a couple of puffs. "I told you that I made a vow to seek the Truth, wherever it may lead. Well, my search has led me here, to this place. Captain Threader, I understand your reluctance. Believe me, I too, like any man facing such uncertainty, have fears, even doubts. Yet, I am prepared to risk all, everything. And for what? For this thing that may not even exist? Yes. And I tell you why." More puffing. "Think of it—the ancient wisdom of Atlantis, passed down for countless generations, possibly crossing into an entirely different culture, embraced by a great Essene teacher, and given to the very Master himself. I swoon with the possibilities. If this scroll is there"—he stabbed the cigar toward Kyropos—"then what can I say? I, Father Jon Basil Andros, was a mere five kilometers from such a treasure, and I did not attempt to retrieve it? No! I do not think so. I am not a brave man, but how can I fear the loss even of my own life, when I have already given it for the sake of Truth? Yes, Niki. I am with you. In the name of Truth, in the very name of our holy God, I am with you." With his cigar hand, he made another sign of the cross, leaving a smoke artifact of the sacred symbol dangling in the air. "And may God be with us."

I looked at Threader, surprised to see tears streaming over his cheeks.

"Damn, Father," he said, blinking, wiping his nose with the back of his hand, "something tells me I'm in the company of a very great man." He stepped up to Father Jon and engulfed him in a hug. Then, he took a step back and looked at us all as if we were some second-rate crew he'd been forced to take on. "What the hell are we all doing standing around gawking? We got to go get us a scroll!"

THREADER MANEUVERED *PENELOPE* TWO MILES from a sheer cliff face that made Kyropos inaccessible by sea. The doomsdayer fanatics were least likely to post a lookout on this side of the volcano. Here we waited for the cover of darkness.

Threader and Father Jon busied themselves repairing the Zodiac, while Niki and I sat on the deck watching Kyropos spew ash so thick it created its own lightning. Thin fingers of lava oozed down the face of the cliffs and dripped in a hissing fury into the sea. The mountain grumbled like a red-eyed pit bull, teeth bared, ready to attack.

A plan began to form in my mind. To minimize our risk of being spotted by the fanatics, Father Jon and I would paddle in on the Zodiac. Niki and Threader would stay on board, keeping *Penelope* rigged and ready for as quick a getaway as a sailboat would allow.

The hardest part of the plan would be to convince Niki to stay on board *Penelope*. She knew better than anyone that Threader could handle the boat alone. Watching her face in the softness of the waning daylight, I could tell that she was pumped, ready to go, strong and brave, capable as anyone of carrying out the task at hand. Unfortunately, the strongest, bravest, most bullheaded person in the world was no match for a bullet, and I assumed those fanatics, overly anxious to meet their Maker, were of a mind to shoot first and ask questions later. The situation made me realize how much I cared about what happened to her, bullheaded or not. Maybe it had to do with my traditional upbringing, or that protective male instinct so deeply embedded in my genetic makeup, but I was determined to do everything within my power to keep her out of harm's way.

She turned and caught me looking at her. I didn't look away.

"Well, Stuart, you finally get your wish: a full view of an active volcano. How does that make you feel?"

My eyes lingered in hers while I thought about it. Strange how fear of fanatics and volcanoes so easily melted. I was safe in her gaze, and she was safe in mine, secure in that mystical aura of familiarity that gently wooed and caressed our souls like the ticking waves that lapped at *Penelope*'s hull. There was a lot about my feelings for Niki that I did not understand. She was different from other women, and I wanted time to know what made her that way.

"I suppose if I was a volcanologist," I said, pulling out of her gaze and turning back toward the spectacle of Kyropos, "I'd be on the verge of an orgasm about now. Terrifyingly beautiful—that's the closest I can come to describing it." I didn't look at her when I added, "Reminds me of someone I know."

I could feel her eyes still on me when she slipped an arm through mine. The warmth of her bare skin on my arm made me tingle. I could think of no immediate reason to resist. Marion was an abstraction, a floating piece of last night's dream that bore no connection to the living pulse of this electric moment.

"I never thanked you for what you did today," she said, a fingertip playing gently with the hair of my arm. "You saved my life."

With the possibility that Niki was right about Marion leaving me, the barriers between us were crumbling; red lights were turning green, though I still carried enough of that weight of responsibility for Marion to keep plenty of flashing yellows going.

"Don't thank me yet. This day's not over."

"Then I have time to decide *how* I will thank you."

Her playfully seductive tone disarmed me and sent my mind careening through intimate possibilities. Suddenly I had us in bed together, kissing, caressing, making love under the blanket of a warm sea breeze. What a delight that would be. I had to make a conscious effort to look up at the yellows still flashing, urging me to douse that vision and proceed with caution.

"Right now I'd settle for a glass of wine in one of those quiet little beachfront tavernas on Santorini, watching the sun go down."

"That would be nice." Her hold on my upper arm tightened ever so slightly. "I would be sitting with you?"

Nothing would have pleased me more, but I couldn't get myself to say it, not out loud, not to her. Time to lighten things up a bit. "You buying the drinks?"

"Perhaps," she said, with an eyebrow cocked in a way that said she understood what I was doing.

"Perhaps? Doesn't sound like you're sure you want to be there."

"Me? Not sure? Yes, I buy. You have my word. Do you wish for me to sign a contract?"

Her annoyance at my petty humor was delightful; it made her so cute I wanted to throw an arm around her and give her a good squeezing. "Okay, you'd be there."

"And when we finish the wine?"

Instantly, we were back in bed, engaged in the full array of bedroom pleasantries. She was on tiptoe, trying to peek into my mind as if it were an open window. I quickly drew the shade and threw the problem back on her. "You're the one doing the thanking."

She slipped into a momentary silence, head tilted, the corner of her mouth raised into enough of a smile to show that I was supposed to be in the spot she was in.

"I will have to think about this," was all she said.

With the Zodiac patched and sitting high in the water, Threader called everyone around the table to outline his plan. I hoped it'd be better than mine.

"This is Kyropos," he said, pointing to a map he'd scrawled on a piece of cardboard. "We're somewhere out here on the western side. That band of yahoos is most likely gathered right here." He drew a circle indicating the spot. "Now here, in the cliff wall, there's a string of caves."

"I remember," I said, images of the caves and their loitering, robe-clad occupants suddenly impinging on my mind.

Threader, annoyed, was doubtful. "How the hell can you remember caves you ain't never seen?"

"There's a big cluster of boulders right here." I tapped the point on the map. "It's a *feeling*, Threader."

Threader studied me as if I were a two-headed goat. He made an *X* at the spot. "Don't tell me how the hell you know it, but you're right. Now, if we can get here"—he pointed to the *X*—"we can see what's going on and figure out what to do next."

"Not we, Threader," I said, recalling my plan. "Father Jon and I will go in. You and Niki will stay with the boat and keep it ready for our exit."

"Is that right, Adams? Thought we settled the authority issue a while ago."

I'd gotten a few more details of the plan worked out. "Think about it, Threader. No one knows how to handle this boat as well as you. You get us in close; the father and I paddle the Zodiac to shore. You and Niki circle out here and wait. We signal with the flashlight when we get the scroll, we paddle back out, you swoop in and pick us up, and we head home."

A few moments passed as everyone considered the plan. Niki was the first to speak.

"It is a good plan, Stuart Adams. But you leave out one thing."

"You're not going," I said, anticipating her response. "You'll be safer on the boat with Threader."

"Ha! You will not tell me what I will or will not do. How about if you stay on the boat and I go? Then I would know that you would be safe. You think the whole world should take your orders? I do not take orders from you. If you go, I go. It is final."

She crossed her arms and glowered at me like a five-year-old brat refusing to eat spinach. I glowered right back, knowing I'd have better luck staring down a marble statue of the Great Mother.

"All right," I said, finally. "You want to go? Fine. But when we get to these rocks"—I drove a finger hard into the map—"that's where you're staying. You're going to watch us go in, and you're going to signal Threader when we start coming out. Now you either agree to that, or I'm going to hog-tie you, put a gag in that mouth of yours, and lock you in your cabin."

She leaned forward, her eyes fixed murderously on mine. She spoke in slow, lethal tones.

"You will not be hog-tying me."

For a long time I held her beautifully scorching glare. *If anything happened to her ...* I didn't finish the thought, but it wouldn't have mattered if I had. If she was set on going, no one was going to change her mind. I just slumped back in my seat, closed my eyes, and laughed out a defeated breath of consent.

Chapter 18

IN COMPLETE DARKNESS, THREADER UNFURLED just enough of the jib to ease the *Penelope* in toward the glowing spectacle of Kyropos. In my backpack I carried a hammer, a chisel, a waterproof bag, and a photograph of the scroll. We'd need the tools to deal with the plaster patch. The bag was for the scroll, essential against any possibility of the fragile artifact getting wet. We'd use the photograph for scroll verification.

I intended to avoid an encounter with the fanatics, but just in case, I stuffed Vito's pistol under my belt. Niki had her knife and the flashlight. Father Jon carried a small wrecking bar and a pair of binoculars.

Niki and Father Jon climbed into the Zodiac. When I stepped in, I noticed that Father Jon was using the wrecking bar to poke at something in the water. "What is it?" I asked.

"I do not know," said Father Jon. "It is something hard with little spikes poking out all over."

Threader's jaw dropped. "Father! Stop poking that damn thing! That's a mine!"

"A what?"

"A mine! You're gonna blow us to kingdom come!"

Father Jon recoiled as if he'd been bitten by a snake. He stumbled over Niki and plunged backward into the water. When he came up thrashing and gasping for air, the wrecking bar was gone. Niki and I lugged him back in the boat before he drew every shark in the region.

Threader, ignoring the choking monk, studied the mine. "Looks like World War II vintage. They're still finding the odd one. Probably rusted from its tethering cable." He tossed me the end of a rope. "Here, tie her on. I want to know where this baby is." He secured the other end of the rope to the deck railing and then used a grappling hook to push the mine away from the *Penelope*. "There. That ought to keep you out of mischief."

We paddled to shore and picked our way over ground spastic with tremors. From the cluster of boulders, we could see the torch-lit camp of the Children of Light. There was a puzzle. The fifty or so white-robed figures were lying like spokes in a wagon wheel around a large, flat stone. Father Jon studied the group through the binoculars.

"What are they doing?" Niki asked.

"I do not know. They are … they are lying facedown, their heads pointed toward the center rock … an altar, perhaps. They could be praying. I cannot tell for sure, but it … it looks like there is something on the altar. Vessels … many vessels … like the chalice for wine."

I glanced toward the beach where four cabin-type cruisers lay anchored. "What about the boats? Anyone over there?"

"No movement. Nothing."

"We'll go in and have a look," I said to Niki. "You gonna be a good girl and stay put?"

"Yes, daddy. Your little girl promises to stay put." She wrinkled her bratty face. "Satisfied?"

It was the best I was going to get. I pulled the pistol from my belt, and the father and I started to our feet.

"Wait," Niki said. With no warning, she grabbed the front of my shirt and pulled me in for a long, hard kiss. "Stuart, promise me you will come back."

"I'll be back," I said, recapturing my breath. "I've never been known to miss a free drink." The tension between Niki and me was growing, and I wasn't sure how to stop it, or even if I wanted to.

The father and I were a hundred yards from the camp, and still there was no movement from the fanatics. Strange. We eased in: fifty yards, twenty-five, close enough for me to toss a fist-sized rock a few feet from one of the figures. No response.

"Wait here," I said, and I crawled to within a few yards of one of the prostrated figures, a man. He didn't move—no sign of even a breath. I stood slowly, crouched, and trained the pistol on the middle of his back, not knowing exactly what I'd do if the man moved. I tapped his foot with my own. Nothing. I knelt again and felt the leg of the next person, a woman. Her flesh was cool, stiff. I stepped to the next body and pulled back the hood. It was another woman, probably in her twenties. I laid the backs of my fingers over her cold jugular. I was touching a corpse.

Father Jon, his face pale even in the glow of Kyropos, joined me. "They are ... they are dead?"

"Looks that way."

The father surveyed the bodies, stepped carefully to the altar, and lifted one of the chalices to his nose. "I do not know what this is. It is not wine. Poison perhaps."

"Suicide?"

"It would appear to be so. I must have a prayer."

"You do that, Father. I'm going to have a look around."

I plucked a torch from the sand and trotted toward the wall of caves, the same caves, I suddenly realized, that I'd seen in my vision on the Rock. I stopped at the mouth of one of the caves. The ground heaved, and a flurry of stones peppered the area around the entrance. Going in was risky, too risky, but I had no choice. The shaking subsided. I stuffed my fear, ducked inside, and swept the eerie darkness with the torch and the pistol.

The cave was a large open chamber with a series of smaller rooms carved into the back. The rooms, all of them, had cots, neatly arranged in straight, barracks-like fashion. The fractured ceiling was a moving jigsaw puzzle ready to collapse. I scoured the walls, but there was no plaster patch.

A massive stockpile of arms filled the next cave: machine guns, pistols, shotguns, bazookas, ground-to-air missile launchers, wooden boxes filled with ammunition. There was enough firepower to equip a good-sized army, but there was no plaster patch.

Another cave, more weaponry. I started to leave, but something in the shadows caught my attention—a knee-high opening in the back wall.

With my heart about to pound through my chest, I pushed past my fear of being buried alive and squeezed through the hole. In another room, I stood and drew shallow breaths from the dead air, scared as hell.

I was staring at a room lined with rough wooden shelves, filled with hundreds, maybe thousands, of books. I laid the pistol on a shelf, planted the butt of the torch into the sandy floor, and lifted one of the leather-bound volumes. The musty smell of antiquity greeted me when I cracked it open. I couldn't read Greek, but I knew I was looking at hand-copied lettering of that language, a calligraphic masterpiece. I wished Niki could have seen it. The brittle pages wanted to crumble in my fingers. I'd once done research on the lost library of Alexandria, mysteriously destroyed centuries before. Was I looking at a salvaged remnant of the half a million volumes, the crowning prize of that ancient intellectual world? Niki probably would have known.

There was no time to ponder the mystery. I spotted a second room and ducked in. Shelves filled with scrolls, thousands, lined the walls like neatly stacked firewood. Overwhelmed by the sheer number, I started to reach for one but stopped when a flicker of light suddenly danced through the entrance. I figured it was Father Jon, but I reached for the pistol anyway. I'd left it in the first room. I was relieved to see the father's face appear through the opening, a torch in one hand, one of the old books in the other.

Father Jon held up the book, his eyes twinkling in the torchlight. "Did you see this?" He was breathless with excitement. "There must be hundr—" He suddenly noticed the hoard of scrolls. "Mother of God!" He moved toward one of the shelves like a witness to the Resurrection. With trembling hands, he laid down the book and lifted one of the scrolls. "Aramaic," he announced just above a whisper. "Isaiah." He turned a slow, gaping gaze on me. "We do not have Isaiah in Aramaic, only Hebrew ... and Greek. The world, it ... it has never seen this."

Then, another shock wave rocked the room. The stone above our heads cracked with the earsplitting blast of cannon fire. The ground shook and threatened to knock us from our feet. A bed-sized chunk of ceiling moved directly above the father. I grabbed the back of his shirt and yanked just as the monster dropped, burying the entire rack of scrolls in an impenetrable grave.

Through choking dust, I could see Father Jon scramble over the heap, clawing violently, futilely, at the huge slab. The light of the remaining torch was enough for me to see that the walls had become a web of newly opened fractures.

"It's no use," I screamed above the horrific din. "This place is gonna go!"

The words had just left my mouth when the shaking resumed. I grabbed Father Jon's arm and forced him back through the entrance.

That's when I saw it—a mailbox-sized hole in the wall. Even through the thick dust, I could see that the outer rim of the hole still bore the remains of a plaster plug, cracked out, no doubt, in the last few minutes.

Enormous slabs of stone groaned and shifted overhead, dropping bushels of dirt and rock over everything. I scrambled for the hole and thrust my hand into the opening. I felt a soft, cylindrical package about two inches in diameter. I snatched it out. There was no time to put it in the backpack. I stuffed it inside my T-shirt and then dashed for the opening. Just then, something hit me in the back of the head with enough force to send me to my knees. Dazed, I crawled through the thick curtain of choking dust until I reached the entrance. I stood, but a blast of hot air slammed into my back and threw me facedown into the sand.

"Avalanche!" I heard Father Jon scream.

In the next instant, the father was tugging at my arm. Coaxing me to my feet, Father Jon led me like a stumbling invalid over corpses and stones to the fragile protection of a huge boulder near the water's edge. We hunkered into the sand. The doomsdayer boats blazed at the shore, victims of the shower of flaming missiles that rained down in every direction. We were like insects cowering behind a tiny stone about to be buried alive in the horrific onslaught. There was nothing we could do but wait.

Then, the hideous roar subsided. I glanced around the boulder. I could see that the avalanche was spent, but it had swallowed the caves and the corpses.

Father Jon slumped against the boulder and stared blankly at the burning boats.

"God is with us this day," he said. "But, to think that I had in my hands the book of Isaiah ... in Aramaic ... it is ... it is almost more than I can bear." With both palms, he tried to wipe the strain of remorse from his face. "I will go to my grave regretting that I put it back on the shelf."

A stabbing pain erupted in the back of my head. I pulled the leather package from my shirt and handed it to Father Jon. "Maybe not all's lost," I said, leaning my head gingerly against the boulder. "I've got a feeling we got the brass ring."

Father Jon studied the leather object; then, with the dexterity of a surgeon, he carefully untied the thong and he unrolled the wrapping that protected what appeared to be a parchment roll. Slowly, he unfurled a portion of the scroll.

I removed my backpack to get the photograph and the waterproof bag. When I handed the photo to Father Jon, I noticed something odd in one of the shoulder straps, a tiny bulge, as if a pebble had somehow gotten wedged between the two layers of fabric that formed the strap. At the top of the strap, on the inside, I noticed a patch of black fabric adhesive tape. When I peeled it back, I saw that the tape covered a small slit. I worked the lump out through the slit. The tiny object was no pebble, but a black capsule, an antitheft device installed, no doubt, by the retailer. It was an expensive backpack, but it was still odd, I thought, that they'd go to that much trouble to guard against shoplifters. I tossed the capsule.

"It … it is Linear A," Father Jon announced in an almost breathless whisper." It only took another moment for him to let out a gasp. "This is it! My God, we have the scroll!"

My sudden flush of joy was countered by the sight of blood oozing down the front of my shirt. The falling rock had opened a gash in the back of my throbbing head.

Then, the beach trembled, and I could hear a new wave of rock cascading down the cliffs.

"Get the scroll in the bag," I said, struggling to my feet. "We've got to get out of here." When I stood, a wave of blackness washed over my vision. I thought I was going to faint. Father Jon zipped the scroll in the waterproof bag; he started to hand it to me but stopped.

"You are bleeding," he said, looking at the front of my shirt. "Give me the backpack. I will carry the scroll."

"I'm all right," I barked. I stuffed the scroll in the backpack and slipped it on. "Let's get the hell out of here."

We ran over the undulating sand toward the rocks where Niki

waited. When we reached the rocks, a blaze of blinding light blasted into my eyes. I threw up an arm to block the beam.

"Niki, turn that thing off."

A man's laugh, sinister, chilling, stopped me cold.

Gustavo Giacopetti.

Chapter 19

THE FLASHLIGHT BEAM DROPPED, SWEPT across the ground, and then stopped on Niki's face. Through inky blotches, I squinted to see Niki standing stiff, gagged, hands tied behind her back, one cheekbone badly swollen. She hadn't been taken peacefully. Giacopetti stood behind her, clasping a handful of hair, the point of her own knife pressed against her throat. Somewhere in the blackness, Vito and Apollo lurked, though I was still too blinded to see them.

I started for Giacopetti. I had caught only a glimpse of Vito's face when he swiped a pistol across the side of my head. I staggered against the excruciating pain, but I willed my body to remain standing. The blaring light returned. The patch of blood on the front of my shirt grew rapidly.

"What a surprise," Giacopetti said. "If it isn't Mr. Adams. My, you do not look so well. Perhaps you are surprised to see us as well?" He lifted a telephone from inside his jacket and held it up. "One of the *many* perks of my position," he said, grinning like an alligator. "Satellite telephones and good friends with fast boats make a wonderful combination. Don't you think?"

I could just make out the grumble of the idling motor.

"Let her go," I demanded.

"Let her go? But why would I do that? We are just starting to get to know each other, the doctor and I. She has much to say, this one, so much, in fact, that, unfortunately, we were forced to silence her. But, I believe the lovely Dr. Mikos has something that she would like to tell you." Giacopetti slipped the knife blade beneath the gag and cut it. Niki spat it from her mouth. "Better? Ah yes, such a beautiful mouth." He stroked her cheek, and she pulled away, her eyes flashing with hatred. "Go ahead, my feisty little angel. Tell Mr. Adams what you have learned."

"Captain Threader," Niki said, her face distorted in anguish. "They … they have killed him."

I squinted out over the water. I could see the *Penelope* engulfed in a firestorm.

"It is a shame about your Captain Threader," Giacopetti said. "I do not think he will be leaving the boat this time. But then a captain is supposed to go down with his ship, is he not?" He laughed like the fiend that he was. "I have another amusing revelation for you, Mr. Adams." He held up the telephone so I could see its blue LCD screen. On the screen I could just make out a bold black arrow. "Voice communication is not all this telephone is good for." With the tip of the knife blade, he pointed to the arrow. "Here we have a marvelous feature, an innovation of my government designed to track stolen artifacts that we equip with tiny transmitters. Allow me to demonstrate." He studied the screen. "You, for example, left your transmitter about a hundred meters due south from here."

The capsule. It was no antitheft device. It was a transmitter. I'd been a walking GPS unit since Rome! That's why Giacopetti had never made a surprise visit to Sarnafi. He'd been tracking our every move.

"You look unpleasantly astonished, Mr. Adams. It may surprise you even more to learn that Colonel De Santis of Vatican security is a business associate of mine. It was one of his sons that … *borrowed* … your backpack."

Kyropos bellowed.

"Well now, I could stand here all evening and chat with you, Mr. Adams, but Kyropos urges us to complete our business. I assume you found the scroll, so if you would just hand it over to Vito, the beautiful doctor and I will be on our way."

I wanted to tear into Giacopetti, but with twenty feet and a pair of crack marksmen cocked and ready, I wouldn't make it ten steps. I had no other choice. I pulled off the blood-soaked backpack and held it out to Vito.

"No!" Father Jon screamed and lunged for the backpack.

Apollo came down hard with the flashlight to the back of the father's neck, sending him sprawling to the ground. In that same instant, I charged Giacopetti, screaming and slinging the pack into his face. The hammer inside the pack must have found its mark. Giacopetti let out an agonizing yowl, dropped the knife, and clutched at his face. A nanosecond later, Vito pounced from behind, locking me in a bear hug. Apollo lumbered toward me.

In a rage, I came up hard with a foot to Apollo's crotch. The big man doubled, and I landed another solid kick to his face. Apollo's head snapped back, and he stumbled to the ground. I tore free from Vito's grip, spun, and delivered a series of savage blows to his face. A jolt to my kidneys forced me to my knees. I rolled to see Apollo standing over me, his gun ready to fire.

Then, the big man stiffened and gasped. Blood suddenly poured over his lip; his eyes almost bulged from their sockets. He made a half turn, clutching at the handle of Niki's knife protruding from the center of his back. Apollo took two wobbling steps and crumpled.

Father Jon stood over him, his mouth wide open, his eyes insanely distorted.

Vito was on hands and knees searching frantically among the scattered rocks for his gun. I had to get to him before he found the gun. I lunged, and at the same instant the ground heaved, throwing me into a bruising cluster of rocks. In the next second, Vito was looming over me with a huge rock poised to crush my skull. Feet away, the earth split and belched hot gas from its fiery throat. Vito turned in horror. Another jolting ground shift sent him plunging headlong into the gaping inferno.

I staggered to my feet and surveyed what was happening. Giacopetti and Niki were gone. I was standing on a swaying island of rock connected to the main ground only by a boulder that had fallen and lodged in the chasm. It quavered, ready to drop.

"Hurry!" Father Jon screamed. "You must cross now!"

There was no time to think. I ran, planted a foot on the boulder, and started to launch myself to the other side of the chasm. The boulder gave way. I had just enough momentum to make the edge, though my legs dangled over the scorching heat. Father Jon slapped a hand on my back and pulled me up.

Bruised and bleeding, I scrambled to my feet. "Niki! Giacopetti took her."

"And the scroll," Father Jon yelled back. "We must hurry."

We were too late. We reached the shore just in time to watch the boat speed away.

"The Zodiac!" I yelled, scanning the empty beach. "We've got to get to the Zodiac."

"It is not there," Father Jon called back. "Giacopetti must have—"

Something the father saw out in the water stopped him. I followed his gaze to the irregular blinking of a tiny white light.

"It is a signal," Father Jon said. "Someone is signaling Giacopetti."

Then, a flash and a huge orange mushroom obliterated the blackness. Seconds later, the thunder of the explosion rolled in off the water; the remains of Giacopetti's boat rained down in a shower of flames.

Against everything my eyes told me was true, I screamed out over the water. "Niki!" The sound of my voice was swallowed in the growing fury of Kyropos, but I screamed her name again. I couldn't stop myself.

"The mine," Father Jon said, in an anguished whimper. "It must have burned free from the rope and drifted out."

The father's speculation was all too plausible. I closed my eyes and imagined the scenario. All the strength drained from my legs. I sank to my knees and pushed fingers through my soggy, blood-caked hair, stopping short of the stinging gash in the back of my head. Slumped, face cradled in palms, I no longer cared that the earth was tearing itself apart.

MUCH TIME PASSED BEFORE I could lift my face. All emotion had drained from my being. My ears rang, and I had a splitting headache. I was in dead shock. It was all I could do to speak.

"The search for truth, Father, is this where it ends?" The question seeped from a black sludge of remorse pooled in my gut. Five less minutes in that cave, and Niki would still be alive. "A cruel finality that leaves you holding nothing? Is this where it all leads?"

The father melted into a cross-legged heap next to me. His eyes, zombielike, swollen orbs still fixed on the flaming disaster, scarcely blinked. When he spoke, his voice was dry, small, and cracked beyond recognition. "I … I do not know how to answer this question."

"Maybe that's what she was trying to say. It's all about the journey. It's got to be, because the destination"—I drew a shallow, choking breath—"the destination sucks."

Father Jon lowered his face into his hands and wept softly.

I lay back in the sand, watched embers float eerily through the air, and listened to the building fury of Kyropos. "You know, Father, it's a strange thing. I've spent most of my life trying to get somewhere. I wonder how much I've missed." Another explosion sent a huge flaming ball over the ocean. Normally, I would have been awestruck by such a sight. Now, I watched in a kind of passive curiosity as the missile plunged into the water. "Maybe it's the fear of dying that's been driving me, like I've got to hurry up and grab on to something big, leave some kind of a mark before I check out." A numb chuckle escaped through the dryness of my parched lips. "Jesus. Here I am, number called, standing next in line at the counter, my time to check out. You know what? I'm not even afraid, not anymore." I rolled my head to face my unresponsive friend. "Is this how it is before we die, Father? We just kind of lose our ability to feel?"

Father Jon raised his anguish-cracked face slowly from his hands. "Oh God, what has happened? The scroll is lost forever."

Did I hear him right? Niki was dead, and he was worried about the scroll?

"Who gives a damn about the scroll?" I said, my voice bitter with resentment.

He just glared at me, detached, cold, overwhelmed, I figured, by shock. Then he stood, staring at me, shaking his head as if I was the pathetic fool too dense to grasp the value of such a priceless treasure. The look on his face left me with no doubt that, to him, the loss of the scroll far outweighed the mere loss of a single human life—even Niki's.

Suddenly a dam of primordial rage threatened to burst in me. I wanted to kill him.

His own animal instincts must have sensed it, for, without saying another word, he quickly turned away, vanishing into the darkness of the beach.

I started after him, but in a moment of clarity, I regained enough of my sanity to stop. I would kill Father Jon? I sunk back into the sand. My stomach rolled, and I thought I might vomit. I suppressed the urge, closed my eyes, and pulled my knees hard into my chest to quell the trembling in my hands.

The ground shook violently. I turned and saw that a massive bulge had formed in the side of Kyropos. The magma chamber had risen into a gargantuan boil about to burst. I was too exhausted to feel anything but the numb realization that I had come to the final moments of my life.

I lay back in the sand thinking of Marion, and I wondered how she'd get the news. Barnes would find a way. He'd have to reach beyond his own grief for Niki, but he'd do it. I turned back toward the sea. *Penelope* still burned, though it wouldn't be long before she slipped away, taking Threader's remains with her. That was the way he wanted it: go down with dignity on a good boat.

Father Jon had been gone for only a few minutes when I saw him returning. His eyes were still downcast, and he kicked the sand as he approached. I gathered my legs and stood, hoping he had reclaimed some of his sanity. If we were going to die together, it seemed to me that it would be best to do it as friends.

Then, a movement fifty yards offshore drew my attention. I squinted into the dismal black and watched until I was certain that I was looking at the flailing arms of a swimmer.

"Father!"

Father Jon came up beside me, his eyes wide with hope. I pointed. The father still had the binoculars around his neck. He took a step forward and raised them.

"Niki!" he said in a gasp of disbelief. "It is Niki!"

I took a running dive into the surf. By the time I reached her, she was so exhausted she could barely keep her face above the surface. The straps of the backpack had tangled around her neck and one arm. I grabbed her shirt at the shoulder, drawing on strength I should not have had. Minutes later, my feet touched sand. I ripped the backpack from Niki's delirious grasp and flung it to Father Jon.

I scooped Niki into my arms and slogged toward the beach. We fell into the dry sand, sobbing ecstatically and grasping desperately at each other. Father Jon, busy tearing into the backpack, was no doubt checking the scroll for damage. The wide-eyed glow on his face told me that it had survived the ordeal unscathed.

Niki pushed away from me and stood on unsteady legs. "Captain Threader. He … he signaled to me. Our code. He flashed his name."

"The light," Father Jon said, slipping on the backpack. "That is what we saw."

Exhausted, I was relieved that the father had taken responsibility for the scroll; I was still confused by his odd behavior but even more confused about the fate of Threader. "I thought Giacopetti kil—"

"No," Niki said, cutting me off. "Giacopetti must have thought he killed him. It was Captain Threader. That … that mine. He had it tied to the front of the Zodiac. I could barely see it. The instant before the impact, I grabbed the backpack and dove from the boat." She buried her face in her hands, sobbing. "He … he was truly a brave man."

In that instant, I caught a faint beating sound. It faded and then returned, growing more distinct by the second. "Listen," I said, searching the sky. "I think I hear a chopper."

All eyes went up.

"There!" Niki shouted. "I see it! Someone is coming."

A light from the chopper splashed over the beach. We ran to meet the aircraft with shouts and waving arms, watching in disbelief as it touched down in a whirlwind of sand. A man in fatigues, armed with a machine gun, emerged, ducking beneath the spinning blades.

"Stop!" the man shouted suddenly, unleashing a warning burst of machine gun fire. "Come no closer."

We froze in startled confusion. The ground trembled.

"Stay where you are," the man ordered. "I have come for Raphael."

"Raphael is dead," Niki shouted to the pilot, her voice barely penetrating the roar. "Please, we need your help." She took a step toward him.

"I said stay where you are!" the man screamed, leveling the barrel of the machine gun straight at her. "I swear I will kill you."

I threw a hand on Niki's shoulder and pulled her back.

In a bold move, Father Jon began walking straight toward the man. What was he doing? Was he delirious? Did he think he could buy our safety with his spiritual status?

"Father Jon," I yelled. "Come back. Don't do anything stupid."

The father kept walking. Expecting another burst of gunfire, I pulled Niki closer and braced to throw her on the ground. I didn't want her to see her friend cut to pieces in a spray of bullets. She trembled beneath her wet clothing.

Father Jon stepped boldly in front of the pilot and stood motionless for a few seconds. The man showed no reaction and made no move to stop him. Then, the father said something, nodded slightly, and a smile came over the pilot's face. The monk had mastered the situation. Suddenly I knew that bringing him along had been the right thing to do. I relaxed when the father turned slowly toward us, a big smile of pride covering his face. We had the scroll, and now we had a way off Kyropos. I could scarcely believe our good fortune.

Then, Father Jon did something I didn't expect. He reached beneath his shirttail and pulled from the waistband of his shorts the pistol I'd left in the cave. Why hadn't he given it to me sooner?

Kyropos roared again, and the ground shook violently. It was time to get out of there. What was taking Father Jon so long?

Still smiling, Father Jon explained, "My friends, there is something that I have been meaning to tell you. I know this may come as a bit of a surprise, but I am the one they call *Raphael.*"

Chapter 20

FATHER JON'S STUNNING REVELATION ECLIPSED even the horrifying roar of Kyropos. His words and actions just didn't register. Worse still, the pilot of the helicopter was not there to pluck us from the jaws of certain death. It was too impossible to imagine. Then, I remembered the father's steely eyes, the hardened face that I suddenly did not know. I remembered my first impression of him, the pleasure he seemed to take in disguising his role as a monk. Now it was all so clear. How could I have allowed myself to trust the son of a bitch?

I glanced at Niki, and she at me. Her face was drawn, bruised and swollen, smudged with the fine grime of ash that thickened the air. Mine must have looked the same. She turned back toward the father, pale, swooning like a victim of fever. If I hadn't been holding her, we both might have collapsed.

"Father Jon," Niki said, her voice full of pleading, "what are you doing? What are you saying? I … I do not understand."

"Of course you do not understand," Father Jon said with a heartless sneer. "Everyone, including your father, believed that Gustavo Giacopetti was the great Rafael. Who would ever suspect a humble little monk from Santorini?" His laugh was suddenly menacing, his expression hard. He fondled the pistol as easily as a set of rosary beads. "*I* am Rafael," he said, thumping his chest with the pistol. "*Raphael, the brilliant mastermind of the world's most successful smuggling ring*— that is how the newspapers describe me. Giacopetti was a bumbling idiot, a brainless thug that thought he was smart enough to get the scroll and leave me here to die. But look!" He shook the backpack. "See who has the scroll! See who is alive and who is dead! Satan rest his rotten soul."

At that moment, I realized we were staring at the tortured face of a madman.

Then, Father Jon reached into the pocket of his shorts and produced a wafer-thin cell phone. He unfolded it and held it up. "The wonders of modern electronics."

"Your little walk on the beach?" I said, remembering that I'd thought he'd needed the time alone to grieve. "You were calling your buddy."

"And you were sniveling about the great injustices of life. Very depressing. As you can see, there are no injustices ... at least not for me."

"And your little speech on truth?" I shouted back. "All one big lie, right?"

Kyropos bellowed, and every head turned.

Father Jon, pistol ready, nodded to his pilot, who had already scrambled into the chopper and was beginning to throttle the engine.

Father Jon pulled open the passenger door to board. "A big lie?" he shouted. "By no means. You see, I have already secured a buyer for the scroll. You will be disappointed to know, of course, that he does not happen to live on Pialigos. He is, in fact, Russian. But he promises that he will give the scroll a very secure home. Two hundred million dollars—that will buy one hell of a lot of truth."

Suddenly the ground quavered violently, nearly knocking us from our feet. Father Jon stepped into the helicopter.

"What are you going to do about us?" Niki shouted after them.

"I do not think I will have to do anything—this time," Father Jon shouted back. "Kyropos seems eager enough to finish this unpleasant task."

Niki looked puzzled. "What do you mean, 'this time'?"

"You still do not understand?" Father Jon said. "Your father. His documentation. He would have upset my network. I could not allow him to do that."

"You?" Niki pulled herself from me. "You killed my father?"

"I assure you," Father Jon said through a soulless grin, "he felt no pain."

"Bastard!" The word exploded from Niki's mouth. She started for the chopper, but the spinning blades kicked up too much sand. She threw up an arm and was forced to turn away. As the chopper lifted, the blast of sand subsided. Niki screamed curses at the fleeing men.

"I will kill you!" Niki shrieked. "I will hunt you down, and I will kill you." She kicked the sand and stood working her fingers, grasping nothing.

Father Jon waved through the bubble of glass, and Niki, exasperated, dropped to her knees and buried her face in her hands, sobbing.

An instant later, a tremendous explosion split the air, shaking the entire beach. Kyropos coughed like some alien monster dying. A gigantic amoeba of sprawling lava surged through the sky, engulfed the chopper like a toy, and then plunged with hissing violence into the black water.

Niki stood and I stepped next to her, both of us shocked to see two men vaporized before our eyes. Added to this was Father Jon's stunning revelation. The filth of deception that I felt would not compare to what must have been going through Niki at that moment. She'd befriended the murderer of her father, shared secrets, and invested a trust reserved for the rarest and closest of friends—a priest, for God's sake. Now I understood why he expressed more concern for the scroll than for Niki. He'd never cared about her; he'd only used her to get his hands on the scroll. He'd succeeded, but his success was fleeting. Justice had been done, horrible justice, for the world would never know the treasure it had just lost.

Now there was nothing to do but wait. Our only good fortune was that the wind carried the ash and the poison gases away from us. If the wind shifted, it would be a slow, choking death.

I couldn't bear the thought of watching Niki die. I took her in my arms, and she nuzzled her face in my chest; in that moment I knew that ours was not the embrace of two souls merely clinging in fear against the onslaught of terrifying forces. It was the rising of a deeper connection. Niki lifted her face, and our lips met. For me, there was a profoundly satisfying sense of fulfillment in that kiss, as if every struggle I'd ever had with love was utterly and completely resolved. I knew she felt it too, and I wanted to see it in her face. I pulled back and touched the tears that streamed down her cheeks.

Like a thousand Aegean sunsets, the beauty of her soul burned indelibly into my mind. Somehow it no longer mattered that we stood at the end of our earthly lives; it only mattered that we had arrived at this moment together.

Her eyes searched and locked on something in mine; her lips quivered as she struggled for words.

"Don't say anything," I said, pulling her back to my chest. Words could only diminish what I felt. I closed my eyes wanting only to die with that picture of her face in my mind.

Niki pulled away from me again. "There is something that I must tell you."

I waited, but she was suddenly distracted, attentive to some sound mixed in the roar of the volcano. She pushed away from me and took a few steps toward the water. "Do you hear it?"

"Hear what?" I moved beside her.

"Look!" She pointed. "Another helicopter!"

I heard the beating of the blades first. Then I spotted the blinking lights of the chopper. It couldn't be true. A spotlight flooded the beach. We shielded our eyes and stood in absolute awe watching the heavenly craft descend like a lumbering angel through a stinging cloud of sand. By some inexplicable miracle, this angel bore the wings of the United States Air Force.

THE MEDIC ATTENDING THE GASH in my head explained that Threader had sent out the Mayday. Niki and I pieced together the rest of the story. Giacopetti had put a bullet in Threader, torched the *Penelope*, and swooped in to relieve us of the scroll. Threader revived and called in the Mayday. Somehow, he swam to Kyropos, retrieved the Zodiac, and then paddled back to the *Penelope* undetected by Giacopetti's driver. He managed to tie the mine to the front of the Zodiac, position himself for the ambush, and pray that Niki had seen his signal.

Safe in the chopper with Niki asleep against my chest, I wondered what she had been about to tell me just before the rescue. Part of me wanted to wake her and find out. Another part was afraid of what she might say. Was she involved with someone? If so, why would she lead me on?

The scroll was lost. My reason for staying on Sarnafi had disintegrated into a disappointing end. What next? Would Niki want me to stay? Had Marion left me? What would I do if she hadn't?

A wave of exhaustion pushed my eyes closed, and in a swirl of unresolved questions, I tumbled into deep sleep.

THE SUN WAS COMING UP when the pilot dropped us off by a roadside just outside of Perivolos. Flat with fatigue, Niki and I trudged to the dock and caught a ride to Sarnafi with a fisherman setting out for his day's work. The fisherman explained that Sarnafi had sustained only minor damage from the tsunami. Pialigos had dodged it altogether. Just then my only care was that there was at least one undamaged bed that I could fall into.

When we approached Sarnafi, we could see Barnes's boat moored offshore. Nicholas was sorting through what was left of the dock. The gazebo had vanished.

"I was on Santorini when the wave hit," Nicholas explained, "so the boat was spared. The dock and the gazebo, they were not so lucky. But no matter—such things can be rebuilt." He took a deep breath and placed a hand on Niki's shoulder. In a somber tone, he explained, "Mr. Barnes, he is not so good. His heart, I think it gives him problems."

Nicholas wasn't the kind to issue false alarms. Niki didn't wait for him to retrieve the golf cart and drive us to the villa. She threw off her exhaustion and shot up the stairs in a near run. My body was made of lead, and it was all I could do to keep up, but I stayed with her. There was no way I was going to let her face this crisis alone.

At the patio, a worried Dora scurried from the house. "Niki, thank God you are here," she cried out, wringing her hands. "Mr. Barnes, he has been asking for you. For days now, he asks only for you."

We scrambled through the house straight for Barnes's bedroom. Through the half-opened door, I could see him lying in his bed, perfectly still, eyes closed, his skin white as death.

Were we too late?

I watched Niki take slow, tentative steps across the room, lowering herself gently, tenderly, to a seat on the edge of the bed.

I leaned against the casing of the door, needing a moment to indulge in some good old-fashioned self-pity. After all we'd been through—cheated out of the scroll, losing everything but our lives and the clothes on our backs—and this is what we got? Barnes's corpse?

Damn you, Barnes. How could you dump this on us now?

Niki was as tired as I was, drawing on hidden reserves of strength. She had to be hovering somewhere near her emotional bottom. Her father had been murdered, one friend had been killed on Kyropos, and another friend had betrayed her. Now Barnes was either dead or close to it. Incredibly, she was ready to meet the situation head-on. I'd never witnessed this much strength in anyone—man or woman.

In contrast, my mind was so fogged, so flaccid with defeat, that I was sure I couldn't fill half a thimble with what I had left to give. I pushed myself away from the door and stood directly behind Niki. I could see her face in the large mirror of a vanity on the other side of the bed. Pale and drawn, her eyes circled with fatigue, she searched anxiously for any flicker of life that might stir in the still remains of her old friend.

Barnes surprised us both when his eyelids suddenly twitched and fluttered open. For the next few seconds, I watched his glassy eyes wander like two lost spirits across the ceiling. He rolled his head slightly, and his eyes settled on Niki. A frail smile of recognition brought some life to his pallid face.

"Niki, darling. You're safe."

"Yes," Niki said, in a gasp of relief. "I am safe."

Barnes closed his eyes, and I could see his lips move slightly. He might have been muttering a prayer of thanksgiving. When he reopened his eyes, they'd gathered a little more life—not that intense, green-eyed, soul-unhinging glare, but enough to know that R. Wesley Barnes was still in there someplace.

"We ... we were getting a little worried about you," he said, though I could barely hear him.

"Do not worry for me," Niki said, pushing wild strands of white hair off his sweat-beaded forehead. "I am fine. We are both fine."

She turned and shot me a glance, her eyes bright with a lot more hope than I believed Barnes's condition warranted. As much as I admired her faith, I knew he was teetering on the edge. It wouldn't be long before he tipped. He looked like death, like he was living on borrowed minutes. I had to push aside that bout of realism to give

Niki a nod and a smile of assurance that said I thought everything was good.

"How did … how did it go?" The question slipped like a dry leaf through Barnes's cracked lips.

"We have it, Rufus," Niki lied. Then, in what looked like an effort to strengthen the deception, she clasped his hand with both of hers. "We have the scroll. There is no need to worry. I will … I will tell you all about it—later."

Something told me she wasn't as optimistic as I'd thought, as if she wasn't so sure there would be a *later*.

"I knew it," Barnes said. "I knew you'd do it. The Pialigarians … they're going to be okay. You'll … you'll get the scroll to New York?"

"Yes," Niki assured him. "I know what to do. Everything is taken care of. You can rest now."

"You make sure that … that the first … translation … gets to Adams."

"Yes," Niki said. "He is right here. Everything will be just like you said. It is all taken care of. Everything is fine."

Barnes turned his feeble gaze on me and smiled as if I'd just entered the room. Even with the life draining from his eyes, he still managed some humor.

"No soap-on-a-rope after all, huh, Adams?" The effort of a chuckle cost him a lung-rattling coughing spell.

I waited for the coughing to subside. I was reluctant to spar with him, but he settled and looked as if he was waiting for something more from me than a smile.

"I guess a few convicts are going to be a little disappointed," I said, hoping he wouldn't laugh.

He didn't. He kept his reaction to a smile and wheezed out a couple more breaths. "You done good, Adams. I thank you for it. Bet you got you one hell of a story."

Recent events flashed through my mind: Niki's brush with death, Threader's murder, Father Jon's deception and horrific demise. Giacopetti and his henchmen, all dead. The disintegration of the scroll. I just nodded and tightened one side of my face into something that looked like a smile.

"One hell of a story," was all I said, and the comment seemed to satisfy Barnes. Our business arrangement was complete. He had his scroll; I had my story.

He turned his attention back to Niki. "Niki, darling, there's something I should have told you years ago."

"No," Niki protested. "You need to rest. You can tell me when you wake up."

Barnes gathered the strength to make a slow, side-to-side motion with his head. "This can't wait. I may not ..." Another wheezy breath. "Niki, this isn't gonna be easy. I need you to stop fussing over me and listen real good."

Stiff with concern, she nodded her agreement, but it was a reluctant nod. "Okay. I listen." She leaned in close, as attentive as if she'd just risen from a good night's sleep.

The urgency in Barnes's tone made me afraid for her.

Barnes closed his eyes like a man searching for the courage to divulge his dark deathbed secret. There were a couple more labored breaths, a few more moments of hesitation. Then, he said it.

"Niki. Alexios wasn't your father."

Did I hear him right? Was it his medication talking?

I looked at Niki in the mirror, and she was still looking at Barnes, her expression unchanged, as if she was asking herself the same question. She sat still for a few moments longer, and then she turned to me, frowning, her face dark with a mix of fatigue and the confused question, Did he say what I thought he said?

I responded with a light shrug, just enough to show her that she was going to have to get some clarification. She turned back to Barnes, let out a bewildered laugh, grew more serious, and leaned in closer.

"Rufus, I ... I do not understand what you are trying to say. Of course Alexios was my father. I think perhaps ... perhaps you should try to get some res—"

"Please, darling, you're not listening to me. What I'm trying to say ... no ... I'm telling you that Alexios wasn't your daddy. He raised you. Done a damn good job of it too, but he wasn't your daddy. He was your uncle."

I shifted my eyes between Barnes's determined face and Niki, sitting still, scarcely breathing, dumbstruck with fatigue and the truly bizarre concept that had just pelted her frazzled brain.

Barnes had to be delirious, cracking maybe. Or it was all just a real bad dream. If we could just get some sleep we would wake up to a more suitable reality.

God, we needed sleep.

I noticed Barnes drifting again, maybe this time for good. He caught himself and came back, his eyes a little sharper. He started going again, but he regained enough clarity to drop an even bigger bomb.

"Niki ... I'm ... I'm your father."

His words dangled like a shard of broken glass in a weather-beaten window frame. Now I was afraid to breathe, afraid the slightest movement could dislodge it, send that shard plunging straight down through Niki's heart.

I could see Niki's mouth open in a slow, trembling gape. Nothing came out when she tried to speak. She cleared her throat and spoke as if every remnant of strength had finally gone from her being.

"What ... what are you saying? That ... that cannot be ... possible."

Tears dropped from the corners of Barnes's eyes. Another bomb. "Your mama was Celia's sister. Her name was Anna. That's ... that's where you got your name. Anna Nicole. The name of a beautiful, beautiful woman, just like you. Thank God you got her looks instead of mine." His attempt at a smile was broken in quivering anguish. "Alexios, he introduced me to your mama. Hell, I didn't even know she was pregnant with you 'til I heard she'd died in childbirth. Alexios ... he told me that Celia couldn't have children and that they'd take you if it was all right with me. At the time, I was hopping all over the world ... couldn't have given you any kind of a home. So ... I agreed. I ... I sent money. Paid for your school ... everything. Always figured one day I'd tell you. But hell, they did such a good job of raising you, I didn't ... I didn't have the heart, didn't want to hurt them ... or you. That's why Celia doesn't like me. She thinks I abandoned your mama. I swear I didn't know." His eyes narrowed and fixed firmly on Niki's. "I ... I just hope ... I just hope you don't hold it against me."

I couldn't begin to fathom what must have been going through Niki's mind just then. Even if she was rested and sharp, this was nerve-shattering, mind-blowing stuff.

I watched as Niki—her face tear streaked, broken in anguish—

clutched Barnes's hand as if she didn't know whether to hug him or press a pillow over his face.

"I ... I do not know what to say," she said in a heartrending whimper. "This is ... this is so much ... so much ..."

"You don't have to say anything, darling." Barnes squeezed out another cough. "I ... I just wanted you to know, that's all. You had to know. Everything I got ... it's yours ... all yours. The houses ... every last penny ... it's all taken care of." He started to drift, but he forced his eyes to stay focused on hers. "I ... I love you, darling. With all my heart ... I ... love ... you. I ... I just wanted you to know."

Wes Barnes tried to force one last smile. Instead, his head rolled slightly, and his eyes widened and stopped on something beyond the wall across the room, something beautiful that I knew I could not see even if I turned to look. His face radiated with the same otherworldly light that I had witnessed at my father's passing. Barnes closed his eyes and let out a long, shuddering breath that I knew would be his last.

Niki collapsed, clutching in pure anguish at Barnes's lifeless body.

I stood numb and motionless and swallowed at the growing ache in my throat. The cracked echo of Barnes's last words lingered in my mind and mingled with Niki's sobs. There was nothing for me to say—nothing for anybody to say. Rufus Wesley Barnes was dead, and that was it.

I ran a hand over Niki's back and wondered if she could feel, through the muddle of pain, shock, and brain-numbing fatigue, even a small portion of the comfort that I so desperately wanted to impart through my touch.

It was the least I could do for the archaeologist who was beginning to unearth some forgotten piece of my heart.

Chapter 21

BARNES'S FUNERAL WAS A SIMPLE ceremony of scattering ashes at sea. A priest from Santorini performed the duty from the boat belonging to Feodor. Aside from Feodor, the only other attendees were Nicholas and Dora, Niki, and me.

The priest also read a piece Niki had written in honor of Blake Threader. Among other things, she wrote of his great bravery and how he had made the ultimate sacrifice so that she may live.

I was grateful to him for that. Threader had his faults, to be sure, but he also had a level of integrity rare among humans. Rigging that mine to the Zodiac in itself would have required extraordinary effort. To think that he'd probably done it after taking a fatal bullet … well, it drove home the fact that there was, as he had said, only one Captain Blake Threader on this planet. I had the good fortune of knowing him.

Nothing was said about Father Jon. I still wasn't sure why he'd killed a man to save my life. I wanted to think it was because he had at least some shred of decency left. The sad truth, more likely, was that he thought he still might need help catching up to Giacopetti. He played out his little charade until he got his hands on the scroll.

A week after the funeral, Nicholas and I were busy rebuilding the gazebo. The smell of wood, the feel of a hammer in my hand, and the sensation of trickles of sweat creeping down my bare back were all pieces of the kind of therapy I needed. It gave me a way to sort through the loss of a couple of friends and to process some of the experiences of the last few weeks.

But the job was winding down, and the time was coming when I would have to make a decision. I needed to get back to Colorado and get started on the book. We didn't have the scroll, but we did have one hell of an adventure. It wasn't going to be the *big book*, but there was a good chance it could hit the top twenty, a feat that would certainly put a grin on the face of Claudia Epstein.

I was starting to get pissed at Marion. I knew she was getting my telephone messages, and I was sure my letter had reached her by now. Why hadn't she called?

I didn't know what to do. Niki was reeling from her losses, still in shock over Barnes's bombshell. She was in no shape to talk.

Nicholas and I were close to finishing the gazebo. We'd underestimated our materials, so Nicholas had taken the boat to a lumberyard on Anafi to pick up the rest of the flooring. I worked alone, nailing down what flooring we had.

It was Thursday, and Feodor had arrived with the mail. He handed me the bundle.

"I still can't get over Mr. Barnes," he said. "It won't be the same here without him."

"Yeah," I agreed. "We're gonna miss the old coot."

"And the *New York Times*"—he held up the week's accumulation—"it has lost a very faithful customer. They should at least write of his death. The obituaries, you know. He was a good man—a little strange, but a good man."

"Barnes broke all the molds," I agreed. "No doubt about that. Hey Feodor, you got time to hang around for a beer?"

"Not today," Feodor said, stepping back toward the cockpit. "Today is the birthday of my youngest granddaughter. I promised the wife that I would be home early. If you are here next Thursday, I will take you up on it."

"I don't have my crystal ball," I said. "But if I'm still here, I promise I'll be waiting with my fishing pole and a couple of six-packs."

He stood staring at me for a few long seconds. "If I do not see you, good luck. I hope your book is a huge success."

I thanked him and shoved his boat out into the surf.

"I almost forgot to tell you," he said, starting the engine. "There is a letter for you. Dallas, Texas."

Marion.

I lifted the letter from the stack, set the rest of the mail on the floor of the gazebo, and then settled into the sand just out of reach of the surf. My hands trembled as I opened the envelope and removed the single page. I hesitated before unfolding it, closed my eyes, and braced myself for what I was about to read.

Dear Stuart,

    I want you to know that I did get your messages and your letter. I haven't called because I wasn't sure what I wanted to say. Now I am. We had something very good between us, and I have really enjoyed our time together. You are a special man, and I will always remember the time I spent with you in the mountains.

    Stuart, I don't know how to say this gently, but I have met someone, a new client that lives here in Dallas. I don't want to hurt you by saying this, but my feelings for Roger are unlike anything I have ever experienced. I hope you understand. There is so much I could say to you, but I will leave it at this. Thank you for the times we had. I pray that you will find the kind of love that I have found with Roger.

    Sincerely,

    Marion

That was it? I didn't even rate a full page?

For the longest time I sat still, as if something in the rhythmic swish of the sea might soothe the stinging mix of anger and regret that burned like an ulcer in the pit of my stomach. Who was Roger? *Damn* whoever he was.

"*Stuart!*" Niki's voice was barely audible over the surf. I turned to see her calling to me from one of the landings of the stairs. "Would you like … ?" Her words drowned in the next wave.

"I can't hear you," I shouted back.

"Would … you … like … a … beer?"

"Yes. Bring the whole case."

"What? What … did … you … say?"

"Yes, beer." I downed a pantomimist's version of a cold one. "I … would … like … a … beer."

Moments later, she was coming across the beach with a bottle in her hand. Her white shorts and red sleeveless blouse added as much cheer to her appearance as she did to mine. She sat in the sand next to me and handed me the beer.

"You do not look so good," she said, glancing at Marion's letter. "Is something wrong?"

Yes and no, I thought. I wasn't sure where to begin. "You first. How are you doing?"

"Good now. I laugh, and then I cry. Mostly I am better, but I never know. So much to think about." She pushed her bare toes through the sand. "I miss Rufus badly." Her eyes welled with tears.

I ran my hand down her back and squeezed her side lightly. I figured we both needed a little humoring, so I held up the beer bottle. "I hope you don't think this is the drink you promised."

"I would not think you would let me off that easy." She wiped away a tear before it fell, sniffed, and then smiled. She took another sip and handed the bottle back to me.

"You're right. I'm not letting you off that easy."

"Lately, I do not think that I would be a fun date. But that does not mean that I am trying to renege on a promise."

"A fun date? After what we've been through, a fun date with you would be sitting on a quiet beach, drinking a beer, not worrying about getting shot, incinerated, drowned, crushed, boiled alive, thrown in prison, or stabbed in the neck. Just you and me, sitting in the sand, with nothing to do but look out at the sea."

"So, you are saying that I am fulfilling my promise to buy you a drink, just by bringing you a beer?"

"Nope. Besides, you're drinking half of it." God, she was beautiful. "What I'm saying is, I'm giving you all the time you need to pull everything back together. Then I expect you to pay up."

"This is sweet of you." She leaned over and gave me a light, lingering kiss on the cheek. "And what if I do not pull everything back together? Will this keep you from going back to your mountain?"

I looked at her for a few seconds, and then I slipped Marion's letter into Niki's hands. She read it, folded it carefully, and gave it back to me, her eyes flickering with uncertainty. "I am so sorry. This must be difficult for you."

"Yeah, difficult because I should have been the one writing the letter."

"You have already decided?"

"It's one hell of an ego bruiser, but Marion is right. I'd probably be a lot happier for her if I could just punch this Roger guy in the face."

"That makes no sense."

"It's a guy thing. We do a lot of things that don't make any sense. Like hanging on to people we're not really in love with. Doesn't make any sense, but it's never stopped me."

"You were not in love with Marion?"

Something told me she already knew the answer to her question. Women just seem to know these things. "You asked me that once already, remember?"

"At the café in Rome. You did not answer."

"Guess I was afraid to hear what I might say."

"But you only admit it now, after she has left you."

She had her facts straight all right, but she was making it sound as if I'd planned it, as if I was waiting for a safety net to appear before I bailed. She was wrong about that one. Wasn't she?

"To you, yeah," I said. "To myself, I reached that conclusion the night I told you I was leaving Sarnafi. Your book and that bottle of ouzo helped me see it."

"My book?" she said with a curious frown. "How did my book help you see?"

"The *romantic* part you said I should read. You know, Anatolios and Panagiota. It got me to thinking. If Marion were ever to leave, would I jump off a cliff rather than live without her?"

"There are plenty of cliffs here."

She wanted me to confirm that I'd given up on Marion. "I don't think I'll jump."

"And the ouzo, how did it help?"

"That stuff makes you honest. I decided there would be life after Marion." Since Kyropos, I'd wondered what she had been about to tell me just before our rescue. Now that some of the air was cleared, I thought it would be a good time to bring it up. I took another swallow of beer. "There's something I need to ask you."

"Oh?"

"When we were on Kyropos, you started to say something. You gonna tell me what it was?"

She looked at me for a few moments before turning her eyes back out to sea.

"I cannot. Not now."

"Why?"

"Because."

"*Because* is not an answer. I said so myself, remember?"

"It is an answer this time."

No, this wasn't going to do. There was too much going on between us. We needed to get it out in the open. "Well, Niki, there's something I think we have to—"

She pressed a pair of fingers to my lips, stood, and started for the house in a determined march. I called to her, but she waved me off, and all I could do was watch her go.

Experience had taught me that the best course of action in a situation like this was to take a large swallow of beer.

I downed the bottle, lay back in the sand, and took another dose of regret from Marion's letter. Even in that moment of defeat, something of a weight suddenly lifted, and I drew one of the deepest, most satisfying breaths I'd taken in a long time. I waded a few yards into the surf and read the letter one last time before laying it flat on the warm surface of the water. The action of the waves began immediately to carry the letter out to sea. Something in me drifted with it: a burden shed, a weight lifted, some invisible threshold crossed. Then, a small breaker formed on the next wave, seized the letter like a white hand reaching from the depths, and snatched it from my sight.

I WORKED THE REST OF the day alone, doing everything I could before Nicholas arrived with the new materials. He showed up a little after five, and by five thirty we'd finished unloading the boat. Nicholas headed for the house, and I for the cottage and a shower.

I was surprised to see a pair of slacks, a shirt, and socks laid out on the bed. A new pair of shoes sat on the floor. There was a note lying on the slacks: *Candlelight Dinner, six thirty sharp.* Niki's odd behavior suddenly began to make sense. She'd been waiting for a certain door to close before opening a new one.

I picked up the shirt—silk—a tastefully subdued combination of blues, browns, yellows, and reds that formed a handsome array of figures lifted from a Minoan fresco. The trousers, sandstone in color, were made of fine wool, delicately textured, velvet to the touch. The shoes were brown slip-ons made of hand-sewn, expensive Italian leather.

After a shower and shave, I got dressed and stood admiring myself in the mirror. Everything was a perfect fit. I felt classy, well dressed, on my way to share a fine seafood dinner with a very thoughtful lady. She did good.

The door to the main house was open, and I could hear Dora in the kitchen singing to herself. I knocked as I stepped in. "Anybody home?"

Dora emerged wearing an ankle-length flowered dress with a brightly colored apron. Her hair was all done up, her face adorned with makeup. When she saw me, her eyes lit up; her fingers flew over her mouth and then melted slowly down her chin.

"Signor Adams, you are … you are so handsome!"

"Well, you're not looking too bad yourself, Dora," I said, grinning. "Are you busy tonight?"

"Me?" Her darkened eyelashes fluttered; the blush of her pendulous jowls deepened with playful scorn. "You are being ridiculous. It just so happens that another, much younger and more beautiful lady is to have the honor of being swept from her feet by you."

I stepped past Dora and inhaled deeply of savory aromas rising with shimmering waves from the hot oven. "Do you mind if I do a little sampling? This smells so good I can hardly stand it." I started to lift the lid off one of the steaming pots.

"Oh no you don't," she scolded, pushing my hand and the lid back down. "You are not to be in here. The food, it will come soon enough." Dora took me by the back of the arm and ushered me to the foot of the stairs that led to Niki's room. "You have more important things to think about than your stomach. Now go."

Climbing the stairs made me short of breath. My heart was pounding. I was as nervous as a red-cheeked schoolboy picking up his first date. I walked lightly down the hall and paused at Niki's door. I knocked, but there was no sound, only the lilting strains of piano music playing through unseen speakers throughout the house.

I started to knock again, this time a little harder. I stopped when I heard footsteps—high heels on a wooden floor. I swallowed as if I had a hunk of dry slate for a tongue.

The door opened and there she was, a stunning force of absolute beauty. Her hair was captured in elegant, loosely bound strands, pulled to the top of her head, accentuating the soft features of her face and the delicate grace of her slender neck. She wore a string of pearls and matching earrings and bracelet, their muted iridescence radiant against her sun-bronzed skin. Her dress was fluid silk, ankle-length, strapless, sapphire in color, low enough at the top to offer a generous hint of her voluptuous breasts. A slit ascended from the hem to just above her knee, permitting a tantalizing peek at a perfect set of legs. Her shoes were thinly strapped, open-toed heels, sensual on her feet.

"Well?" She held her arms out like a ballerina and did a slight curtsy. "What do you think?"

There was playful uncertainty in her voice, as if my gaping jaw gave her the impression that I was too dumbstruck to form an opinion.

"What do I think?" I searched for the right word. Fortunately, there was only one. "*Beautiful*. Niki, you are absolutely beautiful."

She laughed, a short burst filled with pride. "And you! Just look at you!"

I liked what I saw in her eyes when she said it.

"I don't know how you did it, Niki, but everything fits. You're amazing."

Her face shimmered when she took my hand. "Come, I have something to show you."

It was the first time I'd seen her room—a spacious, stand-alone apartment, really. It had a high beamed ceiling, beige stucco walls, and wood floors with cheerful rugs scattered in all the right places. Potted fig trees and paintings—mostly island landscapes of mountain and sea, local scenes—dotted the spaces between bold pieces of mahogany furniture. There was a large mahogany bed covered with a flowered spread, positioned to capture the seascape through an open pair of wood-and-glass doors. A bank of large windows let in a flood of early-evening sunlight, filling the room with golden cheer.

Niki led me past the bed, through the glass doors, and out onto the patio. Beneath a cover of latticework entwined by flowering vines, there was a table set for two, a bottle of white wine chilling on ice, two empty glasses, and a vase filled with red roses. A rainbow of potted flowers adorned the patio's concrete railing and filled the remaining nooks.

"You see?" she said, waving an arm across a hazy vista of sun hovering over ocean. "Perhaps it is not a taverna on Santorini as you suggested, but we do have our own sunset, our own sea, and …" She finished her sentence by tilting her head toward the wine.

"Guess a guy's got to be flexible," I said, stepping to the table and lifting the bottle from the ice. "Fact is, I wasn't particularly stuck on the idea of a taverna on Santorini. Beach, sunset, and the company of a gorgeous woman who buys the drinks—that's the basic vision I was getting."

"Then I am happy that you are so flexible," she said, handing me a corkscrew.

I filled our glasses and offered a toast. "To the journey."

"To the journey," she said, clinking her glass to mine.

We sipped the wine and relaxed in each other's gaze.

"Do you want to know something?" I said, my mind drifting over our shared experience of the last several weeks. "You and I, we haven't known each other all that long, but we've got one hell of a history."

Her eyes turned reflective. "You are right, maybe more than you know."

"You gonna explain that?"

She took another sip of wine. Her glass dangled loose in her fingers as she stepped to the patio railing. She spent a long time lost in the pastel distance.

"Do you remember when we first saw each other in the airport?"

"I do. You gave me the distinct impression that you hated my guts."

She laughed. "I am sorry, but that was not my intention. I was afraid of you."

"Afraid? Of me?"

"You asked me if we had ever met, and I said that I did not think so. But I was wondering the same thing."

"I was familiar to you?"

"I cannot explain it. I mean, I can, but—"

There was a knock on the door.

"*Mezedes*," Dora's muffled voice came through. "Are you ready?"

"Yes, of course," Niki called back. "The appetizers," she said, going for the door. "You are hungry, no?"

Chapter 22

I PUT HER PUZZLING COMMENT aside long enough for the two of us to rave over Dora's cart. It was packed with small dishes of sardines, spiced cheeses, clams, mussels, and a variety of greens and sauces—enough food for six people.

"I guess we're expecting company?" I said, helping Niki into her chair.

"We are not expecting company," Niki said before taking another sip of wine. She turned to Dora. "You would quickly send them away, no?"

"Do not worry, my dear. There will be no company tonight. No distractions." An impish grin covered her face. "Unless, of course, you create them for yourselves. Now, enjoy." Dora headed for the door. "I give you time; then I bring the main course."

When the door clicked shut, I nipped a bite off a sardine and restarted our conversation.

"You said you knew me. You mind explaining?"

"I am not so sure that it is a good idea."

"You're the one that brought it up."

She forked a clam from its shell and ate it.

"Do you remember when we were on Pialigos, walking to the boat, and Euphemia took you to the side?"

"Doubt if I'll forget that any time soon."

"What did she say to you? Do you mind telling me?"

"She got kind of crazy. Said walking that labyrinth is my destiny, something to do with restoring the human spirit. Said I won't sleep right until I do it. According to her, I don't have a choice. My eyes are gonna be opened if the Great Mother has to pry 'em with a screwdriver."

"She did not say that."

I shrugged. "That was the drift."

"Did she ... did she say anything about ... me?"

"No. Was she supposed to?"

"Only if she wished."

"You going to tell me what this is all about, or am I going to have to get you down and tickle it out of you?"

"Ha! You would not think of running such a risk." She took another bite. "It is nothing. Eat."

She was looking for something; I just wasn't sure what.

Through the remainder of appetizers, our dinner, and the start of our second bottle of wine, we turned the conversation to everything from commentary on the sinking sun to her explanation of the difference between our main course of Greek lobster and the more conventional brand that I'd known.

"You notice there are no claws," she said, the scientist suddenly appearing in her voice. "But you also notice it has great bulk. The meat that is lost in the lack of claws is compensated for in a greater size and by the fact that you can find meat in the head and in the antenna."

"Head?" The thought conjured up a musty green mush that I vowed would never touch the tip of any fork of mine again. I guessed she saw something of that memory in my face.

"It is not like you think," she said, the flutter of her eyes betraying a few memories of her own. She cracked the shell. "You see, sweet white meat, just like the tail."

After desserts of coffee ice cream on a dark chocolate nut truffle, we relaxed in our chairs and basked in the pleasure of a perfect meal, wrapped in the warm blanket of fine wine.

She was talking softly about something; I was drifting, lost in the face of an angel half-hidden in the timid light of a rising moon. Her voice trailed off when I stood, took her hand, and eased her into my arms. In slow, timeless movements, we danced to the delicate strains of music that sweetened the night air. I brushed my lips over her ear.

"I love you," I whispered, breathing the soft fragrance of her hair.

She pulled back slightly and looked at me, her saucer eyes misted by the truth of my words.

"I love you," she whispered.

I kissed her, a light, titillating touch of our lips. Passions rose, and our bodies tensed. Fingers, no longer satisfied to caress, searched eagerly through clothing for a tighter, closer, softer hold. I pressed my mouth hard against hers, gathered her in my arms, and carried her to the bed. There we made love, our bodies and souls intermingling, merging one into the other, a mystical union, full and natural, as ancient and as healing as the murmur of Aegean waves rolling gently through that moon-shadowed night.

MY EYES FLASHED OPEN. I sat up gasping for breath, sweating, Niki clutching my arm.

"It is all right," she said, her tone urgent. "You ... you were having a nightmare."

The sound of her voice drew me back into our reality. "Yeah," I said, blinking at a dissipating wall of rage-distorted faces. "A nightmare."

She pulled me back to the pillow, slipped an arm around my waist, and squeezed my side.

"You are trembling."

"They were gonna kill me," I said.

"Who was going to kill you?"

"I ... I don't know. Bunch of people. A crowd. They were angry ... throwing rocks and ... and yelling. They wouldn't let me talk. At first, I couldn't see them. Everything was ... black, like ... like I was blind or something." I rolled my head toward Niki. "You were there. You were wearing a dress, white, but it was torn ... dirty ... like you'd been ... beaten." The image angered me. "I couldn't do anything. You were screaming my name, but ..." Something suddenly came to me.

"But what?"

"Anatolios."

"Anatolios?" Her fingers tightened on my side. "That is the name I called you?"

"Yeah."

She snuggled into my shoulder and stroked my chest. "What did I do?" Her voice was quiet, almost a whisper.

"At first, I could only hear your screams. Then, I saw you. You were pushing your way through the mob. They tried to pull you back, but you ... you got away. You ran at me ... full force. But it was like ... like you were moving in slow motion. I could see the terror in your eyes, the movement of your mouth, your flexing muscles, all in slow motion. When you hit me, we started falling. Down ... down like it was never going to end. Then I woke up."

Silence drifted between us. Niki sniffed, and I realized she was weeping. I rolled over and stroked her hair.

"Hey, it was just a dream."

"No. This was not just a dream. Think about it. *Panagiota*."

She offered no further explanation. I started to press her but stopped. Suddenly I knew. I got out of bed, paced the room, moved to the window, and stared out. A lone cricket chirped. Faint shadows cast by the falling moon reached for the sea. I turned to Niki, now sitting up, clutching the sheet over her breasts. "You?"

She draped herself in the sheet and joined me at the window. "I had to let you come to know for yourself. I ... I was Panagiota."

"You knew that?"

"Yes. Since I was a child I have known."

"That's what you were trying to tell me last night? The thing about the airport?"

"Yes. The very moment that I saw you, I knew you were Anatolios. I *knew* it. That is why I was so cold to you. I was frightened. Do you understand? I knew who you were in that very instant that our eyes met."

Remembering those feelings of familiarity started a chill down my spine. "There was something going on. I ... I didn't know what it was."

"Now you do."

"Kyropos. I felt it then." I remembered the moment we kissed. "And last night ... when we made love. I ... I've never felt what I ... what I felt for you. *Never*. Niki, there's something between us, something ... ancient." I slipped my arms around her.

Fear flashed through her eyes; she pulled away and turned toward the sea.

"Niki, what's wrong?"

"I ... I am so afraid."

"Afraid? What's there to be afraid of?"

"I am afraid I will lose you."

"Lose me?" I turned her by the shoulders and forced her to look at me. "I'm not letting you go, not ever again."

"But … you do not understand."

"There's nothing to understand. I love you, Niki. Not even the fires of hell can separate us. That's what I understand."

She broke, sobbing. I held her tight. "Niki? What is it? You've got to tell me."

I could smell the delicate scent of her tears when she lifted her face. "According to Pialigarian prophecy, there will be two signs given to announce the Prophet's return. The Dream Child will have the last dream. This is the first sign."

"Euphemia's dream."

"Yes. The second prophecy foretells Panagiota's return to Pialigos to announce the Prophet's coming."

"That's why you wanted me to meet Euphemia." Another piece of Niki's mysterious behavior suddenly fell in place.

"I knew you were Anatolios, but I wanted her to see. She saw it too. Stuart, the second prophecy has been fulfilled."

Anger toward the insanity of the idea sizzled in my gut. "You're saying that the only thing left for me to do is walk that labyrinth, get whatever the hell I'm supposed to get, and use it to save all the lost souls wandering aimlessly through their empty lives?"

"It is beyond our control," she insisted. "This is your destiny, the path of your labyrinth. I cannot tell you how afraid I am. I do not want to lose you, ever again. But, you have to do this. For the world. For us. You … you cannot avoid the Walk of the Prophet."

"To hell with the world. To hell with the walk of the damn Prophet. I'm not doing it."

It didn't make any sense. I'd never even heard of a Pialigarian until I came to the islands. Why would somebody like me be responsible for fulfilling their wacko prophecy? It was crazy. This whole thing was crazy. My walking that labyrinth wasn't going to accomplish anything, except maybe get me killed.

"Do you want me to die over this?" It was a hurtful thing to say, and I knew the answer before the question flew out of my mouth, but I was too angry to stop it.

"No!" She was horrified. "Do not ever say that again! I do not want you to die. Ever!" She scampered across the room and threw herself into the bed, sobbing.

The anger still boiled. "Then forget all this crap about labyrinths and prophets," I said, my voice growing louder. I stepped toward the bed, stopped at my trousers crumpled on the floor, snatched them up, and drove in a leg. "We're not going back to Pialigos. And I'm sure not walking that labyrinth." I grabbed the rest of my clothing and started for the door.

Her head came up. "Where are you going?"

I wasn't sure. "Walk. Outside. I've got to get outside." I started to go.

"Stuart, I love you. I love you, so very much."

Her words, pleading and filled with fear, stopped me cold and brought me to my senses. I took a calming breath, stepped back to the bed, sat next to her, and ran my fingers through her hair. God, how could I hurt her like this?

"Niki, I love you. Why do you have to keep talking about all this … this …" I didn't finish the sentence. She obviously believed everything that worried her. "Look, I need to walk, do some thinking. There's a hell of a lot going on that I don't understand. The only thing I really know is that I love you. Whatever all this other stuff is, I know I love you. Nothing's ever going to change that."

"Do you … do you want me to come with you?"

Her tear-filled eyes sparkled with some unseen light. I wanted to crawl back in bed with her, hold her.

"Niki, I want to be with you. More than anything. But I … I've got to sort this out … get it all straight in my head." I ran the backs of my fingers over her cheek. "Do you understand? I've got to think. I need to be alone."

I felt her head nod in my hand. I gave her a slow, assuring kiss on the lips, stood looking at her for a few more moments, and then I turned and left the house.

BY 3 AM I WAS in my T-shirt and cutoffs, headed for the beach. All that night I walked barefoot in the surf, trying to pull the pieces together. The light of morning came sooner than I expected. Tortured by restlessness, I just kept walking, for so long I lost count of how many times I circled the island. Dora called down from a lookout point in the cliffs announcing breakfast. I waved her off.

Hours later, Niki appeared on the patio outside her room, watching me. I stopped to look at her across the distance, trying to fathom a relationship that could last over two thousand years. I could scarcely grasp it, though I knew it was true. All the fear, the struggle, and the indecision I'd had with other women now made sense. I'd been waiting for Niki, and she for me. Our walk through one ancient life had ended abruptly, tragically, but our walk through eternity was a never-ending journey. Looking at her—arms crossed, her long hair lifting in the breeze—I knew that we could walk a hundred million years and never sound the depths of our love. In that moment, I understood that I was looking at an integral piece of my own soul, a spiritual companion whose essence was interwoven into the very fabric of my being. Everything in me screamed to go to her, hold her. I couldn't. Not now. I forced myself to turn away.

All that Euphemia predicted was happening. Too restless to sleep, wracked with self-doubt, running as hard as I could away from this incomprehensible madness, I plodded through the sand for the rest of that day and all of the following night, stopping only for short but futile periods of rest.

The night gave way to the frail light of another morning. Exhausted, I dropped to my knees and cradled my face in the palms of my dirty hands. Hunger knotted my stomach. My brain, wired for an emotional collapse, began to shut down. I was ready to quit; I couldn't even remember why I'd started.

Through eyes bleary with fatigue, I gazed over that indistinguishable smudge that was the sea. Something caught my attention: a strange shift in the water. *Dolphins*, I thought, as I watched the rippling surface. But it wasn't dolphins; it was something else, as if some sort of design was attempting to impose itself on the surface. Impossible. Almost delirious, I relaxed my vision and peered into the chaotic scramble. Huge, concentric lines began forming a very definite pattern. Dizzy with fatigue, I stood, careful not to blink away the strange phantasm. Then, everything came into focus. I was staring at a watery outline of the Labyrinth of the Cave.

A child stood at the center of the labyrinth, her arms opened toward me, beckoning. I rubbed my eyes and took a teetering step toward the labyrinth. It was the little girl who had given me the pink quartz. I reached into my pocket and felt the soft stone in my fingers. The child needed me. The people of the island needed me. Walking the labyrinth made no sense, but I knew I had to do it.

Suddenly my eyes blurred with tears. When I blinked them away, everything vanished—the girl, the labyrinth—only the natural surface of the water remained. I stood staring at the water for a long moment before turning for the house.

I found Niki asleep beneath a blanket in a chair on her patio. She stirred when I laid a hand on her shoulder. I gave her a few seconds before I whispered in her ear, "Niki, I've got to do it."

"Do what?" She stretched and spoke through a groggy yawn. "What do you have to do?"

"The Labyrinth of the Cave. I know now. It'll be all right."

She straightened, her eyes filled with sudden urgency. "You … you are certain?"

"Yeah. I'm certain."

She took me by the hand, and, without a word, she led me to her bed. Beneath a blanket of strange and tender peace, we spent the next few days and nights, sleeping and making love as if there was a two-thousand-year gap we suddenly had to close.

NIKI AND I HIRED A seaplane to fly us to Pialigos. Little in the way of conversation passed between us during the flight. For me, it was enough just to be with her, hold her hand, and indulge in the beauty of her face painted in the soft morning light filtering through the plane's window. If she was worried, she didn't show it. She seemed at peace with her thoughts, satisfied to turn an occasional reassuring smile in my direction.

I would have expected the same kind of serenity from Euphemia. Instead, she greeted us at the dock with the nervous energy of a Broadway producer whose star was late for opening night.

"Come," she said, clutching urgently at my arm. "We must begin the preparations at once." She maintained a stiff and determined pace on our hike to the monastery.

With matters now out of her hands, Niki lagged behind, her mood, I sensed, growing more somber as we approached the monastery. She was a hundred yards back when Euphemia and I reached the

Labyrinth of Roses. The single-minded priestess didn't wait for Niki
to catch up before she began ticking off my itinerary.

"Now listen carefully. You will go into solitude. A girl named Lia
will take you to a hut. This will be your dwelling place for the cleans-
ing period. Here you will fast. It is critical to have all toxins removed
from your body and your mind. You will drink only a tea. Everything
is prepared. Near the hut is a mineral pool. You will follow a trail
through a small canyon. The pool is at the end of this trail. The water
is quite hot, and you must enter it carefully."

"Enter it? You mean … I've got to sit in hot water?"

"Stuart, this fear of hot water is a remnant of your past. To succeed
in the Walk, you must confront it. You will enter the pool at sunrise,
again at noon, and once again at sunset. Stay in the water for as long
as you can. Stand. Cool down, and then get back in. Do this for one
hour, three times a day. The minerals in the water will draw all impu-
rities from your body. When you go back to your hut, you will find a
jar containing the tea placed on a large flat stone. It will taste strange
to you. Bitter. Drink it slowly.

"During this period, observe your mind; see that it is filled with
needless chatter, like the wheel of a cart always turning. Let it go.
Seek the stillness of your inner being. There is great power in stillness. When the time is right, you will find a ceremonial garment and
a new tea next to the hut. This tea will be different. It is an ancient
concoction of herbs designed to enhance soul memories. Once you
drink the final tea, put on the garment and wait. Someone will come
for you."

Her intensity was starting to make me nervous.

Niki approached, and I could see she'd been crying. I started for
her, but Euphemia raised a hand of caution. "There must be no distractions," she said.

I ignored the warning and took Niki in my arms. "Hey, you're not
wussing out on me, are you?"

"Now, I am the one who is afraid," Niki said. I could feel her
trembling.

I buried my face in her hair. "Yeah, well, if you want to know the
truth, I'd rather be drinking a glass of wine in one of those quiet little
beachfront tavernas on Santorini, watching the sun go down."

I felt the *whoosh* of a crying chuckle escape across my chest. She pulled back and looked at me through large wet eyes. "Would I be sitting with you?"

"You buying?"

"I buy last time." She sniffed.

"All right. I'll buy."

"And when we finish the wine?"

"You know, now that you mention it, I've been giving that some serious thought."

"Oh? How serious?"

"Very serious." I cleared my throat. "I was kind of wondering what you might be doing for the next two thousand years."

"That depends."

"On what?"

"On what you say next."

"How about, I love you. Would you consider marrying a guy like me?"

The fear melted from her eyes; her face brightened with joy. She glanced at the emotionless face of Euphemia, and then she quickly turned back to me.

"Yes. Yes, I would most definitely consider marrying a guy like you."

Euphemia, her eyes full of caution, took a step toward us. "We must take this one moment at a time. There is much to do." She turned to Niki. "You must not forget that there is danger in the Walk of the Prophet.

"What?" Niki's eyes widened with something more than uncertainty—a hint of betrayal, maybe. "But ... he cannot fail. You yourself said so."

"The preparations, they are critical. There must be no distractions."

"You ... you are saying ... he could—"

"I am saying there must be no distractions." Just then, a girl of about twelve—gangly, light brown hair cropped below her ears, big teeth—appeared and stood waiting. "If you are ready," Euphemia said, now anxious to separate us, "Lia will escort you to the hut. She knows only a few words of English, but she has her instructions. Do exactly as she says."

Niki and I held each other for a few more moments.

"Don't worry," I said. "I'll be back."

"You had better be." Niki found the courage to force a smile. "You are buying."

I FOLLOWED LIA ON A wordless thirty-minute hike to the tiny white building that would be my home. For how long, I didn't know. Lia pushed open the door of the hut, and then she stood back and motioned me to have a look. Inside, there was a cot, a small wooden table, and a chair. A short stack of clothing lay on the cot; a pair of sandals rested on the dirt floor.

"Your clothing," Lia said, both hands, palms up, extended toward me.

Unsure about what she meant, I pointed to the garments on the bed.

"My clothing. Thank you."

She shook her head and then held out her hands again. "Your clothing."

"Thank you." I was pointing to the cot, smiling. "My clothing. Thank you."

She tugged at the tail of my T-shirt, her way of telling me that I was missing the point. "Your clothing," she repeated.

I was beginning to understand. "You want … *my* clothing? *My* shirt? Why?"

She waited. Reluctantly, I pulled off the shirt and handed it to her. She took it and nodded again.

"All of it? You want all of my clothing?"

She said nothing.

Jesus. "I'll … um … I'll just step inside and …" I slipped through the door, removed my cutoffs, and tossed them to her. "There you go." Left only with my briefs and tennis shoes, I snatched up the shirt and pants from the bed, covered myself, and peered through the crack in the door. "Okay, you can go now. I'll just put on these—"

"Your clothing."

The girl's face held an uncompromising, no-negotiations frown. I pulled off my shoes and tossed them out to her.

"There you go, kid," I said, determined to hold on to my underwear. She waited. "No! That's it. That's all I'm giving you. Now git. Git on back home."

She didn't budge.

"All right. You want it all? Fine." I did the one-legged, underwear-removing hop, yanked off the briefs, hooked the waistband over my thumb, stepped outside, and shot them like a rubber band straight at the wide-eyed little bugger. They billowed like a parachute and landed squarely on her head. "Satisfied?"

She shrieked and tore at the shorts, and then she disappeared up the path, giggling all the way.

I slipped on the loose-fitting pants, shirt, and sandals and then went outside to have a look around.

The hut stood in the cool shadows of the surrounding cliffs, a mix of red sand and stone slabs with shrubs, gnarled cedars, yucca, and tufts of spiny grass growing from crevices. A faint trail led away from the hut, into the cliffs. I followed it through a corridor heavy with sulfur-tainted air.

I knelt beside the pool and plunged my hand through curls of steam. Apprehension tugged at my breath. I slipped off my clothes and eased into the water. I broke into a sweat, stood to cool off, and then forced myself to sit back down, repeating the process for what I figured was about an hour. Heavy with exhaustion, I dressed and headed for the hut.

As Euphemia had promised, I found a small clay jar filled with a pithy tea sitting on a slab of rock near the hut. The tea had a bitter edge, though not unpleasant. I sipped it down as quickly as it cooled, headed for the cot, and fell into a deep sleep.

In the days that passed, it felt as if forty-seven years of toxic sludge melted from my senses. The sky, the earth, the wind, the birds, even the insects, all became objects of intense fascination. I discovered that I could sit quietly for hours, listen, watch, and feel everything that transpired around and within me. Sitting in the hot pool actually became a pleasure that I looked forward to. I understood what Euphemia meant when she said, "There is great power in stillness." I began to see how I'd weakened myself by creating some busy, all-important identity that had formed a barrier between my mind and the larger, universal soul of the cosmos. The Great Mother? The Zadim was calling, had been calling all along, and I was finally starting to tune in to it.

The last light of the day was already showing itself in soft streaks of pink easing across the sky. I waded from the pool, got dressed, and headed back to the hut and the usual jar of tea. The jar was there, but so was something else, something that gave me reason to pause. It was a neatly folded piece of clothing. I picked it up slowly and let it unfold to its full length: a simple, white, cotton, hooded cowl, with strips of fabric attached as ties. I'd been given the ceremonial garment that I would wear on the walk.

Suddenly I could draw nothing more than a shallow breath. I slipped out of my clothes, pulled the robe over my head, and knelt at the rock. In trembling hands I held the jar of tea. The aroma was definitely different, sweet with a trace of mint. I sipped it, savoring its soothing flow through the growing tightness in my stomach. Like a man condemned to a firing squad, I glanced repeatedly at the path where the escorts to my execution would soon appear. I gulped the last swallow and paced to quell my apprehension. What had I done to myself? I took another step and swooned under a sudden feeling of lightness in my head. I sat on the rock and closed my eyes. The tea must have contained some kind of narcotic. Thinking turned to dreaming, and dreaming to near unconsciousness.

I did not care that my body was suddenly folding, crumpling to the ground.

Chapter 23

THE FIRST THING I NOTICED was the humid, sulfuric air that flooded into my nostrils. Immediately following was an ethereal sound, like chanting, a chorus of Gregorian monks, only female. I opened my eyes to an interplay of firelight and shadows dancing amid the jagged ceiling of a cave. I lifted my head to see the statue of the Great Mother looming in a dreamy swirl of vapor. I was lying on the floor of the Labyrinth of the Cave.

There were people—women in flowing garments, priests, a dozen maybe—standing at regular intervals around the labyrinth. The flame of a single candle mounted on a slender pole directly in front of each priest added a surreal appearance to their faces. These were the singers. Directing their voices to the statue seemed to enhance the airy strains they sent reverberating through the room.

I stood, uneasy on my feet. Two women in yellow gowns appeared before me. Neither spoke, but I knew I was supposed to follow them. We walked the few steps to the labyrinth. I stared at the path; it was much narrower than I remembered. Beads of sweat trickled down my forehead. A voice spoke.

"Do not be afraid."

The voice came from behind. I turned to see Euphemia. She was wearing a long white gown with a golden headband, her hair flowing in waves over her shoulders, her smile reassuring.

"Listen to the Zadim," she said. "It will guide you safely on your journey. Now turn around, close your eyes, and see only the path."

I turned back toward the labyrinth. Against every survival instinct,

I closed my eyes to that gurgling death. She lifted the hood of the robe and brought it over my eyes.

"You sure you have to do this part?" I asked.

"You will only succeed if you follow the Zadim," she said, securing the hood with the ties. "Do not be afraid; just listen. It will be like the Labyrinth of Roses. You will see."

I stood in absolute darkness and listened. The only things I could hear were the chanting, water boiling, and the sound of my heart about to burst from my chest. I took a short step and waited, searching desperately for a vision to appear through the blackness inside the hood. Another step. Nothing. This was suicide.

After one more step, the loose edge of the path gave way. I started to fall, but I jerked backward and landed on solid ground. My left leg plunged knee-deep into the scalding water. I screamed and clawed away, gripped with terror. I gathered my feet and stood, completely disoriented, testing weight on my blistering leg.

"Trust the Zadim." It was Euphemia's voice, but now it seemed to come from inside my head. "You cannot fail. *Walk.*"

My leg stung so badly that it made me lightheaded. I tried to will away the pain. Weight on the leg made it throb. I thought of Niki. All I wanted was to get out of this brackish hellhole, hold her in a cool breeze, and drink in the beauty of her face against a lingering sunset. This was madness, an insanely pointless threat to our future together. I'd struggled too long to find her, and now I was risking everything. For what? I clutched at the hood and started to rip it off.

Then, the labyrinth appeared to me as clearly as if I were looking at it with normal vision—maybe better. I forgot about my burned leg; I took a careful step and then another, testing, gaining confidence with my newfound vision. Then, I saw something on the path ahead, a column of light so dense that I couldn't see beyond it. I came up beside it and carefully pushed a hand into the beam. I could feel nothing.

"You are looking at a Station of Remembrance," Euphemia said. "When you step into the light, you will relive significant past-life memories that have contributed to the advancement of your soul. Each has special importance in understanding your destiny. Observe. Listen carefully. Do not be afraid to relive these memories. They are meant only for healing."

I drew a quivering breath and stepped into the light. Everything changed.

"WHO IS THIS STRANGE MAN?"

I was sitting cross-legged before a group of about twelve men. From a clay bowl, I was eating cooked grain and vegetables, and I was drinking water from a skin flask. I was trying to eat with my usual manners, but I was starving, and I consumed the food greedily. My skin was peeling, badly burned by the sun.

The men wore white garments spun of rough wool. Some wore colorless, unadorned vests. They sat in a semicircle talking in subdued tones and watching me with great interest. They seemed to mean me no harm. Still, I was afraid, though I was determined to conceal it.

Other men in the group raised more questions.

"Is he a spy for the Romans?" another man asked. "Was he sent to report our whereabouts to the authorities?"

"No," another said. "He is not a Roman. He has the face of a Greek, but his boat is not Greek."

A third man spoke up. "Why was he drifting alone with no food or water? Who would be so foolish to embark on the open sea without sail or even so much as a single oar?"

I knew from my training as a temple scribe that the men spoke Aramaic. They did not know that I understood their questions or that I could answer them all, for I was too hungry to do more than eat and observe.

Their island was a desolate, forbidding place—red, sparsely vegetated, a smoking volcano whose air stank with the same odor that rose from the fissures on Pialigos.

At the base of a wall of red cliffs were a series of caves. These appeared to serve as the dwelling places for these men. Many others milled about the caves. *Strange*, I thought, *that there are no women among them.*

I concluded that these were ascetics, men who had shied from material distraction, even from the inspiration drawn from natural surroundings. What other type of man would choose such a deprived environment?

Yet, barren as it was, I could hear a flock of goats bleating from somewhere in the distant hills. And the food that I so greedily consumed told me that these frugal men were able to coax enough grains and vegetables from their impoverished land to at least meet the minimal requirements for their existence.

With my hunger satisfied, I set the bowl in the sand next to me. The men watched with intense interest, wondering what I would do next. I was doing the same.

Then, one man stood. "There must be something wrong with his mind. He has not tried to say a word." He walked slowly around me. "Perhaps a demon controls his tongue. Perhaps he is full of demons."

"No," I said in Aramaic. "I have no demon."

An excited murmur rose from the men. The one that made the accusation took a step away from me. "This man speaks our tongue!" he said. "Tell us, who are you, and where do you come from?"

"Anatolios," I said with a brave face. "I am Anatolios, a scribe from Pialigos."

"Anatolios?" another old man said. "But this is the name of a Greek."

"I am not a Greek," I said.

Another man spoke up. "You say you are a scribe." He dangled an amulet in front of me. I quickly recognized it as the warning my priests had forced me to wear. "Tell us," the man said, "what is this that we have found around your neck? We do not know your language."

"It is a message for those who would find me. I was told that if I removed it, I would die."

"As you can see," the man said, "it is removed, and you are not dead. What does it say?"

I knew the inscription from memory. "It says, 'This is Anatolios the ... the blasphemer, banished forever from Pialigos for his failure to follow the way of the Great Mother. Whoever helps this man will be cursed.'"

The men looked at each other, chuckling with amusement.

"We are Essenes," the man said. "We are not afraid of any curse. So, you are banished, are you?"

"Set adrift with no food or water, given over to my fate. As I have told you, I am a scribe, not a sailor. The priests assumed that my lack of experience at sea would force me to drift until my death."

"Well, you nearly succeeded," the man said. "Tell us, Anatolios the blasphemer, who ordered your banishment?"

"The high priestess, of course."

"High priestess? A woman is your ... high prie ..." The man was puzzled, but then he smiled. "You did not tell us that you were banished by a woman. Perhaps we *should* fear this curse of which you speak." There was great laughter among the men.

Another man—tall, his hair and beard long and graying—stood. His eyes were bold but warm, steady with wisdom, yet they burned with a youthful fire. The laughter stopped when he raised a hand. Those who had been standing took their seats. No one had to tell me that this man was the leader of my inquisitors.

"I am Marcus," he said to me, "and I am most fascinated by your story. The philosopher Plato wrote of a great and ancient nation utterly destroyed by a volcano. Only a few escaped the horrific cataclysm. There are those among our brothers of the desert who believe the people of Pialigos are the descendants of these unfortunate souls. Is there any truth to this?"

"I do not know this tale of your philosopher," I said. "But it is true that my ancestors were forced by a volcano to flee their land. Many perished in the great wave that followed. Others fled to Crete or to other lands. Only the people living on Pialigos were spared from death or dispersion."

"Fascinating," Marcus said. "I am curious, Anatolios. What must one do to become banished from Pialigos? You are a scribe, a commander of your language and ours. Surely you are a valuable asset to the needs of your ... priestess. Am I wrong to assume that you have greatly offended someone?"

"Offended? If exposing the great lie is an offense, then yes, I have offended the high priestess. Konstantina is herself the mother of the great lie. I have known it since I was a child."

Marcus sat down. "Please, you must tell us about it. We are all interested in hearing your story."

Another man about my age—twenty-five—with black curly hair and beard and a gentle, pleasing smile, introduced himself as Joshua. "We do not get many visitors," he said. "I agree with Marcus, and I surely speak for us all when I say that I would love to hear your story."

The men all nodded in agreement. I relaxed, for I knew without any doubt that they meant me no harm. To the contrary, their faces reflected genuine interest and great curiosity.

I started to stand, but I was much too weak. Marcus encouraged me to speak from where I sat, so this is what I did.

"When I was very young, still unable to walk, I had been given the gift of writing."

Joshua immediately became incredulous. "You could not yet walk, yet you could write?"

"Yes. I began by drawing figures in the sand. I remembered this from a previous life, when I was the keeper of inventories." I paused to watch the reaction of my audience. I did not know if these Essenes believed that the soul reembodied after death.

"Do not worry, Anatolios," Marcus said, sensitive to my concern. "Many here, I among them, share your sentiments. Please continue."

"One day when I was older, my father noticed this writing of mine, and he became very curious. He asked how I learned to write, and I told him. He explained that the figures I made in the sand very much looked like the sacred writing of our ancestors. When I was five years old, he took me in secret into the temple and showed me the very ornate chests where the sacred tablets were kept. Only the priests were supposed to know how to read the tablets, he explained. He wanted to see if I could read them as well.

"We went into the temple at night. The room was dark, lit only by a few oil lamps. My father carefully removed the lid of the box and lifted me up so I could see the tablets. Though the light was poor, I could read them immediately. My father was utterly confused by what I read. The tablets were nothing more than lists of things like materials for building projects or the censuses of forgotten cities. Some listed the contents of ships. Some were even inventories of grain reserves. My father was deeply troubled by this revelation, but he warned me to tell no one. To do so, he said, could place me in grave danger.

"I told one person only—Panagiota, my friend from childhood. I taught her the language of our ancestors. Aside from my father, Panagiota was the only other person that knew this terrible secret."

Marcus said, "You must have trusted this young woman, Panagiota, very much."

"Yes. I intended to take her as my wife before I was banished." A lump formed in my throat, forcing me to pause. "At an early age, my skill in writing earned me my position as the apprentice to Pericles, the Chief of Scribes. One of the responsibilities of this important position was to accompany Konstantina into the temple's inner chamber. There, she would read from the sacred texts. Pericles, who himself confessed that he could not read the tablets, would transcribe her readings. I was greatly puzzled by this, for the transcriptions were often prophetic utterances or new laws that she said were mandated by the Great Mother or by our ancestors. I could only assume there were other tablets that I had not yet seen.

"When Pericles took sudden illness and died, it became my duty to accompany Konstantina and transcribe her temple readings. She selected one of the ancient tablets, sat running her fingers over the markings, and, with her eyes closed, began speaking. I recorded her words exactly as she had spoken them. She was quite pleased with my work. When she finished, I saw clearly the tablet from which she had read. To my surprise, it was as I had remembered. This was nothing more than an inventory of grains from a certain storehouse on Thera.

"When I confronted her on this matter, she became very angry. Then I knew that she too was unable to read the language of our ancestors, that she was merely inventing the words she spoke. This is how I discovered the great lie and how I came to be here."

Chapter 24

THERE WERE OVER A DOZEN Stations of Remembrance, each appearing as its own single column of light, each presenting me with scenes from my life as Anatolios. These were not merely vivid recollections. I was actually there, hearing the sounds, smelling the odors, and interacting with the people that had been a part of my life. When each episode was complete, the scene around me would fade, and I would again be on the labyrinth's path.

I learned that the Essenes of Kyropos were a splinter group of the parent community that lived at Qumran, near the Dead Sea. They took me in, and for five years I worked among them, sharing the duties of tending the goats, cooking the food, and washing clothing. All members, including Marcus, shared equally the tasks of every aspect of their communal life.

Marcus had taken Joshua and me as his special students, and it was during this period that he taught us the Three Measures of Wisdom. I was so convinced that these teachings were somehow associated with the lost wisdom of my ancestors that I began to record them in a parchment scroll with the dream that someday I would return to Pialigos bearing the gift that had been lost to my people. Because I believed it would lend authority and credibility to the teachings, I carefully compiled them in the script of my ancient ancestors. Joshua, assisting me with the task, quickly learned the language and often practiced making the letters in the sand.

The day came when Joshua announced that he was ready to go back to his homeland and become a teacher. This came as no surprise to Marcus, who had often urged Joshua to do this very thing. Marcus himself intended to retire to the Rock, to the complete ascetic life, and he urged me to go with Joshua. Without the companionship of my friend, Joshua, life on Kyropos would no longer be suitable for me. Though it would mean that I was farther away from Panagiota, I reluctantly agreed. I had no place else to go.

A merchant ship carried us to the port of Caesarea. There, Joshua's brothers and sisters, and a mother overcome with joy, greeted us. His father, a famous artisan in the region, had, sadly, died. The family took me in as one of their own.

For two years, I traveled with Joshua through his homeland. He drew a large following by successfully merging the teachings of Marcus with the Judaism of his people, a system of ideas that people simply called the *Way*. At the request of his closest followers, I recorded many of Joshua's sayings in his native tongue of Aramaic. Few of Joshua's followers knew how to read or write, and these writings became a rare treasure that they guarded jealously.

In one of the Stations of Remembrance, I found myself waking from a fitful, unsatisfying sleep. I was having another dream of Panagiota. Chilled, lying beyond the warmth of our waning campfire, cold smoke hanging like wool in the heavy, predawn air, I yearned for her.

Not far from me, I could see Joshua sitting alone, huddled in his blanket, staring into the dying embers. There were others, a dozen or more, men and women, sleeping around scattered fires. Camped a good distance from the main road, we were hidden in a familiar grove of olive trees that we frequented to escape the crowds.

Joshua watched in silence as I stepped to the fire, stirred warmth from the embers, and added more wood. It was not until I settled back to warm my hands that he spoke.

"You cannot sleep, Anatolios? You were awakened by more thoughts of Panagiota?"

"Yes," I said with a deep sigh. "I would give my very life for the chance to see her face once again."

"And your home? You miss your home?"

My eyes settled in the growing flames; my mind drifted. "There was a place among the cliffs where I could see the sky and the seas come together in an indefinable mist. As a boy, I would sit with Panagiota in this spot and watch the sun rise in the east. We wondered about the strange and mysterious lands and people that we might encounter if only we could sail into that mist." I laughed. "And now, here I am. I have sailed into the mist. I see the land, and I have come to know its people. They are not so mysterious, not so different. It is a strange turn that my heart now follows the sun when it sinks to that very place in the cliffs where, as a boy, I sat with Panagiota, dreaming of all the mysteries.

"I can feel the warmth of Panagiota's hand. I can smell the sweetness of her perfume and feel the gentle breeze that touched our faces. I hear the calming music of her voice, like the song of the birds or the rush of the sea." I turned to my companion. "She vowed her soul to me, Joshua. Before I was banished, Panagiota swore to me that she would touch no man. I miss her more than I can say. My soul remains on Pialigos with Panagiota."

"You must go back to her," Joshua said.

"You know that I cannot."

"But you must. She needs you, Anatolios. Your people need you. You have the Three Measures of Wisdom. You yourself said that this must be the lost wisdom of your ancestors. Send a messenger bearing your scroll. Write a letter and tell her to do what she can to prepare the way for your return. Humble yourself before your priestess. Find your way to this woman you love and to the people you wish to enlighten. I swear to you, Anatolios, the way will be opened."

IN THE NEXT STATION OF Remembrance, I was back on Pialigos with Panagiota, happier than ever. Having seen how the Great Mother had protected me through my trial, Konstantina accepted my return as fate. She forbade me, however, to ever speak of her devious practice.

In secret, I began teaching the Three Measures of Wisdom. The people of Pialigos, including many of the priests, were thirsty for the new revelation. A priestess named Rena, second only to Konstantina, began calling me the Prophet, the one who had come to restore Pialigos to its former splendor. Word spread quickly. Soon great crowds gathered in our hiding places, hungry to hear me speak of the Wisdom.

Konstantina found out, and I was immediately arrested by the temple guards.

"A *real* prophet," Konstantina declared, "could walk the Labyrinth of the Cave, relying only on the voice of Zadim. You will prove yourself, Anatolios. You will walk the Labyrinth of the Cave without the use of your eyes."

I knew it was a death sentence.

When Panagiota came to visit me in prison, I warned her that she must not be caught with the scroll, or she too would be faced with severe punishment. I knew that a merchant ship, due to sail east the following morning, lay in our harbor. "The scroll must be protected," I told her. "Get it to the ship. Tell them to leave it on Kyropos, with Marcus. Tell Marcus that Rena will send for it when she becomes high priestess."

Panagiota succeeded with her mission, but Konstantina found out.

"Did you write this scroll?" she demanded, her eyes flaring, her lips curled and trembling with rage.

"By my hand," I said, "the Great Mother has returned that which was lost to our people. This is my destiny."

"*I am the Great Mother!*" she shouted. "I am the one to decide what shall be returned to my people. You are *nothing*! Your destiny is to die like the worthless blasphemer that you are. You are at *my* mercy. Beg for forgiveness, and I may allow you to live."

"I am at the mercy of the *true* Great Mother," I said. "She alone has the power to deliver me."

"Indeed," Konstantina said. She called for the guards, and they appeared, holding Panagiota. "I want your lovely friend to see how such a great prophet is prepared for his walk of the labyrinth."

The guards rushed into my cell and bound my hands. Another stepped in with a white-hot iron and pressed it against each of my eyes. I screamed at the sound and the smell of my own searing flesh. The pain was too great to bear. I lost all consciousness.

IN THE NEXT STATION OF Remembrance, I stood at the Labyrinth of the Cave before an audience of priests, hands bound, my useless eyes covered with a rag tied around my head. I could hear Panagiota whimpering in agony over what was to come.

"Walk, Anatolios, O great prophet," Konstantina said, her voice seething with contempt. "May the Great Mother lead your every step."

I began to walk. In spite of my blindness, I could see the path. I walked to the center, to the statue of the Great Mother, and I returned without incident.

Infuriated, Konstantina ordered me thrown into one of the boiling pools.

Crazed with pain, I called out in a loud voice. "I will return to destroy the great lie of Konstantina. She is the wicked mother of lies, and she has deceived all of you. She cannot read the texts of our ancestors. No priest can read them. Only I can read them. They are nothing! Lists of grain! You worship lists of grain because of her great lie! I will come back; I will return to bring you the lost wisdom of our ancestors!"

There was an angry cry from everyone in the room: "Kill him! Kill the false prophet! Kill the blasphemer!"

Then, a great peace came over me. Suddenly I could again see with my inner vision. I watched as Panagiota struggled and broke free from the guards. She was screaming my name as she ran straight for me. I called her name. She hit me with her full force, clutching me as we tumbled together into the scalding pool and into the waiting light of the Great Mother.

I COULD SEE THE END of the labyrinth. As far as I could tell, there were no more columns of light. I'd seen the scroll, but I recalled nothing of its content. I knew then that the lost knowledge was lost forever. I had failed.

I took another step and then stopped. The vision of the labyrinth had suddenly evaporated. In place of the melodic chanting was the morbid sound of gurgling water. An appalling wave of emptiness swelled in me. I stood motionless in absolute darkness.

I pulled back the hood. There was no torchlight. Only the dense curtain of black stench greeted my eyes.

Then, it hit me, a thought so terrifying that it weakened my knees. Euphemia was Konstantina reincarnated! She'd planned all along to draw out the Prophet and lure him to his death with fantastic fairy tales and drug-induced visions, an evil scheme designed to ensure that her beloved priesthood would go unchallenged for another two thousand years.

I could barely control the panic as I turned to retrace my steps out of the labyrinth. Then, a tremor, accompanied by the sound of pebbles tumbling into water, halted me in mid-stride. In that same instant, I sensed a faint light coming from somewhere behind me. Thinking it was a rescuer's torch, I turned and peered through the eerie mist. The light emanated from the opening in the belly of the Great Mother.

Then, I heard a splash as more rocks plunged into the water. In the faint light, I could see the path moving, disintegrating. There was no escape. I had no choice but to scramble over the few remaining yards and dive for the center platform.

I landed in a battered heap and struggled to my feet. The tremor stopped. The dim light from the chamber was enough to see that the path, my only way off the platform, had crumbled into the boiling cauldron. I was trapped on an island in the bowels of hell.

I eased around to the entrance of the chamber. The light appeared to have no direct source, just luminous patches, rapidly shifting curtains of colorful energy that materialized and then disappeared— aurora borealis in miniature.

The Throne of Knowledge was made of black granite, rough in all places except for the seat and arms. The back stood about eight feet high and followed the contoured ceiling of the chamber. The throne rested on a circular platform less than a foot in height. I stepped to the throne and sat down. The shifting curtains of light intensified to an excruciating glare, forcing me to shield my eyes.

Then, I sensed a change. Seconds earlier, the air had been moist and putrid. Now, it was dry, sweet, and natural. The gurgle of brackish water became the hypnotic sigh of a breeze rustling through the boughs of a palm grove. The light sting of sand peppered one side of my face.

I opened my eyes and struggled to peer through the glare of light. I was no longer seated on the Throne of Knowledge. I was standing, blue sky stretching over my head, the fronds of palm trees waving gaily in the breeze.

I regained enough of my vision to realize that a sea—not of water, but of sand—stretched to every horizon. I walked in a slow daze around the edge of this desert oasis, trying to figure out where I was and what I was going to do about it.

Shade appeared to be the only amenity in my newfound environment. No food, no water. It occurred to me that I may bake to death, but at least I'd do it in the cheer of broad daylight, a vast improvement over boiling in the stinking black hell of the cave.

Things were definitely looking up.

I noticed something in the distance, a tiny speck that appeared to be moving in my direction. It took several minutes to determine that I was looking at the robe-clad figure of a man. When I saw the beard and sunglasses, I figured he was either a modernized nomad or on his way to the set of a _Lawrence of Arabia_ remake.

The man moved with the kind of confidence I would expect from the owner of the only spot of shade in a thousand square miles. I prepared for eviction. My only request from him would be directions to civilization and a few pointers on traveling through a desert with no food or water, wearing the equivalent of nineteenth-century English-style pajamas with a built-in nightcap.

My concern diminished when the man, now a few yards from me, removed his sunglasses. His brown eyes were warm, crackling with light, definitely friendly, strangely familiar. He pushed back his hood, bowed slightly, and then came up with a smile. His white teeth gleamed in bright contrast to his dark beard. Something in his eyes gave me the impression that he thought he knew me.

"This might sound a little crazy," I said, not knowing if he could understand me, "but do I know you?"

"Yes."

His instant certainty made me laugh—politely.

"I'm sure you're right, but I ... um ... well, I've been through quite a bit lately and I ... I guess my memory's a little fogged."

"Anatolios. Am I not right?"

The face I definitely did not recall. But the eyes—there was something about the eyes. And then it hit me. "Marcus!"

He laughed and threw his arms around me. "It has been a long time, my friend," he said, smiling and holding my shoulders in both hands. "You are looking well. Well indeed."

A million questions clogged my brain, forcing my face into a long and speechless gape.

"You ... you knew I was here?"

"Of course I knew. Just as I know that you are no longer Anatolios. You are Stuart Adams. Is this not correct?"

"Yeah, but ... but you're still Marcus. It's been over two thousand years since I saw you last ... and you look twenty years younger."

"Thank you," he said, smiling proudly. "I take this as a great compliment." He raised a scholarly hand. "The time comes in the journey of the soul, when the shifting identity begins to ... how shall I say ... *stabilize*. Many other things are possible as well, but we will talk of this another day. For now, we have a more important matter to discuss." He motioned, and we both sat in the shade of a palm tree. "You desire to discuss the Three Measures of Wisdom, do you not?"

"How'd you know that?"

"In the same way I know that you returned to Kyropos to find the scroll."

"I found it, all right." Flashing through my mind was the image of Father Jon's doomed helicopter plunging into the sea. "But I lost it again. This time for good."

"True wisdom can never be lost. Truth is like a fig, you see. A man who eats it describes its sweetness. Ten thousand years later, another man comes, and he too eats this fig. Will this man not describe the same sweetness known by his predecessor? He most certainly will. And so, my friend"—he clapped his hands lightly on his knees—"let us turn to the business at hand. Let us taste again the sweetness of this fig of Truth that you seek."

Euphemia hadn't lied after all.

Chapter 25

"THE FIRST MEASURE OF WISDOM is this: There is one underlying reality in the universe, an infinite, creative energy that is the source of all things visible. The material world rises from this unseen energy, like the mist that rises from the warm sea on a cool morning. In the same way that the water in the sea and the mist that hovers above are a singular substance, so the underlying reality and the material world that rises from it are a singular substance, but expressing at different vibratory levels."

"Okay," I said, my readings on quantum physics vaguely dancing in my head. "So what do you mean when you say 'underlying reality'?"

"This is *God*, of course. God is the one underlying reality behind all things."

"That's a little ambiguous. A lot of people would think you were talking about an old man with a long white beard who lives up in the sky, nursing a real bad attitude about the way things are going with all of us."

"Old man? Beard?" He stroked his own. "The sky? But why would they think … ? Hmm. Bad attitude? How could God have a bad attitude?"

"I was hoping maybe you could explain it."

"I see. To understand God, one must take care to free the mind of all human characteristics. Think of God as the Creative Life Force … Spirit, like a breath"—he blew against his hand—"unseen, but you know it is there. You *feel* it. Unlike the breath, however, the Spirit is everywhere, spread out over the earth. It is within everything—every man, woman, and child, every rock and tree. It is, as you say, up in the sky, but it is also in the deepest parts of the sea. No place exists where the Spirit is not. It is present in the wise and in the ignorant and is no respecter of race, class, religion, age—none of these things. The Spirit is the life of all, in all, and through all, and, most importantly, it is working for the good of all. This is the first measure of wisdom. Do you understand this?"

"I think so."

"Explain it to me."

I thought for a moment. "You're saying that the essence of Reality is invisible, like an energy field, a creative life force that produces everything that we see."

"Very good," Marcus said. "Now, it is of special importance to understand that the Spirit, this creative life force, abides within every person as the very essence, the true Self, of the individual. This knowledge, my good friend, is the second of the three measures of wisdom, an understanding of which is critical to a man's happiness. One must learn to still the busy mind, to delve beneath all externally oriented thinking, and learn to commune with the true Self. In the stillness of the mind's depths, the Spirit moves and speaks, not with a voice, but by imparting direct, universal knowledge and unspeakable joy. As the vine sustains the branch that grows out of it, so the Spirit sustains all its offspring. This Spirit, this divine life force, is the essence of every living thing. With disciplined practice, one can know, through direct experience, the will and intention of the infinite Spirit. This direct knowing will free the seeker from all suffering."

"You will know the truth," I said, quoting a biblical verse that suddenly took on a new significance, "and the truth will make you free?"

"Precisely. There is only one true path to absolute freedom, and it is within reach of every living being. And this brings us to the third measure of wisdom. The third measure is very simple, really, almost a restatement of the first two. Yet, it has a place, because it speaks to the connection between the one Spirit and everything in the universe, especially to the individual. All live in a relationship of oneness with the Spirit, and that relationship can never be altered. Nothing a person can do affects the love that the Spirit has for him. If that person thinks he has sinned and he asks the Spirit to forgive him, the Spirit cannot, because the Spirit has never condemned him. He might as well ask the sun to forgive him for creating a shadow. Does the sun care if the man creates a shadow? No. What the man chooses to do does nothing to alter the sun. The sun shines; the man does what he will. The Spirit does not punish the man. The consequences of the man's foolish choices—these are punishment enough. The instant the man turns within to understand his own underlying Reality, the Spirit is there to greet him with open arms." Marcus locked his eyes firmly on mine. "Do you understand all that I have said?"

"I think so. You're basically saying that if people are going to change for the better, they've got to reconnect with this inner Spirit, the true Self. When this happens, everything else follows. Life starts working."

"Yes. This is exactly it. The harmony that is so prevalent in all the universe begins to prevail in the life of the one that discovers the true, unseen Self."

"So," I said, "it follows that if a nation is to become great, truly great, it has to be built by people whose minds are open to this inner Self, this natural wisdom that permeates the entire universe."

"Yes. And the key lies in the understanding that this natural wisdom, as you call it, is found within the depths of every person. When a man or a woman is centered in his or her own inner Spirit— the true Self—then the external life naturally becomes a success. A nation that is composed of such enlightened individuals is a nation destined to flourish with the fruits of peace, prosperity, and creative ingenuity—a great nation indeed."

I huffed out a small chuckle. My head was swimming. "This is strange."

"What is strange?"

"The Three Measures of Wisdom, the secret knowledge, whatever you want to call it. It's so simple, so close. We've been looking for it in all the wrong places, outside of ourselves."

"You are right, my friend. The truth, it is not as great a mystery as one might think." He thumped a fist lightly over his heart. "It is all right here."

Marcus smiled, and I could see in his eyes that he had finished what he was there to tell me. Our time together had come to a close.

We stood and faced each other; he smiled warmly, while I tried to cope with the sudden sadness of parting company with a good friend.

"You will remember all that I have said?" he asked.

"I won't forget a word of it."

"You always had a good memory. This is one reason you were such a talented scribe."

I laughed. "It's funny. After all these years, I'm still writing. Guess some things never change."

"This is true. Some things never change. You, however, you have changed. In your eyes, I see the dawning of something new. I see the eyes of a genuine teacher." He placed his hands on each of my shoulders, and I could feel my eyes fill with tears. We embraced in a back-patting hug. He stepped back, looked at me one last time, and then raised his hood, replaced the sunglasses, and turned to leave.

"Marcus?"

"Yes?"

"There's … there's something I'm not sure about."

He turned to me. "Yes?"

"The people of Pialigos. They … they need help. They thought the Three Measures of Wisdom was their answer. I … I just don't see how this teaching can—"

He smiled warmly and lowered his sunglasses. "My good friend, that which has brought you to this place in your journey knows how to carry you forward. This is true for the Pialigarians as well. The answer is always wrapped up in the problem. It will come to you"— he smiled—"when you are not even looking for it." Marcus winked and replaced his glasses, and then he turned and walked away in the opposite direction he'd come.

I stood at the edge of the oasis and watched him shrink into the distance. I had no idea what I could do for the Pialigarians. I didn't even know what I could do for myself. But suddenly I felt a warm sense of peace about the whole thing.

A dust devil peppered the palm leaves with sand. Once again the light began to grow into a dazzling glare. In complete submission, I closed my eyes and waited for the intensity to pass. When it did, I sensed that something had changed.

I reopened my eyes. I was lying on my back, staring up at the statue of the Great Mother … in the Labyrinth of Roses.

I STOOD, UNSTEADY ON MY feet, wondering how I'd gotten to the Labyrinth of Roses.

It was morning. Artemas, busy working in the garden, was the first person I saw. I didn't want to frighten him, so I waited for him to notice me. When he turned, his mouth dropped open; his eyes nearly popped from their sockets.

"Great Mother! It is a wraith!" He started to flee.

He thought he'd seen my ghost, and I had to look down at my body to make sure he was wrong. "Artemas, it's me," I called out.

He stopped and turned, his eyes narrow with fear. "Stuart Adams?" He took a cautious step toward me, the fear giving way to shocked surprise. "Glory to the Great Mother, it is you!" He leaped on me, locking me in a lung-emptying bear hug. "You are … you are not dead." He pulled away, his face suddenly contorted with a confused frown. "But … how did you survive the earthquake? We … we thought—"

"Earthquake?"

"Yes. There was shaking, and a great thunder rose from the cave. We went to see but … but we could not go inside. The ceiling, it had fallen. Everything had fallen. We … we were certain that you were dead."

"When did it collapse?"

"Yesterday morning; just before sunrise."

His answer meant that I'd been out of the cave for at least twenty-four hours. Yet I recalled nothing beyond my experiences there—walking the labyrinth, the stations of remembrance, my conversation with Marcus. Then I remembered the final *tea,* the one that Euphemia said would enhance soul memories. Had I just returned from a major drug trip?

"Come," Artemas said, grabbing my hand. "Niki is hysterical with grief. She cries in the bed, blaming herself. I am sick with worry for her. You must show her that you are alive." He grabbed my hand as if he'd been charged with the task of keeping me from vanishing into the ether, pulling me urgently through the garden.

"Stuart Adams!" Euphemia gasped, her eyes wide with disbelief. She clutched me as if I was the first glimmer of light after a very long, dark night of the soul. "I knew it could not be true," she said, her voice trembling with relief. She pulled back and peered deep into my eyes, searching. "You were successful? You … you have recovered the lost knowledge?"

"You mean to tell me after that big lecture on my destiny, you're still having doubts?"

"Tell me." She was in no mood for the taunting.

"Yup. Every word of it, right here." I tapped the side of my head with a forefinger; the words of Marcus were still vivid in my mind. "And I'll tell you all about it—*later*. I've got to see Niki first."

She held my gaze for a long, disappointed moment, struggling with the urge to protest. Then, she said, "Yes … yes, of course. You must see Niki. Then you rest, and you eat. We will talk when you are ready."

Euphemia led me to a guest bedroom situated in a section of the house that sat flush with the edge of the cliff. I peeked through the door. Niki was asleep. The sheet was a crumpled heap. Her flowered, knee-length gown was twisted on her body. I stepped closer. Her face was red, streaked with fresh tear tracks. The thought of her in that much pain forced tears to my own eyes. I eased down to the edge of the bed and stroked her face gently. There was a deep ache in her moan, something fighting having to wake up to more pain.

Her eyes fluttered, at first unfocused and then wide with the shock of recognition. She shot up in the bed, gasping. "Oh my god! You … you are—" She didn't finish her sentence. We were too busy throwing arms around each other, clasping, almost tearing at the other with the single purpose of squeezing out the last bit of space that existed between us. "Hold me," she said, smothering me with a barrage of kisses. "Do not ever leave me again—ever."

"I'll never leave you. I want to get married—today."

She pulled back and studied me for a long moment. "No. Not today."

"Yes."

"No."

"Don't argue. We're getting married today."

"You are the one who should not argue. You stink. You look exhausted. You need to rest. I do not want the man I marry to fall asleep at the altar. And there are many preparations to be made."

"I am prepared," I protested. "I've been waiting two thousand years for this. I say we do it right now."

"And what do you intend to wear to our wedding? These silly pajamas?"

She did have a point. "Where's that kid that took my clothes?"

"No, no. There will be no T-shirt and cutoffs, not at my wedding. While you were away, I ordered a fine tuxedo for you and a dress for myself. Dora has them. I will send for her and Nicholas. They will bring these garments. My dress, it is in need of some alterations. Dora will do this. We will marry at a place near the cliffs. Artemas needs time to decorate. Euphemia has agreed to perform the ceremony. The preparations will take time. We are going to do this as it should be done."

I was so tired and happy to see her that I didn't even care that I was losing the argument. But I didn't intend to go down that easy.

"All right then," I said as sternly as if my opinion actually mattered. "But if I have to marry you wearing pajamas, then pajamas it is."

The comment raised a doubtful eyebrow from Niki. "We will see about this. For now"—she pinched her nostrils in a playful gesture of repugnance—"let us think about you getting a bath. It has been some time, no?" We stood, and she helped me ease the robe over my head, a mischievous grin creeping over her face. Then, bursting into laughter, she bolted for the open window, wadded the robe into a ball, and threw it out.

Duped and as naked as a newly plowed field, I half covered myself with folded hands, stepped to the window, and watched my only piece of clothing plummet like a sheet of wet newspaper the thousand feet into the churning sea. One sleeve flapped as if it were waving goodbye all the way down.

I turned a confused gaze on Niki. "Now, what'd you do that for?"

She was still grinning when she took my hand and led me toward the adjoining bathroom.

"I intend to take no chances with a man who has grown so fond of his pajamas."

IN THE SHADE OF HER garden, after I told Euphemia and Niki all that had happened, Euphemia explained that the final tea I drank was an *entheogen,* a natural, psychoactive substance known to induce deeply spiritual experiences.

"It is similar," she said, "to peyote, or the psilocybin mushrooms used by the Native American shaman in their *vision quest*."

"You're saying that the Stations of Remembrance and the conversation with Marcus were drug-induced hallucinations?" I asked.

"Not mere hallucinations," Euphemia insisted. "The tea, as I explained to you earlier, was specifically crafted to enhance soul memories, to recover experiences not registered in the current memory of the brain. These experiences, I assure you, were quite real."

I could believe Euphemia's explanation. If each individual's life really was a continuum—the soul connecting an unknown series of lifetimes—then why couldn't the mind plunge back into the most influential places of its own history? What she didn't explain was how my body was transported to the Labyrinth of Roses. Even during a vision quest, the initiate's body never left a ten-foot circle.

"It could only have been Sargos," Euphemia said. "He must have carried you to the feet of the Great Mother. By many witnesses he was seen returning to the cave ... before the collapse."

"But he would've had to wade through scalding water to get me," I said, remembering the stone path leading to the center of the labyrinth had crumbled.

"Yes," Euphemia said, and her gaze suddenly became downcast.

She excused herself, she said, to meditate on the Three Measures of Wisdom, leaving me with a bitterly humbling image. The man that I'd flippantly called a *nocturnal freak* had waded through scalding water to save my life.

Niki must have noticed the remorse on my face. "There is nothing you can do for him," she said, reaching over and squeezing my hand. "This man, he did a brave and noble thing. We can only hope that he somehow knows how grateful we are."

"I know you're right," I said. "I just wish I could look him in the eyes and thank him."

We lingered in a moment of silent reverence before Niki moved on. "I have been thinking. There is an intriguing detail to your story, one that may have escaped your consideration."

"What detail?"

"You remember Cardinal Sorrentino's letter, the one that suggested Jesus may have gotten the basis of his teachings from Marcus?"

"Yeah. Either Josephus was confused, or his letter is a forgery."

"I do not think that Josephus was confused or that his letter is a forgery. It might surprise you to know that the name *Jesus* is the Greek rendition of the Hebrew name *Joshua*. We know Jesus by this name only because the New Testament writings that we have are copies made in Greek. His family and friends more likely knew him as *Joshua*. Moreover, according to the book of Acts, his early disciples were known as *the followers of the Way*, just like you remembered."

The circuits of my brain popped. I hadn't made the connection. The Jesus I knew was a Sunday school composite of idealized images. Joshua was a man—extraordinary in that he was highly intelligent, compassionate, wise beyond his years, a mystic, a healer, and a natural leader that people trusted, but a man nonetheless. Had I befriended the actual Jesus of history?

I stared like an idiot at Niki, and I was about to begin babbling some kind of a response when two people, a man and a woman, suddenly appeared through the garden gate. The man—eyes hidden behind sunglasses, gaunt, hollow-faced, dressed in a blue Hawaiian shirt and light blue slacks—carried his arm in a sling and hobbled over a cane. I guessed he was in his late sixties. The woman, also in dark glasses, wore a floppy hat and had blonde hair that fell to just above her shoulders. She wore a sleeveless cream blouse, white slacks, and canvas walking shoes, and she had a large bag slung over one shoulder. Younger, probably in her late fifties, she watched the injured man's every step, ready to assist him if he faltered. They stopped directly in front of us.

"Can we help you?" Niki said, standing.

The man smiled and straightened himself with the pride of a wounded war veteran. When he removed his sunglasses, Niki gasped, her jaw dropped, and her eyes went wide with shock. Her voice was little more than a dry whisper when she squeaked out the name.

"Captain Threader!"

I couldn't decide which was more shocking: the possibility that I might have spent time in a past life studying and traveling with the most famous spiritual teacher in the world, or seeing Blake Threader—reduced to a near skeleton but still very much alive—standing before us.

After a long hug, Threader finally came out of Niki's arms and thrust a greeting hand toward me. I grabbed it, unashamed of my tear-streaked cheeks. We were all laughing, crying, wiping our eyes, and sniveling like a bunch of pepper-sprayed lunatics.

When the wave of disbelief started to recede, Threader began to explain. "Niki, Stuart, I'd like you to meet my nurse, Ingrid Weiss. If it hadn't been for her, I probably wouldn't be here."

Ingrid, her German blue eyes animated, offered a more likely explanation. "What the captain really means to say is that if it had not been for his bullheaded strength, he would not be here."

We all took seats, anxious to hear Threader's story. He was going for the Winchester when Apollo shot him. The three Greeks then set the *Penelope* on fire and left Threader for dead. Like we suspected, he'd regained consciousness, called in the Mayday, strapped on a life jacket, and swam for the Zodiac. "I don't know how I done it," he said, when he told us about tying the mine to the front of the Zodiac. "I just knew I had no choice. When I saw Giacopetti's boat coming," he said, looking at Niki, "I signaled with the flashlight and hoped like hell that you seen it. Whatever happened, I figured it'd be better than leaving you with Giacopetti."

"You jumped right before impact?" I asked.

"The instant I seen Niki roll off that boat. If she was gonna die, then I was gonna die with her. But when I knew she was off that boat, I was outta there. And not a second too soon. Took a piece of shrapnel in the leg. Just about bled to death. Lucky for me, a chopper full of geologists got to me before the sharks. Took me to the hospital in Fira. When I woke up, I was staring into two of the most beautiful blue eyes I'd ever seen. I was sure I'd died and gone to heaven."

Ingrid blushed with the compliment. "And I too." She turned to Niki and me. "Blake has asked me to marry him."

A round of cheers went up.

"Heck, Threader," I said, "if there was anything around here to drink besides mango juice, I'd make a toast."

"Mango juice would suit me fine, Adams. No more booze for this old captain. Fact is, Ingrid has got herself a pretty decent little boat. She wants me to get serious about chartering again. I can make it work this time. Got me a damn good first mate."

A beaming Ingrid said, "Blake and I encountered your friends, Artemas and Nicholas. Rumor has it that there is going to be a wedding here on the island."

"Yup," I said, and turning to Threader I added, "I had to twist Nicholas's arm to stand up with me. I'm sure he wouldn't mind giving up the position. I'd consider it a major honor if you'd stand in."

Threader looked at Ingrid. She nodded. "I think we can arrange that. It ain't like it comes as any big surprise. If you recall, I told you that this little girl was in love with you."

"I remember. And I haven't forgotten the thing about the jackass either."

"Yeah? We all have our faults, Adams. Maybe Niki here can do something about that." Threader grinned at me for a moment before turning to Ingrid. He nodded, and from her bag she pulled a two-foot-long rectangular package wrapped in brown paper. She handed the package to Threader.

"Got a little wedding present here for you," Threader said, handing Niki the package.

"Wedding present?" Niki asked. "What is it?"

"I reckon if you open it, you'll find out."

Niki carefully tore away the layers of paper and lifted the lid off the box. Inside was what appeared to be an aluminum container, badly charred but capped at both ends.

"I didn't know what it was," Threader explained. "I was floating out there half dead when I felt this thing bump into my arm." Grinning, he added, "I'm not sure I'm ready to start believing in angels, but somebody must have been looking out for us."

Puzzled, Niki twisted off one of the caps and pulled out the contents. The instant I saw the leather sheath, I knew what it was. Blake Threader had recovered the scroll.

Epilogue

THE NEXT SEVERAL DAYS WERE a whirlwind of activity. Niki and I hired the pilot of the seaplane to fly us back to Sarnafi to check on the legal status of the scroll. Niki had heard that Kyropos was in a no-man's-land, and she called Barry Weathersby, of Weathersby & Rollins, Barnes's legal firm, to see what he could find out. Within hours, Weathersby had returned her call.

"We are in luck," Niki said, hanging up the telephone. Glancing at her notes, she explained, "According to Mr. Weathersby, in 1917 the Egyptian government rejected a bid to annex the unclaimed volcano on the grounds that it had no economic or military value, and because it was completely uninhabitable. They declared the volcano abandoned and derelict." She looked up at me. "The scroll is ours."

With spirits soaring, we flew to Crete and sent the scroll to Dr. Stanley J. Davis, at the Institute for Minoan Research, in New York. Barnes had chosen Davis, a world-renowned paleographer and longtime friend of Alexios Mikos, to head the project. The scroll would be scanned in a high-resolution digital format for translation and further study. The institute would then hold it until a proper facility could be built to permanently house the scroll at the monastery on Pialigos.

I still had a bad feeling about opening the island to tourism, but everyone we talked to agreed that, with tourism a leading money-maker in the islands, it was the only way to salvage the Pialigarians and their culture.

With our legal concerns resolved, I called my agent, Claudia

Epstein, and I told her the whole story. Ecstatic, she called her contact at the *New York Times*, and in two days the scroll's discovery was headline news. The *Times*, who had frequently used Davis as a consultant, touted his credibility and quoted him as saying, "This unlikely source may indeed offer the world one of the clearest windows yet opened into the mind of Jesus." The *Times* was flooded with emails and telephone calls. People wanted to know more. Armed with the article and public reaction, Epstein orchestrated a bidding frenzy between the top New York publishing houses. The book was a sensation even before I'd had the chance to write it.

THE EXCITED BUZZ OF WEDDING preparations transformed the tranquillity of Pialigos. Our wedding's historical significance prompted eager participation from each of the island's 257 inhabitants. The site for the ceremony, a large, grassy knoll bordering the cliffs and offering a stunning view of the sea, had to be prepared. Goats were brought in to nibble the grass into a lawn. Artemas and a crew of workers built and carefully decorated with roses a nuptial arch at the cliff's edge. Planks for seating were hammered together and arranged in two groups to form an aisle leading to the arch.

We had the pilot fly to Chios to pick up Celia Mikos for the wedding. Celia and Niki stood face-to-face, Celia's dark eyes tense with the uncertainty of how her adopted daughter would react to the years of deception. The two women quickly melted into each other's arms, with Niki's assurances to Celia that she held no hard feelings. "You did what you thought was best for me," Niki said. "I could not have asked for a better mother."

"I am sorry I did not have the courage to tell you sooner," Celia said through tears. "I will make it up to you. I will tell you everything I know about my sister, your true mother." After a long embrace, Celia turned to me, looked straight into my eyes, and placed a hand on each of my shoulders. "You will take good care of my child?"

"I'll take good care of your child," I assured her. She pulled me into a hug as Niki, her face beaming, looked on.

Celia drew back, smiling. "You have my blessing," she said. "You have the blessing of my husband."

THE EVENING OF OUR WEDDING brought a spectacular Mediterranean sunset. Soft smudges of pink, red, and gray lay in long, irregular streaks across the blue canopy. Our audience had taken their seats while a band of island musicians played. The band featured a bouzouki, a mandolin-like instrument traditional in Grecian music. There was also a guitar, a stand-up bass, and a percussionist. The woody twang of the bouzouki tugged at every one of my heartstrings. The band members had explained earlier that all their song selections had been composed over hundreds of years, that each one commemorated the love between Anatolios and Panagiota.

When Euphemia gave the signal, Blake Threader and I—decked out in tuxes—followed her to the arch. There, we turned toward the cart path that led to the monastery. Pialigarian tradition dictated that a bride approach her groom in a covered, donkey-drawn cart. According to legend, when Anatolios finally took Panagiota as his bride, her cart would be drawn by a pure white donkey. And so it was. In the distance, I could see the cart appear. The donkey, led by its owner, was indeed white as snow. The cart was covered in flowers and bolts of red, green, yellow, blue, and orange fabric. The musicians churned out their sweetest tunes as the cart bearing my bride slowly approached. It was a warm evening, but my hands were cold and clammy; I had to clench my teeth to keep them from chattering.

The cart stopped at the back of the crowd. Everyone stood in breathless anticipation. My heart raced. Lia and Nitsa, the big-eyed little girl who had given me the pink stone of friendship, stepped from the cart and began walking down the aisle toward us, carefully casting rose petals from baskets they carried.

Niki stepped from the cart wearing a full-length dress of white chiffon with straps that fell slightly off her shoulders and crisscrossed in gathers over her breasts. She carried a bouquet of red roses, and she had a delicate mix of rosebuds and baby's breath woven tastefully into her Edwardian braided hair. Artemas stepped forward as her escort. Niki walked with her head high, her eyes—strong, crackling with life—never once leaving mine. The wailing bouzouki brought streams of tears down even the sun-leathered cheeks of sea-hardened old fishermen.

Euphemia's words passed in a blur, but it didn't matter. I needed no words to confirm that Niki was the first woman that I could love without fear, without reservation. Soon, Euphemia was turning us to face our audience, announcing that Anatolios and Panagiota had at long last come together in marriage. When she invited us to kiss, the audience roared in cheers, and the music flew into a happy, festive mood. The people quickly fell into a double line and urged Niki and me to run through a shower of flower petals. When we reached the end, all the people formed a half circle around us and continued their cheers and clapping, their faces filled with hope for a bright future—ours and their own. It was a time for great celebration. Their prophet had returned with their future in his hands.

Or had he?

For all my joy, something was still missing. The Pialigarians had given me a story. What had I given them? A future of photo opportunities with tourists carrying gift shop bags loaded with fake Pialigarian memorabilia? I was a taker, not a giver, a thief who had snuck in and plucked the last jewel from a pauper's hidden chest. Yeah, I was a prophet all right. I had no trouble seeing into their future. Frail as the flame of a candle in the hurricane of twenty-first-century reality, their culture wouldn't stand a chance.

Nitsa wandered from the crowd and stood looking up at me. Her brown eyes were like a pair of strong hands reaching up and delivering a choke hold to my throat. I could hardly bear to look at her—me, the fraud, the imposter. I scooped her up, and she finished me off by throwing her tiny arms in complete trust around my neck.

"Nitsa, what are we going to do?" I whispered the question into her soft hair knowing she could not understand a word of what I said. "A real prophet wouldn't send you into a future of grubbing money from the cruise ships. I just don't know how to stop it. I really don't."

Niki, overhearing my words, stepped in close and slipped a comforting arm around my waist. "We have found a way to help," she whispered in my ear. "We do not need the cruise ships."

I looked at her doubtfully.

She had a confident smile, and her eyes flashed with unfounded optimism. "During the wedding preparations, Euphemia and I talked. There will be a museum and a retreat center. We will give people something meaningful, something to enhance their lives. The Pialigarians can tell their history through educational seminars. Pialigos is, after all, a monastery. There are already many trained teachers here.

With their lost knowledge now restored, they are all very excited about sharing who they are with the world. You see how the Prophet fulfills his destiny? It is your book that will bring the people here, just as Rufus had hoped. But it will not be the random flood of tourists that you fear. They will come only by reservation. We will not allow the island to be overrun. The future of the Pialigarians will remain in their own hands."

Museum? Retreat center? Seminars? She had it all worked out, and in a way I hadn't really thought about. The wheels of my mind whirred. If the thing was controlled and well-managed, a museum-based retreat center wouldn't destroy the island or the people. It would give them their future without costing them their dignity. It was brilliant.

"Are you sure *you're* not the Prophet?" I said to Niki. "Because right now, it feels like you've got one hell of a lot more brains than I do."

With a teasing smile she said, "There is nothing in Pialigarian scripture that says the Prophet will have a lot of brains."

I frowned, wondering if I should defend myself or give her a hug. I opted for the hug. Then, something in the distance caught my attention. Silhouetted in the orange disk of the setting sun, high on a cliff across a cove, stood the lone figure of a man. Niki saw me looking and followed the direction of my gaze.

"Who could it be?" she asked, squinting into the sun. "Everyone on the island is here."

The Pialigarians began to see him too. One by one, they turned, shielding their eyes against the dying sun, a questioning murmur rising among them.

Then, the man raised his hand. The music subsided, and a deep hush fell over the people. I knew in that instant who it was, and I raised my hand to return his greeting.

"You know this man?" Niki asked.

"It's Marcus."

"Marcus? The Essene? But that is not pos ..." Her words trailed off.

"I know," I said, struggling with the same problem. For me, the line between *possible* and *impossible* had grown thin, nearly imperceptible.

"What would he want?" Niki asked, "Why would he come?"

"Maybe he's giving us his blessing for our new project."

"The retreat center?"

"I told him about the Pialigarians, how they needed help. He said the answer would come when I wasn't looking for it."

A smile shimmered over Niki's face. "His way of telling you to let go and enjoy the journey? So, I am not the only one preaching to you this doctrine?"

"Guess you're not."

"And now you have no excuses. You have discovered your destiny, you have found your lover, and soon you will be rolling in your tub full of money. What more could you want? Even as an American man, you should be quite happy."

"Yeah," I said, ignoring the gibe. "But you're only right on two counts. I'm not sure there'll be enough money to roll in. If we're going to do this retreat thing, it's going to take a lot to get this place up and running."

"Yes, and Rufus has put aside—"

"*No.* I think I'm starting to get the hang of this destiny thing." I turned to her. "Niki, I need to do this."

"You?"

"Yeah. With the help of the book."

"You would commit the proceeds from your book to the Pialigarian cause?"

A couple of Nitsa's playmates darted past. Nitsa wriggled out of my arms and scampered off with her friends. I turned to face Niki. There was a sheen of admiration in her smile.

"Yup," I said with a grin. "Oh, I might save a little to roll in. You know, maybe just enough to get it out of my system."

"I see. And you would be naked?"

"Why? You want to watch?"

"Perhaps I will join you in your tub."

"Yeah? You bringing the wine?"

"Me? I bring the wine last time. Do you forget so soon?"

"You want to join me or not?"

Her eyes flared with playful defiance before they softened. "All right, I bring the wine … this time. But you will owe me."

An excited murmur suddenly rose from the crowd. We turned to see people pointing at the place where Marcus had been. Now, only the sun and the deep-shadowed cliff remained.

I slipped an arm around my wife, and we watched the sun sink slowly into the sea. I pulled her closer and took a deep and satisfying breath. When the last sliver of that blazing disk disappeared beneath the horizon, there was no doubt left in my mind that I had heard the whisper of Pialigos.

God, it felt good to be home.

J Douglas Bottorff is the author of *A Practical Guide to Meditation and Prayer* and *A Practical Guide to Prosperous Living*. He lives with his wife, Elizabeth, in Colorado. Additional information and essays are available on his website, http://jdbottorff.com.